BLOOD OF HERCULES

Also by Jasmine Mas

Villains of Lore

Blood of Hercules
Bonds of Hercules

Cruel Shifterverse

Psycho Shifters
Psycho Fae
Psycho Beasts
Psycho Academy
Psycho Devils
Psycho Gods

To learn more about Jasmine Mas, visit her website, jasminemasbooks.com.

BLOOD OF HERCULES

JASMINE MAS

CANARY STREET PRESS

CANARY STREET PRESS™

ISBN-13: 978-1-335-47472-8

Blood of Hercules

First published in 2024 by Jasmine Mas. This edition published in 2024.

Interior images: VectorStock (chapter opener images);
Maria at Steamy Designs (family tree)

Canary Street Press
22 Adelaide St. West, 41st Floor
Toronto, Ontario M5H 4E3, Canada
CanaryStPress.com

Printed in U.S.A.

Content Warning

This is a story of dark romance and darker obsession. Please note that it contains themes that may be triggering for some readers. There is violence, depictions of murder, stalking, suicidal thoughts, bullying, explicit language and betrayal. For a full list, please see the author's website, jasminemasbooks.com. It's a slow burn, but there are open-door scenes. Please take care of yourself.

Sometimes becoming a hero hurts...a lot.

Beware.

This book is dedicated to all the girls who like morally gray fictional men and who screamed out loud the first time they read "Who did this to you?"

This one's for you.

THE 12 HOUSES OF SPARTA

OLYMPIAN HOUSES

THE HOUSE OF ZEUS.

THE HOUSE OF HERA.

THE HOUSE OF ATHENA.

THE HOUSE OF HERMES.

THE HOUSE OF POSEIDON.

THE HOUSE OF DEMETER.

THE HOUSE OF APOLLO.

THE HOUSE OF DIONYSUS.

CHTHONIC HOUSES

THE HOUSE OF ARES.

THE HOUSE OF HADES.

THE HOUSE OF ARTEMIS.

THE HOUSE OF APHRODITE.

CHTHONIC HOUSE LINEAGES

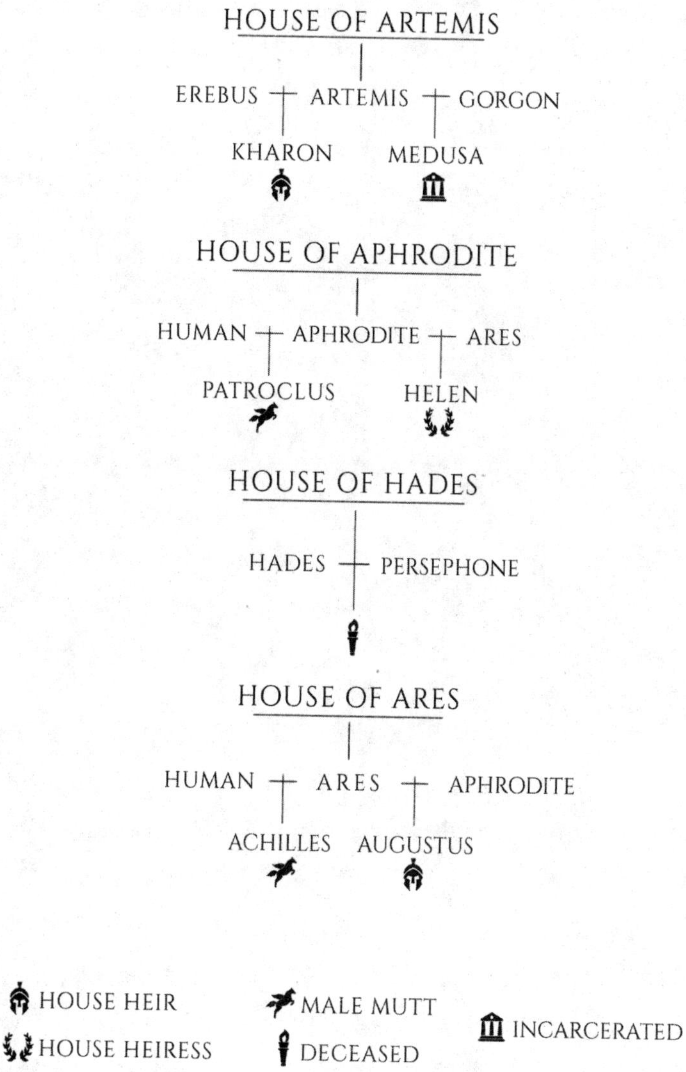

Fides est periculosa ludum—trust is a dangerous game.
She didn't know who was hunting her until it was too late.

OMNISCIENT

Fate

I draped the long toga over my crossed legs and sat completely still in the field. Stones from Delphi were placed in a circle around me.

I'd collected the rocks when I was a little girl, thousands of years ago.

Palms relaxed and open.

Head tipped back.

A smoking pipe hung from my lips.

I inhaled the herbs, and pain pulsed through my closed eyes as I activated my powers.

Glimpses of patterns, numbers, and probabilities flashed through my mind, too many images to comprehend.

The path of existence was nothing but chance, and chance was nothing but a circle of events.

Sharp sensations transformed into agony, but I inhaled smoke and withstood the onslaught.

The nonsensical images changed into cryptic words.

They spoke themselves to me:

The lost one shall change what is before;
Chained to death's soldiers, becoming evermore;
Or Titans will inherit the earth, and there will be nothing but war.

My eyes shot open.

Dark possibilities tasted bitter on my tongue, and I felt the paths forward in the marrow of my ancient bones.

My brand of Spartan power was nothing without action, but I never shied from unsavory choices. It was why I'd survived, while the rest of my kind had perished.

The future hinged before me on a razor-sharp edge: apocalypse and peace were two sides of the same coin.

It could tip either way.

Action was needed. After all, nullum magnum ingenium sine mixture dementia fuit.

There has been no great wisdom without an element of madness.

Gasping out smoke, joints aching as I got to my feet, I tripped and stumbled as I ran through the field, into the palace, then hurried down a long, white marble hall.

My purple eyes and white hair reflected off the mirrored walls.

When I got to the heavy onyx door of the inner chamber, I didn't bother to knock. I pushed against it and threw it open.

The members of the federation were standing behind gold podiums in the grand arena, arguing.

They turned and looked up at me.

Crack.

They fell to their knees.

Pulling the smoking pipe from my lips, I waved it in the air. "The marriage law we've discarded must pass—today," I rasped. "The age to wed must be twenty-six."

The room erupted with a roar. "But we were discussing a century!" someone shouted. "Twenty-six is *far* too young to be bound for all of immortality!"

I held up my hand.

Everyone shut up.

Immediately.

"That's not all," I said. "Kharon and Augustus *must* be professors in the crucible this year."

Everyone blinked with confusion.

"Why?" Zeus asked with narrowed eyes, electricity sparking off his skin as he knelt next to the speaker's podium in the center of the room.

I arched an eyebrow. "Are you questioning my abilities—young boy?"

"Of course not." He lowered his head. "My apologies for my disrespect. I was just curious."

I stared at him. "Don't be."

The silence expanded.

One by one, the House leaders bowed deeply—their foreheads pressed flush against the red marble floor.

Slowly, I walked down the long black-rug-covered stairs that led to the center of the arena.

When I got to the leader's podium, I picked up a pair of scissors and reached into the basket, where the laws that hadn't passed were wrapped in scarlet ribbon.

I snipped.

The ribbon fell away.

The scroll unrolled—"Marriage Law" was printed across it in black ink.

"Pass it," I said as I leaned low and handed the previously discarded law to the still-bowing Zeus. "Pass it now—make the age changes and assign the two new professors."

Electricity sparked across the paper as he took it. Then he immediately resumed his position.

I turned.

Slowly hobbled back up the steps, with immortal beings prostrated on either side.

I scoffed as they cowered—*Kronos, if only you could see what your empire has become… Spartans have become so weak.*

Unlike the House leaders, my word was absolute.

I was the only thing standing between the rise and fall of Sparta.

Kronos save us all.

THE GREAT WAR

SOFTLY IT BEGAN.

Eons before humanity was born, the state of Sparta was spread across thousands of archipelago islands in modern-day Greece.

Sparta was composed of a hundred immortal Spartans, their animal protectors, and local creatures. *Creature* was a blanket term Spartans used to classify all races of civilized people who had special powers but weren't Spartan.

Ruled by an oligarchic federation, Sparta's immortal citizens were content to live quiet, slow lives of island luxury.

They knew nothing of conflict, greed, or jealousy.

All was peaceful.

Then humans arrived.

Humanity was in immediate awe of the immortal people.

Sparta taught humanity art, agriculture, and governance.

Humans worshipped them.

Thus, Spartans became humanity's gods.

Centuries later, Spartans and creatures migrated with the humans to modern-day Italy, enjoying the wealth and status of godhood.

The Roman Empire was born.

But the affairs of man were not to be taken lightly.

The mortal population exploded in size.

In contrast, Sparta struggled with fertility—its numbers stayed around one hundred.

Then humans discovered Spartans weren't completely immune to death—they could be chopped into tiny pieces and scattered, or starved and tortured into comas.

Humanity turned on their gods.

Emperors declared war against Spartans because they wanted all the power and wealth for themselves.

But humanity forgot it was dealing with a race more intelligent than themselves.

Sparta disappeared.

Completely.

Spartans and creatures migrated to Northern Italy and went into hiding in the Dolomites.

But before they left, they destroyed all the advancements they'd shared with humans—the Library of Alexandria burned to the ground and our knowledge of the gods with it. All we had left were the lies.

Without Sparta's guidance, Rome fell.

As the centuries passed, the living gods who had steered humanity toward greatness became nothing but myths. But the myths we told ourselves were wrong. The gods were not as we remembered them in stories and legends: their alliances, their bloodlines, their power. It was all false.

Time trudged forward.

Protected by anonymity, advancing in the shadows, Spartans and creatures amassed unfathomable wealth and created superior technologies.

But Sparta wasn't as peaceful as it seemed.

There were two divisive factions of Spartans: Chthonic Houses and Olympian Houses.

Each House was a separate family bloodline of power, named after its founding leader—a Spartan more powerful than the rest.

All Spartans from Olympian Houses had powers that enhanced themselves, physically or mentally.

They didn't hurt others and instead focused on self-improvement and the sciences.

There were fifty different Olympian Houses, with dozens of members.

Olympians kept their numbers strong by having children with humans, and these half humans, half Spartans were called mutts.

In contrast, the Chthonic Houses were the Spartans with bloodred eyes.

Chthonics had powers that *only* hurt others, such as torture, mind control, pain.

Only four Chthonic families had ever lived. Born at the dawn of Sparta, unlike the Olympian Houses that rose and fell, they remained the same.

Always.

The infamous Chthonic four—the Houses of Hades, Aphrodite, Artemis, and Ares.

Each only had a handful of members, since they rarely procreated with the weak humans, who couldn't handle their powers. A few creatures, those with the *darkest* of abilities, sided with these Houses.

Throughout history, the two factions kept an uneasy truce. Peace was maintained by the federation, which was led by the strongest Olympians.

But at the turn of the twenty-first century, the peace shattered.

The Great War started.

The four Chthonic Houses attacked the fifty Olympian Houses in a bid to overthrow the federation and seize power over Sparta.

Vastly outnumbered, twenty-four Chthonics fought against hundreds of Olympians.

Still, conflict raged for decades because the Chthonics' abilities were so heinous.

The weaker Olympian Houses fell first as Chthonics mercilessly hunted them and scattered their pieces across the globe. The strongest Olympians banded together and sought vengeance.

In 2045, there were only eight of the strongest and oldest Olympian families left standing: the Houses of Zeus, Hera, Athena, Hermes, Poseidon, Demeter, Apollo, and Dionysus.

The war was locked in a stalemate, with numbers dwindling on both sides.

Sparta was at risk of collapse.

The four overpowered Chthonic House leaders remained, but all twenty of their children had been captured and killed.

If the war continued, there would be nothing left to rule, so the two sides signed a ceasefire.

In the new federation, the Olympians held even more of an overwhelming majority.

Peace was reestablished.

A few years later, in 2050, Titans—immortal monstrous creatures—inexplicably appeared on earth and started slaughtering humans.

The Olympian-led federation saw an opportunity to reintroduce themselves to humanity.

The gods rose again.

They also seized the chance to punish Chthonics.

As reparations for the war and their crimes, the federation ruled that all remaining Chthonics—and any sons they bore, as well as the dark creatures who sided with them—were in charge of handling earth's Titan problem.

They called this new organization the Assembly of Death.

But that wasn't all.

The Chthonics and creatures were also forced to fight Titans, *and* one another, in the Dolomites Coliseum. It was a disturbed contest known as the Spartan Gladiator Competition.

The SGC quickly became the most violent tournament to ever grace the face of the earth.

It ushered in a new era of brutality.

Nearly half a century later, Titans still roamed the earth, Chthonics were starting to rebuild their numbers, and Olympians were increasingly bearing less powerful children.

Once again, the federation struggled to keep its power, and the tides of history pointed toward war.

Sparta was more fractured than ever.

To address the growing divide, the federation enacted a controversial marriage law.

Chthonics immediately sought to undermine it.

That is where our story begins.

AB INITIO

"At this century's turn,
all of Sparta applauds;
The federation falls,
to the exposer of gods."

—Fate, 2050

1

SERPENT

Alexis: Year 2090

"Who are you?" a female voice whispered in my ear.

I sat up with a start and blinked groggily.

My wrists throbbed with pain. They were scraped raw.

Grasses and pink summer flowers rustled as a warm breeze blew through the emerald field I was napping in.

Rural Montana was a quiet, eerie place.

Located two hundred miles north of Helena's city lights, the power grid barely sustained our run-down trailer park.

The Titans had arrived in the year 2050, and the world had crumbled.

Kids at school called it apocalyptic core.

I called it hell.

No one knew where the human-esque immortal Titans with razor-sharp teeth, black veins, long claws, and superspeed came from, or why they tore humans apart for fun.

Their existence was unfortunate, if you wanted to live (I didn't).

Father John said the Titans had appeared to "teach humans a lesson." Since we did nothing but perish dramatically and gruesomely...strange lesson.

After all, it was the Spartans who had saved us.

"Can you hear me?" the unknown voice asked louder.

I whipped my head around and searched for the speaker, but there was nobody else in the field.

I groaned as the quick movement made my wrists throb worse.

Father and Mother were making their "special drink" in the bathtub again to deal with hunger—a combination of cleaning supplies, water, and moldy bread yeast—and their behavior had become increasingly erratic.

Case in point, last week I'd looked "wrongly" at Father, so he'd tied me up with a rough rope because I was a "lazy, good for nothing, spoiled ten-year-old bitch."

This morning, I'd gotten tired of being tethered like a dog and had hit my arms down against a rock while pulling until I'd gotten free.

Both wrists were definitely fractured.

At least you've escaped.

The good news: Father was so clueless he probably wouldn't even remember that he'd tied me up.

The bad news: he needed fancy Spartan Federation medication—*preferably death*—but he couldn't afford it.

Someone needed to take care of his mental health the cheap way—hit him over the head with a shovel (that was what they'd done to neighbor Paul: whacked him when he wasn't looking).

"You can hear me, can't you...what—are you?" the invisible voice said next to my ear, and I jolted with fear.

Great, I'm being haunted by a ghost.

I looked around warily.

Barbed wire fence glinted at the distant tree line that surrounded the trailer park, and a tattered white flag hung off a branch displaying the crest of the House of Hades—a horrifying skeleton dog with burning crimson eyes.

It was a hellhound.

Below the flag, a sign warned in bloodred letters, "Spartan Federation Militarized Protected Zone, Titans Beware."

The Chthonic organization of killers—the Assembly of Death—and their symbols (creepy hellhound flags that *no one* asked for) were strung across the protected zones. They were a warning to Titans that even among monstrosities, there were Goliaths.

Everyone knew the twelve Spartan families who ruled the earth.

The eight Olympian Houses were the good guys, since their powers didn't hurt other people. In contrast, the four Chthonic Houses were pure evil.

They were mass murderers with dark powers.

I shivered.

The age of gods and monsters sucks.

Breathing roughly through my teeth, I tried to focus on anything but the agony radiating up my forearms.

What would Emmy Noether and Carl Gauss do in this situation?

Sadly, I was not sure how my heroes—brilliant historical mathematicians—would act.

Sleep would be nice.

So would death.

For now, I'd settle for rereading the public library's autobiography of Emmy Noether for the hundredth time. It was like a gentle hug.

At least, I assumed that was what an embrace would feel like.

I'd never been hugged.

Not yet.

Maybe never, considering I loathed being touched and people didn't like me.

"You smell familiar," the invisible voice whispered louder. "I wonder...what's your name, kid?"

I sniffed my armpit. I'd used the cold garden hose this morning, so all I smelled was sun and grass. "I'm A-Alexis Hert," I said tentatively. The raised scar on my sternum tingled, the one I'd had since I was a baby.

"You can understand me, human? You can speak to me?" The voice was even louder, and I jumped. "I'm Nyx."

"Uh—hi," I said awkwardly.

There was a long pause.

"Why are your wrists bloody?" Nyx asked.

"My foster p-parents are trying to kill me," I said with a heavy sigh.

"You're a strange human." Nyx's voice sounded closer. "You speak of death—but you don't smell of fear. There is something wrong with you."

"There probably is," I said.

Nyx hissed. "Your attitude is unsettling. I've met immortal Spartans who've feared death more than you do."

"Are you a ghost?" I asked.

"No."

"Liar."

The sun was suddenly obstructed by a dark object—it hovered inches from my face.

Slit pupils were stark against neon purple, and a slippery forked tongue dragged across my cheek.

"I told you I was real," Nyx hissed.

A...a...colossal black snake—as long as one of my legs, with twin fangs gleaming, razor-sharp, and purple eyes—hovered inches in the air in front of me.

She looked dangerous.

Predatory.

"What are you?" I whispered.

Her shiny black head swayed back and forth on the summer breeze like she was trying to hypnotize me. "I'm an echidna, an ancient race of invisible snakes. Of course, you wouldn't know—humans know nothing of the ways of beasts."

I swallowed thickly. "Are you venomous?"

The fangs flashed as the snake's head nodded. "Extremely so. Just a graze from one of my fangs would kill you in seconds."

"Wicked," I said with awe. "Want to be friends?" I'd never had one.

Purple eyes glowed.

"Fine," Nyx hissed, her jaw opening as she spoke, "but only because your life seems miserable, and I've been misplaced in this barbaric land with no one to speak to."

"Cool." I reached out and patted her shiny head.

Nyx snapped the air with a click. "*Never* touch me like that or I'll bite you to death, girl—I'm not a common dog." She sniffed haughtily. "This is only a temporary arrangement."

I laughed.

She was funny.

Hours later, after I'd frolicked about with my new bestie and tried to ignore the pain in my wrists, the sun set in a fiery pink sky.

If I didn't get back to the trailer before nightfall, I'd be locked out and forced to sleep in the dark.

I was determined to sleep inside tonight.

"Let's go back together," I whispered. Nyx turned invisible and slithered next to me. Her head brushed against my feet as I ran.

We made it back with light still in the sky—not that anyone noticed.

Mother and Father were sitting in the yard, emaciated and glassy-eyed as they sipped on dirty cups full of their "special drink." Their pupils were blown wide, heads tipped back at an unnatural angle, as they stared up at the clouds.

Living corpses.

I hummed to soothe myself.

"They look—sick." Nyx's wet tongue slicked across my ear

as she rose behind me and followed me into the trailer. "Do you want me to kill them?"

"No," I whispered as I led her down the hall. "That's wrong."

The lamp on the wall flickered weakly with green light, the electricity humming as it struggled to power the decrepit trailer—a mix of metal and wood parts from a time before the Titans.

The singular fan that pointed at the foster parents' bed did nothing to cool the rest of the space.

The muggy summer heat was oppressive.

Nyx clicked her fangs. "Fine—but someday, kid, I'll kill them for you."

I huffed. "You can't. Killing is a sin. It's morally the worst thing you can ever do. Your soul will be corrupted. Father John says so."

"Father John sounds like a stupid idiot—you're too young to know what you speak of," Nyx said. "When you're older, you'll think differently."

She was definitely going to hell for saying that.

Wait—didn't Father John say snakes are evil…am I going to hell for befriending her?

Eternal damnation was surprisingly complicated.

I shook my head. "I will never kill someone," I promised, chest burning with sincerity.

Nyx scoffed.

Gingerly, I settled into the cardboard box that functioned as my bed.

A small piece of white fabric lay at the bottom, and an eight-letter label was embroidered in gold across the front. It was the onesie I'd been wearing when the orphanage found me as a baby—the only possession in the world that was mine.

There was a weird gliding sensation as Nyx repositioned her heavy weight across my lap.

"Can you talk to all people?" I whispered.

"No, kid," Nyx said softly, "it's unusual that you can hear me. I can only talk to my own kind, and there aren't a lot of us."

"Well, I think it's nice," I mumbled with sleepiness. "Now you can't leave me because we can talk—I've always wanted a friend…just no killing…promise?"

"I don't make asinine oaths. Enough chatter," Nyx hissed. "We sleep."

Only later would I realize my stutter had disappeared completely when I talked to her.

Beasts didn't scare me.

People did.

That was how a thirty-pound invisible poisonous snake became my closest companion.

Yes, I befriended the first monster I'd ever met.

Bang.

Bang.

Bang.

I jolted awake a few hours later.

There was a loud thumping noise at the front of the trailer.

Mother and Father swore loudly as they staggered out of bed toward the obnoxious, repetitive sound.

I peeked out the corner of my box. Nyx mumbled against me and shifted but didn't wake up.

A short elderly woman with pure white hair and shocking purple eyes stood at the door.

Her expression was grave.

A skinny figure in a hood stood hunched low beside her.

"What the fuck is the meaning of this?" Mother asked as she stared down at the intruder, much more sober than earlier. "We ain't selling our drink at the front door—you'll have to just wait till Monday and get it in the woods like everyone else in the park."

Beside Mother, Father opened his mouth and slurred out unintelligible sounds.

"Thank you—a very generous offer," the elderly woman said, her tone insinuating it was anything but.

She cleared her throat.

"I'm here because the United States Government, led by the Spartan Federation, has deemed you responsible for a second foster child. Monthly food vouchers will be sent accordingly to cover his expenses. His name is Charlie."

I've never heard of foster kids being delivered to doors.

Before anyone could react, the elderly woman—with surprising strength—shoved Charlie up the steps into the trailer, then slammed the door shut.

Mother scoffed at the child. "They'll be hearing from us. This is fucking ridiculous. We didn't sign up for another one. We can't even feed the other fucking thing."

Nice, I'm an object now.

Father stumbled over to the ratty couch, collapsed on it face-first, and snored.

Mother grabbed Charlie by the scrawny arm and dragged him toward my cardboard box. I closed my eyes tight and pretended to sleep.

"Boy, you can sleep next to… Alex—there's enough room."

Judging from the long pause, she'd struggled to remember my name. *Rude.* I'd been living with her for almost ten years.

Mother stomped away loudly. Broken springs creaked as she got into her bed.

I squinted through my lashes.

Charlie was kneeling in front of me.

I gasped.

His eyes were an unnatural shade of yellow that almost glowed in the dark.

Greasy blond hair hung around his pale pointy face, and dark circles rimmed his sunken features.

"I'm A-Alexis," I whispered cautiously, holding out my

bruised hand. My aching wrist trembled as I waited to see what he would do.

Is he going to mock my stutter?

He stared at my hand but didn't take it.

If his eyes hadn't been open, I would have struggled to believe he was alive because he was so still.

I put my hand down and shifted so there was room in the cardboard box.

We were both small. We could fit.

Discreetly I moved Nyx to my other side so he wouldn't touch her.

"I'm ten," I offered softly. "Are you—also ten?"

Charlie shook his head, then gingerly lowered himself into the space beside me. He still didn't speak.

"Are you younger?" I asked.

He nodded as we sat next to each other in the dark.

"Nine?"

He nodded again.

"I guess you're my younger brother now. Don't worry, I'll be a good sister," I promised him quickly. "I know all about the foster parents. Just follow my lead and you'll be okay. I'll protect you."

"You—don't have to," he whispered softly.

I nudged him with my elbow. "I know I don't have to—but I want to. I'll take care of you."

His eyes got impossibly wide.

"What is it?" I asked with concern.

He shook his head like it was nothing, but a small smile curved his lips.

Warmth unfurled in my chest, and I grinned back.

I'd started the day with zero friends.

Now I had two.

Things were looking up.

2

THE MONSTER

ALEXIS: YEAR 2091

The energy in the trailer was contentious at best and treacherous at worst.

Wind howled outside as winter dumped snow furiously.

The February storm cast everything in shadows. The green light in the corner flickered weakly, barely sustained by the small amounts of electricity allotted to the trailer.

It was the dead of night, which was why Nyx was outside hunting. She said the dark made it easier to kill.

I took her word for it.

"We need to act now," Mother whispered to Father in the trailer kitchen.

What are they talking about? My stomach twisted as a bad feeling scoured my chest.

They thought they were the only ones still up.

Charlie was asleep beside me.

I was wide awake.

Charlie had been with us since the summer, and he was already the best brother I could ever have asked for.

He was quiet and shy, but I didn't mind, since he hung out with me every day and let me help him with his math homework. He never made fun of my stutter or called me stupid.

Actually, he hadn't spoken a word more than the single sentence he'd said when we first met. But I didn't mind.

For the first time ever, I wasn't lonely.

Mother whispered something inaudible, and her tone was dark.

The only problem was—things were *not* great with the foster parents.

There were fewer provisions than ever at the local food bank. Half the food stamps they received for Charlie and me weren't redeemable, since there was no meat and dairy to be had in the winter.

We were all starving.

Even worse than usual.

The icy conditions also meant fewer neighbors left their trailer to buy the foster parents' "special drink."

Mother spoke softly, and I strained to listen.

"We need to get rid of Charlie," she whispered. "No one will know."

Father grunted in agreement.

I froze with fear.

No.

They can't.

But they could.

We hadn't had school in weeks because the roads were too icy to drive on, which was probably why they were making plans now.

A few kind teachers gave us their scraps of food. It was what usually kept us alive. Things were getting more desperate for us with each snowstorm.

Out here in rural northern Montana, in the middle of winter, you could do *anything* to anyone, and no one would know until spring.

Gently I shook Charlie awake.

Bright yellow eyes stared up at me with confusion. He shivered, condensation from our breath lingering in the air. His pale skin was almost translucent.

"Go hide in the bathroom—now," I mouthed. "Lock the door."

Charlie's eyes widened with horror as he took in my tense expression.

"Whatever you hear, do not leave the bathroom," I whispered quickly. "If things get…serious—and there's *no* other option—only then do you use the phone and call the first responders. Dial 777."

The phone was attached to the bathroom wall in a glass case labeled For Emergency Use Only. Every house was mandated to have one in case of a Titan attack.

Mother had installed ours in the bathroom because she said she didn't want to "see the ugly fucking thing all day."

She also said the same thing about me.

Charlie's breath caught as he realized what I was saying.

The phone line connected to local first responders, but they dealt with crises *after* they unfolded. The Titans were the only threat that warranted immediate intervention; for everything else, everyone was on their own.

After all, there were only ten Chthonic Spartans in existence, and only five were currently qualified to hunt down *dozens* of monstrous Titans.

The Assembly of Death was short-staffed.

Since the Great War, only five Chthonic children had been born. *Everyone* knew who they were.

Augustus, Kharon, Patro, Achilles, and Helen.

Technically, there was another child—Medusa—but she was

incarcerated in the underworld, which was the infamous maximum-security Spartan prison.

There were also a handful of creatures who fought for the assembly alongside the Chthonic leaders but they rarely had children.

Also, since Chthonics didn't join the assembly until immortality at twenty years old, there was only *one* Chthonic male heir—full-blooded Chthonic—who was of age right now to fight with the leaders.

Augustus, heir to the House of Ares.

He was the twenty-three-year old son of Ares and Aphrodite.

The next child to come of age would be Kharon, the eighteen-year-old son of Artemis and Erebus.

Augustus's sister, Helen, was the eight-year-old heiress of the House of Aphrodite.

Not much else was known about them because heirs and heiresses were infamous for being reclusive.

They were modern-day Spartan elites, more important and powerful than any human royal could ever have dreamed of being.

The last of the Chthonic children were two rare half humans called mutts: Patro and Achilles.

Patro of the House of Aphrodite was thirteen years old, and Achilles of the House of Ares was fourteen.

They were the future of the Assembly of Death, but until they came of age, there were barely enough monsters to fight Titans.

Humanity was still in grave danger.

The federation kept civilization running, but everything that wasn't a necessity fell through the cracks.

Charlie and I were below the cracks.

We were in the dirt.

"Go—now," I whispered to Charlie, then leaned forward and gave him a big hug. "It's going to be okay."

Both of us were shaking as we embraced.

When I pulled away, Charlie nodded and crawled silently into the bathroom next to where we slept.

Emmy and Carl fought to become pioneers of mathematics. Emmy dealt with evil in her time and stayed strong.

Be like her, Alexis.

I wanted to pretend I hadn't heard Mother, but I had.

I can't do this.

There were two of them and one of me. I was tall for my age, but not that tall. They were still much bigger than me.

Yes, you can.

I took a shaky breath and stood up.

Wrists tweaking with phantom pain, I rubbed at the hair ties that covered the raised skin of old scars.

There would be consequences if I acted—there always were in hell.

You need a plan.

Slowly, I walked out into the kitchen where they were standing sipping their drinks, and I spread my legs wide.

I had no plan.

It took me a dozen tries before I finally found the courage to speak. "If you t-try and h-hurt Charlie, you'll have to g-go through m-me," I said. "I'll tell e-everyone what y-you tried to do, and they'll l-lock y-you up f-forever."

No matter how much I concentrated, my stutter was always at its worst when I spoke to them—Charlie and Nyx were the only ones it completely disappeared around.

As if in slow motion, they turned toward me.

Their eyes were wide and unfocused, pupils dilated. Liquid clung to their lips. Shadows covered the emaciated planes of their wrinkled faces.

"What the *fuck* did you just say to us, girl?" Father asked slowly.

Mother smiled, flashing rotting gums and three teeth. She

threw down her empty glass. It shattered loudly across the cracked tile floor.

I jumped and swallowed a scream.

"How about we just kill you both?" Mother laughed. "We've got nothing to lose—we're fucking starving to death anyways."

Sweat streaked down the side of my face, then froze in the frigid temperatures. Every bone in my body wanted to turn and run.

I held my ground, turning frantically for a weapon—I grabbed the busted metal toaster off the counter and chucked it at them.

Father groaned as it hit him, and he stumbled back.

There was a shocked moment of silence.

Bad plan.

He kicked it aside.

"How…fucking dare you?" Mother demanded. Then they charged at me in a blur of screams and fists.

Far away, glass shards bit into my soles as Mother shook my shoulders back and forth while screaming obscenities. Her breath reeked of chemicals.

Father slammed his fist into my left eye, but I didn't *feel* anything.

Time distorted.

After a lifetime of pain, the brain learns how to suffer. I knew how to stay conscious through a beating. I'd had years to perfect my technique.

The key was tensing your core and buttocks.

Humming.

And nihilism.

Also, role-playing as a tortured nineteenth century musical prodigy in the imaginary throes of writing a violent opera helped.

A haunting melody started playing in my head.

Only I could hear the music.

I dodged, and Mother clipped my left ear with a punch. "You lazy, ungrateful whore, threatening us after everything we've fucking done for you..." A loud ringing cut off her words (a shame; she was making some intriguing points).

I staggered and turned.

Another punch caught the left side of my head.

The kitchen was narrow, and Father was pushed back as Mother kept attacking.

In my scramble to avoid the violence, her fist hit the same spot—everything went blurry, and I couldn't hear or see.

Classical music—delusion—filled the darkness.

Dim light filtered through my abused corneas—half the field of vision was black, and in the other half, I clawed blindly at Mother's face and neck with bloody nails.

I clutched at her shirt.

She screamed something I couldn't hear.

Her fist caught my mouth, and my blood sprayed across Mother's scratched face as I held on for dear life, desperate to stop them from getting to Charlie.

Just keep them occupied. They'll get tired. Then go for an opening.

"Let me in, Alexis—let me in NOW!" Nyx's voice hiss-screamed from outside. She must have returned from her hunt and heard the commotion.

She can help me protect Charlie.

I lunged for the door to let her in, but Father lunged with me. He dragged me back into the kitchen (hell) and threw me toward Mother (a demon from said place).

Her punishing blow caught the side of my head—everything *burned.* I clawed at her as she grappled.

"Kid, let me in right now!" The trailer rocked as Nyx slammed against it.

Mother's fist once again caught my left eye, and lights exploded. Black ringed my vision.

Blood was everywhere.

She screamed in my face—I screamed back. *Oh, look, we're harmonizing. Mozart would have loved this.*

Another blow slammed against the side of my head, and my fingers loosened as everything spun faster.

Stay focused. You're losing it, Alexis. Concentrate.

Panic welled, sharp and hot, like I'd been stabbed straight through the heart. *Charlie's in danger. Don't you dare pass out.*

CRASH!

The world exploded—the window next to us shattered into a million pieces.

Glass rained. *Oh, look, it's a crescendo.*

I staggered backward, slipping on blood and glass as I struggled to catch my bearings.

Shards were everywhere.

The trailer was painted in streaks of red because *something* had come through the window from the outside.

Father pointed at me. Then he was pointing at Mother, and they were screaming at each other. I pointed at the sink and screamed.

They shrieked and jumped back, pushing at each other to get away from the imaginary sink monster. Their pushing turned into shoving, and then a fist was thrown. They fought each other.

That diversion was more successful than expected.

Chest pain randomly skewered my sternum.

Great, I'm having a heart attack at eleven. Any other day, I would have welcomed a cardiac embolism with open arms. But not now. Not when Charlie was depending on me.

Mother grabbed a knife out of the butcher block and swung it wildly, and she yelled something garbled about a red devil as she stared at me. Her expression was wild.

She's lost it completely.

Her mind was poisoned.

I tripped over something solid on the floor as I dodged her swings, and landed on my butt.

She backed away from me.

Shards bit into my palms as a frozen object slapped against my leg, and I stilled in horror. I lunged forward and groped the space, grabbing on to an invisible body.

"I will protect you," Nyx hissed.

Nyx had thrown herself through the window to save me. She was the reason I'd gotten away.

The panic in my chest tripled. *No, she can't get hurt.* I groped blindly at my best friend, wrangling her icy scales with every ounce of strength I had.

"Stay beside me," I whispered desperately. "We need to protect Charlie. Not me," I gasped.

She hissed.

I hummed a frantic tune inside my head.

Evolutionists were wrong; humans hadn't evolved from primates—we'd *devolved* from them.

With my hands tangled around Nyx's icy scales, I dragged us both backward across the floor.

Grabbing at the bathroom handle for purchase, I started to haul us up. The door opened, and we fell inside.

He left the door unlocked for me.

I locked it behind me quickly.

Mother and Father shouted something about a devil as they yelled at each other.

Inside the cramped space, Charlie was curled up in a ball in the corner.

His emaciated body was wedged between the toilet and the wall. Overly large teary eyes looked at me with horror. Then he shook harder and ducked his head like he was trying to hide.

Nyx yanked in my hands. *"Release me,"* she hissed. *"I need to kill those bastards for hurting you."*

Charlie didn't react, and I wasn't surprised. I'd long ago accepted that I was the only one who could hear Nyx.

Everyone just assumed I was a loser who talked to herself.

The loser part was still up for debate (it wasn't; I authored Emmy Noether and Carl Gauss fan fiction in my free time).

I gasped shakily as the pain in my sternum intensified. "Let's protect Charlie from here—let them hurt each other first."

The symphony played faster.

She slithered up my body and wrapped herself loosely around my neck and shoulders like an invisible scarf.

Charlie sobbed harder in the corner.

I would have cried too, but I was too amped up on adrenaline.

Also, I had felt nothing in eleven years.

So, there was that.

Heaving for breath, I staggered over to the toilet and took off the heavy porcelain top. Repositioning beside the door, I raised my makeshift weapon and closed my eyes.

When they walked through, I'd bludgeon them and Nyx would bite them.

No one will hurt Charlie. No one will take him from me. Ever. He's safe. I'll keep him safe.

Pain stabbed my chest.

A panic attack had never felt so sharp.

G-sharp at a crescendo.

With labored breaths, I forced my shaking arms to stay raised while Charlie rocked back and forth in misery.

For him, I can do anything.

We might not be related, but as Father John preached, "The blood of a covenant is thicker than the water of any womb."

Day and night, Charlie and I survived in this hellish trailer together. We shared a cardboard bed. We starved together. Besides Nyx, he was the only person I had in my life.

"What's your plan?" Nyx asked, her invisible tongue brushing against my cheek.

"If they enter," I said, cracking my neck, "we kill them."

Cymbals crashed.

Agony skewered my sternum.

Charlie sobbed louder.

A *lot* was happening.

"Brilliant plan," Nyx hissed.

The foster parents had won; they'd made a murderer out of me.

On the other side of the door, Mother let out an unholy scream, and the hairs on the back of my neck stood up. The sound was so heinous that my panic quadrupled. I gasped with fatigue as my chest ached.

Heavy footsteps pounded.

My arms shook with exhaustion as I raised the yellowed ceramic higher—ready to fight.

Father's voice was close as he screamed, "Kids, help—quick… something is hurting her!"

I stilled.

What had he just said? Had he just asked *us* for help? The ones he was planning on killing? *This man cannot be serious right now.*

Charlie whimpered and curled tighter in on himself.

I closed my eyes and didn't move.

The wails harmonized.

"Children, call 777! A Titan has your mother!" The bathroom door rattled like he was trying to get in. "*Alex*, do something."

I hated that nickname.

We didn't have a mother.

Not really.

A stomach-curdling shriek sounded in the kitchen.

Titans were drawn to blood and violence, but the misery in

this trailer was an almost daily occurrence. *Why would one suddenly attack now? It doesn't make sense, unless…*

I gasped—the window was wide open after Nyx had broken through it, so the trailer wasn't locked up like usual.

A beast had gotten in.

The lid in my hands shook unmercifully. Icy scales slid against my neck like Nyx was repositioning herself to attack.

"Something invisible is tearing her apart—it's—it's—it's one of them…it has to be…please call…*please help*!" Father pleaded through the door.

The door creaked as he slammed against it and tried to get in.

I doubled over with chest pain.

Mother screamed louder, and Father sobbed as he clawed at the bathroom door. "Please, call the Spartans now. Please, children. Her mouth is foaming. It's…horrible."

She was being attacked, and he was at the door. It was really happening—the Titans were here.

I squeezed my eyes tighter.

Charlie sobbed louder.

The orchestra played their final act.

Fists banged against the door, a desperate man pleaded brokenly, and my hands trembled harder.

Blood rolled down my face and dripped onto the floor.

The door rattled.

The dying screamed.

Haunting classical music played.

"You are strong," Nyx whispered. "You are brave." Scales slid across the side of my face like she was nuzzling me. "You can handle anything—the universe is yours to command."

Tears joined blood and dripped down my face.

I didn't move and didn't open my eyes.

The phone on the wall remained untouched.

There was an awful gurgling noise, then…silence. The only sound was Father sobbing brokenly.

The musicians put down their instruments and bowed.

I held my breath as I waited. Waited for him to start making the same sound Mother had made. Waited for the door to break down. Waited to fight a Titan. Waited for death.

Time stretched.

I kept waiting.

"I think it's gone," Father said despondently. Then there was a crash like he'd tripped. The front door slammed, and his voice was muffled as he screamed and begged the neighbors for help.

I didn't lower my weapon.

Charlie sobbed quietly.

The excruciating sensation in my sternum slowly drained away, and everything blurred.

Noises, sounds, movements—it was all a jumbled haze.

Time warped.

Charlie nuzzled sleepily against my side. I blinked into awareness.

Dim green lights flickered above, and a familiar ratty couch was beneath me. Night had fallen in the trailer, and snow fell softly outside in the darkness.

The storm had passed.

Charlie was asleep under my arm, and Nyx was wrapped tightly around my torso, invisible beneath my sweatshirt. The trailer was full of strangers buzzing with energy. One of them said something about the neighbors calling it in.

Two of the strangers turned to me.

I flinched and tried to scoot back on the couch, to put distance between us.

The male and female medics didn't care. They leaned closer and invaded my personal space, the gold lion of the House of Zeus flashing on their ID badges.

If I'd had any energy, I would have screamed.

I barely mustered a grunt.

They dabbed something along the largest cuts on my face, hands, and feet, and I shivered.

"Stay still," the female medic snapped. "This is extremely expensive Spartan healing gel. There's only a small amount left. Once it's gone—you're out of luck." Her lips pursed with disgust.

The problem isn't the medicine; it's that you're touching me.

"You should be grateful we're using it at all," the male medic scoffed. "This bottle is expired. Otherwise, we'd never waste it on you. Olympian Spartan laboratories take *years* experimenting and designing to create these miracle drugs."

I wished it hadn't expired.

With a deep breath, I hummed a classical tune and focused on the positives—a few feet away, Mother was being zipped into a body bag by people in white hazmat suits, and Father was outside in the snow arguing as he was questioned.

Good times.

The trailer door slammed.

"Stay still," the male medic snapped as he squeezed my cheeks and dabbed at my left eye.

He's probably never taken math above calculus. Carl Gauss would never speak to me like this.

A tall policeman—dressed in black with fancy Spartan guns on both hips—knelt in front of me, and the wild horse of the House of Artemis flashed on his ID. It had feral bloodred eyes.

The policeman clicked on a recorder and spoke in a low voice like he was talking to a skittish animal. "We just need you to tell us what happened. Did you get these wounds from your father? Did he hit you?" he asked softly, like it mattered.

We both knew it didn't.

Battery and assault weren't prosecuted anymore—there was only *one* crime the Spartan system expended resources to combat.

"Not my father," I corrected him, and my voice sounded strange. "Foster father, and yes. He hurt m-me."

The policeman's eyes narrowed with interest. "And who hurt your mother? Who killed her? Do you rem—"

"Tell them what happened, Alexis!" Father's voice bellowed from outside. "Tell them it was the Titans. You know I was—" He grunted like someone had hit him.

My brain finished the sentence for him: *sobbing at the bathroom door, begging you to call the Spartans.*

"Ignore him," the policeman said. "Who killed your foster mother? You can tell me the truth. She was...drenched in blood and foaming at the mouth...it was a particularly...*brutal attack.*"

I opened my mouth to say it must have been a Titan, but the words didn't escape.

Charlie could have died tonight. Nyx could have gotten hurt. I rubbed at my wrists and looked the policeman dead in the eye.

"Father killed her," I said calmly.

Red devil eyes flashed accusingly on his badge.

The policeman clicked off the recorder.

"Thank you. That was all I needed. The system will handle this quickly. He'll be transferred tonight to the Spartan Federation Penitentiary—he'll serve life with no parole." He nodded at me. "He's out of your hair."

He stood up and walked out of the trailer.

Outside, Father started shrieking obscenities about killing me (greedy, if you ask me, since he'd already had his shot), but a car door slammed shut and he was silenced.

The female medic stared down at me with disgust, her voice warped as she said, "There was nothing we could do about your eye or ear. You aren't qualified for hospital treatment."

I had no idea what she was talking about.

She walked away with her partner.

I was going to miss her positive energy. Not.

Distantly, I was aware that someone was unrolling yellow tape that read "contaminated zone" along the walls of the trailer, while another person boarded up the broken window.

People shuffled out.

Time passed in a daze.

I blinked.

The trailer was empty and reeked of sterile disinfectant. It reminded me of the "special drink."

Neon-green lights cast shadows over the walls as the line of white electric Spartan trucks drove away into the storm. Snow gathered gently on the windowsills.

The three of us were alone.

It was a dream come true; it was a nightmare.

Shaking, teeth chattering, I pulled Nyx off me and jerkily repositioned Charlie on the couch. Then I staggered over to the trailer door.

It took me multiple tries to turn the three locks.

With trembling arms, I dragged the old armchair across the floor and shoved it in front of the door as a barricade.

Dim lights flickered in a green haze.

Only after I'd tugged the worn, patched blanket off the bed, which none of us had ever slept in, did I lie down beside Charlie on the couch and pull Nyx into my arms.

I couldn't sleep.

When the blinking digital clock said 5:00 a.m., I gave up trying to rest and stumbled into the bathroom.

The pipes groaned as well water sputtered out of the tap. Splashing freezing water on my face, I looked up into the small mirror above the sink.

My mouth opened in an O of horror.

Curls stuck out around my head in every direction, and my golden skin was covered in welts, bruises, and cuts.

That wasn't the problem.

Slowly, I closed my right eye.

The world went fuzzy and dark even though my left eye was still open. I opened my right eye, and vision returned.

Pink water dripped slowly down my face.

Mismatched irises stared back at me in the mirror. It wasn't an illusion—I no longer had two dark eyes.

The left iris was white.

The right iris was black.

The best part—that wasn't all.

Feeling like I was underwater, I lifted my shaking hand up to my right ear and spoke aloud. The sound was warped and staticky. I dropped my hand and repeated the action. This time, I could hear my voice.

I was blind and deaf on my left side.

With a deep breath, I splashed more freezing water, patted down my hair, and pushed my shoulders back.

The girl in the mirror looked calm. Covered in cuts, with eerie mismatched eyes, she was intimidating. Powerful. To her right, the emergency phone hung untouched on the wall.

"Who is she? I must know her name," Carl Gauss would say if he saw her walking down the street in Brunswick, Germany. "That girl will be my prodigy!"

I smiled.

My abusers were gone.

I was free.

In those early hours, I befriended the second monster I'd ever met—myself.

At least, I thought I did.

Later I'd come to understand that I was both very right and very, very, *very* wrong about that assessment. Monsters were tricky like that; by the time you saw them for what they truly were, it was already too late.

Later that day, there was a loud knock on the trailer door.

A middle-aged man with deep mouth wrinkles stood outside in the snow.

"The federation—" in a display of pure class, he spat out a thick wad of mucus "—has identified this trailer as a crime scene and thus uninhabitable."

He pointed to a large white truck with a fancy silver rig on the back.

"I've been ordered to take it away." His voice was warped, and the high-pitched ringing in my left ear worsened.

Snow flurried, and his eyelashes frosted over.

"Where are w-we supposed to live?" I asked on numb lips.

"Not my problem. All inhabitants need to evacuate—now," he said, expression blank. "I'm authorized to use force." His hand rested on a riot stick, which was strapped to his belt.

A few minutes later, Charlie, Nyx, and I stood on the empty patch of dead lawn with the parents' blanket wrapped around our shoulders. A few measly possessions were in a box at our feet.

The truck towed the trailer down the ice-covered road.

"Let's find shelter," I whispered and led my family toward the nearest trailer to beg for help.

We were officially homeless.

That was the thing about living in dark times—life got progressively worse.

Always.

3

SURVIVING HELL (HIGH SCHOOL)

ALEXIS: YEAR 2099

Neon green flickered on the ceiling as the power grid struggled to keep the school's lights on.

It was six in the morning, but homeroom—the period where teachers took attendance before classes started—buzzed with noises.

Who cares if Sarah cheated on Bethany with Eric and that they did butt stuff?

People confused me, but teenagers were downright perplexing.

Sometimes (every day), nineteen years on earth felt sufficient.

I'd seen enough.

Sighing heavily, I tried to focus on solving the equation I'd been working on for months.

Everything was riding on me scoring top .001 percent on the Spartan merit test this June. Every nineteen-year-old on earth took the Spartan test to determine if they could attend one of the three Spartan-run higher-education universities that were left in the world.

If I managed to get in, I still needed evidence of academic accomplishments beyond grades. My work on the Riemann Hypothesis would be my proof.

Charlie was depending on me.

I would not let him down.

Jessica sniffed where she sat next to me on the left. "Does anyone else smell that?" she asked loudly, then tittered with a group of girls.

Thank God I'm partially blind and can't see her expression. A small mercy.

She sniffed louder.

Wishing I could dissolve into tiny pieces and disappear, I sank lower in my seat.

I'd scrubbed in the school bathroom sink this morning.

I cleaned obsessively, but it was never enough because the scent of homelessness lingered on my few articles of clothing no matter how often I rinsed them.

It proclaimed to everyone that Charlie and I lived in cardboard boxes at the back of the poorest trailer park in our town.

Jessica plugged her nose, and her friends pretended to gag.

I hummed a classical tune.

Phantom pains shot up my forearms, underneath the dozen old hair ties that covered my scarred wrists.

I ignored the dirt that crusted beneath my nails, too deep to ever remove.

Ignored the heaviness in my eyelids because I struggled to sleep, worried that every sound in the forest was a Titan coming to hurt Charlie.

Ignored the gaping emptiness in my stomach, since tutoring for other people's food vouchers barely kept us fed and the federation classified illegal child labor as work by anyone who had yet to take the Spartan merit test.

They said it was uncivilized to make kids work.

Hot take, you know what's uncivilized? Forcing homeless children to starve because they have no ability to provide for themselves.

"I swear, she never showers. It's disgusting," Jessica said loudly so the entire room could hear.

There was a fresh round of laughter.

My sternum burned with shame.

It was times like this when I wished I was one of those confident, loud girls. The ones who spoke their minds and didn't let anyone push them around. The strong, fierce femme fatales depicted in old videos and books.

"The smell is awful." Jessica gagged loudly.

I said nothing.

I sank lower in my seat and rubbed my clammy palms against my patched pants. Interacting with other humans was not my strength. Words always got stuck in my throat.

Jessica's desk squeaked as she purposefully shifted farther away from me, like I was diseased.

The pressure in my chest increased by a factor of ten.

Just leave me alone.

Hell, at this point I'd tutored half the school population and was the reason anyone in this godforsaken place could do algebra.

Yes, the bar was set abysmally low. The fall of civilization would do that.

Jessica's desk squeaked louder as she shifted farther.

No matter what I did, I was just the dirty homeless girl who stuttered and smelled.

Humans sucked.

"Ohmygod…everyone!" Taylor screeched with excitement as she ran into the room. "There's a new Spartan Lifestyle Page upload about the Crimson Duo—they have footage of them *fighting Titans*!"

The Crimson Duo—Patro of the House of Aphrodite and

Achilles of the House of Ares—were the most famous members of the Assembly of Death.

The part-human mutts were everyone's current favorite Spartan obsession.

The only thing humans got more excited for was the recorded Spartan Gladiator Competition, SGC, which was held every three years. As it was, the school was already hanging banners, getting ready for next year when the games would be held.

Yay, Chthonic Spartans and dark creatures fighting one another and Titans for weeks on end in the Dolomites Coliseum! Yippee, torture and death. Go sports.

I didn't get it.

Now the class erupted with elated chatter, and my left ear rang with sharp feedback. Chairs squeaked, and desks clattered as the class ran to the back of the room.

My peers (enemies) crowded around the bulky pre-Spartan computers like vultures around a carcass, trying to catch a glimpse at the website, which was devoted to all things Spartan.

The website was the sole reason there was a huge underground market for refurbished early-twenty-first-century computers.

It featured videos, pictures, fan fiction, and quizzes all about the Spartans from the big twelve Spartan Houses.

The website also had some deeper and more *thought-provoking* content on the Spartans—sketches of their naked penises submitted by humans after firsthand accounts.

Not that I'd looked.

Okay, I'd looked once, but I'd screamed and powered down the public library computer.

Fine, I'd restarted it just so I could look again.

Maybe, I'd had a lengthy debate with the librarian over whether penises looked like misshapen snails (she was team sea cucumbers).

Sure, I'd then spent five days in a row checking the page because I couldn't believe men really had such things between their legs.

Yes, this had all happened last week. No, I didn't want to talk about it; I was still mourning my innocence.

"Everyone, *shut up*, I'm trying to sleep," Nyx moaned loudly, purely for dramatic effect, since we both knew I was the only one who could hear her.

Hidden beneath my holey oversize sweatshirt, she coiled her invisible snake body tighter around my stomach. I gasped at the sudden asphyxiation.

"Stop it," I whispered down to her. "I'm trying to concentrate on this equation."

Was I the only person in the world these days who respected math?

"If that girl squeals one more time," Nyx said, "I'm going to kill her. I don't care what you say, kid. It's happening."

I shook my head. "Her name is Taylor."

"Fine," Nyx hissed. "I'm going to kill *Taylor* slowly and painfully—is that better?"

Nyx snapped at the air. Her solution to everything was to bite someone to death. She'd never acted on the impulse, mostly because I physically restrained her from doing so.

Although I had my suspicions that Mr. Jones, the hall monitor, hadn't just "dropped dead randomly" in the cafeteria three years ago after he'd made fun of my stutter, but Nyx swore innocence, and I'd never been able to prove anything.

"Mr. Brewer?" Timothy, the school quarterback (Tim-Tom in my head), asked with a chagrined expression. "Can we play the video on the projector so everyone can see the Chthonics annihilate the Titans?"

"Do whatever you want. You're seniors," said Mr. Brewer, who was eating his breakfast sausage loudly.

"Can I bite a student now?" Nyx asked.

Discreetly, as all teenagers are known to do, I banged my invisible homicidal snake best friend against the desk to stop her from crushing me to death because I wouldn't let her murder my classmates.

Things were not well.

Mr. Brewer turned off the lights, and students whispered with excitement as the projector turned on. The Spartan Lifestyle Page was magnified across the screen.

"I can't believe this is going to be the Crimson Duo," Tim-Tom whispered to his friend. "It's the first sighting since January."

Four entire months—it's a miracle we've all survived.

Warmth slid against the front of my neck. "I want to see," Nyx said as her invisible head peeked out the neck of my hoodie.

I glanced around, nervous that someone had noticed a strange snake-sized bulge in my clothes.

No one was looking at me.

The class stared forward with dilated pupils. The neon-green light of the projector reflected off their glassy, wide-eyed expressions.

Crack.

We jumped in our seats.

On the screen, a Titan flew through the air and slammed against a tree, hideous black veins covering every inch of its exposed skin.

Long black claws protruded from gnarled fingers.

Shouts echoed.

The video had been taken by a Spartan chaser, one of the humans who stalked Spartans across the globe trying to get footage of the Assembly of Death while they fought and captured Titans.

There was a reason the Crimson Duo were famous.

The other Chthonics—the leaders and heirs and heiresses—were rumored to live by an archaic set of rules centered around maintaining honor. They were part of a secretive high society that spent their vast money and resources on being reclusive from humans.

But the Crimson Duo, who were raised by Spartans since birth, were not governed by the harsh honor rules of high society.

They were global celebrities.

The camera angle shifted. A muscular Spartan grabbed the Titan and threw him hundreds of feet across the forest like he weighed nothing. Then the Spartan stalked toward the Titan with his back to the camera.

The Titan moaned in pain and begged, *"Please, no,"* as he clawed at the man's arm with sharp talons.

An obscenely built black wolf walked into the frame and knelt protectively beside the Spartan. The beast growled ferociously. It turned its head toward the camera—crimson eyes and vicious fangs hung below its jaw.

Goose bumps erupted across my arms and legs.

In a blur, the Spartan pulled out a knife and thrust while the wolf lunged. The Titan screamed in agony.

I looked away.

Judging from the noises of awe in the class, I was the only one repulsed.

If Olympians were the heroes whose technologies and advancements saved our civilization, then Chthonics were the new dark gods, revered for their heinous power.

God save us all.

On the screen, black blood sprayed.

The Spartan repositioned to straddle the monster, and for the first time in the clip, his side profile was visible—a black muzzle with a grate pattern was wrapped around the lower half of his tan face.

"Holy crap, it's him," a student said. "It's Achilles."

Everyone knew about Achilles.

He was the only Spartan who wore a muzzle.

The Spartan Federation had constrained him after his terrifying performance in the SGC three years ago because his voice powers did one thing: torture. He'd put dozens of creatures into comas with merely a few words.

He was a monster among monsters.

Which made sense—the House of Ares was nicknamed the House of War for a reason.

Every Spartan to ever come out of that House was psychotic.

Their powers were pure evil, even compared to the other Chthonic Houses.

They tore people to shreds.

For fun.

"He's so hot," Jessica whispered.

"I know," the entire class replied as one.

Since the Spartans were also known for having sex with anyone and everyone—they had no biases about genders and usually dated (were slutty with) multiple people at once—it was a fad for humans to emulate their sexually free lifestyle.

I couldn't have cared less.

Carl Gauss, aka aggressive celibacy, was the only one for me.

Tim-Tom made an inspirational comment about spreading his legs wide and taking it like a champ, and I focused on the less disturbing Titan who screamed as he was tortured.

They were onto something when they started murdering humans.

Statistics flashed in neon letters on the right side of the screen.

- **Name:** Achilles.
- **Nicknames:** The Son of War. The Killer. The Beast of the Crimson Duo.
- **Lineage:** Father—Ares, leader of the House of Ares. Mother—human.
- **Spartan House Affiliation:** Chthonic.
- **Height:** 6 feet, 7 inches.
- **Weight:** 290 pounds.

- **Birthday:** March 23, 2077.
- **Power:** Voice torture ability, details unknown.
- **Animal Protector:** Wolf.
- **Power Ranking:** 95 out of 100.
- **Occupations:** Assembly of Death member. Founded WSDL weapons manufacturing with Patro, Augustus, and Kharon.
- **Net worth:** $3 billion.

Pop. Pop. Pop. Pop.

Achilles unloaded a magazine of bullets into the screaming Titan.

Distinct vermilion eyes were merciless—his eyes were naturally a shocking shade of red, even when he wasn't using his powers—and his long brown hair was tied up in a man bun. He was definitely the reason why half the male students in the class wore their hair in buns.

"Are you seeing this? Do you *see* him?" a male whispered.

"I know. He's…unreal."

"Savage *and* sexy."

The class laughed.

I debated if I should strangle myself now or later.

Pop. Pop. Pop. Pop.

The Titan kept screaming, because immortality meant it couldn't be killed, but it could still be tortured.

The gun clicked.

The beast of the Crimson Duo calmly pulled out another magazine and resumed shooting like he was bored.

Holsters stretched across his bulging muscles, and almost every inch of his powerful body was covered in weapons.

Gold WSDL lettering flashed on the barrel of Achilles's gun.

The *W* and *S* famously stood for War and Sex, an ode to the nicknames humans had given the Crimson Duo, but no one knew what words the *D* and *L* stood for, only that they represented Kharon and Augustus, the secretive Chthonic heirs who were rumored to be even *more* terrifying than the Crimson Duo.

Since Achilles was currently *torturing* a man on the screen, I found that hard to believe.

There was a blur as a second Spartan suddenly came into frame. The Spartan grabbed Achilles's shoulder and pulled him away from the Titan.

A Nemean jaguar slunk forward and sat next to the wolf. They were the same size (the height of miniature ponies but without the cuteness).

"*Ohmygod*, it's him!"

"No way."

"Move so I can see!" someone shouted as they shoved another student out of their chair.

The second Spartan came fully into view—it was Sex from WSDL. The son of the most beautiful woman to ever walk the earth.

The only person with the key to Achilles's muzzle.

Patro.

He fell to his knees and wrapped his hand around the Titan's throat, and his statistics flashed.

- **Name:** Patroclus.
- **Nicknames:** Patro. The Son of Sex. The Leader of the Crimson Duo. The Ideal Man. Achilles's Handler.
- **Lineage:** Mother—Aphrodite, leader of the House of Aphrodite. Father—human.
- **Spartan House Affiliation:** Chthonic.
- **Height:** 6 feet, 4 inches.
- **Weight:** 240 pounds.
- **Birthday:** August 23, 2078.
- **Power:** Mental, details unknown.
- **Power Ranking:** Insufficient data.
- **Animal Protector:** Nemean Jaguar.
- **Occupations:** Assembly of Death member. Founded

WSDL weapons manufacturing with Achilles, Augustus, and Kharon.
- **Net worth:** $3.5 billion.

The Titan kicked its legs and pleaded.

Patro touched his pointer finger to the Titan's forehead—green eyes glowing bloodred as he activated his Chthonic powers—and the Titan said something.

Patro clenched his jaw with anger. Then he turned his head toward the camera.

Short, wavy black hair, full crimson lips, long dark eyelashes, black skin, hollowed cheeks, and deep dimples created a stunning picture.

Students gasped aloud.

"The rumors are true. He really does look like the statue of David," someone said, and the class made noises of agreement.

Desks shifted as they leaned closer.

Even through the grainy lens, Patro's full profile was something otherworldly. He was simply too attractive to be real.

Father John had definitely been picturing Patro when he said, "The devil has a pretty face, and humanity is going to hell for worshipping it."

Patro raised his finger and pointed directly at the camera.

"Holy shit," Tim-Tom whispered behind me.

Heavy black boots stomped into view and revealed bulging thighs covered in weapons, sharp red eyes, and a muzzle.

A fist reared back, and Achilles shattered the lens with a punch—the screen went black.

There was dead silence as everyone processed what they'd just seen.

Lightning flashed outside, illuminating a barbed wire fence, and thunder cracked in the darkness.

Rain poured harder.

"*Ohmygod*, did you guys fucking see that? Holy crap, I can't breathe right now. That was the hottest thing I've ever seen in my entire life. I can't even—"

RINGGGG.

Homeroom was over.

Students buzzed with excitement as they packed their bags and filtered out, but they made a point of leaving a large space around me, like I was Pestilence himself.

The sky lit up a sinister shade of green that matched the flickering lights in the classes and halls.

"Well, kid, that was more entertaining than usual," Nyx said from my neck, and I discreetly shoved her back under my sweatshirt.

I grabbed my bag and headed for the library. "It was horrifying," I whispered.

A student gave me a weird look.

"If by horrifying you mean *brilliant*, then sure," Nyx said and mumbled something upsetting about a woman having needs.

I tuned her out.

Faces blurred as I moved through the flickering-green-lit crowded halls, my thoughts racing.

Technically, I'd finished high school three years ago, but only nineteen-year-olds could take the Spartan merit test and graduate.

I spent my days in the library, studying for the merit test and self-teaching myself advanced classes from old college textbooks.

Titan screams still rang in my ears as I walked faster among the crush of bodies.

Men in all black stood along the walls with their hands resting on top of gun handles, "WSDL" engraved in gold on their holsters.

The Minotaur of the House of Ares and the skeleton hellhounds of the House of Hades flashed on their ID badges.

What was left of the US government made state workers wear the symbols of the Spartan Federation, especially the Chthonic Houses. At the end of the day, it really meant nothing, but it made people feel safer.

One mercenary made eye contact with me.

He looked away first.

Men always did. They liked to pretend otherwise, but my different-colored eyes freaked them out.

The mercenaries were bait.

Titans were lone hunters—but since they were powerful immortals who were barely slowed down by advanced Spartan weapons, the lack of numbers didn't matter.

A single Titan could destroy an entire city if it wanted to.

When they'd first emerged in 2050, governments had tried dropping nuclear bombs on them.

It had been a disaster.

There was an infamous image of a lone Titan emerging from the blast, disfigured but still moving, eyes locked on the injured humans caught in the blast zone.

The mercenaries in the hall were five seconds of decoys at *best*, but apparently armed men glaring at students made everyone feel safer.

The hall was a blur of strangers.

A hand grabbed my shoulder, and I lunged back and slammed into a locker.

"Whoa, calm down, it's just me." A boy moved into my personal space.

He loomed above like a dark cloud. "It's me, Josh—don't you remember?" His smile faltered. "You tutored me last month for my math test. Which I got a sixty-five on, by the way!"

I stared at him blankly. *Does he want me to speak?*

People didn't talk to me outside of my tutoring service; they talked at me.

They commented on the holes in my clothes and asked if I really lived with feral dogs in the woods.

They joked that I had fleas.

Josh tipped his head back and burst into laughter (nothing was funny). "I'm so *excited.* It's my highest grade ever." He patted my shoulder.

The locker rattled behind me as I flinched away.

Since I was tall for a girl, most of the guys in our school were near my eye level, but Josh was built large.

"I know we agreed to leave your payment in your locker," Josh said with a strange expression. "But I wanted to talk to you in person."

He handed over three food vouchers.

I took them quickly and folded them carefully in my pocket, then pushed away from the lockers as I hurried past him toward the library.

"Wait up!" Josh—who I now vividly remembered because he thought six times seven was sixty-seven and didn't believe that zero was a number (someone needed to put him down)—ran up beside me on my left.

I couldn't see him.

My chest tightened with panic.

"Stop worrying. He smells weak. You have nothing to fear," Nyx said with a hiss. "But… I will bite him to death for you because I'm generous and helpful. You're welcome."

"You're not biting *anyone,*" I whispered.

"What was that?" Josh's voice was muffled and distorted, so it took me a second to decipher what he'd asked.

I didn't answer.

The metal detectors of the library came into view, and I hurried my pace.

Josh stepped in front of me, and he reached for my face.

I swallowed a scream.

I froze.

Waited for the blow.

He wrapped his finger gently around one of the gold curls

that had escaped my hoodie. "You know—you're *not* how they say you are. Your eyes are actually really pretty," he said softly.

Thanks, and you're actually really stupid.

Internally, I scoffed.

Externally, I was silent and frozen with fear.

"Wait, kid," Nyx said. "Isn't this the guy who couldn't multiply?"

Her voice pulled me out of shock, and I took a lunging step toward the library.

Josh moved with me. "So, what do you say? Are you interested in…" He wiggled his eyebrows up and down, then paused like he was waiting for me to say something.

Wait. He wants the two of us…to do it.

I shook my head in horror.

I'd rather die.

Gruesomely.

Right now.

Here in this very hall.

In an alternate universe, I was brave enough to tell him all that to his face.

Josh's congenial smile flatlined at my expression.

In this universe, I silently shoved past him and ran into my sanctuary, chest heaving.

This is why I don't interact with people.

"No running in the library!" Dorean the librarian yelled as soon as I crossed the threshold. "This isn't an unprotected zone, Alexis. Have some decorum. We *aren't* Titans."

Dorean glared up at me, wrinkly features pursed with annoyance. A Spartan gun gleamed on the hip she'd gotten replaced last year at a fancy Spartan research institute. Rumor was she'd donated a kidney to get off the waiting list.

Smart woman.

I basked in her impressive presence.

Dorean was the type of woman I aspired to be.

Strong. Bold. Intimidating. Able to verbalize her intrusive thoughts.

It was dead silent in the library because only a handful of students were granted access after *the incident*—Dorean had caught Jake Dalmer getting a hand job under a desk, and she'd shot him in the penis. Point-blank. No hesitation.

Thus my hero.

"The principal wants to see you." Dorean (community legend) handed me a hall permission slip and startled me out of my daydream.

"Thank you f-for your service to the school," I said instinctually.

Dorean rested her hand on her gun and raised her eyebrows. The message was clear: *Get out of the library or I'll have to take action.*

Understandable.

She was the only person besides Charlie that I liked.

I lingered at the library doors until the hall cleared. Then I hurried through the school. Eyes wide, head turning to make sure I was alone. If Josh appeared again, I'd start sprinting.

When I entered the principal's office, Charlie was sitting next to a boy who was covered in blood.

Wind rattled the bars on the window as the storm raged outside.

The principal's face was ruddy.

"Even though he's eighteen, as Charlie's guardian, it's your job to punish him," he said as soon as I stepped inside the small office. "Brandon pushed Charlie, and then Charlie took it upon himself to *beat* him bloody."

All three of them turned toward me.

The principal stared at me like *I* had some authority over the situation, like we weren't just two homeless kids who shared a cardboard box.

"They are waiting for you to say something," Nyx hissed under my sweatshirt, and I was grateful for the cue.

"I will punish Charlie," I said. "His behavior is—" I searched for an appropriate word "—condemnable."

The principal exhaled and sat back in his chair. "Ms. Hert, you're the smartest student this school has ever produced. Please ensure it doesn't happen again. Your brother is also one of our top students, and I don't have the time or energy to deal with this foolery—we have *Titans* to worry about."

He waved his hand at the grown boys dripping blood all over the floor.

Everyone in the room waited for something.

I waited with them.

"Say something," Nyx hissed.

"I u-understand," I said.

I didn't.

A few hours later, I climbed out of a rusty yellow school bus, another relic from pre-Spartan times.

We thanked our bus driver, and he flashed a single black tooth while grunting either a pleasantry or a vulgar swear word (it was definitely the latter).

Warm spring rain poured down, but neither Charlie nor I minded; anything was better than the freezing cold of winter.

Nyx grumbled about drowning to death.

For a wild *snake*, she was surprisingly high-maintenance.

Charlie shuffled closer to me as we walked into the trailer park, shutting the barbed wire gate behind us with a click.

Somehow, someway, the gate had kept out the Titans the entire time we'd been homeless.

It was a miracle. Yet I still stayed awake each night drowning in anxiety. The fact that something hadn't happened in the past didn't affect its probability of happening in the future. That haunted me.

I flung my arm up across Charlie's broad shoulders. He was

skinny but built wider and taller than I was, like if he got proper nutrition, he'd have an impressive physique.

I pulled him close.

He hunched low.

There was something fragile about his larger size, like he feared his own capacity for violence.

Now his pale knuckles were coated in dried blood, yellow eyes sharp.

Charlie's coloring was so different from my own golden skin and hair that people at school were surprised when they found out we were siblings.

But trauma bonds didn't change your appearance, just your souls.

"Are you mad?" he signed with his long fingers.

When it had become clear eight years ago that Charlie didn't speak, the two of us had learned sign language from an old library book.

I frowned at him with confusion and signed back, "Why would I be mad?" I always signed as I spoke, so he wouldn't feel alone communicating with his hands.

"I beat that kid until he was covered in blood," he signed with a frown—his hand motions jerky. "I didn't mean to, but my mind blanked, and suddenly he was Father, and I just wanted to protect—"

"Didn't he push you first?" I asked.

"Yeah," Charlie signed slowly.

"Then it's his fault," I signed. "You're allowed to defend yourself. It's not okay for anyone to touch you without your permission—*ever.* Don't forget that."

Charlie pulled me into a full hug. His body engulfed mine, and I leaned into it.

I loved his hugs.

We held each other.

When he finally leaned back, he held up his arm, showcasing the black "C+A" tattooed across his forearm.

I tapped my matching tattoo against his.

It was our thing.

A man waved out of his trailer window, and we waved back.

It was the kindest soul in the entire park.

Last year we'd borrowed a stick-and-poke tattoo kit from him. He was the only person who gave us cardboard boxes and blankets.

Without him letting us inside his trailer during the coldest, snowiest days of the year, we'd both be dead.

He was our savior.

Our personal saint.

He was also covered head to toe in animal skulls and satanic symbols, which, if you didn't think about it too hard, was inspiring.

A pentagram was stark on his forehead as he watched me and Charlie dip behind the tree line.

Behind carefully placed branches, we pulled back the tarp that protected our network of cardboard boxes from the elements.

The floor was covered in old blankets and rugs we'd stolen from trailers right after people died in them, just before the federation hauled them away.

Fluffy—the eighty-pound husky Charlie had named—stood up and flung himself at me like a battering ram as I fell to my knees.

I kissed his muzzle as he shook his butt with excitement.

Fluffy had been abandoned by someone in the park three winters ago and had wandered into our shelter and refused to leave our sides.

I'd been worried about feeding him, but it turned out that he liked the dead squirrels and rabbits Nyx brought for us.

Sometimes Charlie and I ate them when we were extremely desperate, but too much made us sick, so we left them for Fluffy, who never got affected.

Now, three years later, Fluffy was the best fed out of all of us.

Speaking of food, I pulled up the corner of the piles of carpet and hid our new food vouchers in an old glass beer bottle, since they were only redeemable on Fridays.

Today was Monday.

We only had four more days of hunger to get through. Three, technically, because Monday was almost over, and we'd get a meal on Friday.

Seventy-two hours of starvation.

Not long at all.

I clicked on the cracked solar-powered lantern we'd stolen, and flickering green light filled the space.

A few minutes later, I lay on a pile of blankets, with an invisible snake around my neck, nuzzling my face; a husky draped across my lap; and Charlie sitting up beside me with his homework spread across his own lap.

Classical music played on our old beat-up solar-powered radio.

It leaned against the right side of my head, and the vibrations tingled through me.

Charlie gnawed on one of the jerky sticks I'd stockpiled so he could have some food daily. He was a growing boy, so he needed the protein more than I did.

Hunger flared, but I focused on the softness beneath me and the cardboard over my head.

We're the lucky ones. The foster parents are gone. We're free of their abuse.

The rain pattered soothingly across the tarp.

Charlie signed math questions, and sequences of numbers floated around me as I thought about the Riemann Hypothesis.

Nyx's scales were smooth against my face, and Fluffy rubbed against my legs, getting hair everywhere.

Gratitude flooded me.

I was surrounded by my family and safe. Everything was going to be okay.

If only I'd known how wrong I was.

4

THE SPARTAN MERIT TEST

ALEXIS

"*Five minutes* until the test is over," the proctor announced from the front of the gymnasium. Mercenaries stood around the perimeter with their Spartan guns on display.

"Finish writing your answers," she said. "Remember, after pricking your finger, do *not* press your finger to the paper—squeeze your finger and let your blood drip into both bubbles… you only need a small amount."

Papers rustled as hundreds of students flipped pages.

My hand cramped around my pencil as I wrote desperately. Twelve hours of testing had taken its toll.

The clock ticked.

They couldn't have given us another hour?

I focused desperately on finishing my essay on the physics of quantum mechanics—the answer had to be written in Latin.

As the Spartan merit test progressed, the difficulty of the questions increased exponentially.

Halfway through, every question had to be answered in Latin. Judging from the amount of flipping the other students were doing, I was the only one on the last question.

"Three minutes left!"

Crap, what is the Latin word for "quantum chromodynamics" or "quarks"?

Sweat dripped down my sides.

A translation was on the tip of my tongue, but the time was taunting me.

"One minute left!"

I scribbled down "parva pila," which translated roughly to "small spheres." It wasn't exactly correct, so I hastily scribbled out the context and hoped it would be enough to—

A bell rang.

"Time's up—everyone put your pencils down!" the proctor announced. "Teachers will come around and collect your tests. Make sure your name is written on the front page. Take the time now, if you haven't already, to prick your fingers and fill in the two bubbles on the last page."

I slumped over in my seat and pulled my hood up over my head, gasping like I'd run for miles.

If you didn't score high enough, you and Charlie are doomed.

My hands trembled.

Breathe, calm down. It didn't seem too difficult, and you got through everything.

"Is it finally over?" Nyx asked from underneath my sweatshirt. "I don't know what's going to kill me first, the hunger or the boredom."

"I told you to stay at home," I whispered.

Nyx coiled tighter around my stomach. "And leave you to fend for yourself?"

"I'm nineteen—I don't need a *babysitter.*"

"Kid, I'm not a babysitter. I'm a full-time nanny, without any of the benefits of getting to kill people. My life is tragic."

"Oh yes, such a calamity." My teeth chattered from the adrenaline of taking such a long test. "Also, what nannies get to kill people?" I asked in confusion.

"The good ones," Nyx said. "Who actually protect the children—obviously."

Nothing was obvious to me in this situation.

"You're so weird," I whispered.

The student sitting in front of me turned around and gave me a strange look.

They wrinkled their nose.

I sank lower in my seat, rubbing at the hair ties on my wrist. The holes in my sweatshirt sleeves mocked me.

You've survived high school. You never have to see these people again.

An unfamiliar teacher walked slowly down the rows, collecting tests. She stopped and asked each student a question, so it took forever.

I tapped my foot to a classical melody only I could hear.

The ancient AC sputtered loudly and barely cooled the humid room. Gym lights flickered neon green and hummed as the power grid struggled to sustain so much electricity.

It was late June and humid.

I was trapped with hundreds of students, in the middle row, surrounded on all sides.

When the teacher *finally* got to me, I picked up my booklet and handed it to her, eager to be done and get out.

She took it with a smile and moved to the next—

"Wait." She handed me back my test. "You forgot to prick your finger—good thing I checked. Make sure to do both bubbles."

Taking the sheet from her, I picked up the small finger-prick device we'd all been given and jammed it down on my finger. Blood spurted out.

"Oh, sweetie," the teacher gasped. "Be gentle with yourself."

I barely felt it.

"It's f-fine." I held my dripping finger over the two bubbles on the back.

Quickly I handed the paper back to her.

Wiping my finger on my sweatshirt, I waited for her to walk away.

She didn't move.

I looked up at her. *What is it now?*

Her face was pale, and the paper was shaking in her hands as she trembled.

"What's happening?" Nyx hissed. "Why did your heart rate just increase?"

"I don't know."

The teacher didn't move—she looked like she'd seen a Titan.

Her eyes flickered to my face, then back to the page, and her pupils were blown out. A tendril of smoke curled off the paper like it was on fire. She took a step away from me like she was afraid.

"What is it?" I asked.

Nyx's warm scales slid against my neck. "What did you do to her?"

"Nothing." I gripped my wrists tightly as phantom pain spiked up my arms. "I didn't do anything."

The teacher opened her mouth and closed it, like she couldn't find any words. Students turned to see what the holdup was.

Whispers started.

The hairs on the back of my neck stood up.

The entire gym stared at us.

"Steal a gun from a mercenary," Nyx said. "Shoot her in both legs, then run for it. Do it quickly. I'll cover you."

My eyelid twitched. "You can't just *shoot* people," I whispered (I wasn't built like Dorean).

Nyx hissed, "Sorry I'm the only one of us actually trying to problem-solve."

"Shooting people is not problem-solving," I hissed back.

"That sounds like something someone would say—" Nyx paused dramatically "—who'd never actually *solved* a problem."

"You're insane."

"If I had opposable thumbs, the things I would do," Nyx said. "The sexual moves I would try out, the *positions* I would—"

"Please stop talking," I begged.

Miraculously, Nyx listened.

Mr. Brewer walked quickly down the aisle toward the rapidly paling woman holding my test. "Julie, what is it? Why did you stop collecting the tests? We have to get out of—"

She showed him the test, and he went dead silent. There was a rapidly growing hole on the page, and it was steaming, like someone had dripped poison on it.

Mr. Brewer staggered back.

"Protocol," Mr. Brewer blurted out loudly, and every head in the gym turned to stare at him. He pulled a small handbook out of his back pocket and flipped through it. His hand was also shaking.

I wanted to retch.

"We need to call it in." Mr. Brewer grabbed the teacher's elbow and steered her through the desks toward the far wall of the gym. They stopped in front of the emergency phone.

Mr. Brewer took the hammer off the wall. *Crash*—he shattered the glass around the phone.

He dialed three numbers, and someone answered on the other side.

"Per protocol," Mr. Brewer said with an unnaturally high pitch to his voice. "I'm reporting that we had a student whose blood turned the bubble yellow, and…then it burned through. No—it's not the bottom creature bubble. No, it didn't set the page on fire. It's the…top bubble."

The page disintegrated to ash in his hand.

"Yes…yes…yes…the page just disintegrated," Mr. Brewer said into the phone.

Students turned in their desks and openly talked to one another as they glanced back at me with disgust.

Nyx clicked her teeth. "Everyone mind your own business," she hissed.

No one heard her.

"The coordinates are…" Mr. Brewer squinted at the phone panel and read, "…46.5891 degrees north and 112.0391 degrees west—yes, we are 100 percent sure…yes…understood."

He hung the phone back up on the wall.

BOOM.

There was an explosion.

The gym shook. Desks clattered. Green lights turned off, then flickered rapidly.

A flash of white light burned my eyes, smoke billowed, and air gusted in a sharp burst like a bomb had detonated.

Two men stalked out of the smoke. They were Goliaths: extremely tall, covered in layers of muscles with tailored suits contoured to every curve of their unnaturally powerful bodies.

They glowered.

The lion of the House of Zeus was embroidered on their chest pockets in gold.

"Where is he?" one man shouted.

The room went dead silent.

His voice echoed.

From their outfits, impressive physiques, and lack of crowns, it was obvious who they were—Olympian Spartan mutts from the House of Zeus.

Mr. Brewer pointed directly at me.

A pencil dropped off a desk, and students jumped at the loud sound. Nyx slithered tighter around my neck and hissed, "Stay away from her!"

The two towering men stomped toward me.

I tasted blood.

"Take off your hood, son," one of them bellowed. "Look us in the eyes when we speak to you!"

He ripped my sweatshirt off my head, then froze.

"It's another *girl*, Boss—fuck…not *another* one," the other man said with a gasp.

The boss frowned. "I see."

They moved closer.

I was surrounded.

Nyx tightened around my neck and hissed louder, "I'll bite them. Then you run. Just tell me when."

Neither man reacted to her threat.

I couldn't have responded even if I wanted to.

The boss scowled and spat, "Under article three of the test, impersonating a Spartan, and using Spartan blood, is a capital offense punishable by death—are you aware?"

"Holy shit, kid," Nyx said, "I had no idea… *Did you know?*"

The room spun faster.

"Yes or no?" he shouted in my face, his voice explosive and cruel. "We need your informed consent that you are aware of this. Answer me!"

The student in front of me burst into tears.

Another kid sobbed.

"ARE YOU AWARE?" he screamed, his spit spraying.

I blinked. "Y-yes."

Something silver flashed through the air, and my hand was held upward in a vise grip.

A thick needle was stabbed into my hand.

He pushed a syringe.

Silver liquid was emptied into my veins—iciness spread beneath my skin.

I stared at it blankly.

An orchestra played Chopin's funeral march.

The Spartan spoke, and it sounded like he was talking underwater. "Per the Spartan Federation's merit test law, we're giving you enough purified adrenaline to kill a Cyclops...*if* you're actually an abandoned Spartan mutt—which is extremely rare—then you'll survive." He sounded doubtful as he held up a timer.

"But—if you're a *human* who *illegally* obtained Spartan blood on the black market and are lying to me, then you'll be dead in three minutes."

He clicked the timer on.

There was a retching sound, and more students cried, which was confusing, since they weren't the ones who had seconds left to live.

I stared at the needle in my hand blankly.

Damn.

My heart sank.

Charlie's going to be devastated.

Also, Carl Gauss proved the fundamental theorem of algebra at twenty-one, and I haven't discovered anything new in mathematics yet. How embarrassing.

The Spartan interrupted my mental breakdown.

"Humans are ridiculous. Another *simpering* girl trying to get close to the Crimson Duo. It's a fucking epidemic." He scoffed. "Kronos save us from that stupid web page. You've thrown away your life, young lady—and for what? Now you're dead. You're probably still fantasizing about them like an idiot—"

If I die right now, I'll never solve the Riemann Hypothesis. Just a few more months and I would have had it.

The Spartan shook his head with disgust.

"There hasn't been a female mutt in centuries," he said. "And while there are some heiresses, they're the most honorable and pure of us all—you're nothing like them."

He gagged after he spoke, like the thought of comparing me to them made him sick, then continued ranting.

"An heiress would *never* be caught dead participating in any Spartan initiations, or found in a—" he looked around the room with disgust "—dump like this."

He shivered dramatically and muttered about dishonor and protecting the pure House ways.

He shook his head again. "Mutt or heiress, no Spartan would *ever* voluntarily abandon a female baby—it's blasphemous." His expression was horrified. "Our female numbers are so low."

We stared at each other for a long, awkward moment.

Is he waiting for me to say something?

I didn't speak.

Unfortunately, he took that as a sign to continue. "Guess what, you're not even the *first* one to do this—last year we had *eighteen* fraudulent positives, all simpering girls…do you think we like to waste resources leaping across the globe, only for you to be fangirls who we have to fucking *murder*? Kronos, it's embarrassing the state humanity has fallen to. Fun fact, because you're about to be six feet deep, mutts used to microdose on this stuff to compete with heirs, but that stopped because every single one of them went *insane*. Not that you need me to lecture you on insan—"

The timer beeped, and the Spartan who'd been standing silently gaped at it. "Boss…look." He held it up with wide eyes.

They stared at it.

Looked down at me.

Glanced back at it.

"Stand up," the boss said softly to me.

Is he going to break my neck because the drugs didn't work?

I didn't move.

Crap. I'm not mentally ready to be snapped.

I covered my trachea.

"Alexis, you need to listen to him," Nyx said with urgency. "Stand up now."

With shaking knees, I pushed out of my desk and flexed my core, unsure what proper neck-breaking decorum was.

Should I try to crack it first to get it loose? Should I turn in the same direction to make it easier?

The Spartans stared down at me like they were telepathically willing me to drop dead, and I waited for them to attack. Somewhere in the afterlife, Carl Gauss waited for me (I was delusional).

We…kept…waiting.

I hummed with desperation.

Who knew getting murdered would be so awkward?

"Fuck, Boss, holy Kronos—this is going to…it's going to change everything. This is *huge*."

The boss cleared his throat. "I know."

He gently pulled the needle out of my skin. "Per article three," he said, "you have been confirmed as an abandoned female Spartan mutt. You are hereby declared a citizen of Sparta."

Wait…what?

"Are you nineteen years old?" he asked softly.

"Yes," I whispered on numb lips.

He swallowed thickly. "Are you already associated with any of the twelve Spartan Houses, including heirship or sponsorship?"

"No."

"Do you have any reason to believe that you are an heiress to a House?"

"No."

"Under the article three amendments, all Chthonics are required to compete in the SGC at eighteen years old. They are also required to join the Assembly of Death, if they survive the crucible. Do you have any reason to believe you are Chthonic?"

"No."

"Have you, at any point in time in your life, been recruited, lived with, or had any contact with a Titan?"

Foster Father begging at the bathroom door, "Please call the Spartans now. Please, children." Foster Mother howling in agony as she was ripped to pieces.

"N-no," I said.

"Do you have any reason to believe you failed to fill in both bubbles—and you also have a creature heritage?"

"No," I whispered hoarsely. *This is really happening.*

"What's your name?"

"Alexis." I cleared my throat. "Hert."

He took a step toward me. "Per article three." His tone was grave. "Alexis Hert, you are now a candidate to initiate at the Spartan War Academy…immortality is not a right, but a privilege. May the fates guide you, child of Kronos."

Time to panic.

He grabbed my arm and whispered, "Domus."

The world exploded.

Smoke whipped around me. Agony flared along every one of my nerves, and I opened my mouth to scream, but darkness tore me to shreds. Reality morphed into a—

The excruciating pain stopped.

Loud noises thundered all around.

I stumbled.

We were no longer inside a green-lit gym.

We were outside.

The Spartan boss, the same terrifying man who'd screamed in my face, cupped my cheeks gently. "Good luck, child. You're going to need it." His voice filled with regret.

Sighing, he walked away.

The sky was gray with a rainy drizzle, and the air had a slight chill to it, like it was still spring and not late June.

There was wet sand beneath my feet.

Ears ringing, my jaw dropped as I spun in a circle.

A sparsely filled stadium towered around me, but the regal-looking people and animals in the stands chanted loudly, "Amor fati, memento mori…amor fati, memento mori…amor fati, memento mori!"

Goose bumps prickled.

Remember death, love your fate.

No.

It couldn't be.

It was.

The crowd was full of Spartans, their animal protectors, and creatures dressed in all-black robes.

Boys my age already stood on the sands, like they were waiting for something to begin.

They all turned and stared at me.

The highly upsetting chant echoed all around.

Jagged mountains towered behind the stadium, and the sun peeked out behind the clouds, but it had been late at night in the school gym.

The skyline was strangely familiar.

Oh my freakin' god.

It hit me like a cigarette pressed against my flesh. At first, I felt nothing. Then the excruciating pain was overwhelming.

I staggered backward.

The Italian dolomites pierced the sky, which meant the awful agony had been the Spartan teleportation system.

We'd *leaped* halfway around the world.

I breathed shallowly as my heart twisted.

Charlie was hundreds of miles away.

Around me was the Dolomites Coliseum where the SGC was held. It was also where young Spartans and creatures were rumored to fight to the death in a secret hazing process that was more rumor than reality.

I have a bad feeling it's about to be confirmed.

A horn blared loudly.

The sparse crowd pumped their fists, and twelve flags were raised around the arena.

An ancient immortal civilization cheered.

Sparta.

Eight colorful Olympian House flags waved with about a dozen people in each section.

The gold lion of the House of Zeus.

The rainbow peacock of the House of Hera.

The purple owl of the House of Athena.

The green fish of the House of Hermes.

The blue dolphin of the House of Poseidon.

The brown pig of the House of Demeter.

The yellow eagle of the House of Apollo.

The purple-and-green goat of the House of Dionysus.

In contrast, the Chthonic Houses stood out among the Olympians like a sore thumb. Half the coliseum had empty seats, which separated them from the rest of the colorful crowd.

There were only ten Spartans in that section.

Total.

A handful of terrifying creatures in long black robes stood among them.

Four black flags waved, and their symbols were all equally spine-chilling, each covered in blood with gruesome red eyes.

The charging Minotaur of the House of Ares.

The skeleton hellhound of the House of Hades.

The rabid horse of the House of Artemis.

The black swan of the House of Aphrodite.

Even from afar, the Chthonic Spartans looked menacing. The men and women were taller and stronger (*more attractive*, the teenage pervert inside me noted unhelpfully).

Dressed in black three-piece suits and dresses, they stood with their arms crossed in various poses of boredom.

They were the only section not cheering.

However, it was their animals that *really* set them apart.

Most of the Olympian section was filled with colorful bird protectors: crows and ravens with flaming wings, lion tails, and strange beaks. There were also a few gargoyles, pink monkeys, and other strange-looking creatures among them, but the vast majority were birds.

But underneath the black banners of the Chthonic Houses, the animals were…different.

They were land predators.

Big jungle cats.

A brown dog with three heads towered.

A shaggy wolf stood next to a sleek jaguar, and a tan man with a muzzle leaned against a stunning black man with short, wavy hair.

Holy crud, it's the Crimson Duo.

Memories of a Titan screaming as he was tortured played in my mind.

Shaking with fear, I ripped my gaze away from them and looked around the arena. There were barely any women in Sparta.

It was even worse in the arena.

About fifty boys stood with me on the sand, and they were all staring at me.

I was the only girl.

Please tell me I'm lucid dreaming right now. Please, don't let this be real.

Three boys wore small gold laurel-wreath crowns—the symbols of Olympian heirs—and they looked around cockily, heads held high like they were better than everyone else.

ROAR.

A menacing animal growl reverberated through the air.

The crowd went dead silent.

A Nemean lion slunk forward on a white platform that extended from the bottom of the stadium, and it shook its majestic golden mane.

To the right, a beast of a man in an all-white suit walked beside it.

He wore a magnificent gold laurel crown covered in sparkling jewels (much fancier than the boys' in the sands). The famous headwear indicated that he was the leader of an Olympian House.

He was *the* Spartan royal.

The famous leader of the Spartan Federation.

Curly gold hair, a matching full beard, shocking gray eyes, and glowing skin were unmistakable. He wasn't very tall, but he was wide and stocky.

Power exuded from him.

He stopped at the end of the podium, framed by two towering white columns, and spread his arms wide.

Electricity leaped across his glowing skin like he was a live wire. Zapping noises echoed as the energy mixed with the rain and created sparks.

It was the most godlike Spartan to ever walk the earth.

It was Zeus.

His Olympian powers were legendary; the electricity he naturally generated enhanced his speed, intelligence, and strength. He was simply better than everyone…ever.

"The House of Zeus welcomes all of Sparta on this summer equinox." Zeus's voice projected around the coliseum.

"With our Olympian labs and scientific advancements, we are mightier than ever!" he shouted. "We are the *gods* of this new age."

Sand vibrated as the Spartans stomped their feet, and the drizzle became a heavy rain. Sparks leaped brighter on his shoulders.

Zeus smiled widely and waved to the crowd.

"The twelve ancient Houses of Power stand before me united and stronger than ever, and it is my *greatest honor* to welcome all of you—Spartan generals and the trainees who are working to obtain general status so you, too, can someday be members of our illustrious federation."

Spartans cheered and stomped. Animals flapped their wings and roared. House flags waved.

Zeus turned toward the sand. "And a *special* welcome to

this year's initiates—the heirs, mutts, and creatures of the new generation. In this Kronos-blessed coliseum, you are all equal. There are no Chthonics this year, but there is an *impressive* array of Olympians."

His white teeth flashed.

After the Great War, Spartans had struggled to produce heirs, and it was rumored that they were getting desperate, creating as many mutts with humans as possible to keep their race going.

Since only three boys on the sands wore crowns, that rumor seemed to be true.

Only two wore the black cloaks of creatures.

Bolts of electricity twined around Zeus's arms as he once again spread them wide. "Memento homo quia pulvis es et in pulverem reverteris!"

Remember you are dust, and to dust you shall return.

It was strange hearing Latin spoken aloud. The fact that the words were spoken out of order made my head pound as I struggled to translate them.

This is real.

They are speaking a language that's dead to humans.

I took another step back.

Zeus's golden curls rose with static electricity.

"Welcome, initiates, to the Spartan War Academy's initiation massacre. *If* you survive, you'll have the honor of participating in the crucible—the most rigorous test of intellect in the entire world. This initiation massacre is a sacred privilege."

My eyes widened.

What had happened to a good old-fashioned welcome lunch?

The crowd (bloodthirsty monsters) cheered louder and clapped in cadence with their stomps.

"You're all nineteen years old." Zeus nodded like our age was of grave importance. "Your powers have developed by now. *However*...most of you will not reach the age of immortality until you're twenty. So this is your reckoning—the first, and… for most of you…last hurdle you will ever face."

Wet sand vibrated beneath me.

I debated raising my hand—*What do we do if we have no powers? Can we opt out of the massacre?*

Also, who was going to tell them my entire life was a hurdle? I hadn't stopped hurdling since I'd come out of the womb.

Zeus tipped his head back, sparks streaming from his mouth as he bellowed to the sky, "As Kronos declared at the dawn of time—*immortality is not a right, it's a privilege!*"

The crowd shouted alongside him, and I winced as the feedback caused a sharp sting.

What's the next step after panicking? I need to do that.

Zeus looked down at us. "Initiates, do you have what it takes—TO BECOME A GOD?" he bellowed at the top of his lungs.

My gut reaction is no.

The sky opened up, and rain poured harder. Cold droplets splattered across my face, and neon-blue bolts exploded around Zeus.

"This is concerning," Nyx whispered against my right ear.

I nodded numbly.

I had a bad feeling I was about to unlock a new level of suffering.

5

THE INITIATION MASSACRE

ALEXIS

In the pouring rain, a lithe, pale figure with long, inky hair sauntered slowly down the podium toward Zeus.

He wore a ruby crown with tall, jagged silver spires, which was the famed symbol of the Chthonic House leaders.

He was an entire head taller than Zeus.

The man's countenance was abrasive.

Menacing.

If he was a musical melody, he'd be the Locrian mode—the darkest musical scale played on a piano.

Dark fog swirled around the man's feet, and his eyes were an insidious shade of black.

A monstrous three-headed dog added to his daunting visage. The terrifying animal followed him with matching black eyes.

The man and his beast were notorious for running the underworld, a maximum-security prison that only housed immortal inmates in the North Sea. The place where Titans and incarcerated Spartans were tortured. It was where Medusa was infamously imprisoned.

Beside him walked a short woman with dark skin in a pink dress.

She was his foil: pretty and delicate.

A small laurel crown sat atop her curly blond hair—signaling she was an Olympian heiress—and a dog-sized dragon was perched on her golden-tan shoulder with its tail wrapped around her neck.

Heiresses were super rare and highly sought-after because of all the Spartan fertility issues.

As the woman stood on her tiptoes, whispering, his expression softened, and he wrapped his arm around her protectively.

Hades and Persephone.

Their love was legendary.

Persephone was the daughter of Demeter and Iasion—a dark creature who was rumored to have power over plants.

Because of her heritage, Persephone was uniquely powerful and beautiful.

That was partly why Hades and Persephone were so infamous.

It was also because everyone knew Hades would do *anything* for Persephone. Humans had been killed and Spartans had been imprisoned for merely looking at her wrong.

Plus, Spartans were known for their promiscuity (they had both male and female lovers in the *multiples*). As a result, few Spartans took marriage oaths, and even fewer took an oath with a single person. Hades and Persephone were one such singular rarity.

The rest of the House leaders were in relationships, such as Zeus and Hera, but they didn't take Spartan oaths and were known to have affairs with other Spartans and humans.

It was rumored that centuries ago, it was the norm for Spartans to take marriage oaths, and the largest wedding was between *seven* people.

Hades clapped Zeus on the back in a warm greeting, towering over the shorter, gold-skinned man.

While none of the separate Spartan families were related, they were rumored to be as close as brothers, and their collaboration had ended the Great War.

The hair on the back of the dog's three necks stood on end as it growled at the lion. The beasts stood eye to eye, teeth bared.

As Zeus walked away and his lion followed, a feeling of certain doom settled into my bones.

I took another step back in the sand.

Rain soaked me to the bone.

Hades spread his arms wide. "The initiation massacre begins now. Like always, weapons are *not allowed*—whoever wields one will be killed." His voice projected around the coliseum like a gunshot.

He looked down at us and his face was carved from marble, emotionless and cruel.

"Use your fists and your wits," Hades said. "The adrenaline pumping through your veins will keep you going when your body would otherwise fail—above all else, this is a mental test." His voice rose. "Spartans are gods…remember…there is no such thing as a stupid god!"

The crowd roared.

Shadows stretched around Hades.

"This is your chance to prove your worth!" he bellowed, and black fog gathered at his feet.

The inky fog poured down the high walls into the sands where we stood.

His legendary power streamed toward us. No one knew exactly what it did, but everyone knew to fear it.

The House of Hades was known as the House of *Death* for a reason. Their abilities were as scary as the House of Ares.

Chthonics are all evil.

My breath left my mouth in an unnatural frosty puff as the fog rolled in and the temperature plummeted. I rubbed at my chest, heart racing uncomfortably fast from the adrenaline they'd injected into my veins.

Thunder cracked.

I was painfully alive.

As the black fog approached, it carried voices—*a woman wailed, a male begged me to call the Spartans, a young boy sobbed, a strange male shrieked in pain, and Nyx hissed in confusion.*

I turned to run from it, but there was nowhere to go—the screaming fog surrounded me on all sides. Dark and solid. It trapped me.

My teeth chattered.

"FIGHT TO THE DEATH!" Hades bellowed, his voice warping with a strange cadence, and three dog barks boomed.

"Immortality is not a right, it is a privilege… Immortality is not a right, it is a privilege…" echoed through the coliseum.

Off to my right, a boy bellowed, and flesh smacked in the fog.

I turned my head and squinted.

To my left, a boy's shriek was abruptly cut off.

There was a grunt, then silence.

Lightning flashed, and electricity filled the air. My wet hair fizzled. I turned in a circle and squinted into the fog, but I couldn't see anything.

"You need to get ready—stay alert," Nyx said.

"Ready for what?" I whispered.

A boy appeared out of the fog, charging at me.

I turned to run—he slammed against me, and my face banged against wet sand. My limbs tingled from being body-slammed. He was all over me. He was *touching* me.

There was a moment of pure shock.

I froze.

Nyx yelled something at me, but I couldn't hear.

Fists slammed into the side of my head, and the ringing in my left ear got louder. Another blow caught my chin.

He was still touching me, and I didn't want it.

Something inside me snapped.

Bucking against the boy's hold, I swung and kicked blindly. Scratched. My fists landed against thick muscles. We grappled, rolling through the wet sand.

He punched me in the stomach with insane force.

I tasted vomit.

Nyx slid against my neck.

My attacker collapsed on top of me, convulsing.

She'd bitten him.

I shrieked through my teeth as I shoved his body away and scrambled to my feet, heart racing, frosty breath uneven. I struggled to catch my bearings and think. My skin crawled where he'd touched me.

I rubbed my hands across my grit-covered arms like I could wipe the disgust away.

"Thanks." I gasped for air.

"Kid, you need to stay alert and run," Nyx said. "If they get close, I'll bite them so you—"

Two bodies slammed against me.

Then a third.

A fourth.

I lost count. Boys fought everywhere. There was no tact, no dodging and expert maneuvers like the fiction books described in the library.

There was no honor.

We were animals.

Cymbals crashed, and haunting music played.

Hell was not a place; it was cracked bones and hoarse shouts in the middle of a scrum. It was fighting in a melee of screaming black fog that sounded alarmingly like my foster parents.

Sanity disappeared as I punched, kicked, and scratched blindly in the middle of the chaos. Blood sprayed. Rain poured. Thunder boomed.

Baptism by fire.

A fist pummeled my face. My nose broke, and blood splattered. Copper flooded my mouth.

Someone pulled him back into the fog.

Hands tried to wrap around my throat from behind, but Nyx was already there, and they convulsed with a scream.

My ragged breath puffed in the air.

The temperature was below freezing as the fog rolled over me like a sadistic blanket—*a woman wailed as she died.*

"Filthy abandoned mutt," someone growled.

The ringing in my left ear was now a high-pitched burn.

I turned and ran.

Stumbled. Dodged. Sprinted in a stupor across the wet sand through the opaque fog. *Away. Away. Away.* I needed to get *away.*

The ignominy was too much to handle. I pulled at my hair as I ran, retching with shame that I didn't fully understand.

Lightning flashed, and thunder boomed.

Everything was distorted.

Between the voices in the fog and the fighting bodies, I couldn't tell what was *real* and what was in my head.

I screamed into someone's bloody face; they screamed back.

A boy kicked me, and my forearm cracked.

I barely noticed. I was used to violence, but not like *this.* The adrenaline had me sprinting as fast as I could when I shouldn't have been able to stand.

Nyx's invisible scales slithered against my neck as she lunged in every direction.

Hands held me down—they fell away, convulsing.

I backed away through the fog, trying to put distance between myself and the fighting.

I bumped into something and jumped.

Whirled around.

"No. No. No." A boy in tattered black robes sobbed into his hands and didn't move. Somehow, he hadn't felt me knock against him. "I didn't mean to. I swear… I didn't mean to."

He was on his knees, all alone.

Tiny black horns protruded off his head.

He's a creature.

The black fog writhed around him like it was attacking him.

"No, I'm so sorry! I'm so sorry!" he choked, and lightning illuminated his distraught features. "I'm so sorry. I lied—I meant to do it!"

He punched himself in the head.

Thunder rolled.

Dark music played.

Blood splattered across the sand as he pummeled himself to death with his own fists. His horns landed in the sand.

"Oh dear," Nyx whispered.

Turning, I ran but slipped.

I caught myself with my hands in the deep puddle. Pain streaked down my arms. When I got back to my feet, my arms—fingertips to elbow—were coated in red.

Thick raindrops splattered across it.

I stared down at the puddle of viscous blood I'd fallen into. Teeth chattering, I spat sand out of my mouth. Shaking with horror. Gasping as I struggled to inhale.

I can't breathe.

"I'm so sorry," Nyx said despondently. "If I'd known, kid… I would have prepared you."

I stared dumbly at my trembling hands.

"In my experience, those with power suffer for having it," Nyx whispered.

Screaming fog wrapped around my legs. I slammed the edge of my palm against the side of my head to make the noises stop.

They didn't.

I was covered in open wounds and drenched head to toe in blood, and not all of it was mine.

Gore was caked beneath my nails—the ones that hadn't been ripped off.

"But I don't have any powers," I whispered.

Scales slid against my neck. "It's in your blood, whether you want it or not," Nyx said. "You do. You always have—you just haven't known it."

"TWENTY COMPETITORS REMAIN." Hades's distorted voice cracked like a whip. "ONLY TEN WILL MAKE THE CRUCIBLE—PROVE YOURSELF NOW OR PERISH."

I wiped crusted blood from my throbbing nose.

The "C+A" tattoo on my forearm flashed, and my vision blurred. *I miss Charlie. I miss Fluffy.* The urge to fall to my knees and crawl into the fetal position was overwhelming.

Maybe in an alternative world, I did.

In this world, a large body came barreling out of the fog. Yet again.

A fist caught me on the left side of my head. I kicked out and scratched as arms wrapped around me and wrestled me to the ground. They ripped at my hair, trying to get purchase on my head to snap my neck.

Nyx hissed and lunged.

Like the others, the boy collapsed.

I shoved his body off and lay on my back in the rain, gasping as I tried to catch my breath—a leg kicked out of the fog.

This new attacker slammed a steel-toed boot against my side. Ribs cracked. A second appeared and kicked before I could get to my feet.

"An abandoned female mutt—you're clearly an *abomination* who was abandoned for a reason. Our Houses taught us how to deal with defects like you," he snarled.

A third joined.

Thunder boomed.

Nyx lunged off my neck. *Thwack*. Her weight slammed down against my chest.

I stopped feeling the blows—didn't notice my blood spraying across their shins—as panic filled me.

Rain poured harder.

"NYX!" I screamed as I grabbed at her invisible body. She was icy and limp in my arms.

No. No. No. No. No. No.

The feeling inside my chest was overwhelming.

I shrieked like an animal and clawed with my nails at the legs of the beasts who'd hurt Nyx. My arm cracked as a boot hit it, and I didn't care.

NYX!

Scrambling, grappling, screaming, I clawed at the men with my remaining nails—tore their skin off their bones as they swore and tried to shake me off. Lunging forward, I bit them with my teeth.

Their blows did nothing, because I *knew* how to take a beating.

One of them slipped and fell. I threw myself to my feet and lunged after them. They scrambled back.

Three against one.

They hurt Nyx. She's always been there. Curled around me in a cardboard box.

I bared my teeth and shrieked at them as my heart burned like it was breaking into a million pieces.

The three of them took a step backward and gaped at me.

I took a step forward.

Rage filled me.

Someone shouted—all four of us whipped our heads to the right.

A shadowy figure was silhouetted by the fog. There was movement, and his hand extended toward my attackers.

Glowing red light reflected off the black fog.

I forgot how to breathe.

Pain stabbed my chest.

The boy in the fog had Chthonic power—he could hurt us, and we'd have no way of stopping him. As if to punctuate that thought, my three attackers fell to their knees and cried out in pain as they stared up at me with horrified expressions.

Zeus said there were no Chthonics this year. Does no one know what he is?

Foam dripped from the dying boys' lips, and their bodies arched like they were on fire as they stared at me and bellowed.

The fog in the immediate vicinity thickened and rushed toward me like it was attacking. Male voices in the fog shrieked at me.

I closed my eyes.

The screams intensified: real and imaginary.

Panic stabbed hotter through my heart.

Icy fog twisted against my skin.

I was frozen, glad they were dying but unable to stomach the sight. Finally, the three of them let out the most god-awful stomach-curdling wail, then fell silent.

Rain splattered softly against sand.

It's over.

Panic abating, I cracked open my eyes.

The pale Chthonic boy stepped forward out of the fog. A few scraps of his clothes were left around his shoulders, but the rest had been torn off. He glared at me with a disgusted expression. Loathing rolled off him.

Lightning cracked, and a crescendo of thunder made the sand vibrate.

I stared back.

Waited for him to make his move.

He took a step—

"THE MASSACRE IS OVER." Hades's voice crackled through the air like electricity. "THE FINAL TEN HAVE QUALIFIED FOR THE CRUCIBLE—CONGRATULATIONS."

The black fog cleared. It retracted up the walls and curled around Hades's feet. The awful screams dissipated. The temperature returned to normal.

Mangled bodies were strewn everywhere.

Everything—the sand, the fallen, the ten of us standing—was coated in red.

"Welcome to Sparta!" the crowd cheered as they waved their House flags through the rain.

I looked down.

My clothes were torn and hanging off my body as rags, but at least the hair ties still covered the raised scars on my wrists.

I was half-naked, covered in scraps and streaks of sand, but I couldn't find the energy to care. *Free the nipple and the lips (vaginal)?*

My head spun, and the world kaleidoscoped.

The adrenaline was still affecting me.

Nothing seemed real.

I exhaled with relief as I felt Nyx slither up my legs and around my neck. "Need…rest," she whispered weakly.

Through the rain, Hades stood calmly on the edge of the podium with his heinous black fog swirling around his ankles.

His power had felt like insanity.

Father John was wrong; the devil was real, but there was no god to stop him.

The leader of the House of Hades stared down at the sands with an uncaring, ruthless expression.

Nothing could save humanity from *him.*

He was the reason Nyx was hurt, the reason so many were dead.

I'd never hated anyone more.

"*Congratulations* to our ten Spartans who showcased the mental and physical fortitude of gods," Zeus said, sparks leaping off him as he stepped beside Hades with a smile. "Welcome to the crucible. Survive this next year, and you will be named a citizen of Sparta. Immortality is within your grasp."

The coliseum cheered louder.

I could still feel the black fog wrapping around me like a vise. *I'm losing my mind.*

Zeus beamed at the crowd and glowed brighter. "Thank you all for joining us. Sparta, and the Spartan Federation, are stronger than ever because of you! Now, honored Spartans who've been chosen as mentors, join me now on the sands."

BOOM.

Zeus and a dozen men jumped over the edge of the wall and landed in the sand with bent knees. Their animals followed.

The wall was at least five stories tall.

I stared at the approaching men blankly. Everything was fuzzy.

Time warped.

Zeus was speaking on the other side of the sand. "Being a mentor is a great honor. As you know, if your initiate survives the crucible, you will be granted general status…the highest demarcation a Spartan can reach, and a chance to join the federation!"

The Spartan men who'd leaped from the stadium fell to one knee and bowed their heads toward him. "It is our honor!" they chorused back.

They knelt in blood.

There was a muffled sound. "What…name?"

A diminutive elderly lady stepped out from my left side. "What's your name?" she repeated. Her hair was bright white, eyes a strange shade of violet.

I stilled.

She looked familiar, but my head was rushing with adrenaline, and I couldn't remember why I recognized her.

Zeus droned on about honor.

The lady held a pen over a scroll and looked at me expectantly. A yellow raincoat was draped over her, and she wore neon-orange galoshes. She looked ridiculous.

"*What* is your name?" she repeated. "You're the last one on the list…we have to write ya down, make this all proper."

A manic snort escaped my nose.

"Snap out of it, girl." My head snapped to the side as she slapped me across the face.

Who does that to someone they just met?

Dorean would—I missed her.

As I rubbed my aching jaw, the little old lady (violent assaulter) grabbed the mangled remains of my sweatshirt and pulled me down to her level with surprising strength.

"The fates are rooting for you—don't you *dare* make us regret backing you, Alexis Hert."

I yanked out of her grasp.

If she already knew my name, why did she ask? I would have asked her, but it turned out even a massacre wasn't enough to overcome my fear of speaking to strangers.

Her eyes glowed an unnatural shade of electric blue. "Tell me your name?" Her voice register dropped three octaves. "Tell me *now.*"

"Alexis H-Hert," I whispered.

Her blue eyes faded back to violet as she patted me on the cheek and smiled sweetly. "And don't you forget it, dearie." She leaned close and whispered conspiratorially, "*Girl to girl*—I'd take a chance on the killers, if you know what I mean—even with their hounds." She winked and wrote my name on her scroll. "Don't let their…*passion*…scare you away."

"What?" I asked.

She wiggled her brows and waddled away, stepping on bodies as she headed toward Zeus.

She might be worse off than neighbor Paul, pre-shovel.

I'd only ever heard of Chthonic eyes turning red when they used their power. What did it mean that her eyes turned blue?

What can she do? What is she? Why does she look so familiar?

A strange sensation skittered down my spine.

It felt like—

"Fate has written these ten Spartans into our ranks," Zeus announced as he held the scroll, then read off it. "Maximum, mutt from the House of Hera."

A short naked boy with blue streaks in his blond hair and brown eyes stumbled forward.

"Your mentor is Ryax," Zeus said, "another mutt from the House of Dionysus."

A Spartan man stalked forward with an albino crow on his shoulder. He glared and looked intense. *I'm glad I didn't get him as my mentor.*

The crowd cheered.

Lightning flashed across a gray sky and thunder boomed.

My teeth chattered.

Names were read, men stepped forward, but I barely noticed. Everything was falling to pieces around me. Nothing was real.

"Drex Chen," Zeus said, and I jolted because I recognized the naked Chthonic boy who stepped forward. It was the one who'd killed my three attackers.

No one in the crowd cheered.

Zeus's smile slipped.

"Abandoned mutt!" someone yelled.

That must be why I don't know about him. Am I the only one who knows he's Chthonic? That's not good.

Zeus nodded toward a handsome blond man with deep golden skin and storm-gray eyes. A gold-headed vulture sat on the man's shoulder. "Your mentor is Theros, heir to the House of Zeus."

This time the coliseum erupted in cheers.

Theros frowned, the small gold laurel wreath gleaming atop his head, but then his face transformed with a brilliant smile, and he waved to the crowd as he walked over and clapped Drex on the back.

Zeus cleared his throat. "Finally, we have Alexis Hert—the fates have…blessed us. Please *welcome* the first female mutt in centuries."

There was a splattering of awkward applause as hundreds of Spartans scrutinized me. Drex looked over at me with a pinched expression.

The air hummed with whispers about me being unwanted. Since I lived in a cardboard box behind a trailer park, their judgment was easily ignored. Their derision held nothing compared to Jessica, my high school bully.

"Because of her and their…special circumstances, Alexis's mentors are—" Zeus paused and stared at me with an inscrutable expression "—Patro, the mutt of the House of Aphrodite, *and* Achilles, the mutt of the House of Ares."

The Olympian section was mostly silent; there was a smattering of applause.

But the Chthonic section stomped and screamed at the top of their lungs, waving their flags.

Two tall shadows stepped forward from the edge of the arena.

They stalked across the bloody sand.

The hairs on the back of my neck stood up.

As the two men headed in my direction, they were somehow more feral than the monstrous wolf and jaguar that walked beside them. Both animals bared their teeth as they stared at me.

Run while you can.

I took a step back.

They stopped an arm's length away—one handsome as sin,

the other savage with a muzzle stretched across his jaw. The videos didn't do their size justice. I had to tip my head back just to see their faces.

Close enough to maim me.

They towered above me in their perfectly tailored suits. On their wrists, gold cuff links glinted with diamonds, but unlike everyone else, they had weapon holsters strapped across their chests, thighs, and arms. They were covered in guns and knives.

Lucifer himself would have been less intimidating.

"You're ours now," Patro said slowly, his voice cold.

What a way to greet someone.

He took a menacing step closer.

"Let me be crystal clear," Patro snarled. "We own you—and we won't go easy on you because you're an abandoned *girl*." His lips curled.

"Also—you disgust us, we don't like you, and we *never* will, so rid yourself of all romantic delusions. Here's exactly what's going to happen...you're going to survive the crucible and make us generals. Then—we're going to *forget* you ever existed. You're Olympian, and we're Chthonic. We don't give a single shit about you. Got it?"

Green eyes flashed with warning, like flickering trailer lights in the middle of a storm. Unsettling and sinister.

He bared his teeth.

The internet was right; Chthonics were evil.

"Understand?" Patro leaned forward, and Achilles grabbed his shoulder like he was holding him back. The muzzled man glared at me, and his red eyes made it clear that he would eviscerate me to protect Patro.

They loomed over me, radiating hatred.

"You disgust me too?" I started at my audacity.

Their eyebrows rose.

I swallowed the urge to beg for mercy, but I refused to cow before brutish men.

"*Good*, glad the feeling's mutual," Patro said with deceptive softness. "But that's not what I asked... I asked if you *understood* me."

He leaned his head to the side tauntingly; "Achilles" was tattooed in red letters down the side of his neck.

The son of the most beautiful woman in the history of the world radiated hatred.

Chills traveled down my spine.

"Yes, u-understood," I whispered and ducked my head.

Zeus said something, and they stepped forward, repositioning so they flanked me on either side. Millimeters away.

Close enough to kill.

The shivers worsened.

On my right, Patro leaned down, and the frosty scent of mint burned my nose. "You don't want to mess with us..." The unspoken *we'll hurt you* hung in the air between us.

He didn't need to say it; he wasn't the first person to threaten me.

I shifted away from the chilly breath fluttering against my temple, and my side bumped into Achilles. I jumped and took a step forward to get away.

Patro grabbed my arm and yanked me back between them.

"Smile," he ordered under his breath. "Everyone's looking—pull yourself together."

The jaguar hissed with warning.

Patro was *touching* me. My skin prickled, and sweat broke out across my body. There was something off about him, something...cruel.

Panic mounted.

I never should have talked back to him.

What was I thinking?

I pulled away and bumped into Achilles again. He glared down at me with heartless eyes ringed in dark circles. He smelled like amber and fire. Heat radiated off him.

A chill surrounded Patro.

Fire and ice.

"I said—smile," Patro ordered harshly.

The edges of my lips pulled up, muscle memory taking over. There was comfort in wearing a mask and pretending everything was all right. I'd done it every day of my miserable life.

Zeus droned on. "If an initiate survives the crucible until the January Citizen Initiation Ball and the graduation ceremony the next morning, then they will be an immortal citizen of Sparta. Their mentors will be named generals...and given a seat in the Spartan Federation."

He cleared his throat.

"If an initiate is Chthonic, and there aren't any this year, they will be enrolled in the Assembly of Death at the graduation ceremony."

They definitely don't know the boy who saved me is Chthonic.

I looked over at him, but he was staring down at his blood-covered hands with a wide-eyed, shell-shocked expression.

His secret wasn't mine to tell.

At least there was *no chance* I'd end up in the Assembly of Death, and I most likely wouldn't survive until January.

A silver lining.

Yay. Lucky me.

A wolf growled at my feet, but I didn't look down.

"Kid, why is that dirty mongrel growling at you?" Nyx's voice hissed, and I slumped with relief because she sounded healthier.

Patro's grip on my bicep was the only thing that kept me standing. "Get it together." His voice was sharp, like a serrated knife.

"You're okay?" I asked her quietly.

"*Of course* I'm okay." Nyx coughed. "Stupid boy knocked me out—it takes more than a child to kill me, *obviously*."

Warm scales slithered across my neck in a suffocating hold,

and a forked tongue licked tears off my face. "Uh—kid...why are the *Crimson Duo* standing next to you?"

"They're my mentors," I whispered.

Patro dropped my arm and shifted closer so our sides were touching. "Stop mumbling nonsense to yourself and stand up straight."

I inched away from him.

He inched closer.

"You're screwed," Nyx said in a matter-of-fact tone. "That man is *not* well. You can see it in his eyes. He wants to devour you. Violently."

I grimaced.

Charming.

Zeus glanced at me. "Initiates, you will spend the next two weeks living and healing with your mentors as they prepare you for the crucible. Additionally, over the next year, you will spend three days every two weeks training and strategizing with them."

Scales slid across my neck, and Nyx said, "I don't see this ending well."

A manic snort escaped my nose.

"What's so funny?" Patro's voice was icy.

Does he even have to ask?

I was half-naked in front of hundreds of Spartans standing next to the Crimson Duo—who already *loathed* me for being Olympian—and Zeus was talking about how we'd be spending copious amounts of time together.

"Initiates, your adrenaline will wear off soon," Zeus announced, power sparking off his golden skin.

"Mentors, heal them and lead them—and remember..." He raised his hands to the crowd. "Immortality is not a right, it is a privilege!" The coliseum chorused in unison with him.

Zeus smiled, his skin glowing.

Calloused fingers wrapped around both my biceps.

"Domus," Patro whispered, and we leaped away.

White-hot pain flared along every one of my nerves. Smoke filled my lungs. Darkness tore me to shreds. Reality morphed into a—

The agony stopped, and the hands released me.

I dropped to my knees, smoke billowing around me.

"Welcome home," Patro said cruelly.

I did the next best thing to dying—I fainted.

6
HEALING

Alexis

"Take the drugs," Patro ordered for the millionth time.

He glared down at where I was sprawled lifelessly on the bed, imitating a corpse.

A sheet was draped across my torso, preserving my nonexistent modesty (I still couldn't believe I'd stood half-naked in front of a stadium full of people), and a wood ceiling towered at least three stories above me.

I didn't know rooms could be so tall.

I was lying on the biggest bed I'd ever seen in my life. It had a masculine black headboard and a fluffy white comforter that felt like silk. Nyx was asleep under one of the pillows.

The bed was decadent, a luxury I'd never experienced.

It was also covered in my crusty dried blood.

"No w-way," I said forcefully, because there was no chance in hell I would be knocked out around strangers. For all I knew, they could try to harvest my organs.

No one's taking my kidney. Especially not for free. I could get at least ten food vouchers for it.

Patro raked his hands through his disheveled hair. "You're being impossible."

I tried to shrug, but the movement made me ache.

Instead, I hummed softly (manically).

The adrenaline they'd dosed me with had worn off as soon as we'd leaped away from the coliseum, so when the doctors had finally arrived, I'd been writhing in pain.

The last few hours had been a blur of torture.

"Hold her still," said the Spartan doctor who looked like a middle-aged man but was likely hundreds of years old. The fish of the House of Hermes was embroidered on his breast pocket, and a snowy owl perched on his shoulder. "Don't let her move."

Achilles grabbed my legs and held me down.

The urge to scream at him to release me bubbled up my throat—I forced it down and hummed louder.

Patro tentatively grabbed either side of my waist, like he didn't want to touch me.

The feeling was mutual.

Across the room in front of the fireplace, a jaguar raised its head off its paws and stared at me with icy emerald eyes. It hissed in my direction. Next to it, a wolf with red eyes flattened its ears and bared its teeth at me.

Opening my mouth, I asked if—

The doctor *rudely* jammed my dislocated shoulder back into my socket, and throbbing pain radiated down my side.

I whimpered.

A wolf's deep growl vibrated through the room.

Sharp feedback burned my left ear.

The doctor glanced back at the animal and took a step back from me. "All her dislocated bones have been reset. I just need to wrap any fractures."

As if she heard him, the other doctor walked in. She had a

green crow on her shoulder and a clipboard with a long page in her hand. The winged abomination (I'd never liked birds) glared at me as she held up the page to her colleague.

They both gaped at it, looked down at me, then stared at the paper.

"What is it?" Patro asked with annoyance. The doctors had been stitching and setting my bones for hours, and he was clearly losing his patience.

She turned over the sheet. It was an X-ray of my body—they'd scanned me with a fancy handheld Spartan machine—and there were red arrows drawn on it in permanent marker. "The arrows are where her bones are fractured," she said.

There were a *lot* of arrows.

My wrists and forearms were practically covered in red.

"How the fuck are you still alive?" Patro asked softly.

I've been asking myself that for years.

Achilles stared at me from the end of the bed. Since he couldn't speak with the muzzle, it was unclear what he was thinking.

I was jealous.

If I had a muzzle, then people wouldn't expect me to talk to them.

I wonder if he'll let me borrow it.

"Do you know how many broken bones Achilles and I had—between the two of us—after our massacres?" Patro asked through gritted teeth. "Guess how many."

Both doctors backed away from the bed and glanced anxiously at the men.

Achilles crossed his arms.

He'd taken off his suit jacket and tie and unfastened his cuff links. His sleeves were rolled up to his elbows, revealing an intricate tattoo on his right forearm. A weapon holster hung loosely across his wide chest.

"*Guess* how many," Patro repeated harshly.

He snapped his fingers in front of my face.

I glared at him.

Green eyes flashed.

"Zero," he enunciated slowly. "We survived because we broke *everyone else's* bones—that's how it works."

I gritted my teeth, sweat dripping down my brow as another wave of pain coursed through me.

Turning, Patro slammed his fist into the wall next to the headboard and breathed roughly like he was trying to get control of himself.

Across the room, a clipboard clattered, and the Nemean jaguar rose to its feet.

The doctors plastered themselves against the wall, as far from the raging beast (Patro) as they could get. *Relatable—take me with you.*

The jaguar slunk lazily toward them, its long tail swishing back and forth. Every few seconds it hissed in my direction. The doctors stared at the animal with wide, panicked eyes, and their birds flapped their wings.

Patro gritted his teeth. "How the *fuck* did you qualify for the crucible?" he asked slowly.

I sighed, and my lungs rattled audibly.

"I'm good at enduring," I whispered. It was half true, after all, and I wasn't about to tell them about Nyx and put her in danger.

For some reason, even among overpowered Spartans, I was the only one who could hear her.

"Check-fucking-mate. Stupid, conniving, weak Olympians," Patro said as he looked down at me with disgust. "You win this round, Zeus."

What is he talking about?

Heaving, he loosened his tie and made eye contact with Achilles.

They stared at each other for long moments, and the silence between them was electric.

"We're fucked," Achilles signed with long, fluid hand motions.

"Should we kill the doctors?" Patro signed back. "They know how weak she is. If the other Houses find out, it will be used against her."

My heart leaped in my chest. It took every ounce of control I had to keep my expression blank and not show that I understood sign language. It was perturbing how casually they talked about cutting people into little pieces.

I held my breath and waited for his response.

"Yes," Achilles signed. "We'll kill them later."

I swallowed a scream.

Evil.

Chthonic.

Monsters.

I would definitely *not* be asking if I could borrow his muzzle.

My mentors turned toward the cowering doctors at the same time.

"Wrap her breaks," Patro said coldly. "Now."

The doctors nodded and bowed their heads. Then they hurried to my bedside. The jaguar chuffed at them as they passed.

A cool paste was rubbed across my skin, and a strangely flexible but firm white cloth was wrapped around my arm.

The woman looked over at Patro and said, "The good news is not all of the arrows were fresh breaks. About a quarter of them were older fractures."

I didn't react.

The foster parents had been cruel, but the Montana winters had been crueler. Snow and ice made your bones brittle.

Patro said slowly, "How is the fact that she has a *history* of being weak supposed to make me feel better?" His words dripped with venom.

The doctor opened and shut her mouth.

Patro took a step toward her like he was going to attack, and she cowered. Achilles shook his head, and Patro rolled his eyes and leaned back against the wall, which had a hole in it from his fist.

He stayed there while the doctors wrapped my right forearm, both shoulders, left femur, ribs, three toes, eight fingers, and my head.

When they were finally done, the doctors didn't waste time fussing over me. They said it would take about two weeks for my bones to heal, and after a week, I was supposed to take the bandages off to let the bones breathe, which made zero sense.

Then the doctors sprinted out of the room, and there was a boom in the hallway as they leaped away.

Smoke billowed in from the open door. I would have yelled, "they're going to cut you into pieces," but my mentors would probably snap and kill us all in a fit of rage.

Although, at this point, that might be preferable.

I resumed staring at the shockingly high ceiling while Patro launched into a lecture about how to block punches; at least, that seemed to be the gist.

I tuned him out.

I'd reached my daily limit of interacting with people.

If broken bones made Patro think I was weak (his disgusted expression made it clear he thought that was why I'd been abandoned), then he was going to *lose it* when he found out about my blind eye and deaf ear.

Not that they held me back—I'd adapted to my new reality—but something told me Patro would not see it that way.

He'll kill me. I'll never tell him.

The paste tingled pleasantly, and the numbing sensation penetrated deep. Everything got hazy.

Floating on clouds.

My eyes closed, and I fell into a deep, healing sleep, cradled in the luxury of a bed.

Days blurred.

I was lost in a fever dream.

I woke up gasping for air, covered in a cold sweat, but fell immediately back asleep.

The process repeated.

Scales slid along my neck and whispered that everything would be okay. During a rare moment of lucidity, Nyx said something about Medusa.

"But she's in the underworld," I rasped quietly, my throat like sandpaper. "She used the Titans to attack the House of Zeus." I tilted my head up.

Nyx hissed, "I *don't* believe it." She snapped her teeth with a click.

I opened my mouth to ask more, but my head dropped back.

Nightmares pulled me under.

This time, death himself hovered over me with his hand possessively on my ankle. He had pale skin and hateful bloodred eyes, and he watched me without blinking. A foreign sensation of intrigue and curiosity filled my chest; it was *obsessive.*

I'd never felt anything like it.

Death stayed for hours.

At some point, he left.

Everything warped and shifted. Black-painted nails dabbed a cold rag across my forehead. A raspy male voice whispered insults about pathetic abandoned Olympian mutts.

I raised my bandaged middle finger into the air, delirium making me bold.

He laughed darkly.

At least Satan finds me funny.

His insults got meaner, but I sighed with relief as the cloth cooled my fevered flesh. He dragged it softly across my face, like I was made of glass.

Darkness twisted.

"I'm glad you're back, but what are you going to do?" a harsh male voice asked.

There was a long pause. Then another voice said, "She'll perform for us—we'll make sure of it."

"Good fucking luck. A pathetic waif like her?" There was a dark, gravelly laugh. "You're gonna need my help."

The other man sighed and muttered, "You're a lucky bastard, already being a general, not having to deal with this bullshit."

I drifted away.

A piano played in another room, and the haunting melody resonated like honey. Tears gathered in my eyes. It was so beautiful. The music vibrated through me and chased away the nightmares.

Time passed.

"Nero, Poppae, stop growling at her. Really—you're going to ignore me?"

I dreamed of falling from the clouds.

Plummeting.

Right before I hit the ground, a faceless man caught me. He was cruelly beautiful with stunning blue eyes—it was death again.

A fallen angel.

He placed his thumb roughly against my tongue. Fingers gripped my chin and kept my mouth open as they put pills in my mouth. He tilted my head back and tipped water down my throat.

I choked and sputtered.

"Go—to—hell," I coughed as I tried to open my watery eyes.

The thumb dragged out of my mouth. "Where do you think I came from, carissima?"

A deep chuckle echoed as sleep pulled me back under.

Two animals growled, and the sound was deep and vicious. *Otherworldly.*

A tall figure hovered over me.

"Charlie?" I asked. "You—here too?"

The voice muttered something about fools, and I tried to reply, but the dreams pulled me away.

A piano played.

I woke up with tears leaking out of my eyes.

In the dark, I sat up gasping, covered in sweat. A breeze caressed my skin, and I flopped back with my eyes closed, unable to hold myself up.

My vision unfocused.

Voices whispered.

A cup was pressed to my lips.

Familiar calloused fingers wrapped around my jaw and tipped my head back. Then they traced along my cheekbones. Icy water soothed my ravaged throat.

"Thanks," I whispered.

"Don't thank me yet," said the raspy voice. "I have a gut feeling we're not going to get along. An innocent like you should be *very* afraid of a monster like me."

Opening my mouth, I tried to ask what he meant, but nothing came out.

The nightmares smothered me.

Blood was everywhere. Fists and cigarettes against my skin. My chest hurt as she died. Was I hurting her? Crimson eyes glowed as a hand touched my leg, and a foreign curiosity burned inside my chest.

The urge to devour filled me—it felt like someone else's emotion. A dagger was pressed into my sternum, and I waved bloody hands. A man screamed.

Sitting up, I clutched my frantic heart.

Wide awake, I heaved as I rubbed the throbbing scar on my chest.

Bright sunlight burned.

The crusted sheet from the doctors was still draped over me, and the high-ceilinged room was warm. A breeze filtered through open French doors that led to a patio. I hadn't noticed them before.

Morning rays streamed in with blinding brilliance.

Water lapped.

I squinted—my right eye adjusted to the light.

Holy crap. Past the deck, turquoise-blue waters filled the horizon. Lush green leaves framed the windows.

The never-ending sea was close enough I could walk out and fall into it.

It was breathtaking.

Divine.

I'd seen pictures of large bodies of water, but nothing could have prepared me for real life. The scents of salt water, the sounds of lapping, the way it stretched across the horizon to eternity.

The door squeaked, and I clutched the bloody sheet to my chest.

Patro stood in the doorway with a glass of water and washcloth. His dark skin practically shimmered in the sunlight, and his high cheekbones were sharp enough to cut glass.

It was shocking how closely he resembled the statue of David.

Green eyes narrowed. "You're awake." He turned and left the room.

I blinked.

His voice was soft, chilly in its cadence—nothing like the deep rasp that had insulted me in my dreams.

I must have been hallucinating.

Nice, I'm already losing my mind. Nineteen is not my year.

A few minutes later, there was a loud explosion in the hall, and the same doctors from before hurried into the room. Achilles and Patro followed with their terrifying beasts at their heels.

At least they haven't killed the doctors...yet.

"Have you been giving her the weight-gaining nutrient pill

like we instructed?" the male doctor asked as he pulled supplies out of a bag.

Achilles and Patro glared at him.

"Right, of course you did," the doctor said shakily. "Since it's been a week, we'll need to take the sheet off so we can remove her casts."

"No," I rasped loudly, clutching the sheet tighter.

Father grinning as he leered over me and pushed a cigarette against my stomach. Mother's fists slamming against the side of my face.

My flesh was mine, and no person was seeing it unless I wanted them to.

Unlike Charlie—whose entire back was a mutilated twist of scar tissue, which he'd never spoken about—I had dozens of small, mostly unnoticeable scars. The raised ridges on my wrists were the most prominent.

My midsection was littered with the most marks.

Thin, faint scratches from moving tree branches with pointy ends. A puckered red circle from a cigarette. Tiny dots where broken glass pieces dug into my back as I scrambled across it. A jagged divot where I'd fallen on ice. Then there was the puckered scar on my sternum, the one I'd had since a baby.

But I still felt protective of my skin.

The events of the coliseum were different. I'd been pumped full of adrenaline and covered in enough blood that no one could see anything.

This was personal.

I was *me* again.

Achilles stopped at the edge of my bed and stared; his muzzle obstructed his expression.

I waited for the attack.

I'd seen what he'd signed to Patro.

He was vicious.

White-knuckling the sheet, I prepared to fight if they tried to take it from me. They would win…eventually, but I could make it hurt. Straightening my spine, I breathed in deeply. Tensed my thighs.

"Everyone out but you." Patro's voice whipped through the room as he pointed at the female doctor.

The male packed up and *ran* out of the room as fast as he could. Slowly, the Crimson Duo followed him out.

Patro stopped at the door and looked back. "She's under the protection of the Houses of Ares and Aphrodite. Do *anything* to harm her, and no one will ever find you."

The woman gulped.

"Understood?" Patro bellowed, eyes filling with blood, and I jolted at the ferocity of his voice.

"Yes. Of course. I'm from the Assembly of Healers. I've taken a healing oath," she said quickly. "I would never do anything to—"

Patro slammed the door shut and cut her off.

She exhaled and tipped her head to the ceiling like she was praying.

I would have joined her, but I was 99 percent sure God had abandoned me. Also, I was nervous about the fact that she'd be touching me. It was better than a man—but not by much.

There was one thing I'd learned over the years: most people didn't like me.

The wolf and jaguar growled viciously at both of us, then sat down in a corner of the room.

After a long moment of collecting herself, the doctor gathered her tools and turned to me.

I stared at her with trepidation. *Please don't steal my organs.*

The post-Titan world was full of people posing as doctors so they could harvest people without their consent and make money off their parts on thriving black markets.

The doctor smiled.

I tried not to scream for mercy.

She touched my arm, and I breathed shallowly through my nose. She cut off a bandage, and I watched her scissors like a hawk, waiting to see if she was going to go for my skin.

"Be careful around the Crimson Duo," she murmured as she leaned across me.

I jolted at her close proximity.

"They're dangerous," she murmured as she kept cutting.

No way, they seem super nice.

"I mean—look at who they're *friends* with." She moved to my leg bandage and mumbled something about "heir psychopaths who everyone's obsessed with" under her breath.

She shivered dramatically, then pulled the sheet down to work on my ribs.

I closed my eyes and pretended I wasn't exposed before her.

She picked up my hand and went finger by finger. "Frankly, Kronos help us, I don't think the muzzle's enough for Achilles."

Apparently, she took my lack of response as encouragement to continue.

Picking up her bag, the doctor moved to the last bandages on my head. "You know—" her voice dropped to a whisper, like she was afraid of being overheard "—rumor is they were going to send Achilles to the underworld after his performance in the SGC…a Chthonic *mutt* like him, with that type of power—you're just asking for a repeat of the Great War."

She shook her head and leaned closer, scissors snipping along the side of my head.

"I mean, they founded that horrible weapons company with Augustus and Kharon—who are *actual* sociopaths. I've heard they've even been diagnosed. I mean, look at what they chose to represent themselves."

Her nose scrunched with disgust.

Something tells me the *D* and *L* of WSDL don't stand for "dazzling" and "lovely."

I was too afraid to ask.

She brushed hair off my forehead. I tried not to retch while she acted like we were besties.

Help?

This friendship was upsetting.

She continued, "The fact that Patro took a Spartan oath to only take the muzzle off Achilles if necessary is pure insanity. Everyone knows that *bad things* happen to people who take Spartan oaths outside of marriage and animal bonding." She smiled down at me. "I'm probably boring you, since you already know all this."

Actually, madam, I know nothing, and I can't tell if you want my kidney or not.

Also—please kidnap me away from here. I'd really appreciate it if you did it quickly, before my mentors come back. Thanks.

I desperately tried to find the courage to speak.

The bandage fell off my head, and she clapped. "Now, your bones are mostly healed, but they'll still be very weak for the next seven days, so take it easy."

She squinted down at me.

"You know, it makes sense that you break easily—the House of Zeus is known for its fertility issues. All the recent mutts have…*struggled.* Thank goodness for Theros—he's the first heir they've borne in centuries. The Olympian Houses have all had—difficulties with their progeny's strength after the Great War."

Thank God, there's hope yet. Maybe Sparta will fall and I can live in peace.

"But the new marriage law is going to fix all that, thank Kronos." She beamed. "Everyone's talking about it. It's *genius,* making all citizens of Sparta take a marriage oath when they turn twenty-six. Well, everyone but the House leaders—obviously. No one tells them what to do."

I frowned.

Excuse me? A marriage law at twenty-six? I'd be a child bride.

I never wanted to get married.

Having to touch another person *sexually.*

Hard pass.

"The best part," the doctor continued, oblivious to my mental breakdown. "They put in a clause that listed out all ten of the Chthonic names, and stated they were restricted from *only* marrying someone on that list. Chthonic leaders refused to comply if Chthonics were wholly forbidden from marrying each other, so the federation compromised and added the 'only.' Either way, they must marry an Olympian."

She scoffed.

"The technicality doesn't actually matter—the next generation of Chthonic blood will be diluted with Olympian blood. There's no way for them to find a loophole. The federation claims the law is for Sparta's fertility struggles, but *everyone* knows it's really to force the Chthonics into alliances with the Olympians—it's brilliant."

She moved to brush more hair off my forehead, and I dodged her hand.

Her eyes narrowed.

"Well," she huffed. "I tried to help you." As she packed up her supplies, she mumbled under her breath, "Even though you're just a filthy abandoned mutt."

Short friendship.

"Be c-careful," I said in a rush as I gripped the sheets tightly. "They're going to hurt you."

She scoffed. "You don't know *anything* about the ways of the great Houses. You're the one in danger, not me."

The door slammed open, and my mentors entered.

She jumped with a yelp. "Pleasure to assist the great Houses," she said with her head lowered as she bowed to the men. "Please tell the House of Hades about my services to the great Chthonic families, and let the Assembly of Death know if they ever—"

"Get out," Patro cut her off, his demeanor cold. Achilles

stood at his side, arms crossed and vermilion eyes glinting with danger.

Guilt filled me. *I tried to warn her.*

She gasped and scurried away.

"Nero, get out of the room," Patro snapped at Achilles's wolf, and it reluctantly walked away after giving me a side-eye. "Poppae, you too," he said, and the jaguar obeyed.

The three of us were left.

Alone.

Help.

7

STRATEGIZING

ALEXIS

"I tried to wipe away some of your blood, but I figured you wouldn't want someone bathing you while you were unconscious," Patro said, and Achilles crossed his arms beside him. "That's why the sheet is still gross."

He almost sounds...kind?

"Uh, thanks." I propped myself up on the pillows as awkwardness stretched between the three of us.

Maybe he's not so bad. Maybe they were joking about killing the doctors, and I was just being dramatic—

"You smell and look repulsive." Patro pointed at a door on the far wall. "Use the shower and make yourself presentable. Being around you in this state is disgusting and a dishonor to our Houses. If you were an heiress, the leaders would pass out with horror when they saw how impure you are."

Never mind. He's definitely evil.

"Also, try not to slip and break your neck," he said. "That would be inconvenient."

Purposefully try to die in the shower. Got it.

Clutching my sheet closer to my chest, I waited for them to leave.

Patro narrowed his eyes. "Understood?" he asked softly.

"Crystal clear," I whispered. For some reason, I couldn't hold my tongue around him.

"Good."

"Great."

"Fantastic."

"F-fabulous."

"Stupendous."

"Superb."

Achilles grabbed Patro by the elbow and pulled him out of the room before he could argue further. When the door shut, I sat back with a sigh.

The annoying part was, Patro was right. My hair was matted with blood, and I felt disgusting. I needed a wash badly.

"Nyx," I whispered into the quiet room.

The silk pillow on the far side of the bed shifted. "What?" Nyx asked.

"Do you want to shower?" I asked, since she liked it when I threw well water on her during the hot summer months.

"Do I *want* to shower?" she scoffed. "What kind of ridiculous question is that? Of course I do."

An hour later, I stood on shaky legs under a waterfall of hot water with an invisible snake wrapped around my neck. Classical music played in my head as water blasted from the ceiling *and* walls.

It was heavenly.

Tears filled my eyes as years of grime washed away.

Judging from the happy noises Nyx was making, she agreed with me. There were multiple bottles of products, which I wasn't sure how to use, since Charlie and I had rationed a stolen bar of soap for years.

Charlie.

My heart ached.

I wanted to demand my mentors find out if he was okay, but I'd just fought to the death and watched a stadium cheer over the murder of dozens of boys, and those were their own kind. They wouldn't care about a human.

The risk of the Spartans hurting him was not one I was willing to take.

He was eighteen and knew how to fend for himself.

But he's all alone, missing you.

The shower spun around me. The music died. My breath became labored as I put my hands on my knees and dry-heaved.

"Kid, what's wrong?" Nyx asked.

"Charlie," I gasped, my chest burning with the beginning of a panic attack.

Nyx whispered a steady stream of encouragements about how capable my little brother was until I could breathe again.

Blindly I grabbed one of the bottles off the shelf and lathered the soap all over my hair and body.

It smelled like mint.

I scrubbed with all my might.

Digging my nails into my skin after the dirt and blood were gone, I focused on the invisible fog. It still clung to me, insidious and cold. Voices whispered across my flesh. *Mother's dead because you—*

"You're clean. Calm down, Alexis." Nyx's voice brought me back to reality.

Both of my forearms were covered in red marks.

My vision warped, and for a second, it looked like poison spreading beneath my skin.

I whimpered.

"Snap out of it, woman!" Nyx shouted.

I inhaled shakily and stood up straight, pulling myself together. "What would I do without you?"

"Struggle," Nyx said.

I tipped my head back and closed my eyes. "Nyx—is my power the fact that I can talk to you?"

She slithered around my neck. "When we speak," she asked slowly, "do you feel a tingling, like a euphoria in your head?"

I exhaled, and water sputtered off my lips. "No." All I felt was crushing despair.

"Then it's not your power."

I opened my eyes and stared at the spray. "Then what is?"

"Kid, if I knew, I'd tell you. I've seen crazy things in my life, but these last two weeks take the cake."

We both sighed.

I perked up. "Are you my protector, then? Like Nero and Poppae and the birds on the doctors' shoulders? Are we somehow bonded, and is that why—"

"No," Nyx hissed and cut me off.

I jolted at the vehemence in her voice.

"No," she repeated more softly. "I'm already bonded to another."

My heart sank.

"Who are they?" I whispered, jealousy burning my chest.

"I'm bonded, kid—I want to tell you, but I'm physically not able to." Nyx's scales slid against my neck, like she was rising. "Spartan oaths are serious business. They swear fealty above all to their animals, and when we accept them, we're tied to the same oath. But my person is…gone. The oath won't let me speak of them, not directly."

Does that mean she's spoken about them indirectly?

"I understand," I said, even though I didn't.

"Don't worry about it, kid. I'm still with you. I'll always be with you."

"Yep." I wiped at my eyes, grateful for the shower. "Of course."

"I swear I'm not trying to change the topic," Nyx said slowly. "But do you think the jaguar could be interested in me?"

I hiccupped on a watery laugh. "You can't be serious."

"Have you seen her fangs? Those canines are *lethal*. Razor-sharp. And her quads are insane."

"You're out of your mind." I laughed, aware that she was distracting me, but still grateful for it. "I thought you were into men?"

Nyx hissed. "Don't be a closed-minded prude, Alexis—it's not cute."

I chuckled weakly.

After my skin had pruned and I'd run up what must have been a small fortune on the water bill—I tried not to feel bad about the cost but definitely did—I stepped out of the shower.

Pulling a fluffy towel off the wall rack, I marveled at how warm it was, then held the luxurious item up in front of me.

Weight left my neck as Nyx flopped into it.

After we were both dried, I investigated the marble bathroom. New products were laid out across the sink, presumably for my use.

I pulled a brush through my wet hair and pretended not to notice that the handle was engraved with gold.

Then, feeling like a thief, I piled fresh hair ties on both wrists before I could talk myself out of it. I was used to picking up people's old ones off the ground, so seeing a stack of new ones was too good a chance to pass up.

I brushed my teeth until my gums bled.

Then repeated the process three more times.

When I finally emerged from the bathroom, my emotional support sheet was gone, and someone had replaced the comforter with a fresh white one.

The room itself was minimalist with high ceilings and a low bed.

Everything was pristine.

It was paradise.

Charlie.

Guilt filled me, and I tried not to think about him all alone in our cardboard boxes.

A pile of clean clothes was also waiting for me on the bed, and there were sports bras in every size with the tags still on. I pulled on the smallest one—grateful neither of them had paid close enough attention to notice.

A T-shirt fit nice and oversized like I liked, but the only pair of sweatpants had to be rolled at the waist and tied off to avoid a flashing situation.

As I pulled them on, I noticed the shirt smelled like amber and fire, and the pants smelled like mint. I sniffed them a couple times—just to confirm.

After what seemed to be ages of primping, I felt reborn.

I went out onto the deck.

I'd always loved swimming in the murky pond behind the trailer park, but I couldn't even *imagine* what it felt like to float in the turquoise sea.

Verdant foliage spilled over the sprawling house, which was built on the lower side of a lush hill.

It was breathtakingly tropical.

The warm sun was divine against my tender skin, so I gingerly lay down on the plush lounge chair and closed my eyes.

A smile curved my lips.

I drifted off.

"Why do you look like Zeus?" Patro barked, and I jolted upright.

The Crimson Duo loomed above me—completely blocking out the sun with their freakish size.

"What?" I asked with confusion.

"Same ridiculous golden skin and curls." Patro glared down at my now dry hair like it morally offended him. "You even have one of his gray-white eyes. Although—" he narrowed his eyes "—he would never abandon a daughter unless there was something extremely wrong with you."

A phantom pain spiked my left side, right where Foster Father had slammed his fist.

I didn't correct him about my eye color.

Everyone always assumed I was born with heterochromia. *Some wounds are so visible that no one can ever see them.*

Patro squinted at me like he was trying to figure out what was off about me (so much—I could make a list). I cleared my throat and tried to change the topic.

"You could do a paternity t-test to check," I offered tentatively.

It seemed ridiculous to assume my parentage based on mere coloring. Everyone knew genetics wasn't a zero-sum game. It wasn't *he also has golden skin—boom—you're related.*

Achilles and Patro looked at me like I was stupid, which was still up for debate.

"No." Patro made a *duh* face. "We can't just *test* your blood. You're not just a weak human anymore. Spartan blood is too acidic to test. Obviously."

Literally nothing is obvious about Sparta.

Patro pursed his lips and sighed dramatically. "Moving on—the real question is, why would Zeus pair you with us and not Theros?"

Achilles looked at him pointedly and arched his brow. "He's weak and pathetic," he signed. "Just like her."

It took everything I had not to make a face. *That was just uncalled for.*

"I know he's incompetent," Patro replied aloud. "But he's their heir, so why wouldn't he—" His mouth dropped as he looked down at me. "Unless he actually *wants* you to succeed."

He wrinkled his nose. "But he abandoned you and hates us. It only makes sense if he's trying to kill you off and screw us."

At this point, it feels like everyone is trying to give me father issues.

Patro rubbed his temples like he was either thinking or had a tumor that was causing him pain.

I prayed for the latter.

Silence stretched, and it got awkward again.

Or maybe it's always been awkward? I tended to have that effect on people, especially men. It was probably my giant boobs, curvy body, and bubbly, extroverted personality.

"Is th-this Crete?" I whispered, naming the first Greek island that came to mind.

Both men frowned at me. Well, I assumed Achilles was scowling; it was hard to tell because of the muzzle.

Does it ever chafe?

"No, this isn't *Crete*. This is Corfu," Patro scoffed like I'd asked the dumbest question in the world. "The House of Hades owns Crete—obviously."

Voices, cold, black fog everywhere, a boy with horns punching his head during the massacre.

"Don't make that disgusted face," Patro snapped. "You're not good enough to lick the boots of Hades or Persephone—they're the best of us," he said, almost wistfully.

If they were the best, I didn't want to know the worst.

Achilles sat still like he was carved from marble, and Patro lit a cigarette that smelled like cloves and tobacco.

I scrunched my nose at the smell.

Patro blew smoke in my direction and flipped me off.

I grimaced and looked away.

After a tense moment, Patro took a long drag and said, "Moving on—so, daughter of Zeus and a random human whore who probably wanted a taste of fame but found ruin because he didn't want you, what's your power? Please, enlighten us. Personally, I can't *fucking wait* to hear this."

"Swearing is a sign of a weak mind," I whispered, then clapped a hand over my mouth, horrified that I'd spoken my thoughts aloud.

I was losing it.

Patro crossed his arms and mocked, *"Swearing is a sign of a weak mind."* His smile was venomous. "Grow the fuck up. What's your motherfucking power? Tell us, fucking now."

I took a deep, steadying breath. "I don't have one."

Patro's right eye twitched, and Achilles remained motionless.

"What do you—mean?" Patro asked softly, cigarette quivering between his lips.

I stared down at my feet. "I don't have any powers."

A sea breeze blew warmly and whipped our hair.

Patro crushed his cigarette, walked inside, and screamed in the other room at the top of his lungs.

I was surprised he didn't punch the wall like a psycho.

There was a crunching sound and a bellow—there went the wall. *Classic.*

One mental breakdown later, about ten minutes give or take, the Crimson Duo once again sat across from me on lounge chairs.

Patro rubbed his bloody knuckles and asked, "Olympians always say their power feels pleasurable and bubbly...are you *100* percent sure you've never felt this?"

If I was being completely honest, I wasn't sure I'd ever felt "pleasure." The closest I'd come to enjoyment was when Tim-Tom had gotten suspended from school for a week because he'd chanted "peace, love, and butt stuff" and started a mini riot in the halls. Yes, that had really happened.

High school was a bizarre place.

"Yes," I repeated.

"Are you kidding me?" Patro shouted, and stood up. Achilles put a hand on his thigh and pushed him back down.

"What does using *your* p-power feel like?" I asked, because

Nyx said it was important to make conversation and not stare at people in silence (I wasn't convinced).

Patro breathed deeply. "It's…intense," he said through gritted teeth. "Painful and all-consuming, in a way that Olympians could *never* understand. But that's not any of your business."

He shook his head and narrowed his eyes cruelly.

"The only women Chthonics are heirs," he said vehemently. "A half-human female Chthonic is literally impossible—our power would *rip* you to shreds from the inside out. It would tear you into pathetic pieces and boil your womb. You can't even fathom what we feel."

Riveting. Sounds like an average menstrual cycle.

Not that I'd had many. Because of starvation, I could count on one hand the number of times I'd had my period, but each one had been highly traumatic.

"So—to be clear." Patro paused and breathed roughly. "You have no powers, no training, no House backing, and a history of broken bones? That's what you bring to the table?"

I also have a blind eye and deaf ear, and Tim-Tom once told me that I had the build of a sick giraffe—I'm still not sure if he meant "sick" in the "cool" or "physically ill" sense.

Patro's eyes twitched like he was having an aneurysm.

I waited with anticipation.

Sadly, he did not drop dead.

There's no justice left in this cold, cruel world.

After long, drawn-out moments of uncomfortable eye contact, I sighed and offered, "I do well in school. That could be something I use to my advantage."

Patro sliced his hand through the air like a knife. "Spartans are *known* for their intelligence. Do you think anyone in the crucible is going to be dumb?" His eyes widened with horror. "Do you even know what the crucible is?"

I knew a trick question when I saw one.

My lips stayed closed.

He covered his mouth. "You *don't* know—you have no clue what's in store for you." He turned. "She's dead."

Achilles nodded in agreement.

"That's what I always say!" Nyx called from the other room.

I pressed my fingers into my forehead and prayed a meteor would fall from the asteroid belt and strike me dead.

Please, God, hit me with your best shot. I'm ready.

"You're pathetic. Even for an Olympian, you're an embarrassment," Patro snarled. "And that's saying something."

God did not, in fact, hit me with his best shot.

"I never asked for any of this," I said, my unused throat burning from the force of my outburst. "I thought I was fully human *last* week."

"Oh yes." Patro waved his hands in the air. "It must have been *so* difficult, growing up as a pampered human with *no* responsibilities other than going to school and living a charmed life. Cry me the River Styx."

I fisted my hands so I wouldn't punch him.

You should have never spoken.

Nero glared up at me from the ground and bared his teeth. He reminded me of Fluffy, just with razor-sharp fangs, red eyes, a mammoth size, and the ability to rip out my throat with one bite.

Also, unlike Fluffy, he *loathed* me.

It hurt.

The quiet stretched as Patro and Achilles seemed to be having another silent conversation.

I leaned back on my lounge chair and sunned myself (dreamed of death and tried to make a bigger target for the asteroid). *Fingers crossed.*

Patro stood up abruptly and left the deck.

I glanced over—Achilles was glaring at me.

He didn't look away when I held his gaze.

Not a good omen.

"Here," Patro barked as he came back out and dropped two books onto my lap. One had a painting of a disemboweled corpse on its cover; the other had a drawing of a Spartan helmet.

Something tells me these aren't going to be my Emmy and Carl fanfics.

"Do you have any math b-books?" I asked before I could stop myself. My stress levels were at an all-time high; I needed numbers to calm me. I also needed to stop talking to the man who was likely going to snap and kill me.

Patro made a face. "No, because believe it or not, I'm not a *loser.* Also, this isn't leisure reading." He pointed to the graphic cover. "It's an original founder's manual on the crucible, but it's in Latin, so I also gave you the translated version."

"I can read Latin," I whispered.

"Sure you can," he scoffed with disbelief. "We'll reconvene once you've read them and are no longer an ignorant savage."

I ran my fingers along the rough yellow pages of the original. *How old is this book? I'm holding history in my hands.*

I barely noticed the men leaving.

An hour later, I was nauseous and sweating.

The Latin was rough but comprehensible—unfortunately.

I wish I was illiterate.

The book had started with,

> All Sparta is divided by one mental test, one of which paranoia inhabits, sleep deprivation another, and starvation the third. What others in their own language call "pain" is, in our Spartan War Academy, the crucible. The River Styx separates the dolomites from the academy; the drowning and running separate them from the mind. Of all these, the cunning are the bravest. Because they are farthest from civilization and refinement, their minds don't break when the rest shatter.

It got progressively worse from there.

The book detailed ad nauseam the importance of pain, suffering, dirt, fear, and hunger. Confusingly, it referred to the crucible as a mental test, but then constantly described it as a war.

Later the book repeated, "It is the right of the crucible to break those it has conquered so they have no shelter from themselves. If you must break a man, do it to reveal power; in all other cases, kill him."

Charming.

And the last line read, "There are no stupid gods because there are no stupid Spartans. The crucible or death; there is no third option."

Sweat streaked down my spine. I opened the English version of the book, hoping I'd made a mistake translating.

It was exactly the same, except the English author used the terms *slaughter, murderous*, and *revolting* more frequently.

I pushed both books off my lap, unable to stomach them.

The crucible almost sounded worse than high school.

I collapsed back on the chair with Nyx wrapped around my throat. The sun set over the Ionian Sea, and a graveyard of stars made an appearance.

I barely noticed.

Time warped around me.

Crickets chirped and waves lapped as I drowned in the night sounds.

When I finally dragged myself into the bed, head fuzzy with heavy thoughts, there was a strange creaking coming from the other side of the wall.

A low, masculine groan and a shout.

Heavy panting.

Someone cried out, like they were in pain.

Then the creaking resumed.

Before I could wake up enough to investigate, nightmares pulled me under.

Crimson eyes glowed from the end of my bed.

There was a weight on my ankle, fingers wrapped around in a vise. A foreign feeling of interest and curiosity filled me. The obsession burned me alive.

Skeletons growled.

The night breeze dragged across my skin like it had claws.

"You're going to survive," the familiar raspy voice ordered. "You're going to do it for them—or I'll bring you back to life and make you wish you were dead. Then I'll make him break your mind. Obey—you don't want to test me, carissima."

"Wake up!" Patro shouted.

I sat up with a gasp.

Holy crud, I've never had dreams like those before.

Patro loomed over the bed. "I assume you read the books I left you," he said without preamble. "Do you understand the crucible?"

Slumping back against my pillows, I nodded weakly. "Mental test, pain, suffering, starvation, paranoia, death, blah, blah, blah."

An average day living in the forest.

Patro huffed, and for a second, it almost looked like he smiled. "That's a pretty accurate summary."

I grimaced at his expression—cheerful people freaked me out. *What do they have to feel good about these days? Genuinely. I want to know.*

Luckily, Patro's face contorted with disgust (understandable), and he grabbed a thin textbook off the bedside table. "Read this today—it covers the four disciplines of the crucible."

I reached for it.

"You've never heard of them," he said. "The curriculum is purposefully kept a secret so no initiate can have an upper hand, which actually helps in your case. The book just outlines the names and gives a general description of each class. It's nothing you, or anyone else your age, have studied before."

My interest piqued.

What could possibly be taught that I've never even heard of? The Spartan merit test covered a dozen different subjects.

Patro must have mistaken my silence for disinterest.

"You *need* to know the four classes," he said with a huff. "*First*, Thagorean—advanced math coupled with philosophy. *Second*, Lost Classical Lore—which focuses on archaic history in Latin. *Third*, Discipline and Power, D and P for short—the most useful class by far, since it covers powers, Spartan oaths, mental shielding, and leaping."

"You said there were four?" I asked.

Patro smirked. "The fourth is less of a class and more of a long challenge, which starts after the summer. It's bonding with an animal protector."

I glanced over at the pillow I knew Nyx was sleeping under.

"Oh," I said, spirits sinking because I didn't want to bond with some random animal.

"Since Zeus seems to be your father," Patro said with a frown, "as an Olympian with a strong bloodline, I'm sure birds will flock to you, and you'll have your pick of them."

I couldn't find the energy to nod.

I'd never been a bird girl.

No, it wasn't because neighbor Paul (pre shovel-to-the-head incident) used to scream from his trailer porch that birds were government surveillance drones.

It was just—no one had proved birds *weren't* spying on us.

Also, why were they always flying around? Where were they going? What were they doing? Why were they always singing? Suspicious.

Morning chirps echoed through the windows, and my eyes widened. *They've got us surrounded.*

Patro scowled like he was waiting for me to say something.

"Yay, b-birds," I said tentatively. "Go pigeons? They're definitely *not* watching us and sending information back to the—"

Patro left the room.

That was weird, Alexis, even for you. Tone it down.

Sighing, I lay down on the deck and read my new book.

Time resumed its leisurely stroll (death march).

Over the next five days, I took copious nutrient pills, and my bones healed. My collarbone and ribs also stopped protruding so severely. I almost looked healthy.

But a new fear ate at my nerves because the crucible—a mental test akin to war—was fast approaching.

Each night, I drowned in nightmares where a raspy voice taunted me.

On the last day before I was supposed to leave, the Crimson Duo once again sat across from me on the terrace.

Green leaves rustled on the surrounding hillside.

The sea sparkled like diamonds.

"You won't survive the Spartan War Academy without a power," Patro said in a grave tone. "They will literally *kill* you if they think you're powerless. No questions asked. So don't tell anyone."

I gulped.

"My brother, Augustus, is teaching D and P this year," Patro said with a fond smile. "He's very even-mannered and honorable—but he won't suffer fools. If you're powerless...let's just say—you don't want to be. Although he's usually protective of women because of our sister, Helen. Still, he'll exploit your weaknesses ruthlessly to make you better."

I shivered.

Augustus is the thirty-one-year-old eldest Chthonic heir.

Literally everyone in the world knew about the infamous son of Aphrodite and Ares.

There were wild stories circulating about his "sinful handsomeness, disturbed power, and divine rage," but he was notoriously private, so none of them had ever been confirmed.

The Spartan Lifestyle Page had tried and failed for years to get photos of him, since he was part of the upper crust, the secret royal society of Spartans who cared about honor and purity.

They're all delusional.

Neighbor Paul (pre-shovel) seemed more grounded than the Spartan heirs.

One thing was for darn sure, Augustus was *not* someone I ever wanted to meet. As the son of two heirs, he could have chosen to be the heir to the House of Aphrodite or Ares, but he'd been named the latter.

He'd *chosen* the House of War.

Enough said.

Patro continued, "The good news for you is that asking another Spartan about their power, without them offering to discuss it, is considered taboo. Your incompetence shouldn't pose too much of a problem—at least, for now."

"Okay," I said slowly. "So, what is our overall strategy?"

The men glanced at each other.

Patro ran his hand through his hair. "You survive." He shrugged.

"That's it?" I gaped at him, fury filling me as I fisted my hands.

Patro rolled his eyes. "After the first two weeks, you'll have another few mentor days with us. Once you've experienced a…*taste of our culture*, we can reassess. Make it until the end of July, and then we'll talk."

I saw red.

"You're giving up," I whispered. "You didn't even bother."

Green eyes flashed like lightning in a fog. "Don't you fucking dare *tell* me what I'm doing. We have more here to fucking lose than you do."

I crossed my arms and glared at my feet. "My *l-life* is at stake."

Patro leaned forward. "Our *world* is at stake. If we're named generals, then we get seats in the Spartan Federation, and Chthonic power increases. In contrast, your life means nothing to anyone in Sparta." His tone was vicious. "Grow up and figure out how to make it matter."

I scowled. "I want a strategy. Now."

"You want to know what *my* strategy was?" Patro bared his teeth. "Beat everyone in everything—separate myself as smarter, stronger, faster, tougher from day one… I made it so they couldn't ignore me. I couldn't fall behind, because everyone was chasing *me*."

"What happens if you fall behind?" I asked.

Both men looked at me with pity.

"They kill you."

There are no stupid gods because there are no stupid Spartans. The crucible or death; there is no third.

The book's words haunted me.

Patro smiled meanly. "You want to know what Achilles's strategy was?" he asked sarcastically. "The same fucking plan as mine. We were the best of the best—something someone like *you* can't even imagine."

He spoke like I was lesser than him.

Unimportant.

Replaceable.

Filthy.

Patro continued, "Survive—if you last fourteen measly fucking days, then we'll consider a plan."

He stood up, and Achilles followed him out with the animals. None of them looked back.

I'd never felt smaller.

That night, I barely slept.

Before the sun had risen above the horizon, Patro burst in and ordered me to wake up and get dressed.

"It's an exercise toga," he said as he handed me a thin scrap of black fabric made of a buttery-soft elastic material like nothing I'd ever felt before.

It looked like a dress but had built-in shorts and a built-in bra, *thank God.* It hung across my shoulders without sleeves, bunched in layers at the waist, and fell to my knees.

"There are no shoes—you don't get to wear them during the crucible," Patro said. Then he left so I could change.

I dressed in the strange garment, checked to make sure the hair ties covered the marks on my wrists.

"I'm r-ready," I called out.

I wasn't.

The Crimson Duo grabbed my arms, and we leaped away in a cloud of smoke and agony.

When I got my bearings—my toes squished into grass, and the Dolomites Coliseum gleamed gold far off in the distance—I glanced over. The men were already gone.

Booms echoed as Spartan mentors arrived and left.

Silence descended.

Nine boys stood next to me in a line, all cold-blooded murderers with death on their hands.

Only one boy in the group wore a gold laurel crown. Of the three Olympian heirs in the massacre, he was the only one who'd survived.

I turned around—my breath caught.

An architectural marvel was carved into the side of the mountain before us. It was an edifice of tall columns, gold foil, arched gables, and water fountains that stretched hundreds of feet above our heads.

We were standing on the lawn of the Spartan War Academy.

The crucible had begun.

8

THE SPARTAN WAR ACADEMY

Alexis

I shivered in the damp cave air.

Even though it was the middle of July, the mountain rocks were icy beneath my bare feet.

General Cleandro—an imposing bald man in a long black toga—led us down a shallow flight of stairs, which went straight into the carved-out mountain.

A mammoth hawk the size of a midsize dog sat on his shoulders and glared at us with beady eyes.

Good birdy. Please don't use your razor-sharp talons to scalp me.

The hawk snapped its beak like it was hungry for my brain juices.

"Disgusting creature," Nyx hissed into my ear, and I had to agree.

In the center of the short stairwell, a narrow basin was cut through the rock, and long crimson candles hung from the ceiling, dripping wax into the channel.

Dim light flickered.

Wax ran red.

Evocative music intensified as we descended into the darkness, and for the first time in a while, it wasn't in my head.

At the end of the stairs was a long, cavernous room.

The basin expanded into a long, shallow pool of red wax with thousands of candles hanging above it, and a narrow walkway led to five doors.

My jaw dropped.

On the high ceiling above the pool, dozens of full-size marble and bronze sculptures depicted men and women in battle—it was a melee of bodies, swords, and shields.

Crimson dripped below the fighting statues, off the candles and into the water…*as if they're bleeding.*

But what was below them took my breath away.

It's beautiful.

In the pool, there were statues of female musicians. Motorized harps and violins played in their hands as red wax dripped across their faces. Their gowns were carved into the stone in exquisite layers, which created a sopping-wet effect.

It was art, beyond imagination.

"Initiates, stand in a line!" General Cleandro barked, his voice echoing off the rocks, a sharp contrast to the poignant melody playing behind him.

He frowned down at us as we filed into a line, deep wrinkles stretched across his forehead. He seemed to be in his sixties, which meant he was probably hundreds of years old.

"There are five doors—" he gestured behind him "—beside the sacred pool: a classroom, a library, a bathroom, a bedroom, and a tunnel that leads to the creature menagerie."

His dark eyes narrowed as he walked slowly back and forth before us.

Whatever he saw, he didn't like.

Touché.

"DO YOU UNDERSTAND ME?" he bellowed.

My left ear rang with sharp feedback as his warped baritone voice echoed louder than should have been possible.

"Yes, General!" we chorused.

The music intensified.

We waited.

General Cleandro's sandals scuffed across the rock, and the chilly underground air prickled across my skin.

Finally he scoffed and said, "Luctor et emergo."

I struggle and emerge.

A new melody played as General Cleandro glared down at us with disgust, and the hawk on his shoulder wore a matching expression.

The tune was gentle and hypnotizing.

Everything was surreal.

"Humans—" he spat like it was a filthy word "—take *eight* weeks to heal a single broken bone. They can also only go *twenty-one* days without food…*ten* days without sleep, and only…*three* days without water."

Wax rained behind him.

The musicians looked like they were crying tears of red.

I wanted to cry with them.

Candlelight cast strange shadows across the room.

"Are you human?" He lunged forward and screamed into the face of the initiate to my left, spit flying, cheeks bright red.

Technically, nine of us were half-human because we were mutts, but even I had enough social awareness not to point that out.

He repeated, "ARE YOU A HUMAN?"

The high-pitched ringing in my left ear stabbed hotter, and I gritted my teeth. *"No, General!"* we chorused.

He resumed pacing before us with his expression cold as ice.

"Unlike humans," he said, "Spartans can live forever…we heal bones in *two* weeks, we can go *sixty* days without food, *thirty* days without sleep, and *two* entire weeks without a single drop of water."

He narrowed his eyes.

"But you're only nineteen and not full Spartans yet. Some of your minds and bodies are stronger than others. Soon enough, we'll find out who has what it takes."

He stopped in front of me. "Do you know what happens when a human surpasses those time frames—girl?" His tone made it clear that I wasn't welcome.

Their suffering ends, as it should.

"They d-die, General!" I answered, keeping my expression relaxed and nonconfrontational.

To my right, an initiate snickered at my stutter, but I kept my face a blank mask. I was used to the ridicule, the taunts, the name-calling.

Nyx hissed in his direction, but per usual, no one reacted.

There was a blur of movement from my left, and it was too close to dodge.

Crack. General Cleandro slammed his fist into the head of the boy standing next to me, and he collapsed to the floor from the force of the blow.

"WHAT'S SO FUNNY, INITIATE?"

The initiate scrambled unsteadily to his feet. "Nothing, General!"

"WHAT HAPPENS—" he leaned down so his face was pressed against the boy's, nose to nose "—TO SPARTANS WHO SURPASS THEIR LIMITS?"

"They go into a coma, General!"

"No. The key is that they *live*, initiate," he snarled. "Snicker in front of me again and I'll cut your tongue from your mouth."

"Yes, General!"

I hunched and made myself a smaller target.

General Cleandro resumed pacing in front of us and said, "Some of you have the misconception that this is a generic military boot camp, but this is *not* a pathetic human physical test. This…is the most civilized test in the world."

He paused.

"WE SEPARATE THE ANIMALS FROM THE GODS!" Rocks vibrated from the force of his bellow.

It took everything I had not to clutch my left ear and wince.

General Cleandro whirled around and stopped in front of the blond initiate in the laurel crown.

"Cassius Hermes—I hope you know that being an heir means *nothing* down here," he snarled in the boy's face. "There is no dishonor here, no fancy golden rules. I don't give a flying shit if you have perfect posture, wear diamond-encrusted clothes, know how to eat a fourteen-course meal, or court another heir with ancient jewels so he agrees to suck your sorry, limp dick for all of eternity—DO YOU UNDERSTAND, HEIR?"

"Yes, General!" the initiate shouted, Olympian crown glinting as he held himself perfectly still.

Diamonds in clothes and a fourteen-course meal can't be real—right? Also, do Spartans really trade jewels for sex?

I pursed my lips.

Can I do that instead?

Sadly, the opportunity to join the Spartans giving fellatio—and not competing to literal death—did not present itself.

Disheartening.

"This is a *mental* test." General Cleandro backed up and addressed all of us. "Until next January, you will not eat when you are here, unless we say so—spoiler, we won't. You will also not bathe, and…you will not sleep unless you're seconds from death. Also, if you're injured, you'll heal yourself. There will be no doctors to coddle you."

The song changed, and the energy in the mountain shifted.

It was ominous.

He showed his teeth. "What you will do is study until your

eyes bleed, and then—" he smiled maliciously "—you'll study fucking harder."

This is exactly why I avoid people.

"The crucible trains the mind." He smiled. "The question we answer in this mountain—how will you react when everything crumbles around you?"

He lunged forward like he was going to hit us, cackling as we flinched back.

"If you manage to survive the crucible," he said with deceptive softness, "you'll graduate and be named a citizen of Sparta. You'll be an immortal god."

His smile was wicked.

"But that's a big *if*...remember—" He thumped his fist against his wide chest and bellowed, "THERE ARE NO *STUPID GODS*—BECAUSE I MAKE SURE THERE ARE NO *STUPID SPARTANS*!"

I flinched again.

This was not good.

"Welcome to the Spartan War Academy. Follow me." He stalked along the edge of the pool, stopped at the first door, and opened it. "This is the sleeping quarters."

Inside the dark, low-ceilinged room were ten cots laid out across the rocks, nothing more.

The door slammed shut in our faces.

"I advise never going in there," he said. "Not if you want to survive. Don't tempt yourself with what you can't have. It will make you weak."

He moved on to the next door. "This is the bathroom—a privilege you don't deserve. Back in my day, we shit in a hole." He puffed up his chest like he was proud of that statement.

Were people okay?

The room was tiny with nothing but a rusted toilet that would probably give me diseases and a broken sink.

"Luxurious," he spat, and shook his head with disappointment.

He moved to the next door. "This is the classroom."

It was another windowless, cave-like room. The only difference was that the red candles hung from the ceiling, along the perimeter of the wall, and their wax dripped into a smaller basin. Smoke from the candles hung along the ceiling in a misty cloud. My eyes watered.

There was a desk with a chair and a chalkboard on the front wall.

Ten separate piles—each with a notebook, three textbooks, and one pen—were spaced out across the floor.

There were no other desks or chairs.

It was barren and cold.

Dark.

Damp.

Depressing as heck.

Honestly, it has the same vibes as high school.

"This is where you'll be spending most of your days." General Cleandro vibrated with barely constrained glee.

He could also benefit from a few whacks of a shovel.

He led us to the fourth door. "This is the library, the second place you'll be spending all your time."

My head tipped back, eyes widening.

It was palatial.

Towering stacks of books, velvet chairs, mahogany desks, and fireplaces with flickering flames filled the long, narrow space. Unlike in the other rooms, the rock ceiling towered high above. Much larger red candles hung down the center of the stacks, and their wax dripped into a long, narrow pool.

The scent of old parchment filled the air, and the roaring fireplaces chased away the underground chill.

It was lovely.

A few women in white togas milled about, putting books on the shelves and translating texts at desks. I almost cried because I wasn't the only female around.

"Here is our new batch of initiates," General Cleandro announced, and a few women looked over, but most ignored us.

"You'll show the muses respect," he spat. "Or you'll be killed."

It was potentially *not* a good sign that he sounded hopeful.

Before I could devolve into a full-on panic attack, we followed him to the last door, which opened to a long, dark tunnel.

"As I said before," he said as his hawk (government surveillance drone) stared at us. "The animal menagerie is down this hall. But you won't be seeing the animals until September, so this door should have no use for you."

He paused.

"Some of you won't live that long, so you don't need to worry about this hall at all." He smiled meanly. "Well, I hope you've enjoyed your tour. There is no kitchen or bath house—because you will *not* eat or clean yourselves while you're studying here."

The door shut with a thud.

I wanted to cry.

"Your studies start now."

His expression was cruel. "You will attend the classes: Thagorean, Lost Classical Lore, and Discipline and Power, in that order. The sessions will last for varying amounts of time determined by your two professors, and I will announce when you have breaks and for how long they will last...it's all quite simple."

Simply awful.

"Oh, one more thing." He took a step closer. "You have three guest professors filling in this year—General Pine and General Augustus will be your classroom professors, and General Kharon will be working the circuit."

Initiates whispered with horror around me.

Augustus and Kharon—both *the infamous Chthonic heirs are teaching us?*

General Cleandro bared his teeth. "We use the Socratic method here. You'll be called on at random, and if you answer a question wrong, your mentors will be notified. They'll lead your entire class through the circuit—which is a run through the mountains and swim through the River Styx, where Kharon will be waiting for you."

There was a long, awkward pause.

"Any questions, initiates?"

Someone whimpered, but no one spoke. *What idiot would ever ask him something? You'd be eaten alive.*

Drex, the other abandoned mutt, who I was pretty sure was secretly Chthonic, slowly raised his hand.

General Cleandro arched his brow. "What?"

Drex cleared his throat. "What about Titans on the circuit? I didn't see any fencing outside marking this a protected zone."

Great question.

General Cleandro burst into laughter.

After five long minutes of howling, he wiped tears out of his eyes and scoffed. "Of course these lands aren't in a pathetic human protected zone. We're *Spartans*. The Titans fear us, not the other way around."

The other initiates chuckled.

"However—" the general smiled cruelly "—some Titans have been known to…attack the weaker initiates up in the mountains. So keep your eye out."

No one was laughing now.

Cassius raised his hand, laurel crown gleaming. "But, General, isn't it the job of the Chthonics to fight the Titans? Not Olympians, like ourselves? That was the entire point of the Assembly of Death."

General Cleandro's smile fell.

He scoffed, "This is about separating the weak from the gods—if the Titans picking you off helps do so, then so be it. Understood?"

"Yes, General."

Actually, I don't understand, and I have a lot of questions.

A muse walked up to General Cleandro, and he turned away from us to talk to her, but his hawk swiveled its head fully around and kept staring at us.

Yep, that is 100 percent a robot.

"At least Augustus is known to be honorable and fair," whispered an initiate to my right. "He's the sanest heir the House of Ares has ever borne."

A boy with curly brown hair replied, "Yeah, but we have to deal with *Kharon*—I thought it was a rumor meant to scare us this year. Kronos save us, he's almost as unstable as Medusa—and she sided with the fucking Titans."

They nodded in agreement with grave expressions. "Kharon's literally *the Hunter* and Hades's favorite soldier. Why would he agree to work the crucible?"

"Probably because he's *insane* and likes torturing Olympians." All the initiates shivered dramatically. "That's what happens when Artemis procreates with Erebus—they say Kharon is more monster than man. Rumor is that Artemis birthed him to punish Olympians for killing her daughters in the war—he's her vengeance."

I blanched. *That doesn't sound good.*

Tim-Tom loved to theorize that Kharon's creature heritage gave him a massive dick. In contrast, Father John preached he was a descendant of the devil.

I pursed my lips; technically, both could be true.

Mental note—start praying for my soul.

Aggressively.

General Cleandro whirled around with an intense glare that immediately shut everyone up. Then he led us into the chilly, austere classroom.

He grunted as he sat down at the only desk in the room—

positioned in the front so he could loom over us—and kicked his feet up.

We awkwardly sat on the floor next to the ten piles of textbooks.

A few initiates sneered at me and snuck glances at the heir, but for the most part, everyone stared at the front with nervous anticipation.

The tension was palpable.

The door slammed open, and everyone jumped.

A man in a long white toga entered the room. "Hello!" He smiled and waved.

Young—with a pleasant face, short brown hair, and kind brown eyes—the new teacher seemed friendly. A shiny black raven sat calmly on his shoulder.

His congenial expression seemed genuine.

What a creep.

"Hello, initiates," he repeated gleefully. "Welcome to your first day of the crucible. My name is Pine."

He clapped with excitement, like we weren't literal hostages being held in a cave against our will.

I want whatever fancy Spartan antidepressants he's on.

"I'll be teaching your Thagorean classes during the circuit." He chuckled. "More commonly known to some of you as advanced mathematics, or as I like to call it—fun."

No one laughed.

He wrote his name on the chalkboard in big, loopy writing.

"Like most of you," Pine said, "I'm a Spartan mutt. However, *unlike* most of you, I'm a mutt who was born in less-than-ideal circumstances."

His gaze darted around the room, then lingered on me.

We're not bonding over abandonment issues.

He quickly looked away.

"All right, everyone." Pine clapped. "Turn to page one of your textbook. We're going to go over the basics of the philosophy and ethics of mathematics. In my class, these two principles will combine into glorious equations."

Pages rustled as we cracked open the heavy tomes.

"Don't worry," Pine said cheerfully. "This is not a simple math class where normal, *boring* math has no object permanence. Every number and symbol we use will be tied to a real-life ethics problem."

Interesting. Maybe this won't suck?

Judging from the frowns and groans of boys around me, I was in the minority.

Pine immediately launched into solving an equation.

Drip. Drip. Drip. Candle wax fell in a relaxing rhythm. Classical music drifted in from outside, and Pine's teaching cadence was pleasant as I took copious notes.

This doesn't seem too bad at all.

"Alessander Poseidon." Pine stopped teaching and pointed at a short initiate who sat in the back of the room. "What did I just say the function of Platonism was?"

The raven on his shoulder tilted its head to the side, like it was also waiting for an answer.

Alessander's face paled. "You said…it is the postulate of the—square root?"

Pine arched his brow, his smile falling. "Not even close."

He turned and nodded to General Cleandro, who gleefully tapped a small black paging device.

Hawk wings flapped with excitement.

BOOM.

A tall man with gray eyes appeared in the front of the room in a cloud of smoke. A pink ferret the size of a small cat clung to his arm.

He'd leaped straight into the mountain.

"Vorex, heir to the House of Poseidon," General Cleandro said to the new man. "You're the mentor of Alessander, correct?"

"Yes, General!" Vorex held up his palm and bowed his head, laurel wreath gleaming even in the shadows.

His pink ferret nodded up and down.

Aw, cute.

General Cleandro stared at him. "Lead the class through their first round of the circuit. And you might want to advise your mentee about paying attention in class. He's a fucking imbecile."

Not cute.

"Yes, General!"

Vorex gave Alessander a hateful look that promised retribution.

I shivered because Patro hadn't been physically violent with me—yet.

"GET UP!" General Cleandro bellowed in his booming voice, and we scrambled to our feet. His hawk screeched louder. "FORM A LINE BEHIND HIM!"

My left ear burned with pain.

We followed Vorex, who jogged out of the room.

"Stay here," I whispered to Nyx as I forced my stiff legs to cooperate.

Scales tightened around my neck, and I choked. "*No way* am I leaving you alone, kid."

That was unfortunate.

A few minutes later, we emerged from the mountain, and I struggled to adjust to the warm weather and bright daylight. The July sun was scorching, and grass squished as we ran across it.

It was a shocking contrast to the dark, chilly classroom.

Vorex cut toward the nearest mountain and led us along a dirt path.

In school I'd participated in a grand total of one gym class—I'd been starving, and the movement had made me want to pass out, so I'd hid behind a shed, doing math problems, for the rest of the year.

They'd never assigned it to me again.

Now I suffered for my inactivity.

I ascended the side of one of the dolomites, my lungs burning, calves and thighs cramping, as sweat dripped. I pumped my arms desperately.

One by one, the other initiates passed me.

Nyx was deadweight around my neck.

Halfway up, the temperature cooled, and my sweat froze, making it hard to open my eyes.

"Are—you—" Gasp. "—trying—to—kill—me?"

"Stop talking," Nyx snapped rudely. "You need to conserve your energy—concentrate, kid."

I breathed heavily (asphyxiated) and *concentrated* on not committing amicide.

My lungs rattled.

Vorex yelled something, but I couldn't hear him over my suicidal thoughts.

The path narrowed. On the left was a jagged cliff—one wrong step and I'd be dead. *Hopefully.*

I hugged the side of the mountain, since the blind spot on my left made it hard to judge depth.

One foot in front of the other. Coming down will be easier. Just get to the top. Don't stop.

I tried to think positive thoughts.

How do I summon a Titan so he kills me? Immediately.

I failed.

The space between me and the last initiate was widening, and I gritted my teeth, moved my legs faster, desperate to not lose the group.

Nyx felt like she weighed a million pounds.

Near the top of the biggest freaking mountain on earth, the boys *finally* stopped running. They were keeled over, hands on their knees in a circle.

When I approached, a handful looked over and watched me, their eyes filled with hatred.

"I didn't know a Spartan woman could be so pathetic-looking," said a tall initiate with red hair. "Aren't they all supposed to be stunningly strong and beautiful? No wonder you weren't wanted."

He had *big* Jessica and Tim-Tom energy.

Two other boys in the group shuffled closer to him and laughed. "Good one, Titus," one of them said.

Ears ringing from exhaustion, I stared at them incredulously.

Drex rolled his eyes and didn't join them.

"How is it possible that you look weaker than a human?" Titus said louder as he glared at me. "Aren't you embarrassed?"

Ignore him. He's not worth your time.

He spat at my feet, then lunged forward and yanked on my ponytail.

I stumbled away from his disgusting touch.

"How is it possible that your brain is *smaller* than your tiny balls?" I shouted aggressively and shook my fist at him.

In my head.

In reality, I said nothing, because I didn't like interacting with people. Also, I couldn't breathe. So there was that.

My legs gave out.

Knees banging against cold rocks, shaking palms digging into pebbles, I lowered my head and dry-heaved. Mucus dribbled attractively out of my mouth.

Ah, womanhood.

Titus sneered, "Of course you'd be a useless bitch who couldn't even swallow." His cronies snickered.

My eyes ached from the force of rolling them back in my head.

"Do you want me to bite him?" Nyx asked as I lowered my body and groaned in pain.

"No," I whispered. She'd killed enough people for me in the massacre.

Also, I wanted to be the one to choke the light out of his eyes.

I do?

Mental note—physical exertion makes me homicidal. Avoid anything above a brisk walk.

Titus said something else, but I stopped listening, because I had free will.

Coughing, I spat more mucus onto the rocks.

Should I be concerned that it's bloody?

"That's it, let it out," Nyx said. "Take deep, calming breaths. It's totally normal to spit up blood. Very common."

"I'm going to kill you," I whispered as I swatted the air in front of my neck like I'd seen a bug. "Slither on the ground beside me."

Nyx grunted as I hit her head, and scales tightened around my throat.

"Don't be ridiculous," she hissed as she loosened her grip. "I'm not some common dog—you will carry me, and you will enjoy it."

"You're the worst," I whispered.

The boy throwing up next to me gave me a strange look.

I made a face back at him.

"Everyone, listen up," Vorex said, standing tall with his hands on his hips, looking bored. His ferret hissed, flashing long, pointy fangs.

He wasn't even sweating. God had his favorites—I was not one of them.

Another initiate keeled over and emptied his stomach.

Relatable. Let it out, brother.

Vorex rolled his eyes as he looked down at us. "Right now you're going to *pull yourselves together* and follow me back down the mountain. We'll have another break at the bottom, so stop acting so dramatic. This will be the *easiest* lap of the circuit you ever do."

He gestured up to the blinding sun. "The weather's perfect."

Spoiler, he was deranged.

The weather was heinous. I'd describe it as a burning day in hell before I used the term *perfect.*

Vorex trailed off and muttered something under his breath about pathetic, weak bitches.

I would have been offended, but I was too busy trying to find my will to live, like the aforementioned pathetic, weak bitch. The edge of the mountain was looking mighty tempting.

"Let's go." Vorex stretched his heavily muscled body, then started jogging easily down the side of the mountain like he was weightless.

The rest of the group groaned as they followed, and I obeyed sullenly.

Alas, the journey into hell continues.

9
The Crucible

Alexis

Wiping away spit, I accidentally made eye contact with another initiate as I followed (fell in a forward direction while somehow staying upright) the group down the mountain.

The boy shuffled toward me, curly gold hair plastered with sweat to his pale skin.

"We got this," he said as he raised his hand toward me. It was bloody from where he'd fallen and cut himself.

I tripped and stumbled away to avoid being hit.

My palms scraped across sharp rocks as I barely caught myself, then staggered back to my aching feet.

There was an uncomfortable pause because he was *still* holding out his hand for a handshake.

I didn't take it.

He gave me a strange look.

Embarrassed, I jogged faster (increased from an injured snail's pace to a somewhat healthier snail's pace).

Unfortunately, he fell into step beside me on my left side, hovering in my blind spot.

Unease skittered down my spine.

Panic pulsed in my chest.

"I'm Christos Zeus," he said. "Nice to meet you."

I grunted and kept my eyes away from him so he'd get the memo.

"Alexis, right? I've heard about you—I'm also a mutt." He pointed to his corkscrew curls as we descended the mountain and said, "Since they think you're also from the House of Zeus, that would make us half siblings."

He grinned like something was funny.

Nothing was humorous these days. People needed to learn to accept the energy of the dark times.

Charlie was also halfway around the world, probably worried sick.

"I already have a brother," I whispered.

"Well, either way, I'm sure we'll be great friends." Christos patted my back, and I jumped, falling over rocks as I staggered, trying to get away.

He laughed.

I didn't.

"Cheerful idiot," Nyx hissed.

I would have said something in agreement, but I was too busy trying not to *die*.

Time stretched as the sun marched slowly across the sky, a frantic melody played in my head, and I learned something very important: running downhill was *not* easier than running uphill.

There was no justice in this cruel world.

Hours later, calves cramping, chest heaving, I collapsed on all fours at the bottom of the mountain, where the group was resting.

Christos fell to his knees beside me. "Whoa, that sucked." He coughed.

I moved away from him. My roster of friends was full. Yes, Nyx took up every spot. She had a big (deranged) personality.

Titus said something derogatory about women belonging on their backs.

"Stand up!" Vorex ordered too soon, and I joined in the chorus of groans.

He gestured to the dark blue water behind us. "That is the River Styx—do you all see the boat with the man standing on it?"

A tall, wide-shouldered figure was upright in a thin boat. Covered head to toe in the black cloak that signified he was part creature, with a long pole in his hand, he looked more shadow than man.

"That is Kharon, the heir to the House of Artemis and the deadliest Chthonic assassin on earth," Vorex said with a grimace. "If you stop swimming...if he catches you...you *will* die. The fact that he's agreed to be the ferryman of the circuit this year is *not* good news for your chances of survival."

Kharon's boat turned in the water toward us.

A hair-raising growl echoed, and everyone looked around warily. *Where is that sound coming from?*

Vorex frowned. "They call Kharon the Hunter for a reason. You don't want to be caught by him. He's more creature than man."

An initiate shivered with fear (it was me).

But apparently, we didn't look properly terrified, because Vorex continued, "He's the only Spartan who doesn't have an animal protector. Do you want to know why? Because all the monstrous creatures are *afraid* of him. He's one of them...but worse."

Kharon stared at us across the River Styx and smiled.

Is he looking at me?

I discreetly moved to the side so I hid behind Christos.

Vorex grimaced as he continued, "Rumor is, he has a dungeon in his villa at Lake Como where he tortures anyone who angers him."

Kharon is definitely still looking at me.

I blanched and crouched lower.

Please don't take me to your dungeon.

"All right." Vorex shrugged. His ferret crawled onto his shoulder and stood up tall. "Everyone, get in the water and swim to the academy."

He pointed to the very end of the rippling water, where the carved side of the mountain was barely visible.

The distance was *far.*

Nyx slithered down my side onto the ground. "I'll swim beside you, kid."

I slumped with relief at the release of her crushing weight and sat down, but didn't have time to enjoy it.

Christos once again offered me his bloody cut palm.

Sighing, I took it.

Scrapes burned on my hand as they reopened.

"What are you waiting for? Go—go—go!" Vorex shouted. "Swim like your lives depend on it."

The ten of us ran forward into the river. Icy water jolted my exhausted system into panic mode. It was like face-planting onto concrete.

A sharp pain stabbed my chest.

With all my strength, I threw my arms forward and kicked as I fought to get away from the flailing bodies.

It was a frenzy.

Arms elbowed. Skin smacked. Water splashed. Hands yanked on feet.

The pain in my sternum worsened.

I found some separation, grateful for the long summer days I'd spent swimming in the pond behind the trailer park after the foster parents were removed from my life.

As the swim continued, the gratitude died.

The panic in my heart became a blinding pain.

We were going *against* the current—on the shore, it had looked like the water traveled lazily in a slow, peaceful motion, but it was anything but.

With every stroke, I turned my head to the side and gasped, desperate to fill my deflated lungs with air, but it wasn't enough.

I battled the water.

When I inhaled as I turned my head to breathe, water filled my nose, and I choked. Coughing, I flipped onto my back. Sinuses burning, I desperately sucked in air.

A loud splashing sound caught my attention—I leaned my head up to look around.

Christos was beside me, treading water, moaning pitifully. "Help!" he screamed, foam dripping out of his mouth as he splashed like he was in agony.

Someone's hurting him, but who?

His head bobbed under as he looked at me with frantic desperation.

I tried to reach and help him.

He pulled away and screamed louder, fighting against an invisible monster.

A shadowy boat appeared, seemingly out of thin air. My eyes widened.

It was the *who.*

"Swim!" I screamed at Christos desperately as I tried to hold him up.

He pulled us both under. When we resurfaced, he screamed louder, splashing as he struggled against me.

"S-swim," I begged him as I sputtered.

He kicked at me.

A tattered dark cloak blew menacingly on the mountain breeze as Kharon leaned low in the boat.

Panic made white-hot agony burst through my chest.

I swam away from Christos, desperate to put separation between us.

Kharon stared down at me. His head tilted to the side with interest, like he was observing something unique.

I looked around, but everyone else was swimming yards away.

He was looking straight at me with glacial blue eyes.

Glaring at me.

Focused.

Like he was hunting me.

A heart attack ripped through my sternum, and everything got hazy.

I struggled to breathe.

The water swallowed me. When I resurfaced, Kharon's eyes were filled with blood, and his long, pale finger was touching Christos's forehead.

Christos let out a hideous shriek, like a single touch had ruined him, and he splashed wildly as dozens of birds flew off a tree on the riverbank.

Kharon smiled, pulled his hand away, and stood up in his boat.

He stared down at the drowning boy dispassionately.

Christos wailed like he was being torn to shreds from unseen forces. Blood poured as his skin was ravaged.

Foam dripped off his lips like he was a feral creature.

His shouts got more desperate.

More hopeless.

Stabbing agony skewered my chest.

Christos disappeared under the water—he didn't come back up.

I wanted to cry.

"We're going to be friends." Why had I refused to talk to him?

Kharon Artemis slowly raised his cloaked head and stared directly at me, sharp, blood-filled Chthonic eyes glowing.

The son of Artemis and Erebus was evil incarnate.

Kharon's lips pulled up into a knifelike smile, and the nose of his boat turned in my direction. Water splashed all around the vessel.

His smile was that of a predator who'd locked on his kill. *He's headed straight for me.*

My eyes widened.

"Swim, Alexis," Nyx hissed from somewhere nearby. "As fast as you can, *right now*!"

I didn't need to be told twice.

Kicking with everything I had, arms slapping at the water, head downward, I didn't breathe for minutes at a time.

I swam like the devil was chasing me.

He was.

The world blurred in a frantic haze.

Finally, knees sinking into warm mud, I crawled out of the water across the riverbank. Vorex pointed at a pile of foil blankets, and initiates scrambled for them, but there weren't enough for all of us, and I wasn't fast enough.

Icy scales slid up my torso as Nyx wrapped herself around my neck.

Numbly I staggered to my feet. Dripping water, convulsing with shivers, I limped behind the group.

We formed a line in front of the academy entrance.

General Cleandro looked pissed. "If I find out that one of you took it upon yourself to try to separate your weak classmates…"

What is he talking about? It was Kharon. I saw him. He must have done something with his powers to hurt him.

The general narrowed his eyes. "Then I won't be happy. You don't need to do a single fucking thing but worry about yourselves. Weeding out the weak is *my* job…or do you not think I can do my job?"

"No, General!" we chorused, our voices cracked and raw. Someone coughed up water (it was me).

We'd gone from ten to nine, in just one day.

A pervasive deadness filled my chest.

How am I going to survive this place?

The doctor had said that the House of Zeus was known for its fertility issues, and recent mutts struggled. Now her words felt sickly prophetic.

Another one was dead.

Am I next?

"I was originally going to give you all a break, but now—" the general's smirk was cruel "—you will attend Lost Classical Lore with Professor Augustus."

The setting sun cast long, sinister shadows.

"MOVE, INITIATES," the general bellowed. "WHAT THE FUCK ARE YOU LAZY FUCKERS WAITING FOR? FUCKING MOVE."

Unsurprisingly, we all moved.

Back under the mountain, the dripping wax, life-size sculptures, long crimson pool, and melancholic music were depressing.

It was also freezing.

Slipping, I winced as the raw cuts on the bottoms of my feet scraped against the rocks. I sat back down on the hard classroom floor (fell over and somehow landed on my butt).

My hands were also covered in wounds. Blood, river water, and despair dripped off me.

Our breaths were loud and raspy, and someone coughed every other second.

The mood in the room was *misery*.

The door flung open.

A man entered.

His energy was vicious.

Unlike with Pine, everyone in the room immediately sat up straight, even General Cleandro.

It was him.

The infamous assassin, rumored to have dark powers.

The heir to the House of Ares.

Augustus.

The son of Ares and Aphrodite looked more like a savage warrior than a professor.

Evil incarnate.

A thick scar slashed across the top of his sharp right cheekbone and ended on his nose—it matched the color of his spiky ruby-covered crown.

I rubbed at my hair-tie-covered wrists. Fear made it hard to breathe.

He loomed high above us with perfect posture. He was about Achilles's height, and his powerful muscles bunched as he walked into the classroom. His hands—the size of dinner plates—clenched into fists.

He had a commanding (terrifying) aura.

Suddenly the description of sinful handsomeness, disturbed powers, and divine rage made perfect sense.

It fit him.

Augustus was a frightening amalgamation of sharp edges.

Dark stubble covered a harsh square jaw. Tan skin stretched across wicked cheekbones. Shadows pooled in the hollows of his cheeks. His black eyes were smoldering. Lips curved viciously.

A severe center part split his two-toned hair—half black and half white—which was pulled back into a long, silky ponytail.

His parentage was immediately clear from looking at him.

He was deadly.

I don't want to be alone with him in a dark alley, or even a well-lit alley. Actually, I don't want to be alone with him anywhere.

Augustus paced slowly at the front of the room, and the hair on my arms and legs stood up.

"You *really* need to get a Spartan gun," Nyx hissed in my ear.

I nodded in agreement.

Two voices whispered near me, and I looked to my left. Nothing was there.

You're losing your mind.

I took a deep breath and concentrated on the monster in front of me.

The very air around him was electric. Dark power hummed beneath his skin, and my mouth prickled like I could taste it.

We were in the middle of a mountain, but we were somehow also in a lightning storm.

Augustus *was* the storm.

A small gray creature with dark stripes darted across the room from the door, and it climbed up Augustus's shoulders. Little hands wrapped around the professor's thick neck, and its eyes were as midnight-black as his.

It was also fluffy.

I gaped at the *raccoon* that Augustus was essentially giving a piggyback.

It was the cutest Chthonic protector I'd ever seen.

"I could eat that creature in three bites," Nyx hissed, and I discreetly slapped her.

"You ruin my life," she muttered, then let out a loud, raspy snore as she immediately fell asleep.

I envied her lifestyle.

Augustus peered down at us while an adorable raccoon played with his long hair.

"You will refer to me as Professor Augustus." His silky baritone voice vibrated through my bones. "This is my animal protector, Poco."

He turned to showcase the creature that I wanted to kidnap and give kisses to.

"He might look harmless," Augustus warned. "But beware, he is a feral creature—touch him and you'll reap the consequences. You've been warned."

Poco the raccoon looked down at us from his high vantage

point—a black-and-white ponytail wrapped around his fist—and flashed a full set of razor-sharp teeth that looked like they belonged in a shark's mouth.

His black eyes flashed as he tipped his head back and screeched.

Avoid the rabid raccoon.

Got it.

"As most of you already know," Augustus continued, "I am known for my honor. I will not torture you just to torture you. Everything we will do in this classroom has a purpose."

Initiates relaxed, some smiled at the professor with relief, and he nodded back at them.

Patro said he was even-mannered; maybe this won't be so bad after all.

"I see we have a…girl—in the class this year." Augustus stared down at me. "That is unfortunate."

Boys snickered behind me.

The professor's attention was intense as he held my gaze. "What is your opinion of women participating in the crucible?"

He waited for an answer.

"It's…good?" I shrugged, not sure what he wanted me to say. *Frankly, I'm not exactly sure what any of this even is.*

Augustus's congenial expression disappeared; pure loathing twisted his features. "So that bastard really had a sanctimonious daughter, just like himself. You really think other women should be subjected to this test?"

Oh no.

I'd definitely given the wrong answer.

I opened my mouth to dispute it, but my mouth was dry, and I was tongue-tied. "Oh, th-that's—" I struggled to speak. "Not wh-what—"

"Save your excuses." Augustus cut me off with his hand raised. "Future generations will have to suffer because of your stunt. Have you thought of that? Or are you just selfish?"

Soulless black eyes bore through me.

Um, I have no clue what you're talking about. Have you ever thought of that?

I rubbed at my hair-tie-covered wrists, phantom pains shooting up my forearms. Then I ripped my gaze away from his and stared at the floor.

Skin prickled under the weight of his fury.

Finally, what felt like *ages* later, he turned his suffocating attention away from me.

With a dramatic turn of his long toga, Augustus wrote, "The Story of The Minotaur" in Latin across the chalkboard. "Turn to page two of your textbooks," he said in Latin. "The story begins with—"

Wax dripped slowly.

Plop. Plop. Plop.

Eyes closing with exhaustion, I held my trembling legs to my chest to conserve body heat as I listened to the sordid story of a feral Minotaur and Kronos.

My brain hurt as I tried to piece together the Latin words that were spoken in a random order and form them into sentences.

It's a dead language for a reason. Someone needs to kill it again. Also, whoever invented it should be stabbed twenty-three times in the back.

Time passed.

I forced myself to concentrate on the words.

Mid-lecture, "Alexis," Augustus said harshly in English, and the change of languages was jarring. "What did ancient Spartans from the House of Poseidon primarily use Minotaurs for?"

Poco hissed on his shoulder.

I opened my eyes. "Entertainment."

Augustus made an unimpressed noise at the back of his throat. "*What* entertainment are you referring to?" He glared at me with disdain.

Vitriol wafted off him.

Why am I so hateable? I'm literally just trying to live a good (short) life.

In the front of the classroom, General Cleandro leaned forward in his seat and pulled out his black device. On his shoulders, his hawk slowly spread its wings.

"Or," Augustus taunted, "just like your father, do you think you already know everything? So you haven't bothered to learn the true intricacies of the Latin language—and you've been sitting here for the last two hours, not comprehending but thinking you're better than everyone, just waiting—"

I shook my head and blurted, "They hunted Minotaurs for sport through the maze at Mycenae on the island of Crete."

On numb lips, I repeated his lecture before he could criticize me further.

"But Minotaurs were sentient beasts who communicated with each other to trap and thwart the Spartans—they b-became the hunters and ripped the Spartans to shreds and blocked the maze's exit. Every time the Spartans healed, they immediately tore them apart."

"*Never* interrupt me again. You're not better than others because you're from the House of Zeus," Augustus said harshly as Poco twirled his long black-and-white ponytail around his little paws.

A few initiates snickered under their breath.

He switched to Latin and asked, "How long were the Spartans trapped?"

I coughed (hacked up a lung for a minute), then said, "They're still there today—the House of Hades has blocked any rescue efforts."

"Why?" Augustus demanded.

I shrugged. "Because they're Chthonic and they h-hate the House of Poseidon?"

Because they're evil.

Instead of mocking my stutter, my classmates nodded in

agreement, and a few even clapped. "Evil Chthonic bastards," someone muttered, then gulped with fear as Augustus glared at them.

Deep lines appeared in Augustus's tan forehead as he turned back to me. "Your answers on what I taught were technically correct, but your assessment was...*disappointing*."

The room let out a collective sigh of relief that we wouldn't be running the circuit, and I glanced guiltily over at Drex, who was sitting next to me. He was staring down at his textbook, ignoring everyone.

Technically, he's Chthonic, but he saved you.

I felt ashamed. Dirty. Augustus was also Chthonic, and I'd just insulted him.

Christos screaming as he died and Kharon smiling. The Crimson Duo torturing a Titan.

Numbness spread.

Father John said evil was the absence of God and that he'd seen the devil in bloody Chthonic eyes.

I'd seen it too.

Augustus switched topics and started ranting in Latin about how sirens were advanced sentient creatures in the same class as Minotaurs, and I sighed with relief.

He didn't call on anyone else and smiled at the other initiates when they asked questions.

He didn't smile at me.

Not once.

An indeterminate amount of time later, which felt like *forever*, Lost Classical Lore ended, and General Cleandro announced we had a three-hour break to study before Thagorean class with Pine. "I expect everyone to spend the time in the library, or there will be...consequences for you."

My gut told me he was *not* bluffing.

But I was so tired and cold I could barely stand up straight.

In the library, I curled up (flung myself facedown) on a maroon velvet settee in front of a roaring fireplace, which was hidden in the back behind the stacks.

A pretty muse with long pink hair stacked books on a shelf nearby. She frowned over at me, but glanced away when we made eye contact.

Most of the other initiates had curled up in front of fireplaces, but two boys sat at the long mahogany desks, working. Apparently, they were paragons of discipline and had enough physical and mental stamina to study.

Not relatable.

I didn't even have enough energy to die, if it came down to it (hopefully it would).

Nothing could have stopped me from falling asleep.

Nyx muttered with contentment around my neck, and I pulled her close like a blanket.

Déjà vu washed over me. Everything had changed, yet *nothing* was different. I was still an exhausted, unwanted little girl covered in bruises, shivering in a cardboard box.

"This place sucks," I whispered. "I want to go home."

"Home is not a place," Nyx said softly. "It's a person."

I closed my eyes. "That literally makes zero sense."

"You'll understand, someday."

Darkness claimed me.

10
TORTURE

KHARON: A FEW HOURS EARLIER

I stood in the boat, dying of boredom as I waited for the idiot boys to finish their first lap of the circuit.

When the federation had randomly forced me to work the crucible this year (a decision that still didn't make any sense), I'd assumed the torturing of Olympian spawn would make it a little fun.

I was wrong.

Ennui had already set in.

My fingers itched with the urge to palm my knife and stab something. Preferably, *someone.*

I wanted to be in the forest hunting Titans.

Needed it like I needed oxygen.

Craved it like a Cyclops desired blood.

Hell let out a yawn of boredom, and Hound flopped over, which caused the boat to rock.

Yes, I'd named my hellhound protectors what they were. No

one else could see them anyway, just another perk of having a monstrous creature lineage.

All three of us were exhausted by the act of standing still.

We weren't bred to be patient.

We were bred to devour.

The violence—the chase—was everything. Every second stuck in the stupid boat was a second I could have been tracking my prey through a forest. Following them for hours, then attacking when they weren't expecting it.

Now I was stuck in the bumfuck dolomites twiddling my thumbs.

Fuck the federation and their political machinations. If they think forcing me to babysit their toddlers will make me more empathetic toward Olympians, they're gonna be in for a rude awakening. I'll kill them all.

The fact that they forced us into the Assembly of Death in the first place proved how brainless they were. The federation thought they were keeping Chthonics occupied by forcing us to fight Titans for a living.

Little did they know, it was *exactly* what all of us wanted to be doing anyway.

We were just sharpening our skills.

Biding our time.

Unlike useless Olympians, Chthonics were handcrafted by Kronos himself. We were born to kill, and we did it well.

It was our *pleasure* to slaughter.

To fight.

The violence was divine.

Sitting up straighter in the fucking dinghy they called a boat, I stared at the towering mountain pass and waited for the Olympian bastards to arrive so I could torture them to death.

I cracked my knuckles.

The fact that the federation was trying to soil our Chthonic bloodlines by forcing us to marry weak, pathetic, whiny Olympians was beyond absurd. Taking a marriage oath and binding my dark soul to one of those fuckers was a fate *worse* than death.

When Chthonics bonded, they got stronger, but when Chthonics bonded with Olympians, they weakened.

It was unacceptable.

I refused to be neutered.

Olympians called their puny characteristics "abilities," but we Chthonics knew the truth.

They were powerless.

They couldn't taste the bloodlust like we did. They didn't crave the games, the hunt. They didn't know the glory of ripping apart prey with their bare hands while their heart pounded with the pain of using *real* power.

They didn't experience the rush of the kill, because they weren't predators like us.

Olympians were the Spartans who weren't strong enough to wield true power.

They were barely better than pathetic humans, and compared to our illustrious bloodlines, they were *nothing*.

I spat into the River Styx with disgust.

The new marriage law was proof of how desperate the federation was getting.

They were doing everything in their power to keep us constrained because they knew we were superior to them in every single way.

It was only a matter of time before we finished what the Great War had started.

Zeus and the other Olympian leaders were barely holding on to their power.

We were all just waiting.

To attack.

I stood straighter, and the ravaged muscles in my right leg tightened, so I rolled my ankle, trying to alleviate the ache.

Fuck the Gladiator Competition. Fuck all the Olympians. Fuck this Kronos-damned dinghy.

My ruined leg was a reminder.

Even as a child, the federation had tried to destroy me. I hadn't been old enough for the crucible, but according to the federation, I'd been old enough to be hunted in the Dolomites Coliseum and maimed like a feral creature.

That was what Olympians did when they realized someone had *real* power—they attacked.

Pain intensified.

Panic clawed at my chest, and I breathed deeply to calm myself down. I rubbed at the brands on my chest.

There was a reason I hunted all day and night; if I stopped moving, I felt the agony. I remembered the trauma. However, if I kept myself distracted, then I couldn't remember. Mostly.

Gritting my teeth, I rubbed at my tired eyes.

I couldn't recall the last time I'd slept. The problem was the second I lay down, my subconscious tortured me with the heinous memories.

So I stayed awake.

I didn't run from my demons. I fed them, and now *I* was the demon.

The Olympians called me many names.

Insomniac.

Sociopath.

Hunter.

Killer.

All of them were true.

Tapping my foot faster, I debated capsizing just to give myself something to do.

Hell and Hound whined as they flopped over with a huff.

The urge to slaughter *anything* pounded through me like a living force, and from the body language of my hellhounds, they agreed. We were not made for this.

Time crawled forward.

I played with my knives.

What felt like hours later, I sighed with relief as the spawn finally made an appearance. I debated shooting at them for fun, but didn't want to deal with the paperwork.

They staggered down to the base of the mountain, then collapsed onto the ground in various states of misery.

I snorted.

The crucible was *nothing* compared to the training at the Assembly of Death. They wouldn't last a second.

Hell growled low in his throat and tipped his head over the boat as he stared at an initiate with his razor-sharp teeth bared.

"What is it?" I asked.

My protectors only ever growled at Augustus because hellhounds were extremely territorial—but only around other predators. Since they were top of the food chain, it wasn't often that they got riled up.

Hell bared his teeth wider, and his head turned toward the lithe figure kneeling apart from the group with their head down. He let out a toe-curling sound of aggression.

I focused on the initiate.

Golden skin practically glowed in the sunlight.

Curls shone like silk.

The initiate looked up. A white and a black eye stared directly at me—the different colors were shocking.

It was *her* again.

Alexis Hert.

The abandoned girl everyone in Sparta was talking about. The one I'd played nursemaid to back at the shanty Patro and Achilles called home, after the massacre when they'd been called away to fight Titans.

I'd thought the hellhounds had been growling because they'd smelled Augustus on me, but it really had been the girl.

Interesting.

She'd been out of her mind with delirium and pain, but even writhing on blood-covered sheets, there'd been something *intense* about her.

It was a feeling without a name.

Whatever it was, as I held her chin and fed her pills, recognition had stirred within me. There was an energy about her, an aura that felt like I'd known her before.

She'd been so helpless, at my complete (nonexistent) mercy, and yet even half-asleep, she'd fought like a wildcat.

I smiled at the memory.

Sparta was small, and there weren't enough Spartans and creatures on earth to keep me entertained, so it was rare that I was interested in anyone.

But with her, I wanted to play.

Even covered in sweat, kneeling in the dirt a few yards away, there was something arresting about Alexis. It went beyond her physical appearance, which resembled a wild thing.

The way she observed the world was intriguing, like she was constantly on alert and surprised by her surroundings.

The last person I'd felt this drawn to was Augustus.

But with him, it made sense, since he was scarred and tormented, just like me. The hardness in his eyes, the blackness in his soul, was what had enticed me in the first place. Like recognized like.

But Alexis looked weak and breakable. She was all long, gangly limbs and wide, innocent eyes.

She came across as a naive.

How the fuck did she survive the massacre? She looks like she's been starved.

Hell growled louder. Hound stood up next to him and let out a warning howl. Their canines flashed as they hunched low, like they were getting ready to fight a ruthless predator.

They were both fixated on her.

What are your secrets—carissima? Are you more than you seem?

Twisted interest burned inside my sternum as a new obsession kindled to life.

Is her innocent air all an act? Is she dangerous?

I smiled wider.

Suddenly, Titans weren't the only things I wanted to hurt.

How fun it will be to crack her open. Break her and reveal all her secrets.

There was a shout. Then all ten of the initiates dove into the river.

My attention was rapt as Alexis swam deftly through the water. I followed in my boat, chasing after her, chest tightening with pure adrenaline and anticipation.

Then a boy near her started screaming. He shrieked louder, the sound of a dying animal, like something, *someone*, was killing him.

I looked around for a source.

Hell and Hound went wild, growling and barking in the direction of Alexis, who had stopped swimming and was treading water next to him.

She lunged at him.

Her face turned toward me.

An *insane realization* hit me, and my breath left my lungs like I'd been punched.

Oh my Kronos—she's killing him.

The boy screamed louder, like he was being torn to pieces as she grappled with him.

Whatever Alexis was doing—she was filthy powerful.

The obsession that had kindled exploded into a bonfire of pure want. I adjusted my belt to loosen the growing pressure in my pants.

Holy fuck, she's murdering him.

She's vicious.

The boy screamed louder while splashing to get away from her.

Alexis yelled something as she drowned him, but I couldn't hear it over the rushing in my ears.

I call dibs.

She disentangled herself and swam away.

Pure euphoria filled me.

Kneeling, I touched the boy's forehead and unleashed my power to finish the job. Pain stabbed through my chest. His screams intensified as I let him see my protectors, and he flailed while Hell and Hound jumped in to feast, but all my attention was still on her.

A plan unfolded before me.

It would work.

It had to.

I was the hunter of my generation because I knew how to play the long game—I always caught my prey.

I'm going to devour her.

I stood up, the boy forgotten, as I slowly turned my boat toward her.

Alexis swam away frantically.

I tipped my head back and laughed as I followed.

Glory be to Kronos. Thank you for delivering this exquisite creature to me like a lamb for slaughter.

It was a great fucking day to be a Chthonic monster.

Alea iacta est—the die was cast.

A great day indeed.

11

HELL

ALEXIS

"BREAK'S OVER!" The general's voice ripped through the library like a nuclear bomb, the ones humans had unsuccessfully used against Titans when they'd first appeared.

I sat up with a start and groaned in pain. It felt like I'd been asleep for mere seconds.

"Ten more minutes," Nyx grumbled as she tightened around my neck. I rubbed at my groggy eyes and moaned louder as I stood up.

Every muscle in my legs screamed with pain. Each step forward was agony, and I wanted to collapse.

I face-planted into a bookshelf.

Great, now inanimate furniture is trying to off me.

My right eye was blurry with exhaustion—my field of vision was 35 percent at best—and my face throbbed where I'd slammed into the bookcase.

"FORM A LINE, INITIATES!"

Judging from the sleepy groans of the other initiates, I wasn't the only one suffering.

Of course, General Cleandro decided it was the right time to launch into an unhinged rant about the importance of mental toughness and being gritty. His hawk bobbed up and down on his shoulder like it was agreeing.

Birds are the worst.

The hawk let out a screech, and Nyx hissed.

General Cleandro went *on* and *on* about being strong.

Personally, I preferred to be mentally weak—it made life more interesting.

Will I kill myself today dramatically or barely survive? Every day was a new mystery.

I didn't remember walking back into the classroom, but suddenly I was seated in my same spot on the cold rocks, shivering and humming to myself. General Cleandro was seated at the front of the room with his demonic bird on his shoulder.

Professor Pine drew equations on the board with his raven staring at us as he taught Thagorean. Numbers blurred together, and my usually neat handwriting was illegible as I haphazardly scratched out notes.

At some point, class ended and Professor Augustus entered to teach Discipline and Power. Poco loped in behind him, clapping his little black hands together like he was excited.

Professor Augustus spoke slowly, "There are some different rules that govern the lives of mutts and heirs, and this is especially true when it comes to females, since they are so rare. For example, a female mutt may participate in the crucible."

He looked at me pointedly, black eyes glinting fiercely.

"But," he continued, "for an heiress to do so would be the *highest* dishonor, and if she survived—which would be highly unlikely due to her genteel upbringing—extreme methods would be taken, like an arranged marriage, to save her honor."

His eyes were full of disgust.

He's trying to shame me in front of everyone.

Blankly I stared back.

I had no honor.

I'd stolen everything I owned.

Lived in a cardboard box for years.

Showered in sinks all winter when the well water was too cold.

His words meant nothing to me. If anything, I was happy for all the heiresses who weren't allowed to participate in this hell.

It was nice that someone was protecting them.

Stay honorable, sisters.

Augustus arched a dark brow at me, then looked away and continued, "Differences in how the rare female heiress is treated aside—there are four things common to all Spartans twenty years old and above, Olympian and Chthonic."

He held up four fingers, lips turning up into a smile as he talked to everyone else.

A headache throbbed as he lectured.

"*First*—immortality after you turn twenty years old." He put down one finger.

"Our bodies get stronger, our senses keener, with age—although Spartans are not infallible and will go into a coma if injured or starved long enough. Cutting our bodies into small pieces and scattering them will also ensure we remain in a coma."

Do they offer that somewhere for free? Or do I have to pay for it?

Smoldering black eyes glanced at me spitefully, like he foresaw a coma in my future.

Same.

His full lips pursed with disgust.

"*Second*—" Augustus put down another finger "—enhanced intelligence."

He scoffed like he didn't think it applied to us.

"*Third*—leaping or teleportation across the globe. When a

Spartan first leaps, they can only go to a place they consider their *domus*, or home. Usually this is to a person you have a strong connection with."

His upper lip furled as he put down another finger.

"Don't be fooled," he said. "Spartan leaping is *extremely* difficult to master. If your focus wavers, you can end up in the wrong location—which most of the time is the middle of the ocean. Some of you will *never* be able to do it. However, we will endeavor to begin teaching you how to clear your mind in the fall—if you survive that long."

He put down his last finger. "*Fourth*, and lastly, Spartans have the unique ability to take an oath."

I rocked back and forth as I tried to warm myself up.

"Spartan oaths...are *extremely* serious." His baritone voice dropped an octave in warning. "The oath is a binding contract formed when a Spartan looks into another Spartan's eyes, and is thought to be an ancient form of hypnotism that changes the neural pathways of our brains."

He spoke slowly. "Both Spartans have to say the Latin words to cement an oath—and you can only have *three* bonds, the golden number, with a single person."

He shook his head. "But this is a relic of ancient days. Today, no one willfully binds themselves outside of Spartan marriages and animal protector bonds—immortality is a dangerously *long* time to be stuck to a promise. That is why this new marriage law has everyone up in arms."

The class whispered to one another.

Augustus frowned, dark eyes flashing.

Since he's past twenty-six, does that mean he has to marry this year? His poor spouse.

He stood up taller and gestured down to where Poco was gnawing with his fangs on a piece of chalk.

When the rabid raccoon saw he was being summoned, he gleefully threw himself at Augustus and raced up his torso. He hung off Augustus's neck, then flung his little head back and forth, trying to eat the long two-toned ponytail.

Okay, that is cute, people. Someone needs to take a picture.

Augustus sighed but didn't stop Poco, like he was used to his antics.

Instead, he said, "An animal protector is gained through taking a Spartan oath. Once again, *if* you survive this summer, you will get access to the creature menagerie located beneath this mountain."

His dark eyes narrowed. "*Don't* think gaining a protector is easy. Some of the strongest initiates in history failed to graduate from this academy because no animal would bond with them." He glared at me.

"Animals can sense both the levels of power in our veins *and* the nature of our souls. They see us better than we see ourselves."

His scowl deepened.

"History teaches us that animals can feel a person's aura," Augustus said. "A protector chooses you—*not* the other way around, like most wrongly believe. When it's clear that an animal wants to bond with you, you lock eyes and say 'domus.' If it agrees to the bond, it will hold your gaze, and its eyes will change to your color as the connection is cemented."

I blamed my state of exhaustion for noticing the dozens of veins on Augustus's tan forearm. It was unfair how attractive he was.

The cute raccoon hanging off him also really helped.

I wonder if there's an inappropriate drawing of him on the Spartan Lifestyle Page?

The baby onesie I'd been wearing when the orphanage found me also had "1/23/2080" embroidered on it in gold stitching. They thought it was my birthday, which meant I was an Aquarius.

An ancient magazine at the library said I had an independent, loyal, quiet, and easily distracted personality.

Apparently, I was distracted by smutty drawings of male genitalia.

I'm going to hell.

"If the animal does *not* agree to the bond—or sees something in your soul it doesn't like," Augustus said gravely, "your mind will boil from the inside, and we will kill you to put you out of your misery."

I choked on my spit.

He flashed a mean glare in my direction.

Ah, what? Repeat that part.

"But you don't need to worry about that right now," Augustus said. "There will be a day in December when everyone bonds with an animal...hopefully."

That "hopefully" is not comforting.

"Enough talk about protectors," Augustus said. "You all need to focus on getting in touch with your power source."

He sat down gracefully at the front of the room, and Poco perched on top of his head, draped over his spiky crown, like an obese hat.

That can't be comfortable.

"Now—we meditate," Augustus ordered.

I closed my eyes and immediately fell into a peaceful, trance-like state.

Just kidding—I fell asleep sitting up.

Clap.

I jolted awake.

"What did you experience while meditating?" Augustus asked as he glared at us suspiciously. Poco was belly-up, asleep, across his head.

No one spoke.

General Cleandro grabbed the black box, and the tall heir

with blond hair shot his hand in the air. He was one of the boys who'd studied instead of sleeping during the break.

Augustus smiled at him. "And you are?"

"Cassius, heir to the House of Hermes." The blond initiate uncrossed his legs and showcased his ankles—flesh-colored wings detached from his golden skin and fluttered at his heels. "When I meditated, I became aware of a pleasurable tingling in my head. I could also *feel* all the built-up power inside my legs."

Nice. He has cankles.

The freakish wings fluttered faster.

Augustus said something about harnessing our powers, but I was too cold and tired to pay attention.

He glared down at me like he suspected I was an idiot—which was ironic because Poco was gnawing on his crown—and I deeply regretted being born.

Time continued its slovenly march forward.

Discipline and Power blended into Thagorean class, then Lost Classical Lore.

I didn't take notes.

The chilled air of the mountains penetrated my bones.

Latin stories about Cyclopes blended into mathematical equations that predicted the future, then were replaced with hours of meditating (sleeping with my eyes open).

Am I even alive?

I couldn't remember.

In the middle of a depressive episode, I raised my hand. "Can I use the b-b-bathroom?"

Augustus arched a dark brow, skeptical, since we hadn't eaten or drunk anything for days, but then he scoffed and pointed at the door.

"Quickly—but don't expect special treatment because you're a girl," he said, and Poco pointed with him. "You're the one who decided to participate in this."

Did I? I don't remember anyone giving me an option. Also, since when does the toilet constitute special treatment?

I hobbled out of the classroom, skin prickling under Augustus's intense glare, then collapsed onto a broken toilet seat and cried.

Rust scratched through my toga and probably gave me a venereal disease, but I didn't even care.

He hates me.

I'm so tired and cold.

So hungry.

"I can't do this," I whispered. "I can't. I can't. *I can't.*"

Sobs wracked through me.

"Alexis Hert." Nyx became visible, purple eyes glowing against gleaming black scales. "You are the *strongest* person I've ever met—and I've met all manner of Spartan heroes."

I cried harder.

She leaned closer and hissed, "You're the same girl who befriended a monster without fear. You've fought every day of your life for yourself and Charlie. You've lived your entire life being strong—don't you dare give up now."

"You're not a monster," I gasped, wiping snot off my face.

"Kid—we both know that's not true."

Tipping my head back, I whispered, "I don't want to live like this. I just *can't.*"

I held my wrists, which ached with phantom pains.

Life was finally supposed to get better—not worse.

I wasn't supposed to feel like this.

Not anymore

I can't do this.

"It's temporary." Nyx's tongue flickered across my tearstained cheek. "Do it for Charlie—he's waiting right now for his big sister to come home to him. Don't let him down."

Sucking in air, I dropped my head into my palms.

My little brother was scared and alone, living in the woods.

Pull yourself together, woman.

I hummed loudly, pressed my palms into my eyes, and focused on a peaceful melody.

Time passed.

Breathing shallowly through my teeth, I wrapped my fingers around the "C+A" tattooed across my forearm. "I *can* do this," I whispered.

"Yes," Nyx hissed. "You can, and you will."

Using toilet paper to wipe the tears and snot off my face, I stood up and slowly hobbled back into the classroom.

As I collapsed back into my seat, Professor Augustus opened his mouth to say something about my extended bathroom break. His gaze met mine, and he closed his mouth, jaw clenching. Mercifully he said nothing.

Whatever he saw on my face kept him silent. But the corners of his eyes crinkled, and his mouth pinched, like he was distressed.

I wiped at a tear, rocking in place.

He snuck glances at me for the rest of class. His expression tightened as time passed, until he was a dark cloud of fury.

What is he mad about now?

The professors traded places—again and again, endlessly. Information was thrown at us in a steady torrent of words and numbers.

Time lost all meaning.

"Leo Apollo," Professor Augustus said, and I barely registered that he was speaking.

"Leo!" Augustus repeated with a sigh.

Titus's crony, a muscular boy with a shaved head, was lying on the ground behind me with his eyes closed.

"Leo," Augustus said louder, but the boy didn't move. Poco chittered on top of Augustus's head with chalk in his hands. "Someone please help him," Augustus said with a shake of his head.

Is he asleep or dead?

"LEO, WAKE THE FUCK UP!" General Cleandro roared, and his hawk (demon) shrieked like a banshee.

My left ear rang with horrible feedback.

Not dramatic at all.

As Leo sputtered awake, Professor Augustus sighed again. Poco got bored and shoved the chalk into his mouth (*I wonder if that tastes any good*).

General Cleandro pressed the button on his awful black box. "TIME FOR THE CIRCUIT!" he bellowed with glee.

Time distorted, as it was known to do in hell.

I blinked.

The sun burned hot and bright in the sky, illuminating the frosted dirt near the top of the mountain. In the valley below, the Dolomites Coliseum was the size of a child's toy.

I looked down. Red footprints followed me on the jagged rocks.

Someone's stalking me. I looked around nervously, then grimaced. They were my footprints.

We hobbled forward slowly as a group.

My legs burned and lungs heaved.

I prayed with everything I had, but in a highly upsetting turn of events, a Titan did not suddenly appear and violently murder me.

There's no justice left in this cruel world.

Dark times indeed.

I didn't remember making it to the top, didn't remember stumbling down the other side, didn't remember half drowning as I swam pathetically through the river, didn't remember Kharon glaring at me as I crawled onto the riverbank.

Or maybe I did remember, and I wanted to forget.

This time there were enough foil blankets after the swim for everyone, but I was too tired to grab one.

Augustus wrapped one around my shoulders aggressively and shouted something.

I blinked.

We staggered into the classroom. In front of me, General Cleandro shoved cups into the initiates' faces.

Augustus swooped in and grasped my chin tightly. He tipped water past my lips. My throat was so raw from breathing haggardly that it *burned.* I tried to pull away, but his fingers tightened.

The rest of the initiates were only forced to take a small sip, but Augustus didn't let me go until I'd finished the entire cup. He glowered and whispered something into my left ear about Chthonics. Thankfully, I couldn't understand what he said.

"Time for your first test," Professor Pine said after we'd reclaimed our spots on the floor as his raven stared at us with intelligent eyes.

Pine handed out paper.

I stared blankly down at it.

Equations? With numb fingers, I picked up the pen. It took multiple tries to get the ink to stay on the page where I wanted it to.

Writing a number took a minute.

Slowly, digit by digit, I went through the sequences, following steps mostly by intuition. Some of it I remembered Pine talking about, but most of it was completely new. Each question was tied to ethical dilemmas with dozens of variables and steps.

The questions made the math on the merit exam look childish.

"Time's up!" Pine announced. "Put your pen down."

I'd barely gotten halfway through.

Time warped.

I blinked, and Professor Augustus sat in front of the class, meditating with his eyes closed. All the initiates were asleep around me.

Augustus shifted, and the scar across his sharp cheekbone was an angry shade of red.

His wide shoulders were in perfect posture.

Since I was half slumped over with my left boob angling toward the floor, this was not relatable.

I squinted at the cruel professor. *Have demons always been so attractive?*

Smoldering dark eyes shot open.

"What—are you doing?" Augustus asked slowly.

I squeezed my eyes shut.

Please don't let him see me. Please don't let him see me.

"Since I'm sitting directly in front of you, obviously I can see you."

Ohmygod, he can read my mind. I need to kill us both.

Hands clapped together. "Alexis, open your fucking eyes. You're speaking aloud and distracting the class—look at me. Now."

I cracked my eyes open.

The class was in a state that could only be described as severely catatonic. *Distracting them from what—death?*

Augustus mumbled something about girls, dishonor, and the crucible.

"Preach, girlfriend," I mumbled back.

His right eye twitched. "Calm yourself," he said with a frown. "Focus on your center, find your inner calm."

"Will do—Captain." I bowed and face-planted onto the floor. "Like a beached whale," I said with my cheeks pressed against the rocks. "Don't worry, the tide will pull me back."

I rolled to my side.

Augustus looked worried.

I made a whale sound.

He did not make one back. *This is why I don't talk to people. They never understand me.*

A muscle in Augustus's jaw ticked as he stood up, leaned over, and hoisted me into a seated position.

The boy in front of me moaned in his sleep.

Augustus gripped my shoulder with painful tightness, and he didn't let go.

"You saved me?" I whispered up at him.

Surprisingly long lashes fluttered. His expression softened. Fingers loosened.

"You saved Big Bertha, the humpback whale."

He dropped me.

I let out the cry (aquatic moan) of my people.

In a surprising turn of events that absolutely no one saw coming, he didn't talk to me for the rest of class.

Time shifted.

"Are you okay, kid?" someone asked.

"Who's asking?" I looked around but didn't see anyone, and the initiate sitting next to me—*I think his name is Drex?*—gave me a strange look. Behind him, a boy stared up at the rock ceiling with drool coming out of his open mouth.

"Kid, it's Nyx," the strange voice repeated. "Keep your voice down."

I didn't know any Nyx.

Pine wrote names on the board, and a four was written beside "Alexis."

I squinted and tried to figure out the puzzle.

Alexis is my name. Satisfaction filled me that I'd figured it out.

"This is the order you placed on the test," Pine said.

What test?

Pine pointed at the drooling boy. "Iason Athena," he said. "You embarrass your illustrious House. You couldn't answer a *single* Thagorean question. That level of ineptitude is unacceptable for a Spartan."

General Cleandro stood up and said, "Iason, you're running the circuit by yourself. I'll be leading you. Get up, let's go."

Iason was dragged out of the classroom with his mouth open and eyes unfocused.

Hours later, General Cleandro came back.

He was alone.

The hairs on the back of my neck stood up, but I couldn't remember why it mattered.

We were given a short break in the library.

Augustus stopped me in the hall, his frown severe.

"Are you all right, Alexis?" he asked silkily, and my toes curled.

"Who—is this *all right* you speak of?" I winced as my bloody feet scraped across the rock floor.

Judging from Augustus's murderous glare, I did not want to know.

"Keep your s-secrets." I patted his disturbingly hard chest.

Augustus stared down at where I was touching him.

Neither of us said anything else.

I couldn't remember who walked away first (he did).

Time got hazier.

More tests were given—we sprinted (hobbled through) the circuit. On the side of the mountain under the dark of night, a bright spot glowed in my vision. There was a light up ahead, and it would be warm.

I just have to get to it.

I never got to it.

Music played frantically in my head.

Three of my toenails turned black after I stubbed my feet into boulders. The River Styx was creepy at night, and I sobbed as I crawled out of the water onto the muddy bank. Two voices growled, then whispered in the darkness.

I growled back.

The bright light still hovered just outside my reach.

"Congrats, you've survived your first two weeks," someone said, but I didn't know who.

I was dizzy with nausea.

Bang. People appeared in a cloud of smoke.

"Fucking Kronos, Alex, are you okay?" Moonlight illuminated emerald eyes, which filled with blood as a finger touched my forehead.

I hate that name.

"I h-haven't b-b-een okay for y-y-years." My teeth chattered from the cold so hard my jaw ached.

"Interesting. She's telling the truth." There was a pause. Then the voice scoffed, "But none of us have been." Foil was wrapped around my shoulders, and the icy pain got a little warmer.

The pretty man with eyes like spooky lights turned to a muzzle.

I grimaced. "G-g-good d-d-doggy."

"Did she just call you a *dog*?" He laughed darkly.

Hands wrapped around my arm painfully.

"Let's go. Domus."

The world warped.

Darkness smothered me, and the music died.

Permanently.

12

MENTOR DAYS

ALEXIS

"Wake up!" a voice demanded.

I groaned and pulled the warm covers over my head, but the slight movement made my arms burn with pain.

I deeply regretted being alive (more so than usual).

"It's almost noon," a voice ranted. "You need to wake up *right now.* We have to fuel your body and strategize. Our future hinges on you getting the fuck up."

A man was speaking, so I stopped listening.

Dreams beckoned me.

The toasty covers were ripped away. It was freezing cold, so I pressed my face into the pillow, searching for warmth—it, too, was ripped away.

Screaming through gritted teeth, I debated waking up, but it seemed like too much work. Sleep reclaimed me.

Hands wrapped around my legs and shoulders roughly. I

was lifted into the air, and mint filled my nose. Someone had picked me up.

Drool dripped down the side of my face, and I prayed Carl Gauss was embracing me. *Please let him have a normal-shaped penis. I can't handle any more trauma.*

I groaned loudly as I was jostled.

"Everyone, shut up!" Nyx yelled from somewhere nearby.

My unsupported neck jiggled, and bright warmth suddenly heated my face.

There was a strange splashing noise.

Abruptly the hands released me.

I was free-falling.

Splash.

I screamed out bubbles.

Underwater and disoriented, I flailed.

Kharon is near. He's going to kill me. Swim. Swim as fast you can before he kills you and—

I burst out of the surface of the water.

Bright sunlight burned my eye as I struggled to catch my bearings and get away from the evil ferryman who was coming after me in the circuit.

Panic intensified.

I splashed harder.

My vision focused. I stood (half keeled over, flailing) in hip-deep turquoise water that was warm and tranquil, nothing like the River Styx.

A lush green hill contrasted with the brilliant sea, and a sprawling white home was nestled among the plants on the island's edge.

French doors were open, leading into a familiar room.

Either I was having a hallucinogenic episode, or I was back in Corfu at the Crimson Duo's home.

The Ionian Sea was peaceful around me.

Sparkling and serene.

If I'm back with my mentors, then it must be the beginning of August.

The bright summer sun warmed my face. In the shadows of the deck, a figure moved. Achilles cut an imposing figure, dressed head to toe in black. A cigarette protruded from the grate of his muzzle.

He puffed out a cloud of smoke.

Shadows moved at his legs—Nero wagged his tail, and Poppae glared.

Water rippled as another figure blocked my sun.

Patro stood over me.

He looked *pissed.*

I opened my mouth to ask why he'd dumped me in the sea, but a groan left my lips. My head throbbed, and white spots dotted my vision.

The world spun.

Every muscle in my body *ached.*

I rested my hands on my knees and coughed raspingly. Red droplets of blood sprayed from my lips, then sank into the clear waters.

It was all too much.

I collapsed backward into the sea and spread my sore arms.

In my head, I floated peacefully. In reality, I partially drowned because I couldn't find the strength to lift up my sore hips.

A tear streaked out of the corner of my eye.

If I hadn't known any better, I'd have assumed I'd been hit by a Spartan truck. It felt like a driver had slammed into me from the side, then backed over my body, then got out of the vehicle and stomped on my—

"Why are you scrunching your face like that?" Patro interrupted my spiral.

I grunted as I tried to breathe. "I'm profiling the imaginary driver that hit me with his truck." I squinted as I thought about it.

A bird squawked as it floated across the cloudless sky, and I studied it suspiciously. *Is it spying on me?*

"Next time," Patro said slowly, "don't share."

"Next time," I whispered, "don't ask."

"How about next time, you wake up like a normal person," Patro snapped. "Then I won't have to dump you in the sea and watch you *drown* in shallow water."

I rolled my suspiciously moisture-filled eyes. "Just let me sleep."

Patro clamped his hand around my ankle and dragged me through the water so I was right beside him.

"No, you need to refuel your body after the academy. That's what these three days off are primarily for. I've been trying to wake you up for *hours*, Alex," he growled. "Nothing worked."

I loathed that name.

His grip tightened, red ink spelled out "LIAR" across his knuckles, and his thumb scraped against my shin bone.

We both stared down at where he was touching me.

It hit me, harder than my imaginary truck driver: he was touching me. *Another person is touching me.*

I shrieked and kicked him in the groin.

Patro groaned and doubled over. *"What the fuck—"* he grunted in pain *"—was that fucking for?"*

Splashing, muscles cramping, I scrambled toward the shore. "Don't t-touch me," I called out weakly.

Patro stood up to his full height, broad shoulders imposing—the sparkling sea did nothing to soften him—and his wet green T-shirt stuck to his chiseled chest like a second skin. It brought out the color of his eyes.

If I didn't know better, I'd have sworn the statue of David was modeled after Patro. He really was sinfully handsome.

Not that I noticed.

"*What* the fuck is actually wrong with you?" he yelled.

"Anger is a secondary emotion," I pointed out helpfully with a dry croak as I backed away toward the land. "You should work on expressing your p-primary emotions...and not swearing."

Nostrils flaring, Patro cracked his knuckles. "Genuine question—what in the *fuckity fuck fucker* is wrong with you?"

I winced.

Why do I keep engaging with the psychotic killer?

Patro narrowed his eyes. "Got something to say?"

The wounds on my feet stung as I kept backing away over the pebbled seafloor, and I shook my head.

The momentary courage was gone.

I should never have spoken.

"You just kicked me, Alex." Patro's voice was cold. "You *spoiled* little brat."

The irony of him calling me spoiled while using the awful name *they* used to use was not lost on me.

"Please don't call me that name," I whispered quietly.

"Kick me like that again," Patro said as he stalked forward through the hip-level water, "and I'll break your fucking leg. *Alex.*"

How the world worshipped the cruel man in front of me was beyond my comprehension. Sure, he was interesting to look at, but so was magma before it burned you alive.

Widening my sore legs, a scarlet cloud rising in the water from the open wounds on my feet, I tried to look like I wasn't five seconds away from passing out and drowning.

Vicious memories played on a loop at the edge of my subconscious.

Patro took another step forward so he was within lunging distance. *Retreat, retreat.* Turning, I sprinted (hobbled slowly) over the pebbles on the shoreline back up to the deck.

There was a trail of red behind me.

Grabbing a towel off the chair farthest from Achilles, I angled myself behind the furniture and Nero, with my head tilted so I could keep my right eye on both men.

I prepared to scream for Nyx.

When Patro charges, I'll bash him over the head with the chair.

The son of Aphrodite stalked onto the deck, and I plastered myself against the wall next to the French doors.

Nero turned his head to the side and looked back at me like he was asking, *What is wrong with you, woman?*

So much.

He bared his teeth and growled, like he wanted to maul me.

I grimaced.

"You're such a drama queen—I'm not going to attack you, Alexis." Patro rolled his eyes as Achilles handed him a towel. "Not right now."

Patro lunged in my direction, and I screamed.

He chuckled as I clutched my chest.

The jerk is taunting me.

Suddenly the old beliefs that women had "hysteria" problems didn't seem so far-fetched.

I could see it.

Case in point, I was a woman, and I was hysterical.

Seemingly done taunting my frayed nerves, Patro leaned on the wall next to Achilles and whispered something in his ear. He stood on his toes to talk to him, and their body language almost seemed...tender.

Almost being the key word.

I cowered as the men stared at me with disappointment, and I tried to act nonchalant (unfortunately, I had not been relaxed a single day in my life).

"When did I get here?" I asked in a pathetic attempt to break the tension, but as I glanced inside the breezy cottage, doubt filled me.

Did I imagine everything at the mountain?

Was it all a bad dream?

Patro's eyes flashed as he ran the towel through his short, wavy hair. "Last night, you finished your first two weeks at the academy." He spoke slowly like I was an idiot.

I started to make a face and mock him, but self-preservation kicked in, and I kept my expression blank.

A soft melody played in my mind, and I hummed.

Patro gave me an unimpressed look like he could see through me.

"We picked you up yesterday at noon," he said. "After you'd run the circuit, you were delirious and caked in mud and didn't recognize anyone—so we hosed you off out here." He held his palms up. "Don't freak out. You were fully clothed."

He raised his eyebrows, like I should be grateful I'd been hosed down like a wild animal (I was).

However, since I'd been tortured into a comatose state, gratitude only got you so far.

"You've been asleep for over twelve hours." Patro scowled. "We only have two and a half days to plan before you have to go back to the academy."

My stomach dropped.

"I don't want to go back," I whispered.

Please don't make me. Please. I'll do anything.

"That's not an option. Grow up." Patro threw his towel to the side. "Let's eat. I'm starved." He walked away into the house, like the conversation was over.

I whimpered.

A cloud of clove-scented smoke billowed out the grate of Achilles's muzzle as he followed Patro inside the house.

"That habit could k-kill you," I said as I followed him. Years of warning Charlie about the dangers of drug use had ingrained the response into me.

Achilles looked back over his shoulder. Up close, his eyes were an extremely unsettling shade of red.

"Patro" was also tattooed in scarlet ink down the side of his neck.

I wrapped my fingers around the "C+A" tattoo on my forearm.

It was a strange coincidence that all three of us had names of people on our bodies, but it didn't make me feel closer to them. If anything, it highlighted the different worlds we came from.

Charlie was a human.

He was homeless.

In a cardboard box, lonely, probably missing me like I was missing him.

I was dealing with billionaires who couldn't die.

Achilles made a scoffing noise and turned forward.

I'm never speaking aloud ever again. It's really not worth it.

I followed them both down a narrow hall.

The ceilings were low, and the floor was a rich walnut color that reflected the sparkling sunlight through arched windows. We entered a sprawling rustic kitchen that had an expansive glassless window overlooking the turquoise sea.

I'd never known a house could be so pretty.

At a wood counter, a young woman in an apron was putting chopped fruit into a bowl. She smiled coyly at the men, looked at me curiously, then hurried out of the room.

Warm aromas filled the air; piles of foods that I didn't recognize were spread across a long stone table. I blinked, but the spectacular feast didn't disappear.

I wanted to cry.

On the other side of the world, Charlie was counting food vouchers and rationing a single box of cereal over weeks. He was lying awake under a tarp, trying to ignore the gnawing sensation of constant starvation.

But here I was, standing in front of enough food to feed a village.

Eat the rich.

There was no justice in our Titan-infested world.

"You need to consume as much as possible to fuel yourself for the next two weeks of starvation," Patro said as he and Achilles sat down and served themselves in a casual display of gluttony. Achilles ate small bites through the grates of his mask.

Head dizzy, aching limbs tingling like I was having an out-of-body experience, I hobbled slowly across the room.

A muffled noise on my left side made me jump.

Another young woman was smiling, cleaning the floor where I walked. She frowned at me, like she was waiting for a response, but before I could figure out what to do, she hurried away with her bloody mop.

I sat down at the table next to the men (fell toward a seat and somehow landed in it).

All thoughts left my brain as my hunger took over, and I shoveled food into my mouth as fast as I could as I tried to consume every delicious—

I blinked.

Time shifted.

Stomach churning, I hugged a garbage bin in the corner of the kitchen and retched into it. Tears streamed down my face. Someone said something, but I couldn't hear.

I'd *never* eaten a big meal before, and my stomach punished me for it.

Eventually I made it back to the table.

Lightheaded, queasy, unwell, exhausted, depressed, and catatonic—exactly how I'd felt after the one gym class I'd attended in high school—I stared at the food.

With shaking fingers, I grabbed a small purple fruit and chewed on it slowly.

Tentatively, I grabbed another fruit, then another.

Three hours later I'd consumed enough fruit, cheeses, and meats to sustain me for months.

When I finished gorging myself, Patro and Achilles were

still sitting across the table, and they wore annoyed expressions. Well, I assumed Achilles was annoyed—it was hard to tell with the muzzle.

I still wanted to borrow it.

Sighing, I slumped low in the chair (almost fell out of it, but the corner of the table kept me upright).

"What?" I asked as they glared at me.

Patro snorted. "You have the weakest stomach of anyone I've ever met and even worse table manners. You need to stop being so dramatic and gluttonous."

I stared at him numbly.

The audacity of men persists.

Patro clapped his hands and nodded like he'd come to a conclusion. "We're fucked—how in all of Kronos's creation did we get stuck with *you* as our mentee? It must be a sick joke. You're the most pathetic Spartan I've ever seen."

A sharp sensation pierced through my heart.

I was tired of everyone labeling me inadequate.

Something snapped inside of me.

Clasping my shaking hands together, I rested them on the table. "Must be so tragic," I whispered, "that your fate as generals rests in my pathetic hands."

Both men narrowed their eyes dangerously.

Smoke billowed out from the grates of Achilles's muzzle. His vermilion eyes were on fire. *"We'll kill them later,"* he'd signed so casually.

I wasn't dealing with men.

I was dealing with monsters.

"Are you threatening us?" Patro asked softly.

"What's my strategy?" I countered.

Patro's nostrils flared, and he gripped the table like he was about to throw it at my head. "Seduce the other initiates," he finally said. "Distract them so they fail."

What?

"No—I'd rather die," I said honestly.

"That can be arranged." Patro lunged toward me threateningly, but this time, I didn't flinch.

Hit me.

I dare you.

You're not the first.

"Then d-do it." My voice was unnaturally cold, and everything went numb. "Kill me right now."

Please.

Patro inhaled through gritted teeth and flexed his hands like he was trying not to throttle me.

Nothing happened.

Coward.

"I want a real strategy," I said softly.

Patro smacked his hand down on the table.

"There are only *three* strategies," he said with a growl. "Fuck them, kill them, or beat them." Green eyes flashed. "Since you can't beat them, and *refuse* to fuck them, you're going to have to KILL THEM." He sat back, panting.

Achilles crossed his arms, biceps bulging obscenely. His gaze was sharp.

The urge to not exist intensified.

I gaped at them in disbelief. "What's even the point of you being my m-mentors? You're useless."

"That's rich," Patro snarled. "Coming from an abandoned female mutt—it's not like you *shouldn't even exist.* Oh, wait."

"Unfortunately, I do," I mumbled.

Patro pulled at his hair. "Spartan heirs and mutts are raised from birth, training for the massacre and war academy. The only abandoned mutts that ever survive do so because their powers are *insane.*"

Drex holding out his hand, red glowing in the fog, three boys falling to their knees, screaming.

"But you—" Patro glared "—are powerless. Frankly, I'm

surprised you survived the first two weeks, and I'm still not believing it's all not been one big fucking fluke."

My entire existence has been a fluke.

Somehow, my life defies all mathematical odds, and it always gets worse.

"Maybe," I said slowly, "I won't...survive the next week."

A beat passed as my words sank in.

Patro's eyes sparked with cruelty. "Are you still *threatening* us?" He leaned forward across the table. Achilles clenched his hands into fists.

An ominous melody played in my mind.

For the first time ever, I felt dangerous, like I was playing with a lit match over gasoline.

This is what power feels like.

I liked it.

Achilles unfurled his fist and put a hand on Patro's shoulder. He pulled him back. The muzzled man drew soothing circles on his spine.

Patro leaned into his touch. "Don't you fucking dare try to sabotage everything we've—"

BOOM.

Smoke billowed from the hall into the kitchen.

Oh great, another Spartan leaped into the house. It's probably the stupid doctors. Well, hopefully they're still alive.

A towering figure in a tattered black cloak walked into the kitchen.

"Honeys, I'm home," a scratchy masculine voice rasped sarcastically.

No.

I didn't blink.

Didn't move.

Didn't breathe.

The newcomer's cloaked head brushed across the ceiling. He was tall and wide, rivaling both Achilles and Augustus for size.

"Well," he chuckled darkly. "This looks *cozy*."

Please, God, kill me.

Do it fast.

Kharon—the Hunter, one of two Chthonic heirs in the world, the son of Artemis and Erebus, the half creature, the murderer of Christos—pulled off his dark creature hood.

A silver ruby-covered crown sat atop messy black hair.

I swallowed a gasp.

Glacial blue eyes were on fire. Pale skin stretched across razor-sharp cheekbones, and dark shadows filled out the perfect planes of his face.

Where Patro was classically handsome, Kharon was *disturbingly* attractive.

Gleaming white teeth flashed as he smiled, the same evil expression he'd worn as Christos drowned.

He smelled like a violent rainstorm—salt tinged with rain—a hurricane.

Like death.

"We weren't expecting you," Patro said with surprise. "Have you come to commiserate over the new marriage law? You *and* Augustus have to technically tie the knot this year because of your ages—what are you going to do?"

Kharon smiled darkly. "Oh—I'm not worried. I think I've found a…solution."

"How?" Patro asked. "They listed all our names. There are *no* loopholes. You can't just marry Augustus, either of us, or Helen—you're stuck with an Olympian or a creature, and *all* the eligible ones are in the Olympians' pockets."

"Are you proposing?" Kharon asked Patro with a sinister laugh. "No offense, but you aren't my type. I prefer my lovers a little more bloodthirsty."

Patro shoved at his shoulders, but a dark blush stained the tops of his cheeks.

I gaped.

Patro is not bloodthirsty enough for him? Who does he want to marry—Satan?

Kharon leaned his hip casually against the edge of the counter and picked up a pastry. "Let's just say there's a loophole in progress. I've got my eye on someone. One might even say I'm becoming—obsessed."

Uh, why is he looking at me?

His cloak parted, and the Latin word "Furia" was tattooed across his throat.

It meant fury, but I'd seen another translation of it somewhere; I just couldn't remember what it was. Some slang use.

It was going to drive me crazy trying to remember.

A silky white button-down pulled across his wide chest, and blue diamond buttons glinted in the sun, barely holding the straining fabric together.

Similarly, weapon holsters stretched over his bulging thighs, holding guns and a wicked-looking knife. Expensive trousers were perfectly tailored.

His dagger was coated with fresh blood.

Whoever he's obsessed with should immediately kill themselves.

"So, what did I miss?" Kharon asked slowly.

"Alex here—" Patro said.

I looked over at my mentor in horror. *Why is he drawing attention to me? Help?*

"—was just threatening us." Patro smirked at me meanly as he spoke to Kharon. "She was saying that she was going to purposefully die so we couldn't become generals."

I bit down on my lower lip and tasted copper.

Kharon chewed carefully.

"Is that so?" he asked slowly, his raspy voice reverberating through the room like a warning. "How—interesting."

Images flashed of blood splattering as a predator feasted on my carcass.

Kharon's expression was blank, *too* blank. Something evil bubbled beneath his surface.

There was a feral quality about him, like he was one wrong move away from shedding a facade of civility and going on a killing rampage.

"I was j-joking." I forced out a pitiful laugh.

Kharon swallowed, and the words on his throat bobbed. "I would hope so," he said softly as he licked sugar off his thumb.

His nails were painted black, and a skeleton was tattooed across the top of his right hand.

Ice-blue eyes held my gaze.

Goose bumps exploded across my body.

For some reason, he was staring at me with laser focus, like he was trying to see into my soul.

I stared down at the table, neck prickling under the weight of his cruel gaze as my life flashed before my eyes.

"Hades," Kharon said softly, "wants me to go over intel and strategy with you two about Titan movements before we go on our next mission."

He's talking about the Assembly of Death.

"I'm gonna crash in my room here at your lovely shed for the next few days," he added. "While my partner is otherwise occupied."

Shed? This is the nicest house I've ever seen. He should see where I live.

Chairs squeaked as my mentors stood up.

I tilted my head to the side to keep them in my peripheral vision as I remained seated.

Patro bowed deeply to Kharon. "We're delighted by your company—we *live* to serve you, oh great fearsome one," he said, voice full of deference. "Not all of us can live in a villa like you."

My jaw dropped.

Do they worship him because he's an heir? Isn't Kharon twenty-six, only a few years older than Patro?

Patro burst into laughter, and Kharon rolled his eyes.

It was a joke.

Who would ever jest with that monster?

"How's the honorable heir life treating you?" Patro asked sarcastically. "I heard you're the most eligible bachelor in high society this year because of the fucking marriage law. How's all the desperate Olympian pussy and dick? I've heard there are even some creatures following you around."

Kharon clenched his jaw. "They're all powerless, simpering fools—too afraid to look me in the eye—but they want the crown and fortune. Also, the thrill of fucking an Assembly of Death member helps. As if I'd ever marry one of those sniveling cowards."

Not looking you in the eyes seems very reasonable.

Also, so does marrying rich so you never have to worry about starving.

I'd do it.

"No." Patro gasped mockingly. "But their Olympian mommies and daddies told them they were special."

Both men laughed.

I squinted, trying to figure out if parents really did that or if that was the joke.

Kharon gritted his teeth. "I'm gonna start *stabbing* the Olympians who approach me at the next moronic society ball."

The men chuckled louder.

I sank lower into my chair and hoped he would forget I ever existed.

"Alex, we'll resume our conversation tomorrow," Patro said.

Why is he talking to me after they were just talking about stabbing Olympians? Why was he looking at me? STOP LOOKING. DON'T TALK TO ME.

Of course he kept going.

"You should get more sleep now that you've stopped being dramatic and have eaten," Patro said. "Also, you might want to take a proper shower—you smell."

I'm going to end him.

I stared at the table, skin crawling from the weight of all their attention. Finally, a bazillion years later, all three of them walked out of the kitchen.

I let out a sigh of relief and rested my head back.

Kharon reappeared in the doorway.

I froze.

He stalked over to where I was sitting.

Glacial blue eyes burned with fury. "If you dare harm yourself," he rasped softly, high cheekbones glinting like razor blades, "I'll bring you back to life and torture you for all of eternity."

My breath hitched.

Long fingers wrapped around the column of my throat like he was demonstrating how he'd do it.

His thumb hovered over my fluttering pulse.

A strange queasiness cramped my lower stomach, and my head spun.

Blood pooled over the whites of his eyes.

The sensation in my stomach quadrupled, and I gasped for air, overwhelmed by the foreign feelings. Something alien and obsessive swirled in my lower gut.

Is he going to use his powers and kill me like he did Christos?

I waited for the pain.

Kharon pulled his hand away and took a step back, eyes returning to normal.

Sweat trickled down the side of my face as I watched him warily.

"Chthonic lives are important," he whispered harshly, still leaning toward me. "Patro and Achilles *will* become generals, and you *will* survive the crucible to make it happen. If you try to deviate from that plan in any way, I'll hurt you. Just for fun."

I blanched.

Long lashes fluttered over the dark shadows that rimmed his piercing eyes. "I promise you—you'll *never* recover," he said raspingly as he backed up and put more distance between us. "It will just be me and you—forever."

Wait, what are we talking about?

"Don't worry—the two of us are going to have a lot of fun in the future," he said cryptically.

I was beyond worried.

His smile was feral. "But if you let yourself get hurt, you'll become my mortal enemy."

I inhaled swiftly.

"Do you *know* what I do to my enemies?" he asked, voice rough and menacing. "Have you heard the rumors?"

He bared his teeth. "Tell me—do you want to find out?"

"Uh, n-no," I said shakily.

"I *know* what you did to Christos." He smirked. "I know you were killing him."

I blanched and shook my head frantically. "No. No. I was trying to save him and—"

"*Stop* with the fucking lies." He made a slashing motion with his hand. "Don't you dare try to play games with me," he said darkly, as if my dishonesty was a foregone conclusion. "I'll back you into the type of corner that you'll never see coming."

Why did he say I was killing him? We both know he did it. Is it because Christos was splashing around and I was trying to save him? How could he misinterpret it that badly?

Kharon's words were saying one thing, but his depraved tone was saying something else.

There were layers of context I was missing.

I opened my mouth to respond (plead for mercy and beg for a quick death), but he'd already disappeared down the hall.

Well…that was a lot.

My head fell forward, and I slammed it against the table.

Kharon's threat was nothing like Patro's; it was infinitely worse.

I could already feel his fingers tightening around my throat, squeezing the life out of me while he smiled.

Long minutes passed as I sat at the table, trying to find the courage to move. When I finally did, I was half-delirious by the time I'd made it back to my bedroom.

In a daze, I stripped out of the stupid toga and staggered into the shower. The water scalded my skin, so I turned it up hotter. Then I yanked it up more, hating that it felt so heavenly.

Sitting down on the tiles, I sobbed under the scalding flow.

A high-pitched ringing stung my left ear.

My head throbbed. My vision was blurry. My abused throat burned from the force of my grief.

I didn't want a *mortal* enemy.

I just wanted to listen to eighteenth-century music and solve obscure math equations. Maybe lie in some flower fields during the summer and swim in a warm lake. Marry Carl Gauss and bear his children in the afterlife.

Is that really too much to ask for?

After partially waterboarding myself, I crawled out of the shower on all fours like a wounded animal and collapsed naked into the bed. I pulled the thick cover up over my head until I was cocooned in darkness.

The dreams came quickly.

The devil stood at the end of my bed, staring at me with glowing crimson eyes. He touched my ankle and morphed into two skeletal monsters that whispered darkly. The foreign curiosity was tinged with mania. The devil wanted to know more about me.

"Why are you lying about who you really are?" he asked.

I woke up screaming, clutching at my chest.

Sanity was slipping away from me.

The Ionian Sea sparkled outside, mockingly picturesque, and nature sounds washed over me peacefully.

Blessedly, I was all alone.

Hours passed, and my mentors didn't make an appearance, but I could hear Patro's voice all day as he talked with Kharon (the devil) somewhere in the house.

Grateful for the time alone to contemplate my impending doom, I spent the hours slowly eating small portions of food from the kitchen, floating in the tranquil sea, and chatting with Nyx.

Every few hours, I took a scalding shower and scrubbed myself raw.

Sometimes I cried in the water, sometimes I laughed, and once (three separate times) I flipped my curls over so I looked like a founding father and pretended to give a revolutionary speech—but each time, my speech was *too* good (the town sheriff shot me for insurrection, and I flailed dramatically in the shower—died—while my fellow rebels watched in horror).

During the day, the feminine urge to lead a fictional revolt plagued me.

At night, nightmares once again tore me to pieces.

It was always glowing crimson eyes and a man watching me cruelly. He touched my leg possessively, and again I felt foreign emotion: compulsion to watch, fascination, a dark obsession.

When I woke up the next morning, the cycle repeated.

I cautiously ate food; sang a depressing song that I made up on the spot, extremely off-key; lay face-first in the sea and half-heartedly tried to drown; told Nyx in detail the plot of my favorite Emmy and Carl fanfic (yes, they whispered calculus problems to each other while riding off into the sunset… on each other); took another shower and fell asleep in it; woke up and chugged ice water; hummed Mozart's Symphony No. 41 until my throat burned; then took another shower because I still couldn't believe how luxurious it felt.

Yet for all my rest (three showers in a row), the pounding ache in my head didn't abate, and it still hurt to walk.

I tried to think about the Riemann Hypothesis, but it felt like I was soiling it, contemplating it in my sorry state, so I gave up.

Later that night, my stomach *burned* with pain, and I sobbed because I was convinced I was dying from stress ulcers.

It was just cramps from eating too much food.

But the metaphysical pain persisted.

The strange grunts and knocking, squeaking noises that echoed against the wall all night didn't help my mental state.

As it was, I woke up the last day before hell with a renewed purpose in life—*I need to off myself before they send me back to that wretched place.*

I ran into the sea dramatically.

Five minutes later, I floated on my back in the warm water with my eyes closed because I couldn't bear to look at the glorious nature.

The sea is my favorite place on earth. I wish Charlie could be here to see it.

August on a Greek island felt like a dream within a nightmare.

It didn't help that I could still hear the unnaturally deep vibrations of Kharon's voice through the open windows. In contrast, Patro's voice was lighter than usual, and he was constantly laughing. Since Achilles was muzzled, I heard nothing from him, but I could *feel* his malicious presence.

I flipped over in the water.

Face-first, mismatched eyes wide open, I screamed out bubbles.

"Do you feel better, kid?" Nyx asked when I came up for air. The water rippled nearby like she was swimming in a circle.

"No," I said honestly.

"You should try eating a freshly caught rat. I swear, *nothing* in the world tastes better."

"Rats are actually highly intelligent animals," I replied numbly. "They've been known to make good companions."

"So?" Nyx asked.

I closed my eyes and pretended I was an astronaut in the early two thousands, floating peacefully through space at the International Space Station. Titans didn't exist, and Spartans hadn't emerged. An old astronomy book in the library said mathematicians often became astronauts—I would have enjoyed exploring the cosmos.

"Hunting is great fun. You should try it," Nyx said.

The illusion shattered.

My best friend was a talking poisonous snake, and all space missions were abandoned after a lone Titan massacred almost every person in Florida—including all the scientists at Cape Canaveral. It was one of the first places they'd attacked.

Apparently immortal monsters were against space exploration and warm weather. *Disheartening.*

Neck prickling like I was being watched, I lifted my head and looked around—but I was all alone.

Nyx rambled on about stalking, and a bad feeling washed over me.

Something told me a hunt had already started, but I wasn't the predator.

I was the prey.

Flipping over, I resumed screaming into the water.

13

TESTS

ALEXIS

Professor Pine gave us a thumbs-up, and the raven perched on his shoulder tilted its head to the side.

Don't give me that look, bird. I know you're a surveillance drone.

"Good luck with Discipline and Power," Pine said as he gathered his Thagorean papers and backed out of the classroom with his robotic spy.

The door closed gently behind Pine, and I groaned under my breath with the rest of the class as we waited for Augustus to make his entrance.

Only eight of us sat in the chilly academy classroom, since Christos and Iason had both been murdered by Kharon.

I was jealous.

Mental note: pray harder for my soul.

It was still only August, but to survive the crucible, we had to make it until January.

There is a negative chance I last that long.

Shivering from the damp mountain chill, I rubbed my eyes. Vision fading in and out from exhaustion, I kept myself awake by examining my classmates.

We'd done roll call when we'd arrived back at the academy a week ago, and I'd made a point of learning their names.

It was always good to know the people you'd die in front of.

In the front row of the class sat two boys: Dimitrios, mutt to the House of Apollo, and Maximum, mutt to the House of Hera.

Dimitrios was tan and lanky with a dark ponytail. In contrast, Maximum was short with brown eyes, blond hair, and blue highlights. (Also, apparently his parents hated him because they named him after a limit. Who did that?)

In the middle row, next to me, was Drex Chen, the only initiate who was Chthonic and a fellow abandoned mutt.

Cassius, heir to the House of Hermes, who had wings on his feet—which got creepier the more I thought about it—sat ramrod straight on Drex's other side.

In contrast, I was hunched over so low that my nonexistent breasts basically touched the floor.

The good news was, those four initiates in the front side of the room seemed to mind their own business. The bad news was, the same could not be said for the three bullies who sat in the back.

Leo, Alessander, and Titus.

Leo, mutt to the House of Apollo, was the muscular boy with the shaved head who'd fallen asleep and laughed with Titus.

Alessander, mutt to the House of Poseidon, was a short, bulky guy with dark hair who'd also laughed.

Finally, Titus, mutt to the House of Dionysus, was the tall, skinny boy with flame-red hair who'd taunted me during the circuit.

I could feel the weight of their angry glares behind me.

They weren't the only toxic men in the room. General Cleandro was at the front desk, idly reading a book, which was probably titled *How to Effectively Torture People While Exerting the Least Effort Possible.*

Case in point, a black box sat beside his feet, perfectly positioned so it was on full display.

The box was a constant reminder that Kharon was out there in his *stupid* boat, with his *stupid* pole, waiting to chase us to our *stupid* deaths.

The intimidation tactic was brutally effective.

Every time the general made a move, I stared nervously at the box.

Its dimensions were imprinted in my brain.

I counted days in my head, although it was hard to keep track of time in the windowless classroom.

Only one more week before a three-day break. Basically six days, because the mentors came at midday last time. So really, it's less than a week. Easy. Not hard at all. You got this.

General Cleandro looked up from his book, and all eight of us froze and ducked our heads. He harrumphed, flipped his page, and went back to reading.

No one relaxed.

Hunger gnawed at my stomach, and my head spun with dizziness.

You don't got this.

The tension in the room was thick enough to cut with a knife because we'd been back for about a week, but we hadn't run the circuit.

Not once.

Dozens of classes, yet neither of the professors had asked us a *single* question.

Somehow, the anticipation was worse.

Instead of being glad that I wasn't running the circuit, I spent every second *anticipating* it. Trying to figure out what General

Cleandro and the professors were thinking. What mind games they were playing.

I was jittery and on edge. My teeth chattered as stress sweat dripped down my face.

Candle smoke made the room hazy, and my eyes watered from irritation.

Turning to a fresh page in my notebook, I ignored the needle sensation prickling down my legs and the fact that my butt had gone numb days ago.

Shockingly, sitting on the floor hunched over a notebook was not an ergonomic position, and if Kharon didn't murder me (he was *definitely* going to), late-onset scoliosis would.

"Are the classes over yet? It's been like a million years," Nyx asked sleepily as she coiled herself tighter around my neck.

"No," I whispered under my breath.

"Kill me," she whined. "I'm so bored."

I rubbed at my aching head. "You're the one with the venom. Kill us both."

Nyx huffed. "Don't tempt me."

The pain in my lower spine spiked as I shifted. "I'm not joking," I groaned.

There was a long pause, like Nyx was considering it.

"Nah," she said finally. Then there was a low hissing noise as she resumed snoring.

I rolled my eyes. "Wimp."

She grunted in her sleep, and I was jealous. I would have done *unholy* things for a sip of water and ten minutes of sleep—like, sell my organs on the black market type of things.

Who needs a gallbladder or a kidney? Not me. For the right price, I might even throw in some fingers and teeth.

I high-fived myself (clapped like a weirdo, and everyone stared at me).

It was official: I was losing it.

Nyx snored louder.

Bang.

"Are we being shot at?" I asked, and Drex laughed next to me.

It was the door.

Professor Augustus swept into the room, his two-toned hair and silver crown shining in the dim candlelight as he dumped a pile of papers onto the desk. Poco was wrapped around his neck like a rabid fluffy scarf.

So cute. He's a raccoon mother.

He nodded to the class with a small smile.

"Instead of starting with a meditation…" Augustus said as he turned and glared hatefully down at me (not cute).

His expression had a strange edge to it that hadn't been there the last class. He was staring at me accusingly, like I'd recently done something unforgivable.

I squirmed with discomfort, neck prickling.

Soulless black eyes stared at me with laser focus.

He refused to look away.

Prayers for whatever cursed soul must marry him this year.

Finally, after what felt like an eternity, Augustus cleared his throat and turned to the rest of the class. "We're going to start with a demonstration," he said, gesturing at the door.

A man walked in.

The newcomer flashed an attractive smile.

It was Drex's mentor, Theros, heir to the House of Zeus. A gold laurel wreath sat atop his head, and it matched the golden feathers of the vulture, which sat perched on his shoulder.

I waited to feel something as I stared at the person who could potentially be my blood relation. I felt nothing.

He wasn't Charlie.

Weeks ago, the doctor had said that he was the only heir Zeus had had in centuries.

He was important.

Augustus gestured to Theros. "As an heir from the House of

Zeus," he said, "Theros's Olympian power is one of the more *useful* ones—he's going to demonstrate how he feels when he engages his abilities so you all can have a reference for *why* we're meditating so much."

Judging from Augustus's disgusted expression as he looked at us, he did not have faith in our rumination abilities.

His smoldering dark eyes were still locked on mine accusingly.

He can't know I spent the last meditation imagining Carl Gauss whispering sweet nothings to me while he proved the existence of algebra…right?

He kept staring.

I struggled to swallow.

What if he's reading my mind right now? What if he's Chthonic and his power is mind control? What if he's going to kill me for picturing Carl Gauss naked? What if he knows I'm imagining him in a dress because he's a raccoon mother—

He arched his brow.

Can you…uh…hear me? I thought tentatively.

He didn't look away.

I wanted to throw up; that was definitely a yes.

Squinting with concentration, I thought loudly, *PLEASE DO NOT TAKE OVER MY MIND.*

The parameters of reality were bleeding around me.

I continued my mental screaming. *BLINK ONCE IF YOU CAN UNDER—*

He looked away, and I deflated with relief.

Thank God he didn't blink. I'm in the clear.

Then the shame hit. I'd officially lost the plot. Just because we'd made eye contact didn't mean Augustus could *read* my mind.

Nyx mumbled something in her sleep and tightened around my neck.

I blamed asphyxiation.

"The floor is yours." Professor Augustus—who I was 90 percent sure *couldn't* read minds (maybe, but I still had some suspicions)—walked to the left corner of the room.

He disappeared in my blind spot, and I was grateful I couldn't see him.

Theros stepped forward. "I'm going to bring you through my meditation process," he said as he puffed up his chest. "I like to start by envisioning a golden ball of light hovering over my chest."

He pressed a hand against his sternum and closed his eyes.

Sounds fake.

"I envision the light growing in size and expanding until it surrounds my entire body."

He paused.

"Then…the tingling starts in my brain."

He spread his arms wide, palms up.

I learned something: grown men should never say the word *tingling* aloud.

It made it weird.

"The feeling is impossible to ignore," Theros continued. "It's an all-consuming relief…like when you *finally* scratch an itch that's been bothering you for hours. I envision the glow solidifying, and the tingling sensation intensifies until I can feel power pounding through my skull."

I'd never experienced anything remotely close to what he was describing.

I'm definitely powerless. There's been a big mistake.

The air around Theros warped like it had thickened around him.

He opened his eyes and smirked cockily.

Augustus stepped forward and said, "Theros has now engaged his ability."

Without warning, Augustus pulled his fist back and slammed

it toward Theros's face. His arm stopped in midair, and a dull vibration echoed, like he'd punched something solid.

Theros spread his arms wide, unharmed by the fist hovering a foot in front of his face. His vulture flapped its wings. "No person or thing can touch me, not once I've engaged my shield." He smirked like he was invincible.

Augustus dropped his arm and smiled back. "How long can you hold it?" he asked.

"My longest is two hours—but who knows." Theros winked (*at me? help*) and flexed. "Every day, I push my limits further."

Augustus's smile disappeared. He glared at Theros like he was dirt underneath his boot. *Why the sudden change in demeanor?*

I would have clapped for Theros, but I didn't have the strength to lift my hands and put them together. Also...people didn't deserve praise.

No one in the class reacted.

We all agreed.

If Theros had given this demonstration at the beginning of the week—before the hunger, thirst, exhaustion, and overall discomfort had set in—maybe we would have been more impressed.

A few initiates blinked rapidly and rocked like they were trying not to fall asleep (I was one of them).

Theros stopped flexing and looked chagrined.

"Please explain to the class the limitations of your ability," Augustus ordered, his features harsh. Any traces of congeniality were gone.

Why did he just look at me when he said "ability"?

Theros's face scrunched like he'd tasted something sour. Next to Augustus's fearsome countenance, he looked like a child playing dress-up in a crown.

Augustus was either unimpressed with the presentation or annoyed that Poco had half his ponytail in his mouth.

Theros's chest deflated under the scrutiny, and he said, "If someone is close enough to me before I engage my shield, I could trap both of us inside it together because when I'm stressed, it's hard to release the shield."

Note to self: stand close to Theros when you try to kill him. I chuckled to myself at the thought, then frowned.

Apparently, I now found murder funny.

This was rock-bottom.

Instead of addressing Theros, Augustus suddenly looked down at me and pointedly held eye contact.

Oh crap, he definitely heard that.

Augustus made a disturbed face, then looked away from me with a grimace.

Now who's the top dog in the classroom, huh?

Was it my imagination, or did Augustus just smirk? I turned my attention to the floor and wished I'd never gained consciousness.

Time passed in a blur of misery.

Just another day in my life.

The professors switched places.

Professor Pine wrote complicated fractions on the board as he ranted about the ethics of utilitarian calculations. I didn't take any notes because I couldn't feel my hands. My mind got further away from me.

Hunger sank its claws deeper into my stomach.

Professor Augustus stood with his shoulders back in front of the room and read in Latin from a thick textbook with Poco flopped on his head.

The same book was open on my lap, and I couldn't remember how it had gotten there.

"Sirens are extremely misunderstood, unique creatures," Augustus said. "They have regenerative abilities, and when a group of sirens was given an intelligence test, they scored higher than Spartans, but because only a rare few of them can understand other languages and none can speak them—they can only communicate in their own incomprehensible language—they have a relegated role in Spartan society."

He frowned as he lectured, and I tried not to fall over.

"Because both male and female sirens are extremely amorous, with overly exaggerated secondary sex characteristics, they're most known for providing sexual entertainment at symposia."

As an unsexy being that just wanted to rot in peace, the siren lifestyle was *not* relatable.

However, since the Spartans had technically kidnapped me from my home, forced me to fight to the death, and were now holding me captive inside a mountain, *torturing* me—I was 100 percent on their side.

Free the nipple, lips (vaginal), and sirens from sexual servitude.

Unfortunately, that was the last comprehensible thought I had for a while.

Professor Pine came in and taught another class, then Professor Augustus, then Pine, then… I lost track of how many times they switched.

"You will now be given a test in each of the subjects," General Cleandro said out of nowhere (literally one second, I saw darkness, and then poof, he was in front of me).

A thick packet was placed on my lap.

"Begin," he ordered.

I stared down at the page blankly.

Someone clapped loudly, and I barely noticed.

"EVERYONE, WAKE UP."

Icy water hit my face—I gasped and blinked back into awareness. Others groaned around me as General Cleandro threw water on all of us from the front of the room.

Hallelujah, it's raining men (I was awake but not functional).

I greedily licked the moisture off my lips, desperate to quench my thirst.

"Your test starts now," General Cleandro snapped. "Wake

up and stop acting like pathetic humans—or would you rather run the circuit?"

Is this a trick question?

"TEST! NOW!" His voice boomeranged around the cave-like classroom.

Papers shuffled.

"SOLVE THE PROBLEMS!"

Sucking in air through my teeth, I squinted at the numbers until they stopped dancing around the page, blurry and barely comprehensible. Ever so slowly, I solved equations.

I found the properties shared between polynomials.

Formalized the sequences into patterns of repeating numerals.

Established their parallel correspondence.

Constructed an axiomatic system.

Doodled a small penis.

"TIME'S UP."

I stared with horror at the detailed, graphic image I'd drawn in the corner of the page.

General Cleandro took the packet off my lap—*that's not good.*

Then I fell over.

Ice-cold water was dumped on my head, and I sputtered awake.

"Here's your next test." General Cleandro handed me another packet. "Keep it together, initiate. Try not to—draw, this time."

Dear God…it's me again.

I nodded jerkily, unable to form the words to explain to him that I wasn't a pervert and it wasn't what it looked like.

Actually—it was exactly what it looked like.

I needed to trade my kidney for a Spartan firearm.

"BEGIN YOUR SECOND TEST NOW!" General Cleandro bellowed.

My left ear burned with excruciating feedback, and I went to cover it, but I couldn't lift my arm above my lap. *Nice.*

Breathing deeply, trying not to pass out, I focused on the

Latin words scrawled across the top of the page: "Write an essay in Latin on sirens and their intelligence and role in Spartan society."

Easy.

I scribbled messily: "Sirens are smarter than Spartans and speak their own language; however, Sparta is a bigoted society, which prejudices them for having exaggerated secondary sex characteristics, aka, sirens have big breasts and big penises, which is likely rooted in male chauvinistic jealousy (from the Spartans, not the sexy sirens). Most things in life are..."

"TIME'S UP."

Wait...what did I just write?

General Cleandro tried to take my paper, and I held on to it for dear life. "No," I grunted, desperate to hold on to my too honest words.

Sadly, he easily ripped it out of my hands.

He walked away, and blessedly, I fell over, head hitting against something soft that grunted. Immediately I fell into the darkness.

"ALL RIGHT, THAT'S ENOUGH REST. I'VE GIVEN YOU AN ENTIRE HOUR... EVERYONE, WAKE UP." Someone kicked me in the side. Hard. "EVERYONE, GET UP NOW." Heavy boots stomped around, and initiates moaned.

A weight lifted off my thighs.

Something caught in my hair, like someone was lying on it, and the pain in my scalp forced my eyes open.

Coughing, I somehow pulled myself back into a seated position.

My stomach revolted, but nothing came out—I hadn't eaten or drunk in *days*—and I shivered from body aches.

I wanted to cry, but I couldn't feel my face or my eyes.

Professor Augustus's voice echoed far away, "Here is the order of how you scored on the test, from best to worst: first, Cassius Hermes. Second, Alexis Hert." He paused to glare at me with disappointment (apparently he did *not* ascribe to the ideology that second was best), then continued, "Third, Alessander Poseidon. Fourth, Maximum Hera. Fifth, Leo Apollo. Sixth, Drex Chen. Seventh, Titus Dionysus. Eighth, Dimitrios Apollo."

"*Dimitrios* Apollo," General Cleandro's voice boomed. "WAKE THE FUCK UP RIGHT NOW!"

The lump on the ground in front of me stirred.

General Cleandro grabbed it and lifted it up. "You're running the circuit with me, son. Let's go." He shook the lump back and forth until it stood on two feet and followed him, albeit shakily (he was dragged out).

"Two weeks have passed," Professor Augustus said, and someone sobbed with relief. It might have been me; I couldn't tell.

"However, we have spoken with your mentors and have decided that you will *not* have a break this week. The crucible will continue for two more weeks."

Someone cried out. This time, it was definitely me.

14

ALLIANCES

Alexis

My stomach turned to ash.

No break, no food, no rest, no mercy.

Sobs echoed.

"Please no," Maximum whispered in the front of the class (relatable).

Professor Augustus sighed. "Pull yourselves together. For Kronos's sake, you're Spartans. Start acting like it."

There was no god in this cruel, monster-filled world.

"Only two more weeks of study." Augustus scowled down at me like everything in the world was my fault. "Then you'll get your days off."

Study was an interesting word choice. I would have chosen *torment* or *hellacious suffering.*

Augustus rubbed his temples. "Stop with the dramatics—or you'll all join Dimitrios on the circuit. Is that what you want?"

The room fell dead silent.

Is there a third option?

"After these two weeks—" Augustus paced at the front of the room "—you'll have survived the summer—the hardest part. The fall is easy. You'll start visiting the animal menagerie to choose the animal you want to bond with, we'll give you more frequent breaks, *and* you'll gain access to the local symposium."

Where all the buxom sirens are subjugated? I'd rather not.

Augustus continued, "There will be food at the symposium."

Sign me up. I've always wanted to meet the sirens. They sound like good, hardworking, big-breasted people.

Augustus narrowed his eyes at me. "Only fourteen more days," he said. "Then your lives will get immeasurably easier. Stop bitching and pull yourselves together—what is a measly fourteen days compared to immortality?"

It sounded so simple when he put it like that.

But my tongue was stuck to the roof of my mouth, and I couldn't feel my limbs, or my face or… *Is that a raccoon eating a candlestick?*

"General Cleandro," he said, "wanted to have you run the circuit, but I petitioned for a break. You have five hours right now to study in the library. Use the time wisely. Calm your minds. It will be okay."

Someone gagged loudly.

It was me.

"Everyone will get a sip of water as a treat." He walked around handing out (throwing) cups of water to us. I barely caught mine and greedily sucked it down.

If a sip of water is a treat, I don't want to know what he views as a punishment.

Augustus mumbled something about an ungrateful girl (he was probably talking about Titus). Then he said, "I recommend using your time wisely and reading ahead in your Thagorean textbooks. It's where most of you *struggled*. You're supposed to be intelligent, powerful Spartans. Man the fuck up."

He turned his head.

"Your...rare abilities," he said slowly as he stared directly at me, not blinking, "won't be enough to carry you forward."

Who is he speaking to?

"Go on, get out of here." He clapped his hands. "Move. It's going to be okay. Focus on gaining control of your thoughts."

My spine screamed as I unfurled to my full height (I stood hunched over with my hands on my knees).

Nyx's weight didn't help.

I took a shuffling step forward, then stopped as I almost lost consciousness. Maximum crawled past me on his hands and knees.

Crap, I should have done that.

Somehow, someway, against all the odds in the universe, I made it into the library (I passed out, and Augustus carried me from the classroom while mumbling something that didn't make sense about dishonor, legacies, and lies).

"Finally, a freaking break," Nyx groaned, and I jolted awake.

I was lying in front of a library hearth, spread-eagle.

Nice.

"How are you still alive, kid?" Nyx asked, and I groaned as I sat up. "Genuine question, because I slept the entire time, and I feel dead."

I grunted in response, lips dry and cracked, tongue too heavy to use.

Who am I?

Slowly I stood up and hobbled across the room. I lowered into a seat at the table (I clipped the chair and crumbled to the ground, then crawled forward and lay atop it, and a muse picked it up with me in it).

When I was finally seated (kinda), I leaned my head back and closed my eyes with relief.

Please, God, give me a sign that it's all going to be okay.

"You think you belong here," a muffled voice taunted.

"You're an abandoned mutt, a nobody. A defect. A daughter of a *slut* who fucked her betters."

Message received, God—things are not going to get better. I understand. Praise be.

I turned slowly to the left.

Titus sat a few chairs down and leaned forward threateningly. He sneered, his expression drenched in shadows, and in the muted firelight, his red hair spiked out like angry flames.

He opened his mouth.

I turned my head forward and sighed with relief as he disappeared in my blind spot.

Sharp feedback rang through my left ear as Titus spoke, and I easily ignored it.

Drex rolled his eyes across from me. "This sucks," he said.

I waited.

Who is he talking to?

He waited.

We both waited.

Nyx made the snake equivalent of a heavy sigh. "He's talking to *you*, kid," she said with exasperation.

Why?

I licked my lips and tried to find some moisture. "Wh-what?" I croaked out raspingly, throat burning like I'd swallowed glass.

"This entire crucible bullshit *sucks*," Drex said. "Don't ya think?"

I nodded jerkily.

Pages rustled and textbooks cracked as initiates opened them up throughout the quiet library. With shaking fingers, I did the same.

Vision blurring, I stared at the book for long minutes until an excessively long Thagorean math equation came into focus.

Sighing internally—it was too much work to continue breathing heavily out loud—I read the directions: "Assign the word problem to variables and solve."

"I propose an alliance," Drex said.

Hmm. The abstraction makes sense, if you divide the prime numbers by—

"He's still talking to you, kid." Nyx interrupted my train of thought.

I looked up with surprise, and the movement hurt my neck. *I'd know if it was broken, right?*

Drex was staring at me, his expression expectant.

"What?" I repeated, chapped lips splitting open attractively.

Drex leaned forward and glanced around like he wanted to make sure no one was looking at us. "We're the only two people who grew up in the human world," he whispered. "There are only eight of us left. We need all the support we can get—*I propose the two of us form an alliance.*"

I squinted. "To do…what?"

Is he trying to recruit me for a cult? I'd read that was a big problem happening these days. Dark times and all.

Titus said something derogatory at the end of the table, and the feedback in my left ear intensified.

Drex's dark eyes darted around nervously.

He dragged a trembling hand through his short, dark hair and leaned closer. "I've only studied up through Calculus III. That was the highest math course my school offered. I need help with Thagorean—*please* tutor me."

He hadn't taken linear algebra, differential equations, or algebraic structures? Thagorean used all those basic principles.

I shuddered in horror.

How can you get through a day without knowing linear algebra? How do you live?

"I can't," I said, barely remembering how to speak.

Drex shook his head with desperation. *"Please,"* he begged. "I'll help you during the circuit and will help you deal with Titus and his cronies—*please*—I'm a quick learner, and I just need the basics. Otherwise, I'll be last and…" He trailed off.

You'll be dead.

"I'm so sorry." I shook my head and looked down at the textbook, the weight of his desperate gaze burning through me.

Memories played of his eyes glowing red, hand outstretched while boys screamed. I shivered and swallowed thickly. *He's evil.*

"Please," he said louder.

I didn't look up.

"Why are you talking to the bitch, Drex?" Titus's obnoxious voice carried loudly through the library. "Do you two abandoned mutts recognize the bitch in each other?"

That doesn't even make sense?

"See, I'll help you with him," Drex said. "Please. I can protect you."

I shook my head and didn't look up.

No one protects me but me.

Drex made a pitiful noise.

Nyx said soothingly, "You don't owe anyone anything. You're allowed to prioritize yourself."

I grimaced.

"However—" Nyx hissed. "I will bite the Titus kid for you… right now. You won't need to worry about him ever again."

"No," I whispered and grabbed at her invisible body.

Nyx made a dramatic noise but didn't struggle. "You stifle my creativity," she said as she nuzzled her face against my palm.

I breathed out as softly as possible, "Killing people is not creative."

"Don't knock it until you try it, kid." Nyx slithered around my neck, her tongue brushing against my cheek. "I'm an artist. The ways I can make a person scream with violent terror."

Unfortunately, that was the last time someone spoke to me for hours. Everyone settled into studies, and no one spoke.

Time moved at a *strange* pace.

Poignant music drifted through the stacks, candlelight flickered, fire crackled, and wax dripped. Everything was drenched in warm shades of red.

"TIME'S UP!" General Cleandro's voice cut through the peace.

I jolted awake—I'd been dreaming that I was sitting at the desk studying, but I hadn't been. He ordered everyone back into the classroom, and we hobbled obediently.

Professor Pine greeted us with a big, toothy smile.

What is wrong with him?

The marathon of lectures continued.

I wished Charlie was with me.

It was after our second meditation session for Discipline and Power that I realized Maximum was the only person sitting in the front row of the class. Dimitrios had never returned.

We were down to seven.

Titus whispered in my ear and yanked on one of my curls when Pine turned his back to solve the equation written on the chalkboard. "You're the next one to die, bitch."

Hopefully.

Time became even more peculiar.

Nyx whispered a steady stream of encouragements and nudged my face every time I started to fall asleep.

Titus's taunts also got bolder and more frequent.

The ringing in my left ear intensified into a high-pitched whine.

A lifetime of partial deafness meant I could read the professors' lips when they were facing forward, but when they turned away, I was lost.

Professor Augustus overenunciated his words, even though they were in Latin, so he was easy to follow.

Professor Pine mumbled.

Time stretched as seconds bled into hours that melted into days.

"Leo, what is the function?" Pine asked so loudly that the sound traveled over the noise in my ears.

The class turned around to look back at Leo (one person turned, two others fell over, and someone hit their head on the wall).

I rubbed the new bruise on my forehead.

Leo was asleep on the ground, arm draped over his eyes with drool running down the sides of his face. There was nothing discreet about his position. From the way his leg twitched, he was in a *deep* REM cycle.

That or he was convulsing and needed immediate medical attention.

Titus and Alessander shook Leo's shoulder, but he didn't wake up.

SNAP. General Cleandro slammed his yellow book shut—I was 110 percent certain he was just pretending to read it—and he picked up the pager.

No.

Please, God, no.

Just make him run it by himself. It's his own fault he has a sleeping problem. Everyone else stayed awake. Please don't make us all suffer. It's not fair—

General Cleandro smiled as he pressed the button.

I shriveled into dust.

BOOM. A tall, handsome man with long, dark hair and a laurel-wreath crown stalked into the classroom with a scowl. He had a colorful phoenix on his shoulder.

"Fox, heir to the House of Athena," General Cleandro said as he greeted the newcomer.

"General, like always, it's an honor." Fox bowed his handsome head. Then his eyes roamed over the classroom. His upper lip pulled back with disgust.

General Cleandro pointed at Leo. "Your mentee seems to have a sleeping problem."

Fox's scowl was downright vicious. He stomped over to Leo and wrenched him up by his toga. He screamed something, and the feedback was excruciating. Then he slapped Leo across the face. Hard.

I rubbed at my wrists.

"ENOUGH LOLLYGAGGING! GET UP AND GO… GO… GO!" General Cleandro's voice exploded through the room as his hawk flapped its wings.

Stumbling—drowning in nausea from the excruciating ringing in my left ear—I followed the rest of the class out of the room.

Fox led, dragging Leo roughly behind him by his ear. His phoenix let out a shrill noise, which almost sounded like a cat's meow.

We ran out of the chilly mountain—straight into hell.

Sunlight blinded, muggy air suffocated, heat punished, and grass squished warm beneath my bare feet.

The sun was bright and high in the sky, and there were barely any clouds.

I'd forgotten what warmth felt like.

Fox led us down the grass path, which transformed into pebbles and slanted up a mountain. His phoenix flew high above, its tail a rainbow of colors.

On wobbly legs, I willed my mind to wander.

I prayed time would warp.

Every second was an infinity—every step was agony.

There was nothing to distract me from the burning in my legs and the heaving *agony* in my struggling lungs.

Sweat poured off my face.

Every step of the ascent worsened.

Wobbling, eyes blinded by exhaustion, I teetered near the mountain's edge.

Far away, on the other side of a mountain, a maniacal, bloodthirsty scream echoed. *A Titan.*

Shocked, I tripped over a rock and plummeted toward the—

"Stay next to me. Be careful. The Titan is far enough away

that it can't get to us." Drex pulled me away from the cliff's edge, then dragged me forward.

I tried to push him away, but he didn't budge.

I shook my head desperately because I didn't have the energy to tutor him. I *couldn't*.

"Calm down," Drex said. "I don't expect anything in return. Fucking relax."

I tripped over another rock, but his hold on my toga kept me upright.

I was incoherent and unwell, spit dribbling out of my lips as I huffed and heaved. Gagged and cried.

Eons later, we *finally* made it to the stopping point at the top. I keeled over. Every breath hurt; every heartbeat sent anguish throbbing through my limbs. I couldn't see anything.

"You're the most pathetic Spartan bitch to ever exist. You don't deserve this. Just kill yourself now and put us all out of our misery," Titus whispered in my ear.

I gritted my teeth.

"Are you sure you don't want me to bite him?" Nyx asked. "I can make it *hurt*."

I tried to form my lips into words, but no sound came out. Weakly, I reached up and smacked at my neck.

"Ow, ow, stop it, woman," Nyx said. "Fine—*fine*, I won't bite him—just stop hitting me."

Titus scoffed, "You're disgusting and weak. Bitches like you are the reason men suffer. You've *stolen* a man's spot in the crucible. You're a thief and a fraud." He tugged on one of the curls that had escaped my hair tie.

Jessica would have told him that she didn't listen to men who smelled like sewer rats.

I missed my high school bully.

Things were truly tragic.

"Let's go. Break's over!" Fox yelled, and there were grunting noises as people stood up. I floundered to find my bearings.

Someone yanked me up, and I fought against their—

"Calm down." Drex grunted as I kicked out.

I stopped struggling. "Sorr—" I rasped, unable to finish the apology.

"It's fine. Let's go," Drex said as his hand once again tangled in the excess fabric at the front of my toga, and he dragged me down the mountain.

Each step was pure pain.

When we *finally* made it to the bottom, I collapsed.

"I'll give you longer to recover before the swim," Fox said, and there was a chorus of relieved noises.

I gave him a shaky thumbs-up.

"Thank you," Leo said. "We appreciate it."

"Shut the fuck up," Fox snapped. "Stop falling the fuck asleep and making me do this bullshit. I thought I made it clear last time what would happen if you did. So shut up, sit down, and think about how you're never going to fall asleep in class again."

Preach, sister.

Leo muttered an apology.

"I just told you to *shut the fuck up*—so why are you speaking?" Fox asked.

There was something attractive about a man who spoke his truth with such charisma. Fox had my vote.

After long minutes of gasping (an hour), my heart rate slowed, and my vision unblurred.

Orange and pink streaked across the sky as the sun set behind the peaks.

It's beautiful.

Tears filled my eyes.

"Oh my Kronos—are you *crying*?" Titus asked, and his cronies chuckled like he was hilarious.

Yeah, cause you're so ugly.

I instantly regretted not speaking the insult aloud.

Once again, Drex sat in front of me. This time, he was cross-legged in the grass on the edge of the river. He was drenched in sweat and nodded at me tiredly.

Without him, I'd have careened off the side of the mountain into the ravine.

You're going to have to tutor him.

"Do you really think you're going to survive this?" Titus asked as he walked over and leered above me. Leo and Alessander stood beside him.

"What's that white shit on your lips?" Titus asked, and I wiped shakily at my dried spit and sweat.

Titus laughed exaggeratedly. "Is it cum?" His cronies chortled.

Drex rolled his eyes.

Bending my knees, I leaned forward and put my head between my legs. *Tell him no one will ever love him.*

Titus laughed louder.

Nyx hissed in my ear, "Are you *sure* I can't bite hi—"

I poked her.

The moment passed, and once again I regretted not insulting Titus. For some reason, Patro was the only person I could insult.

"Rude," she groaned, but her tongue flickered across my cheek. "You're worth so much more than them," she hissed. "Ignore them—a Nemean lion doesn't listen to the ramblings of sheep."

Her words were inspiring.

Too bad Charlie had once said I had the countenance of a platypus and the energy of a deranged squirrel. It was early on in our sign language studies, though, so I wasn't sure he'd meant it. I'd been too scared to ask for clarification.

"Holy fuck. Guys, *look*." Alessander's voice quivered with fear, and all three of my abusers finally went silent.

Thank God for small mercies.

I looked up.

My heart stopped.

Kharon stood a few feet away, his long boat floating along the edge of the riverbank. Ice-blue eyes glared at me.

Never mind.

Close enough to reach out and touch, his black tattered cloak rippled around him like a shadow.

My vision distorted. His pole resembled a scythe.

Titus, Leo, and Alessander backed slowly away from the river's edge.

I was too tired to move.

The breeze blew Kharon's hood to the side, revealing razor-sharp cheekbones and an even sharper scowl.

Long seconds passed as he glared at me.

"What is he doing?" Leo whispered.

He's reminding me of his threat.

I looked away first.

In my peripheral vision, Kharon pushed away from the river's edge with an evil smirk.

Satan: 1.

Alexis: 0.

The rest of the break passed in a tense silence, and even Fox looked unsettled.

But like all good things in life, it came to an abrupt end, and we swam the River Styx (drowned in a forward-moving direction). The water was warmer than last time, but it was still a shock to the system.

Each stroke was desperate and filled with terror. Each ripple was the ferryman hunting. I didn't think he'd kill me—not *yet*—but that didn't mean he wouldn't torment me with a little light drowning.

Kharon seemed like the type who played with his food.

When all seven of us crawled onto the shore as a group, the moon shone brightly above, and there were no foil blankets.

General Cleandro stood on the bank and looked unimpressed as he announced we had another five-hour break to study.

I didn't remember making it inside.

Just had a faint memory of crawling on my hands and knees.

One second I was under the stars, and the next, I was sitting at a table, struggling to read a textbook while tears streamed down my face. Nyx's cold scales were wrapped up in a ball between my feet.

Drex sat across from me, brow furrowed as he took notes.

He was also crying.

"You just got lucky. Your days are numbered, bitch," Titus whispered directly into my right ear.

He stood behind me, and his breath was hot on my neck.

I focused on the text in front of me. *Tell him he's going to die alone. Just say it quick.*

I flipped the page, unable to find the courage to speak.

"I said—your days are numbered, *slut*."

Quickly, call his mom a bad name.

I reached up with shaking fingers to turn the page.

Titus grabbed my arm and stopped me. "You're going to wish you—"

I stared down at where his fingers were wrapped tightly around my forearm.

"Release me," I rasped.

He squeezed tighter. His vile fingers pressed into my skin, nails cutting.

I was back in a trailer.

Titus laughed. "Make me."

I shoved my chair back, whirled, body careening jerkily as I flung myself forward and slammed my fist into the side of his stupid face.

He staggered back from the force.

"Did you just...*punch* me?" He clutched his jaw, eyes wide and crazed.

I swayed back and forth unsteadily, head spinning from the sudden movement, stomach rolling.

His fist flew.

Crack. Sensations exploded across my nose, and blood gushed across my lips. I stood frozen, blinking in shock, stunned by the liquid pouring down my face.

Titus snarled in my face, "Yeah, that's what I *fucking thought.* You're a weak bitch and don't stand a chance against a real man like—"

I lunged forward and slammed my knee into his crotch as hard as I could. He grabbed himself and fell to his knees. I kicked him in the face as he went down.

Crack. Blood exploded as his nose splintered.

He moaned in a fetal position on the floor.

Now—who's the real man?

As I swayed drunkenly, my vision doubled.

There was a muffled noise, and I turned to my left. Leo and Alessander were charging in my blind spot. I squinted my eyes and braced myself for—

Drex flew out of nowhere and threw his fist into Leo's face.

Drex and Leo slammed into the table.

Alessander stopped in surprise.

With trembling arms, I picked up my chair, groaning as I raised it high. Alessander turned back to me. I rammed it down over his head, and he went down like a rock.

Broken chair pieces splintered everywhere.

Leo and Drex pulled away from each other and stared at me. Maximum and Cassius gaped in their seats with open mouths. Muses peeked out from behind the stacks.

Shadows moved strangely in my peripheral vision.

Neck prickling, I squinted into the darkness outside the open library door. *Is someone watching me?*

No one was there.

Titus groaned, and I dropped the broken piece of wood in my hand.

"Wahoooooo." Nyx slithered up my leg. "*That's* my girl."

She made a sniffling noise. "I'm so proud right now…this is the best day of my life. I knew you had it in you, bestie. Pussy power, crush the patriarchy! Don't stop now—murder them all. KILL EVERYONE IN THIS ROOM!"

Grimacing, I keeled over and threw up all over Alessander.

Oops.

I wiped my mouth with the back of my hand, then barely stopped myself from face-planting.

"What the fuck is all the noise?" General Cleandro stomped in, and Professor Augustus followed him with a worried expression. When he saw me, his face transformed into a hateful scowl.

They both stopped.

Blinked as they took in the scene.

Slowly, the two men (towering behemoths who looked like they belonged on a battlefield) walked over to where Alessander was passed out cold, covered in a broken chair and *stuff*, aka, my regurgitated bile. Next to his fallen friend, Titus staggered to his feet, clutching his crotch like a pervert.

"What—happened here?" General Cleandro asked slowly. Augustus glared at me accusingly with soulless dark eyes, rubies gleaming on his head in the library's firelight.

Out of respect for his authority (pure fear), I stared at the floor.

Titus sputtered.

General Cleandro held his hand up. "I just want to remind you," he said softly, "that if anyone has been fighting—for any reason—you will all run the circuit until your feet are bloody stumps…then you'll run it some more."

Titus's teeth clicked as he snapped his mouth shut.

"So I'll ask again," General Cleandro said. "*What* the fuck happened here?"

Cassius spoke quickly. "It was just—"

"Titus." The general cut Cassius off and pointed at the blood-covered boy. "*Titus* will tell me what happened."

The silence was so charged that if a match had been lit, the air would have exploded.

After an excruciating long pause, Titus whispered, "Alessander fell out of his chair. When he fell, the chair also hit me… and…uh…that's why we were both on the ground."

I glanced up.

General Cleandro stared at Titus with an unreadable expression, and Augustus was still glaring at me.

"Be more careful with how you act in the future," the general said. "The furniture can be—*dangerous*."

It didn't feel like he was talking about a chair.

"What are you all waiting for?" He whirled around and glared. "STUDY AND STOP STANDING AROUND."

As General Cleandro stalked out of the library, we scrambled into our seats.

Titus's excuse hadn't explained my broken nose, Leo's black eye, the bruise on Drex's cheek, or how the chair had broken on *top* of Alessander, then covered him in vomit.

But he hadn't punished us.

Augustus lingered in the library with his eyes narrowed.

Help, why is he still looking over here?

Why is he walking toward me?

He stalked over to where I sat and loomed behind me like a dark cloud.

I prayed for spontaneous combustion.

"What do you think you're doing?" Augustus asked silkily, low enough that only I could hear.

Sadly, I did not explode.

I swallowed thickly. "What are you t-talking about?" I whispered.

He leaned closer, breath tickling the side of my ear, and strange sensations fluttered in my lower stomach.

"Why—*the fuck*—are you putting yourself in danger?" he asked slowly, his voice vibrating with vehemence. Quietly, in a deathly whisper, he said, "Chthonics are *extremely* rare and important. Act like it."

Oh, it's because my mentors are Chthonic, and he's worried about them becoming generals.

I waved my hand dismissively. "Don't worry, I'm just defending myself, and I had it all under control. It's fine." My tone was confident, but the blood that gushed from my broken nose onto the table ruined the effect.

Augustus made a rough noise in the back of his throat, and he flexed his hands like either he had rheumatoid arthritis or he was trying not to strangle me (both options were extremely concerning).

"Take better care of yourself," he snarled. "Or—I'll have to take action. This can't continue."

Since it was completely unclear what "this" he was referring to, I gave him a hesitant smile.

He growled and stomped away, then slammed the library door shut behind him.

That went well.

I slumped over, groaning as my face throbbed.

With the two Spartan generals (power-hungry fascist dictators who were definitely suffering from undiagnosed mental disorders) gone, there was a collective sigh of relief in the library.

We rejoiced over our avoidance of certain doom.

Yay, not being murdered in a fit of rage. Wahoo. God is good.

"Wow, kid," Nyx hissed as she slithered up my body. "That was *hot*. Did you feel that tension? I can't breathe."

"First—you're delusional," I whispered. "Second, you're a snake. Do you even have lungs?"

Nyx hissed, "First, I do—rude. Second, please, I'm a *woman*, and it's obvious that man wants to do depraved things to you. Thank Kronos, finally a worthy suitor. I was getting worried you were going to die a virgin. It would have been so embarrassing for our family's honor."

I choked.

What family honor?

"Hey, what's wrong with celibacy?" I asked under my breath. "I told you, Carl Gauss is the only man for me. You *know* this. Also, you've officially lost it—Augustus hates me."

"I never said he didn't hate you." Nyx tightened around my throat. "That's obvious. That man LOATHES you. But that doesn't mean he doesn't want to murder you—in bed. If you *know* what I mean."

Unfortunately, I did. Kinda. But in a very real sense, I had no clue what she was talking about.

I cleared my throat in disbelief and dribbled saliva attractively onto the table.

"You're crazy," I said to Nyx as I tried to wipe the bloody spit away with my arm, and just spread it around, making a bigger mess.

"You're an idiot," Nyx scoffed, and I took the high road (pinched her until she shut up).

Sometimes violence *was* the answer.

Drex made a noise as he sat down across from me.

"What just happened with Augustus?" His eyes were wide, expression confused. "Why was he whispering to you like that? Do you—interact with him outside the crucible?"

I scoffed. "No, that would be horrible."

He kept looking at me weirdly. "He seems very—proprietorial over you."

Not him too.

Shaking my head, I waved my hand dismissively. "It's just because my mentors are Chthonics. All of them are s-super worried about them becoming generals. They've created a very stifling, unhealthy environment. The old boys' club. Ya know."

What am I even saying?

Drex did not look like he knew at all, but he shrugged and opened his textbook.

"Here." I coughed. "Let me explain," I whispered roughly, air whistling through my crushed nose, as I pushed my textbook toward him.

Drex's head snapped up. He looked up at me like I was his savior.

"Alliance?" I croaked out, then clarified, "But not the cult kind. No human sacrifices, flower crowns, or weird circles with sticks."

At this time in my life, I could not handle cult life.

Maybe later, when I had more free time.

"Of course." Drex flashed bloody teeth from his fight with Leo and said, "Us abandoned mutts have to stick together."

Nodding (then regretting it because it jostled my aching nose), I began to slowly explain linear algebra to him. Luckily, he was a quick learner and caught onto concepts easily.

As the next hours passed, a strange warmth unfurled in my chest. The sensation was so foreign that it took me a second to place it.

It was *hope.*

The two weeks were almost over, and soon we'd get to rest. It was already the end of August, and somehow I was still alive. Professor Augustus had said the fall was much easier. *You've already made it through the hardest part.*

Everything wouldn't be so bad, and it would all work out in the end.

Delusion was one hell of a drug.

Spoiler, it would not all just "work out."

15
OBSESSION

Augustus

There was a loud crashing noise and a thud in the other room where the initiates were supposed to be studying.

Someone shouted.

A grunt echoed.

Cleandro and I stopped lesson planning and stared at each other in horror—we sprinted toward the library.

We skidded to a stop in the doorway.

I fisted my hands.

It was the bane of my fucking existence. *Why is she constantly causing fucking problems?*

Alexis was standing in the center of the room.

Her nose was smashed, her chin was covered in blood, and both her eyes were swelling and turning black.

Someone punched her in the face.

Red filled my vision. Pure unadulterated rage burned me apart at the seams, and I rubbed at my chest as I breathed deeply.

Alexis was delicate, just like my sister, Helen, and her soft features were twisted with pain.

Every muscle in my body tensed. Men who hurt women didn't deserve to live.

This is exactly why she shouldn't be participating in the fucking crucible. It's a Kronos-damned outrageous dishonor.

My hands itched with the urge to snap someone's neck, and I trembled from the force of trying to keep myself together.

Cleandro gave me a strange look, like he could see through me.

I ignored him.

He couldn't see *anything*; he was just an Olympian.

He would never understand what it felt like to be me. The power. The rage. The weight of responsibility.

Chthonics were an endangered species, and it was my duty as eldest to keep the next generation safe. They were all depending on me. I wouldn't fail.

Alexis's lips trembled.

I will not fall for her games.

Hatred and something unidentifiable burned in my gut. She was opening up the possibility of Helen having to take part in this depraved nonsense.

I wanted to kill her for it.

When Kharon had told me just what she was, the hatred had intensified exponentially.

How dare she.

She was a mockery of everything I stood for.

No woman, no matter how strong, should ever endure the crucible. It was dishonorable and wrong.

I didn't fucking care if Aphrodite and Artemis said I wasn't progressive. It wasn't about women being as tough as men; it was about the fact that they shouldn't *have* to be.

Spartan women were rare and needed to be protected at all costs. The future of our society depended on keeping them safe.

Now Alexis's two-colored eyes were wide as she stared down at the floor.

Cleandro and I stalked forward into the room.

At Alexis's feet, Alessander was unconscious and bloody.

My jaw dropped as I took in the broken pieces of wood all over the boy, and the piece of wood clutched in Alexis's hand. She'd smashed him with a chair.

Holy Kronos.

Fury warred with grudging respect.

Another figure moaned. Titus was on the ground, blood pouring off his face as he clutched at himself like a weak coward.

She destroyed the sniveling pussy. Both of them. Good.

Sharp emotions strangled me, and I didn't know how to feel.

Everything about Alexis was confusing.

She was shy and timid, but also bloodthirsty and savage. She made idiotic comments, but according to Pine was a prodigy at theoretical math.

I hadn't believed it when Kharon had told me what she'd done on the circuit—now I believed him.

She was clearly here to make a statement about women in Sparta.

Not on my watch.

It was completely fucking unacceptable.

My fingers itched, and I fisted them. The urge to kidnap her and lock her away, then break Titus's mind into little pieces, was overwhelming.

Do it later. Now's not the time.

Pain radiated through my sternum.

I breathed deeply and fought against my debased urges as Cleandro let the girl off the hook.

He should be punishing her for her lack of self-preservation, not fucking rewarding her. She's one wrong move away from death.

Alexis stared at Cleandro with wide, grateful eyes, but there was a dimness in her gaze that was uncomfortably familiar.

Life had hurt her.

Badly.

Just like it had hurt me.

It doesn't matter. Don't feel bad for her. That's what she wants. This is all a game to her.

She didn't make sense.

From what I'd seen, Alexis blundered through life, naive and frustratingly innocent, with no thought for the consequences. Mix in her sanctimonious need to prove women should fight alongside Spartan men, and you had my worst nightmare come to life.

But I was here.

I was the consequences.

I was going to keep her, and all the women under my charge, safe, whether she fucking wanted it or not.

Cleandro walked away, and I lingered at the door, fighting the urge to do something. Instead of following him out like I should have, I stalked forward across the library, unable to avoid the pull in my gut.

Alexis's delicate features blanched as she saw me coming.

You better be afraid.

When I stood a foot away, I leaned close, discreetly inhaling her intoxicating scent. A growl burned the back of my throat, and my fingers itched to find out if her golden curls were as soft as they looked.

Concentrate.

With a low growl, I warned her to take better care of herself. Warned her there would be consequences.

She glared up at me with horror.

Kronos, she made me feel like a monster, like she wasn't the one setting Helen up for pain. I was the one trying to keep everyone safe.

Did she think it was easy?

What did she think, that I'd fucking coddle her? Welcome her with open arms? Applaud as she risked her life like an idiot?

As Alexis stared up at me, her long, dark lashes fluttered. Up close, I could see the gold flecks in her midnight-colored eye.

Her tongue flicked out, and she licked across her blood-covered lips. They were curved perfectly.

My silk boxers grew tight, and I instantly loathed myself.

Fuck, what am I doing?

I was older than her, and I was her professor.

This was wrong on so many levels.

Something about Alexis made me lose all control.

She made me feral with rage.

If I stay in this library another second, I'm going to murder both those boys for touching her, then kidnap and handcuff her to my bed.

I stalked away.

Poco chittered in the hall as he climbed up my shoulders. His weight was familiar. Calming.

I walked out of the mountain, into the warm night, and bellowed with rage. A sea of stars sparkled above.

The Milky Way was streaked with yellow.

Punching stone, I breathed roughly.

Shaking my head with confusion, I headed down the path away from the mountain.

I needed to run the circuit to regain control.

A few hours later, my muscles burned from exertion, and a facade of calm was once again plastered across my face.

Cleandro announced to the library that it was time for a break, hit the buttons on his pager, then leaped away.

The initiates startled awake.

Patro and Achilles arrived first and grabbed a barely conscious Alexis.

My knuckles cracked.

Why the fuck are they touching her so familiarly, and why do I care?

I glared at them, and they looked at me with confusion, then disappeared with a loud bang.

I barely stifled the urge to follow them.

You need a distraction.

The rest of the mentors started arriving. I grabbed Alessander and Titus by the front of their togas and dragged them behind a bookcase.

I threw them forcefully to the ground.

They yelped in pain. *Good.*

Agony exploded in my chest as I activated my powers, yanked them both up, and stared into their eyes.

Pressure burned my skull.

Their mental defenses were nonexistent—I stabbed into their pathetic Olympian minds.

Unlike Chthonics, who fought back, Olympian minds were soft and malleable.

They fell to their knees.

"If you *ever dare* hurt Alexis again, or *any* woman, ever," I bellowed straight into their skulls, "I'll destroy you from the inside out."

They cried out like babies.

I made it hurt.

Blood poured from their mouths, eyes, noses, and ears. It covered them in rivers of red. They choked and gagged, unable to breathe.

If they were human, they'd be dead.

As Spartans, they'd live. Unfortunately.

I straddled them. "Spartans don't hurt women—or I hurt them. Understood? This is just a taste of what I can do."

Their minds trembled with agony and started to crack. They gagged louder.

I rolled my eyes because I'd barely used my power; their brains weren't even leaking out their ears.

They were fine.

The sniveling cowards nodded jerkily as they trembled on the floor, suffocating.

I straightened to my full height and brushed off my hands. "You disgust me." I spat on them, then I stalked away.

"They're back there," I said to their mentors and pointed.

Both Olympians bowed to me, terror written across their faces.

I forced my expression back into a mask of calm.

The men relaxed.

Gullible fools.

I turned around and scoffed. Cracking my knuckles, I palmed my gun. I needed to fight a Titan, or I was going to lose it and start torturing Olympians—more than I already had.

"Domus," I whispered and pictured the feeling of home.

The world exploded in smoke.

I leaped away.

Narrowing my eyes with confusion, I looked around the quiet forest. A tarp was strewn across branches in a purposeful pattern. *I didn't mean to leap here.*

Shrugging, I turned and stalked through the trees.

It would do.

Jumping over the barbed wire fence of a protected zone, I ventured farther into the woods, searching for my prey.

Kronos, I was so fucking angry.

Alexis Hert is going to be the death of me.

Kharon was right; his plan was the only acceptable path forward.

I'll tell him later that I agree. We're going to do it his way.

Things were going to change around here.

They had to.

Aut viam inveniam aut faciam—*I shall either find a way or make one.*

Otherwise, I was going to lose my mind, and people were going to die.

16
HAUNTED

Alexis

"Why is your nose hanging off your face?" Patro asked accusingly, like I *wanted* it to be detached.

Stumbling, I tried to regain consciousness, but after hours of studying in the library (sleeping at a desk with my eyes open and blood dripping from my nose), it was difficult.

The smoke from leaping cleared around us and revealed a familiar woodstove kitchen, covered in golden streaks of light.

Outside the bay window, water glittered a dark shade of blue as the sun dipped over the horizon.

A wolf and jaguar growled at me, and I waved at them in greeting.

We were back in Corfu.

Thank you, God.

I coughed miserably, pain and exhaustion radiating through every cell in my sleep-deprived body.

Patro yanked me upright by my wrists.

Forearms burning with phantom aches, I ripped away from his touch, slammed into the wall, then staggered into a partially standing position.

He said something derogatory, but I missed it over the high-pitched ringing in my left ear.

Also, the morbid despair was loud. *Life sucks.*

My face still throbbed from the library *incident*, where I may or may not have had a violent mental breakdown and assaulted two men (I had no regrets; someone had to do it).

Then, after I'd tutored Drex in math, while mouth-breathing because my nasal passage was smushed, and fallen asleep, General Cleandro announced we'd survived four weeks straight at the Spartan War Academy and could leave with our mentors.

Yay, not.

Personally, I wished I was dead.

Now Patro's expression was somewhere between disgust and hatred as he watched me lean against the wall and struggle to stand. Achilles loomed behind him with a muzzle taut across his face.

Achilles cracked his knuckles. "DEATH" was spelled out across them. The tattoo ink was faded, which was why I hadn't noticed it before.

Since our kind neighbor at the trailer park was covered head to toe in satanic symbols, I was not intimidated. *I hope he's still taking care of Charlie.*

Heartsickness made me nauseous.

"Explain," Patro demanded as he gestured to my ruined nose. "You look like shit."

I started to speak, but rattling coughs exploded from my chest, and blood spattered onto the kitchen floor. I keeled over, gasping, with my hands on my knees.

Nyx's scales vibrated against my neck as she slept peacefully. *Must be freakin' nice.*

Patro sat down at the kitchen table with a huff of annoyance.

"Oh my fucking Kronos." He glared at me. "Can you pull it together for once in your life? It's like you make an *effort* to be pathetic."

Between coughs, I gave him a death glare.

I'd just spent four weeks being tortured without food and water. Another initiate had *died* during the experience; you'd think he'd have a little compassion.

Patro leaned forward and snapped his fingers in front of my face. "I don't have all day."

I purposefully coughed on them.

"Ew!" He snatched his hand back. "Did you just *hack* on me like a filthy, gross commoner—"

BOOM.

More smoke filled the room.

Please, God, don't do this to me.

Not again.

I coughed harder.

"Honeys, I'm home," taunted a deep, scratchy voice straight from my nightmares.

Satan walked into the kitchen.

God is definitely punishing me. First Augustus, now him—why can't I catch a freakin' break?

Glacial blue eyes flashed with danger, and "Furia" was stark against his throat.

White dress-shirt sleeves were rolled up, revealing veiny forearms. *Stop looking at his arms.* Thigh and chest holsters also bulged with weapons.

The spiky crown glinting atop his head was a reminder of just what he was.

Chthonic royalty.

Who knew evil had such wide shoulders and a tapered waist?

I wanted to shoot myself.

"Well, well, well," Kharon said as he clicked his tongue. "If it isn't the troublemaker. You've caused quite the stir. Everyone in Sparta is talking about your little...*performance*."

He sized me up.

"I told you not to harm yourself," he snarled.

Like Augustus, he's upset that I endangered Patro's and Achilles's chances of becoming generals.

"I a-am unharmed," I said as I stumbled and tried to not pass out from sheer exhaustion.

The gold hue of the kitchen darkened to a spectral shade of blue, or at least it did in my imagination. And even with squished nostrils, the smell of a summer storm was heady.

Shadows expanded, and two voices whispered.

No, you're just losing your mind. The voices aren't real. The thought was comforting.

At the table, Patro's frown transformed into a comical look of disbelief as he asked, "What could Alex have possibly done to anyone for *all* of Sparta to have heard about it?"

My mentor laughed like the idea of me doing anything but dying was funny.

"Don't call me that," I whispered.

His smile fell. "I'll call you whatever I want to—*Alex*."

The scar on my sternum twinged, and an icy, numb sensation spread through my limbs.

I wanted to hurt him. Badly.

No. You're not like your foster parents.

I shook my head to dislodge the dark thoughts and sighed heavily.

"Alexis," Kharon said slowly, "punched the Titus boy from the House of Dionysus in the face. Then she got punched in retaliation."

Patro harrumphed.

"Attacking your betters, I see," Patro sneered as he turned to me. "You need to focus on self-preservation. I hope you've learned your lesson...you *don't* want to mess with a Spartan mutt who's been trained since birth to—"

"That's not all," Kharon cut him off.

Copper flooded my mouth from my ruined nose, and I tilted my head back, awkwardly gurgling until I could breathe again. It was a move I'd learned as a child, since Foster Father had woken me up with a broken nose on more than one occasion.

The fact that my face had healed perfectly each time should have been a sign that I wasn't fully human, but I'd been a little distracted trying to survive, so I gave my younger self a pass.

Now all three men (evil Chthonic monsters) gaped at me with varying expressions of disbelief.

You'd think they'd never seen a woman gurgle her bloody spit and nose juices before.

I shrugged.

The key to surviving girlhood in an apocalypse was being adaptable—and period cups. Music also helped. So did Carl Gauss fan fiction.

Kharon took a step closer, leather holsters creaking across his wide thighs, the leather straps crisscrossed right below another bulging—

I was staring at his male thotch (thigh-crotch) region like a weirdo.

Mental note—pray. ASAP.

Nineteen was a strange age.

In an effort to come across as less of a melancholic pervert, I studied the blue diamond buttons gleaming across his wide chest.

Aren't blue diamonds the most expensive diamonds in the world?

I'd read something about the rarity of the blue Hope Diamond, which used to be kept in a museum until Titans had ushered in the era of anarchy and thieves had stolen it.

A dozen *thick* diamonds sparkled on Kharon's shirt.

What are the odds I can successfully steal one and run away? Then Charlie and I can live off the proceeds for the rest of our lives.

The devil approached with perfect posture. His wide shoulders were pulled back (not that I noticed), showcasing the Spartan guns holstered across his chest.

Ten percent chance I can steal a button.

Kharon looked down his aristocratic nose and leaned dangerously close.

His voice was a deadly rasp. "It's *quite* the story, you see. After being punched, Alexis kneed the one boy in the crotch, and then…she kneed him again in the face as he fell."

A frantic piano tune played.

Patro made a noise in the back of his throat. "So? She managed to moderately incapacitate one boy. It's not like she—"

"Then—" Kharon interrupted harshly. "Alexis here lifted a library chair above her head and bludgeoned another boy until he was out cold."

Patro turned and raised his eyebrows.

Kharon leaned close to my personal space.

I narrowed my eyes and craned my neck back to look at him. "It wasn't like that," I said. "I just…hit him once. With the chair. It was more of a tap. A light bop."

"And then, to add insult to injury," Kharon continued like I hadn't spoken, "she puked on the passed-out, fallen boy to assert her dominance over him."

Oh…that's not good.

Patro's jaw dropped.

"Um." I winced and raised my finger. "That's n-not what happened."

Kharon moved faster than my eye could track—he was millimeters away. His body heat burned, and a curious sensation twisted low in my stomach.

"Did you not puke on him?" he asked mockingly, the deep baritone of his voice scratching across my ears.

Fire smoldered inside my gut, and strange sensations made me weak.

"It was an accident." I shrugged casually. "The puke."

Just a girl with a weak stomach, nothing to see here.

A pale hand reached toward my face.

Flinching, I closed my eyes and waited for the blow.

Long, burning-hot fingers grabbed the back of my neck in a vise. Goose bumps exploded down my spine. My knees shook.

Okay, 0 percent chance I steal a button.

Nothing happened.

Great, he's going to prolong my death and make it weird.

I squinted up. Glacier-blue eyes stared down with an unreadable expression, cut jaw clenching.

"On the count of five," Kharon said quietly.

What?

"One," he said, voice cold and raspy. There was a long pause as he looked at me expectantly.

Ohmygod, does he want me to count until he kills me? Who does that?

"Uh, two?" I said.

Yes, I was voluntarily participating in my own murder. No, I didn't want to talk about it.

I flinched and whispered, "Three."

Kharon grabbed my broken nose. White-hot agony exploded, and he reset the bone back into place. Violently.

I yelped and tipped my head back, tears streaming, face on fire. Groaning and clutching at my abused nose, I shuffled backward and knocked into the table.

Patro yelled something.

Tripping, I was face-planting toward the—

Kharon grabbed my shoulders and stopped my descent.

I looked up at him, the queasiness intensifying in my stomach. For a long moment, we stared at each other.

The whites of his eyes turned crimson.

Strange, intense emotions rolled through me. They felt… *obsessive.*

"Don't touch me," I whispered.

"Fine." He dropped me.

I collapsed onto the floor, a tangle of spread limbs and wounded pride. Luckily, I'd turned at the last minute and had barely avoided rebreaking my nose.

Rolling over, I panted.

Nero stood up from where he was lying under the table and growled. Poppae delicately licked a paw and glared across the room.

I think they're starting to like me.

Poppae hissed, then violently hacked up a hairball.

Maybe not.

Thick leather boots embossed in gold—which I probably couldn't afford, even if I sold my virginity *and* all my organs (including my skin) on the black market—came to a stop beside my head.

"Get the fuck up," Kharon snarled. "Right now." His light eyes promised pain.

Strangely enough, I suddenly found the strength to do just that.

"Do you now see what we're dealing with?" Patro said when I was sitting across from him at the table. "This is what I meant."

"I do," Kharon said. "I know more than you think. But do *you* know exactly who she is?"

"What?" Patro asked with confusion.

"My name is Alexis," I said helpfully. "That's who I am."

"Shut the fuck up," Kharon roared at me. "How dare you?" he asked with a snarl.

Immediately I regretted speaking. *Why do I keep interacting with them?* I snapped my jaw closed and stared down at the table, praying for invisibility.

As far as I could tell, every Chthonic spoke in confusing riddles.

Also, they were all lunatics.

So, there was that.

A whack with a shovel would *not* be enough for them. They needed to be hit by a car.

No one else said anything, and we sat collectively in the uncomfortable environment Kharon had cultivated.

Carl Gauss would never act like this.

Moonlight filtered into the darkening kitchen, and my mentors glared at me from across the table. Kharon stayed standing, which was highly unsettling.

My heart twisted with fear.

Think positive thoughts, Alexis. He's not going to kill you. He wants you alive for his friends. No need to be afraid of him.

Crack. A skeleton-covered fist slammed against the table next to me.

He's going to eat your brain. Run. Run. Run.

"Patro and Achilles," Kharon said softly. "Why don't you go get Alexis's room ready for her? I want to have a…chat with her. Alone."

Ohmygod.

"Of course," Patro said with a smile as he offered his arm to Achilles. He turned his head to look back at me as they left the room, and the message in his green eyes was clear. *He's going to eat your brain now.*

Kharon leaned closer, and his breath wafted against the back of my neck.

I swallowed a scream.

His sinister voice was a noose that spiraled around my throat. "You mutilated your fellow initiates," he rasped. "You pretended to be weak, but then…you *tore* them to pieces, easily. It would almost be impressive, if you weren't so far below your potential."

He pounded his fist.

What potential?

Shadows stretched across the table. Something growled.

A scream bubbled up in the back of my throat.

"You're a filthy little liar." Kharon's breath was icy against the side of my cheek, a sharp contrast to his intense body heat. "How dare you put yourself at risk, while bringing dishonor to us all with your little charade?"

He caged me against the table—his stomach muscles bunched and pressed into my back.

"I warned you what would happen. Do you want to be my mortal enemy?"

Sweat streaked down the side of my face as I breathed shallowly.

"I'm not l-lying about anything," I whispered, too terrified to speak loudly. "I had it all under control."

He didn't move.

A sarcastic chuckle burst from his lips.

He doesn't believe me.

"Kharon… I swear it on my life."

The heat dissipated as he abruptly pulled away. "What did you just call me?"

Gasping for air, I needed a second to process what he had asked. "Kharon?" I repeated his name with confusion.

Is he playing mind games?

"My name is not *Karen*," he spat with vitriol, like I'd gravely insulted him. "It's pronounced Ch-ar-on."

I narrowed my eyes. "Okay, but it's spelled with a *K*."

"Say my name," he ordered. "Now, Alexis."

"Kharon?" I muttered.

"Did you just say Karen again?"

"What? No…" I squinted. "Wait, can you pronounce it again?"

Long fingers dug into my scalp. Then he yanked my head

back. He towered above me, torso close to my face, cruel ice-blue eyes full of violent promises.

"Say *Ch-ar-on*. Now."

"Charon." I swallowed thickly. "Sorry, sir."

He inhaled sharply.

His Chthonic eyes filmed over with blood.

A streak of white-hot *something* exploded in my lower stomach. The sensation was powerful and foreign, like it hadn't come from me.

I panted, squinting up at him with confusion.

He released me like I'd scalded him and took a step back. Dragging his tattooed fingers roughly through his messy hair as his eyes returned to normal.

For a long moment, we both breathed heavily.

A strange tension unfolded between us. It was charged. Volatile. *Terrifying.*

"Don't forget what I told you before." His voice was gravelly and had a menacing undertone. "Stop lying. Let harm befall you, and I'll make your life so miserable that you'll pray to Kronos for death."

Too late. I'm already doing that.

Shaking my head, I took a deep, steadying breath.

I will not be gaslit by a man with a skeleton tattoo. I'm better than this. I didn't try to get hurt.

"But," he said slowly, "you did beat those boys to a bloody pulp. I'm almost…proud, carissima. But don't you dare fucking do it again. Remember—I'll be watching you."

Before I could respond (start crying), he stalked out of the kitchen.

I was alone.

His cold, mocking energy still lingered insidiously.

Please don't be proud. Please don't watch me. Actually, never look at me ever again. Also please don't call me "dearest" in Latin. Thanks.

Once again, the infamous son of Artemis and Erebus had left me reeling at the kitchen table.

"Bye, Karen," I whispered spitefully.

The strange sensations in my stomach slowly dissipated. I slumped over with relief. The moonlight and sea breeze felt softer, less insidious.

"Holy crud," Nyx hissed against my right ear. "Wow—talk about a real mate. I haven't felt that type of *energy* around a man in ages. Although Augustus does have similar protective instincts. They're good men, Alexis."

I choked.

Were the good men in the room with us?

"Uh, hard no. He's a literal psychopath," I said in disbelief.

"Exactly," Nyx hissed. "He's driven and relentless—he's not one of those sissy boys today who don't even know how to kill."

What a take.

"Whoever he loves—will be protected for the rest of their lives." Nyx sighed like it was romantic. "He'd be…devoted… possessive—if you know what I mean."

Laughter bubbled up my throat.

No, I did not know what she meant. At all. Head in hand, I chuckled uncontrollably at the thought of Kharon in love. He'd probably kill people, then gift his lover chopped-up body parts.

"You're funny," I said to Nyx as I wiped the tears off my cheeks.

I stopped laughing.

How did Kharon know what happened at the library?

My heart skipped a beat, and I felt sick.

Is he stalking me? Waiting to make good on his threat? Waiting to kidnap me to some lair where he'll torture me for—

No.

Stop it.

I slammed my fist into my forehead to dislodge the insidious thoughts.

Kharon had said that everyone in Sparta knew about it, so one of the initiates had probably said something.

But we just left the academy?

I pulled my fist away from my head and slumped over farther. My limbs heavy, gravity crushed me.

My sanity was fraying.

Suddenly I understood exactly why that horrible book had said the crucible was a mental test.

I couldn't trust my thoughts.

It's fine. You're just paranoid. You're better than this. You've lived through hell already and kept your mind intact. You can do it again.

Determination coursed through me.

I was going to make a change.

Starting now.

With painful slowness, I hobbled over to the piles of fresh-cut food laid out along the kitchen. Chewing slowly, I ate until I couldn't eat anymore, then gulped down a pitcher of ice water, which tasted divine.

Unplugging the shiny radio that sat on the kitchen counter, I grabbed an entire wheel of cheese and carried it back to my bedroom.

With music playing and a chunk of fresh cheese in my mouth, I walked into the Ionian Sea for a night swim.

The moon glowed magically. Warm water lapped softly against the rocky shore.

It was peaceful.

Calm.

I swam leisurely, like I would at the lake in Montana, like I would if I wasn't in a fight-or-flight state and was just having fun.

After the swim, I took a long, hot shower, scrubbing off four weeks' worth of dirt and grime as I hummed along to the radio. I used every bottle of soap, on all parts of my body. Nyx swayed with me.

Then I flipped my hair over and gave another revolutionary speech.

It was my best one yet.

When I finally crawled into the silky sheets, I pulled Nyx close to my chest. "I'm so grateful for every single day we get to spend together. You're my best friend," I whispered.

I wasn't going to let this place make me mean.

"Same, kid." Her tongue flicked across my cheek.

"Love you too, Emmy and Carl," I whispered into the dark as sleep gently pulled me under.

I dreamed of bloody eyes watching; a strange, obsessive mania; two voices whispering; skeletons.

The next morning was sunny and beautiful, so I pushed the nightmares aside.

I'm in control of my mind.

Am I?

No one was in the kitchen, so I shoved slices of meat and fruit into my mouth until my jaw hurt.

Then I found a notebook and pen in one of my bedside drawers and sat by the sea (still eating), working on the Riemann Hypothesis. It wasn't perfect, because I didn't have access to all my past calculations, but graphing numbers came easily.

It was peaceful.

For the first time in weeks, I felt alive.

The rest of the day was spent swimming in my toga (at this point, I was convinced the material had to be imbued with some type of magic). Lazily I did the breaststroke through glittering turquoise waters. It was sometime in early September, so the sea and sun were still pleasantly warm.

Life was different on the island.

The green foliage on the hill practically sparkled in the light.

Twigs snapped loudly. I squinted at the forest behind the house, and two men had long cameras pointing directly at me.

They were *close.*

I screamed and gathered Nyx around my neck, then ran back inside the house.

Spartan chasers.

"What is it now?" Patro asked as he slammed my bedroom door open with Achilles in tow.

They stared down at me with narrowed eyes.

Dripping wet from sprinting out of the sea, I said, "Two men are close to the house on the hill, taking pictures of m-me swimming."

"Unacceptable. We need to do something," Achilles signed to Patro angrily, scarlet eyes flashing. "We need to string them up by their intestines."

I flinched.

Achilles narrowed his eyes at me with suspicion, and I examined a very interesting fleck of dust on the ground.

Nope. I can't understand sign language at all, and you are definitely not a psychotic killer. Nothing to see here.

Patro shouted, "*Fuck*, how do they keep finding us? If this location is compromised, we'll have to move again. This is getting out of—"

"Did you just say they took pictures of you, Alexis?" Kharon asked as he stepped into the room from the hallway. His eyes were covered by thin sunglasses engraved with gold.

Apparently, the devil had spent the night, and also, he looked concerningly good in eyewear.

Humanity is doomed.

Kharon cracked his neck, tattoo rippling as he pinned me with his gaze. "Did they—take—pictures—of—you?" he asked slowly, his expression feral.

Suddenly I was worried about the health of the two cameramen.

I pursed my lips and shook my head no.

Kharon took a step closer.

Achilles pointed at me angrily at the same time Patro said, "She's lying."

I glared at my mentors.

Click. Kharon flicked off the safety on one of his guns. "WSDL" flashed on the barrel as he clipped in a cartridge. Then he rolled up his sleeves.

BOOM.

Smoke billowed in the hall, the faint scents of salt and rain lingering like the aftermath of a summer's storm.

He'd leaped away.

Patro sighed. "We might as well watch the show." He gestured to my deck, and the three of us walked over and squinted at the greenery behind the house.

Long minutes passed, and nothing happened.

"Maybe he couldn't find them?" I said hopefully.

Patro shook his head like I was an idiot. "Oh, he's gonna find them all right. It's Kharon. He's known as *the* Hunter for a reason."

"What makes Karen so special?" I muttered petulantly.

Patro arched his eyebrow. "I wouldn't call him that name to his face. He'll snap, and it won't be pretty."

Too late. Also, news flash, it already isn't.

"Why WSDL for your company?" I changed the subject and pointed between my two mentors. "Why choose *W* and *S* as your monikers?"

Patro tilted his head in confusion. "We didn't." He held up his tattooed knuckles, then pointed at Achilles's fading tattoo. "Death and lies—*DL*—those are the two letters that represent us."

The grates of the muzzle shifted as Achilles made an expression, and something told me it wasn't a smile of love and happiness. Crimson eyes shone with pride, like he was *proud* of being called death.

I shuffled discreetly away from Achilles.

He shifted closer.

Swallowing a nervous scream (hysteria was a lifestyle), I asked, “So what do *W* and *S* stand for?”

Is it War and Sex still, or something else? Stifling and Weird?

Patro never answered because gunshots echoed loudly.

Splash.

The two cameramen slammed into the sea a few yards away, like they’d been thrown. They sputtered and struggled to stand up in the shallow water.

Kharon stalked in after them.

“Who else,” he bellowed, “knows about this location?” He pointed the gun down at their heads with one hand. With his other, he pulled out the wicked dagger from his holster.

The Spartan chasers babbled and cried as they pleaded for their lives, splashing about frantically.

Kharon drove the knife into one of the men’s legs—an ear-piercing scream echoed—then leaned over and said something, too low for us to hear.

The screams got louder.

Foster Mother shrieking.

Rubbing at my wrists, I squeezed my eyes shut and breathed roughly through my nose.

Pop. Pop.

Silence.

They were dead.

Achilles clapped slowly.

Not the time.

“What did they say?” Patro asked.

“That they were alone exploring, and they got lucky,” Kharon answered calmly as he stalked through the water toward us. “They said their boat is parked on the other side of the island. I’ll find it and get rid of it.”

“I could have questioned them,” Patro said. “You know, without all the stabbing.”

Kharon grunted. "Where would be the fun in that?" He spoke casually like he was discussing the weather, not the two men he'd just *murdered* in cold blood for taking a picture of me.

All three men laughed.

I took a step back, trying to separate myself from the three killers.

Kharon stepped closer. His white shirt was covered in gore, and locks of dark hair fell messily in his eyes.

He saw me looking and smiled with teeth. Then he slowly licked the flat edge of his bloody dagger (*that can't be sanitary*). Glacial blue eyes flashed with mania.

"Oh yes," Nyx sighed dreamily on my neck. "He'd be a devoted lover."

She needed an exorcism.

Kharon took a step toward me again.

I took another step back.

"Scared, little girl?" He reholstered his weapons, powerful thighs flexing. "Or is our world too frightening for your delicate female sensibilities?" He laughed like he'd said something hilarious. "You don't have to pretend with me. I *know* what you are."

I shuddered with horror. *What do you do when a monster wrongly thinks you're also one?*

Patro chuckled loudly, and Achilles's eyes crinkled like he also found it funny.

I grabbed my wrist.

Neon-green lights flickering—the sputtering hum of electricity—an old metal roof—rope attached to a spike in the dirt.

A long moment passed.

The devil glanced down at where I cradled my hands protectively, and he clenched his sharp jaw.

Then he turned and stalked away, a slight limp in his gait.

Did he get injured?

BOOM.

Kharon disappeared in a billow of smoke, probably to go look for the dead men's boat or go on a murderous rampage for fun. You could never tell these days.

"Poppae, Nero," Patro called and pointed at the floating bodies. "Dinner."

The animals sprinted through the water.

I turned away and walked numbly back into the house, turned the shower up to scalding with shaking fingers, and sat under the spray. Tears leaked out of my eyes.

When my fingers were pruney and the memories no longer tore my psyche apart, I crawled back into bed.

I lay awake eating for hours as classical music played on the radio. Crickets and frogs sounded.

When the creaking noise started up again—this time, from outside—I looked around, heart racing with paranoia.

The lounge chair in the corner of my room was completely covered in shadows, even though moonlight lit the rest of the room. *Did it just move?*

The hair on the back of my neck stood up. Long seconds passed as I stared at it, unblinking.

Nothing happened.

You're losing it again. It's just furniture. Calm your thoughts.

The creaking noise got louder, and it was unmistakable. Something was out there.

Moving cautiously, so I didn't jostle Nyx, who was snoring beneath my pillow, I gave the corner a wide berth and tiptoed out the open deck door with a blanket wrapped around my shoulders.

Water lapped peacefully at the rocks, and the moon was a glowing silver crescent.

An orchestra played gently behind me.

A few windows down, on a deck similar to mine, figures moved in the night.

I squinted through the shadows.

One dark figure was seated in a chair, and the other was—on the ground? The chair rocked back and hit against the railing with a creak. That was the noise.

A low guttural moan echoed.

Heavy masculine pants blended with the smooth music.

My eye slowly adjusted to the low light. The man in the chair had a muzzle wrapped around his face, and his hands were buried in...wavy hair.

Achilles held Patro's face against his lap.

The son of Aphrodite was on his knees before the Son of War.

Hips jerked up off the chair, the creaking increased, and grunts became harder. Faster. There was a loud sucking noise.

Sweat streaked down my ribs.

The salty sea breeze filled my senses.

I shivered.

Achilles pulled Patro's head back harshly and jerked his hips up so his manhood was outlined in the shadows. Then he came.

Patro panted heavily. "Fuck," he whispered, his usually smooth voice raspy. Liquid dripped off his cheeks.

I waited for him to get angry.

To do something, for being treated so...disrespectfully.

"Fuck, I love you," Patro whispered, voice brimming with emotion. "So much." He licked his lips, then nuzzled his face into the larger man's lap.

Achilles stared down at him—chest heaving—and he cradled Patro's head like he was precious and played with his hair. He used the bottom of his shirt to wipe gently at Patro's face.

"I love you more," he signed slowly.

His actions were tender and delicate, a harsh contrast to his frantic thrusting.

There was something heartbreaking about the two of them. Something impossibly intimate.

Patro gazed up at Achilles with adoration.

The big man leaned over and rested his cheek against his forehead, like he wished he could give him a kiss.

"I love you so much," Patro repeated hoarsely, arms wrapping around the other man's waist.

Achilles nuzzled his head and played with his hair.

Quietly I tiptoed back into my room, chest heaving, stomach twisting, as I struggled to understand what I'd just seen.

I face-planted onto the bed with my arms spread wide.

Soft music washed over me in a gentle hum.

"Nyx, I think I get what you mean," I whispered into the covers. "About the violence being…romantic, and about the—devotion."

There was no response.

Nyx slept peacefully.

Little did I know that statement would come to haunt me.

In ways I couldn't even begin to fathom.

That night, I dreamed of a hand around my ankle, two skeletal monsters whispering to each other, and dark promises. In the background, Charlie was shivering in a cardboard box, begging me to come home.

I woke up sobbing.

17

THE MENAGERIE

ALEXIS

"Remember—do not approach an animal unless it approaches you," General Cleandro said as he led the seven of us that were left deeper under the mountain, down the winding rock stairs. "There are ancient beasts in the menagerie that *will* maul you if they feel threatened."

Thank God.

Approach all the animals until one puts me out of my misery—got it.

General Cleandro walked faster into the dark hall. "These are not your normal animals," he said ominously. "They are carefully bred predators with creature ancestry—but…just because they are distantly related to sentient beings…does not mean they have intelligence."

So the animals were stupid but powerful.

They sound like most Spartans.

The general picked up his pace like he was trying to lose

us in the cramped tunnel, which would have been funny if I wasn't one of the idiots trying to follow him.

"If an animal attacks you," he said ominously, "you have the right to defend yourself or exact vengeance, but no one else can interfere."

That's concerning.

It had been about a week and a half since I'd returned to the Spartan War Academy, and shockingly, my will to live was nonexistent.

Hours of lectures had melted my brain. Not being able to nap during breaks because I was tutoring Drex also didn't help.

The lack of food, water, fresh air, and basic human (Spartan?) rights was not ideal.

The fact that the only toilet was so rusty I'd scraped my butt cheek on it this morning was my final straw.

Yes, I'd had a moment back at Corfu where I'd decided to think positive thoughts and live better. Unfortunately, I was a quitter and had already given up.

I'd accepted the truth—*I am not meant to live well.*

Now I stumbled forward exhaustedly, teeth chattering, bare feet squelching as cuts opened on my raw soles.

Someone's stomach rumbled loudly, and a groan of despair echoed. Lately the other initiates had started complaining more and more that they were starving.

It was annoying.

Don't they know the more you talk about it, the worse it feels?

I shoved gnawing hunger out of my mind and concentrated on not tripping.

The narrow path had darkened, and it was almost pitch black. Stalactites hung low and dripped water from the rock ceiling.

Drex walked behind me and mumbled about how if the tunnel narrowed any more, we'd get stuck—*I'm praying for that.*

Anything was better than sitting through another one of Augustus's D and P lectures.

Apparently, clearing my mind until a sense of peace (from a nonexistent light source shining on the top of my head) settled over me was not one of my strong suits.

I guess I'm not perfect after all.

General Cleandro came to a sudden stop, and shoulders jostled as we ran into one another.

"Everyone be quiet," the general whispered harshly. "There is a beast that will maul you to death inside the menagerie if you make a loud noise."

Thank God.

He pushed open a heavy bronze door concealed in the rock wall of the corridor.

"You're on your own from here," he said. "Spartans with protectors are not allowed to enter. I'll open the door to let you out in three hours sharp. Good luck."

No one moved.

To be fair, only an idiot would voluntarily go inside.

"Move your sorry asses right now," the general whispered harshly. "Or you'll run the circuit until your dicks fall off."

I pursed my lips. So would that affect a vagina as well, or was it just a—

The general grabbed the front of my tunic, lifted me off the ground, and chucked me inside.

Does that mean I'm his favorite?

Ears ringing, I lay for a long moment on—grass that was... warm?

Bright light burned, leaves rustled, and birds chirped above.

With wide eyes, I sat up, mouth open.

I was lying on a path in a forest of flowering trees.

Far off in the distance, there were rolling green hills and a glittering blue lake.

There was a giant hole at the top of the mountain, and sunlight streamed through.

The nature was *inside* the mountain.

It was magical.

Birds with long purple tails and yellow puffs on their heads spiraled lazily above in the pleasant air. Red monkey-like creatures hooted at each other as they raced atop the pink-covered tree branches.

The lake sparkled, and elk-like creatures with strange horns grazed on its banks. A creature with tentacles and a beak slithered out of the water and disappeared into the tall grasses.

Initiates entered and wandered in all directions, heads tipped back and mouths open.

A paradise in the middle of hell.

Smiling, feeling like Eve, I ambled to my feet. There was a low hair-raising growl to my right.

I froze.

A sleek orange cheetah-esque creature with fangs as long as my forearm crouched low and growled, muscles bunched, ready to pounce.

I looked around—it was just the two of us.

"Good kitty," I whispered.

Dagger-like nails exploded from paws, and it hacked violently.

"Bad kitty?"

It snapped its wicked fangs three times, then turned and sprinted off into the forest.

"Wow," Nyx hissed on my neck. "That cat really hated you."

Jumping, I clutched my heart. "Or maybe she was growling at you."

"Please," Nyx scoffed like the idea was preposterous. "She gave me a nod of respect before she told you to get lost or she'd eat your spine."

"Wait—" I narrowed my eyes "—can you speak cheetah-thing?"

"No, I ad-libbed."

Rolling my eyes, I pulled at her. "Okay, well, she was probably threatened by your poisonous self, so get off me and slither around. Be free, birdy."

I tried to throw Nyx into the air, but she wrapped around my arm like a vise.

"Ow, that hurts." I yelped, grateful the rest of the initiates were off exploring so they wouldn't have to watch me fight my invisible frenemy.

"Well, it hurts my feelings that you were going to throw me into the air like a common pigeon," Nyx hissed as she refused to let go.

Grunting, I used my other hand to try to dislodge her from my forearm.

"Just meet me back here in a few hours," I suggested like a reasonable adult.

She tightened until my hand turned purple. I lay on my back and used both feet.

"Fine," she hissed and loosened her death grip. "You clearly don't respect me. I'm going to go maul a rabbit."

She slithered away, long grasses parting around her invisible body.

"Don't try to gaslight me," I whisper-yelled after her. "You treat me like a horse that you can ride whenever you want. Also, leave the nice bunnies alone."

"I bet that cheetah monster needs a friend," Nyx called back.

"You resemble an obese slug."

"Your hair is greasy and frizzy."

I gasped and clutched at my bushy ponytail. She did not go there. She knew they didn't let us shower.

With narrowed eyes, I pointed at the tree she'd headed toward. "Listen here, you—"

"Uh?" Drex asked. "Are you arguing with a tree?"

I whirled around and put my finger down.

"No?"

Drex grimaced. "I understand. This place can really make

you—" he rolled his finger next to his ear "—lose it." A miniature horse (with fangs) galloped by. "Talk later." He sprinted after it.

Sighing, I stomped off down the path, waiting for a cute, fluffy animal to come love me.

I wouldn't have minded a raccoon.

A big dog could also be cool.

A falcon (government surveillance drone) with glowing purple eyes and a long silver tail perched on the top of a tree and screeched down at me angrily.

Then it spread its wings, which were wider than I was tall, and flew away. *Robot design is really getting out of control.*

As I walked through the forest, all sorts of (alleged) birds bobbed their heads angrily, then took flight.

Apparently, I was the opposite of a princess—creatures absolutely loathed me.

Nice.

Not upsetting at all.

A deer with wings stood on the tree-lined path, eating berries off a bush. Pink eyes flashed, and it sprinted away in a blur. *Did it just do a double take?*

The bizarre behavior continued as I walked through the forest.

Whenever I came across another initiate hanging out with peaceful animals, those same animals saw me and panicked, sprinting in every direction to get away.

After an hour of being a pariah of Mother Nature, I collapsed onto the short grass at the edge of the lake.

I'd thought Nero and Poppae hated me because their owners did.

Now I wasn't so sure.

It felt like *I* was the reason.

Water splashed as an alligator (a T. rex?) with ten-foot spikes waddled out onto the bank, saw me, turned around, and swam away frantically.

Moisture burned my eyes.

Why are the animals acting like I'm some terrifying monster?

Apparently I was hard to love.

Purple bees buzzed, and neon-blue butterflies fluttered about.

"Do you want to be my protector?" I whispered pathetically at a chunky bee who could barely hold its round body aloft.

It gave up trying and spiraled to the ground.

Relatable.

A butterfly landed on the end of my nose, and a round beetle, with pretty pink markings and long pincers, settled on top of my hand.

At least the insects like me.

The beetle bit me. Hard.

Slapping a hand over my mouth, screams echoing, I sat up and looked around wildly, worried I'd triggered the monster the general had warned us about.

There was a beat of silence, then a hair-chilling growl.

My heart plummeted.

Great, Alexis, now you've done it. You're unlovable AND dead.

"Nyx," I whispered. "I'm sorry. You don't look like a slug, only when you eat and your belly gets all big. I love you and hope you live an amazing life."

The dangerous sound repeated closer, and the birds perched along the far riverbank took to the air.

I sat frozen.

Tall grasses rustled to my right, and I squinted.

Panic filled my throat.

A small white dog sat defenseless between the stalks, with its floppy ears perked up. *Run away, little guy, before the beast gets you.*

The tiny creature opened its mouth, flashing sharp fangs

much too big for its mouth, and let out a ferocious growl. *Never mind, you are the beast.*

I slumped with relief.

Its eyes narrowed, and it crouched low.

"Come here…you…thing?" I whisper-called, not wanting to upset the poor creature.

While the other animals in the menagerie wore their unique characteristics in a sleek, impressive way, this—dog?—looked like it had been through rough times.

Since I'd also been going through it recently, I tried not to judge.

Clumps of misshapen white fur protruded from its shoulders and butt, and its overgrown fangs jabbed the sides of its muzzle. Its paws looked ten sizes too large for its tiny body.

It looked almost like a husky puppy—if you squinted and ignored the jagged teeth, bulges of fur, glowing purple eyes, and terrifying growl.

"What's your name?" I whispered.

It snapped its misshapen fangs at the plants and shook violently.

"Good job killing that dandelion."

In a demonstration of pure hunting prowess, it pounced on another unsuspecting flower and bit savagely.

Fuzzy white seeds floated in a cloud.

I scooted forward with my hand out.

It took a step back and let out a low warning growl.

With my hands in the air to show I meant no harm, I lay back down.

Content that I wasn't a threat, the puppy resumed hunting (mutilating) the plant population.

Every few seconds, purple eyes looked in my direction, like it wanted to make sure I hadn't moved.

Long minutes passed, and it didn't leave my vicinity. At one point, it rolled onto its back. It was a boy puppy-thing.

"I'm gonna call you Fluffy Jr.," I told him.

Either he identified as something else, or he hated the name, because he walked closer and puked. The fact that it was mostly twigs seemed concerning.

Slowly I got to my feet.

Fluffy Jr. hunched low and snarled up at me, but the effect was ruined because his head didn't clear the grasses, or my ankles. I was 50 percent sure I could take him.

He wiggled his misshapen body and snapped at my feet (*okay, 49 percent*).

"What do you want me to do?" I asked and pointed at the mess of twigs he'd regurgitated. "You did this to yourself."

He hunched low.

I walked away.

"Ohmygod." I turned back as I entered the forest. "Are you hunting me?"

Fluffy Jr.'s ears flopped forward, and he stared at me without moving. Purple eyes glowed brightly.

He resumed growling.

"You're so smart and strong," I praised him, because everyone needs positive reinforcement, as I resumed walking (shuffling forward at a snail's pace because he kept stopping and getting distracted by leaves).

As I cut through the forest, most of the other initiates were spread out in the trees, whispering to animals.

Titus narrowed his eyes at me, but looked away when I raised my eyebrow. He'd been subdued ever since last week's library altercation.

If I'd known all it would take was kneeing him in the crace (crotch, then face), I would have done it ages ago.

"I think the birds really like me," Drex said when I came upon him sitting on an ivy-covered stump. A gold toucan with long silver talons sat on a branch above his head, singing a pretty song.

"What about you?" he asked.

"Oh." I pointed behind me, where Fluffy Jr. was trying (failing) to catch a butterfly. "This p-puppy is stalking me."

Drex did a double take. "Are you sure that's a puppy? What's wrong with its fur, and why is it so—lumpy?"

God forbid someone be built a *little* different during an apocalypse.

Everyone was a critic these days.

We lived in dark times.

"Don't hurt his feelings," I said. "He's just...unique."

The toucan stopped singing and started screeching, which felt like a metaphor for my life.

"I'll talk to you later," I whispered to Drex as I backed away slowly so I wouldn't ruin his bird (robot) bonding time.

Back near the door, the forest thinned, and there were no animals for me to disturb with my apparently terrifying presence.

Fluffy Jr. still followed me, this time with a twig in his mouth. (He was holding it by the end, and it seemed to be half down his throat, choking him?)

"Nyx?" I whispered. "Where are you? I take it all back."

"Do you want me to bite that thing and put it out of its misery?" she asked as she slithered up my body and settled like a scarf.

Grinning, I petted her warm scales. Being snubbed by the rest of the animal kingdom had given me a new level of affection for my best friend.

"No, don't bite him—that's Fluffy Jr.," I explained.

"Oh god, kid," she hissed. "You named it. Look at it—it's an abomination."

We both looked.

Fluffy Jr. gagged on the stick. Then he spat it out and started eating chunks of dirt. Aggressively.

It was hard to watch.

"His fur's just grown in a little weird." I winced. "But who am I to judge another's appearance? Apparently I have frizzy hair."

Nyx hissed, "Your issues can be solved. Nothing is fixing that thing."

"His name is Fluffy Jr." I rolled my eyes. "And he's a dog, a puppy—I think. Maybe?"

Nyx tightened around my neck. "If you bond with that thing…I will kill it."

"I'm not gonna bond with him," I mumbled and kicked a rock. "But all the other animals hate me."

"It's better to be alone than to have to look at that every day." Nyx shuddered.

"I think he's cute," I said petulantly.

"It's not." Nyx's tongue flicked my cheek, and she hissed, "Also, you probably just freaked the animals out with your depressive hormones. Try to think less about death—animals can sense it."

I had no counterpoint.

The bronze door flung open. "Time to go," General Cleandro called from the dark hall.

Distantly, past the lake, a spine-breaking roar echoed. Only an enormous creature could have made that sound.

Initiates sprinted past in a hurry to leave.

Fluffy Jr. whimpered.

My heart broke.

"Next time, I'll break you out of here," I promised. "Try to carry sticks in the middle until then." I picked up a stick and bit down to show him how to hold it properly, then threw it to him and sprinted for the door.

When I looked back, the twig hit him in the face, and he fell over.

Just before the door closed, he had it shoved halfway down his throat with the end poking out like a dagger.

I tried.

In a shocking turn of events (that absolutely no one saw coming), General Cleandro marched us back up to the gallows.

The hours of torture in the classroom continued.

I missed the butterflies.

Pine drew fractions on the board; Augustus guided us through a meditation; Pine rambled on about the ethics of graphs while he wrote out equations that were too long for the blackboard; Augustus told us in Latin about fearsome Cyclops creatures, who looked sentient but were dumb as rocks (he glared at me the entire time).

Is he insinuating I have the intelligence of a Cyclops?

Candle wax dripped. Smoke hung hazily on the low rock ceiling. Classical melodies played, and teeth chattered from the damp cold.

The world was nothing but shades of black, red, and gray.

Without windows, time didn't exist. Only misery did.

"Here are your tests," General Cleandro said an indeterminable amount of time later as he dropped packets of paper onto our laps.

The room shifted back into focus.

Boots scuffed against rocks, and Leo whimpered as the general kicked him. "Stop slouching. Sit up straight and take the fucking test."

A hawk screeched in warning.

Will the drones ever stop spying on us?

Pen fisted awkwardly in my hand, arm shaking, I started on the long Thagorean equation. It spanned multiple pages. One number at a time, I solved it.

The pattern, the repetition, was calming.

"PENS DOWN."

Another packet was placed on my lap. It took long minutes to switch my brain to Latin. Then I scratched out an essay about Cyclopes and their limited intelligence.

"TIME'S UP."

Maximum grunted in the front row as General Cleandro "accidentally" kicked him when he picked up his test.

When the general got to me, I flinched and waited.

He grunted, staring down at me with an unreadable expression as he picked up my test. Then he moved on to the back row.

Alessander, Titus, and Leo all got kicked—hard.

Thank you, God, for being so good to me. I see what you do. Praise be. Sadly, I was too exhausted to celebrate properly (feel anything).

"Everyone, please pay attention." Professor Augustus stood at the front of the class. He glanced at me with a fierce scowl, then looked pleasantly at the rest of the class.

What do they call reverse favoritism? Wait, isn't that bullying? Do they have HR around here? I need to report him.

Stylish black glasses perched on Augustus's nose and somehow contrasted with his scar, making him look *more* uncivilized.

"All of you," he said, "showed a decent aptitude for the material, so no one will be punished for their performance."

He paused.

"That being said, if you're consistently at the bottom, you need to study harder if you want to last till the spring. Here is your order: first, Alexis Hert. Second, Cassius Hermes. Third, Alessander Poseidon. Fourth, Drex Chen. Fifth, Maximum Hera. Sixth, Leo Apollo. Seven, Titus Dionysus."

The one time they decide to not off the person who scored last—there's no justice left in this cruel world.

Drex nudged me with his elbow and grinned. I tried to give him a thumbs-up, but I couldn't get my hands to cooperate, so I held up three bent, trembling fingers.

We both grimaced.

"You all have two hours to study, until nightfall," Augustus snapped, scowling at where Drex was touching me with his elbow.

"As you know," he continued, "as a reward for surviving this far, you get a taste of what Sparta has to offer. A symposium is held monthly at the Dolomites Coliseum. So we'll be attending tonight after your study session."

Didn't they say there would be food there? Bless up. Tears of relief filled my eyes as my empty stomach cramped painfully.

The room erupted in whispers of excitement.

"SILENCE," General Cleandro roared.

You could have heard a pin drop.

Augustus narrowed his dark eyes at me, then smiled at the rest of the room. "You will return to this academy by dawn tomorrow morning. Then you only have one more day of class before you see your mentors."

Shoulders slumped.

"But if you don't make it back by dawn," Augustus warned, "then you'll be a presumed defector, and I've been ordered to personally hunt you down and eliminate you."

Well, that escalated quickly.

Also—tempting.

Should I take the second option?

"All right. Good work, everyone." He clapped his hands. "Go study."

Groaning, bones creaking and joints popping, the seven of us slowly ambled to our feet.

Gravity was a cruel mistress.

General Cleandro left the room, muttering something about using the shitter. I wasn't exactly sure, and frankly, I didn't want to know.

"Alexis—stay back in the classroom," Augustus called, smile slipping off his face. "I'd like to have a word with you."

I closed my eyes and swallowed a scream of frustration. The warmth of the library was so close.

Great, he's going to kill me.

"Yes, P-Professor," I whispered, face warming with embarrassment as the other initiates left and I walked over to the blackboard. Something about stuttering in front of Augustus made me feel like the biggest fool.

Poco chittered, perched on his shoulder, an obese floof of gray and black. *I hope Fluffy Jr. is doing okay.*

I stared at the raccoon as I waited for Augustus to speak, too much of a coward to make eye contact.

"Look at me," he ordered, smooth voice deepening into a snarl.

My head snapped up.

Soulless black eyes narrowed threateningly and held my gaze. The scar across his cheek was an angry shade of red.

I struggled to breathe under his intense scrutiny.

The scent of ozone and electricity filled the air, sharp enough to sting but warm enough to be slightly intoxicating.

He smelled like a lightning storm.

Long seconds passed as I waited for him to speak, and there was a strange tension between us.

It felt…*violent.*

"Zeus has requested to meet you before the symposium," he finally said, voice full of accusation, like I'd gone behind his back.

Silence stretched, heavy and oppressive.

"Okay?"

Augustus inhaled deeply. "As I'm sure you know, women are usually forbidden from attending symposia."

Why does everyone assume I know things?

"However." His black eyes flashed. "The federation has voted to make an exception for you. Because you're an abandoned mutt already participating in the crucible, they do not believe there is any honor to be lost."

Judging from his scoff, he did not agree with their assessment.

Personally, I got where they were coming from. *Never been honorable a day in my life.*

Augustus shook his head sharply. "But you don't have to attend if you don't feel comfortable. It really is not the place for a young woman like yourself. Especially since Kharon has told me about you. On my honor as a Chthonic heir, I can't allow it. I'll inform Zeus to meet you here at the academy and—"

"No, I'll go," I said, cutting him off with a casual (very tense) shrug. *There's food there. I will be present and accounted for. Count me in.* "It sounds—delicious."

Augustus went unnaturally still.

"Excuse me?" he asked softly.

"I'll go," I repeated as my empty stomach growled loudly. "It's fine." *Did he not hear me?*

He lunged forward, posture contorting with fury, face twisting, hands fisting.

I reeled back.

Never mind, it wasn't fine.

Professor Augustus loomed above me, radiating vitriol, like he was ready to commit murder.

Of all the times for Nyx to be asleep, I needed her help now. I'd missed something crucial in the conversation.

Oh my god, he's actually going to kill me.

He took another step forward.

I inched back toward the blackboard.

The scent of electricity increased a hundredfold, like lightning had struck where he stood.

Poco hissed, picking up on the energy.

Augustus abruptly stopped moving and ground his teeth together, then he cracked his neck back and forth like he was getting ready for battle.

The movement made his long ponytail sway, and the two-toned hair shone beneath his crown like silk in the candlelight.

"The symposium," he said, voice menacingly low, "is not the place for a sheltered girl who grew up in the softhearted human world. Our world is...dangerous, especially for someone like you. You should rethink your choices if you know what's good for you. It's my duty to protect you."

What does he mean, someone like me? Is it because everyone thinks I'm Zeus's daughter?

Phantom pains shot down my wrists, and I rubbed at the scars.

An ember of rage smoldered in my sternum as "sheltered" repeated mockingly in my head.

You know nothing of what it takes to survive the human world.

"No offense, Professor," I whispered as I held his burning gaze, tired of being pushed around by everyone. "But I know what's good for me. I don't need your help."

Pride filled my chest.

I'd finally done it; I'd talked back.

Augustus clenched his square jaw, the vein in his forehead jumping. That was the only warning I got.

Blood covered the whites of his eyes.

Heaviness slammed against my mind like a battering ram, and acute pain throbbed at the front of my skull.

The pounding sensation intensified, like someone was hammering behind my eyes.

There was blinding pressure.

The world was on fire.

His lips didn't move, but a distorted masculine voice boomed through my skull. *You don't want to go to the symposium.* Pressure and flames tore through my mind, razing all thoughts. *You will not go,* it ordered.

The voice was right.

I didn't want to go.

The burning pain ratcheted up into an inferno, the order repeating on loop, tearing apart my mind and my will.

Wait—no.

Terror sparked hotter, and I mentally pushed with everything I had, shoving at the intruder.

The pressure in my skull suddenly disappeared.

Staggering, blind, head aching, I slammed back against the board and barely held myself upright.

When my vision finally refocused, I was bent over with my hands on my knees, covered in sweat.

Shakily, I rubbed away the moisture beneath my eyes. My fingers came back stained red—I was crying blood.

It was also trickling out of my nose and ears.

Looking up at Augustus with horror, I slid away along the blackboard toward the door.

His expression was harsh and unrelenting. Unmerciful. Like he didn't regret it. Like he wanted to do it again. Like he wanted to hurt me. Break me. Destroy me. Torture me.

I averted my gaze.

He tried to crack my mind. He tried to...change my thoughts. He tried to force me not to go.

His power was so much worse than I could have ever imagined.

He didn't read minds—he broke them.

Teeth chattering, arms wrapped around my torso, I backed away from the Chthonic monster that had violated my thoughts.

"Can I go, Professor?" I whispered to the floor. I was never going to look him in the eyes ever again.

"No," he said silkily.

Pain throbbed in my temples, and I wanted to scream at the injustice of it all. In three strides he'd crossed the room and loomed over me.

Electricity filled my nose.

His hot breath fluttered against my ear, and I whimpered at his proximity.

"Your scores in Lost Classical Lore are unacceptable." His voice was deceptively soft. "Your analyses are surface-level and argumentative. Your grammar is abysmal, and you write in run-on sentences."

I swallowed thickly.

Numbers had always made sense, words less so.

He leaned closer. "Your work product is…infuriating."

His words were saying one thing, but his body language was saying something else. Once again, there was a conversation happening that I was missing.

Why are Chthonics so freakin' cryptic and confusing?

Rage, violence, and a tangle of sharp emotions too intense to name rolled off Augustus. He was backing me into a corner, a predator playing with its food.

He just violated my mind, and now he's threatening me. I didn't know if I wanted to sob or scream.

"Is that a-all, P-Professor?" I breathed out, barely able to speak.

"For now," he said, but he didn't move, like he knew how much standing in his presence was getting under my skin. "You're dismissed."

I stumbled blindly toward the door, refusing to give the monster my back.

"Oh—and one more thing," he called as I stepped across the threshold, so close to freedom.

He was toying with me.

I whimpered.

"Your Thagorean scores will only carry you for so long. I don't give a fuck that you're a math prodigy." He chuckled cruelly. "You are a woman in a man's world. It's a dishonor on all of us for allowing this to continue. Make smarter choices, or…there will be consequences, Alexis." My name fell from his lips like it was the wickedest of sins. "You're not proving what you think you are for women—you're just screwing yourself."

I don't think I'm proving anything. I'm just trying to survive.

"If you can't take care of yourself," he said softly, "someone else might step in to do it for you. You've been warned."

Blood-covered eyes glowed in my peripheral vision.

I stared at the floor, gasping.

What the heck is happening right now? What does he mean about stepping in?

He was trying to scare me away—right? It didn't feel like that was happening. It felt like I was missing something.

Something big.

It's that he doesn't hate you; he absolutely despises everything about your existence.

I didn't look back as I ran into the library. Collapsing behind the stacks, hand on my frantically racing heart, I struggled to inhale.

It was official.

I was never speaking again.

A muse pushing a cart full of books stopped to give me an odd look, but then she averted her gaze and disappeared.

No one was going to help me.

Not here.

Not in Sparta.

I gripped the lopsided tattoo on my forearm and whimpered. I missed Charlie so freaking much that it hurt to breathe.

It hurt to live.

Gasps turned into manic laughter. Then brutal sobs wracked my chest as I clawed at my wrists, tears dripping red. My ears and nose leaked. A high-pitched ringing burned unmercifully.

There was nothing left of me to ruin, neither body nor mind.

The hairs on the back of my neck prickled, and two voices whispered, but I didn't bother to look up.

I knew nothing was there.

It was all in my head.

I'd lost control.

Of everything.

18
THE SYMPOSIUM

ALEXIS

I dragged my feet over the rolling hills, a wraith of a woman, more dead than alive. Nyx was coiled asleep around my waist.

As a group, we headed toward the spires of the Dolomites Coliseum.

Lights glowed in three of the top arches—the symposium had already started.

The full moon cast strange shadows, and I shivered miserably at the biting autumn breeze.

Augustus (Evil Incarnate) led at the front—he'd changed out of his toga, into a perfectly tailored black suit with ruby cuff links—and the seven of us followed him.

Titus, Leo, and Alessander whispered excitedly. Even stoic Cassius had a bounce to his step.

I hung back, shuffling wearily, as far away from Augustus as possible.

Blood trickled out of my nose, and I wiped it away furiously.

Drex looked back at me with a concerned expression, and I waved him off with a forced smile.

As we trudged through the dark landscape, the hairs on the back of my neck prickled like I was being watched.

I rubbed at my wrists, left ear ringing.

I'm losing my mind.

By the time we crossed the fields and reached the coliseum, I was numb.

Vision blurring, I trudged up the ancient spiral staircase toward the top floor.

When we finally entered the symposium, I faltered.

My mind had been violated over comfy lounge chairs, a sleek bar top, roaring hearths, card games, and drinks.

Wood Corinthian columns, covered in gold foil at the top, were spaced out in a perimeter around the room.

Everyone was in business casual.

We were underdressed.

This is why he attacked me? This mundane-looking club.

I would have laughed, but it wasn't funny.

Augustus walked in and greeted my mentors. Patro and Achilles laughed and smiled when they saw him (I assumed from how Achilles's eyes crinkled that he was smiling).

Why is Augustus a nice guy to everyone but me?

When Patro saw me looking, he leaned forward and arched a mocking brow at me.

I stared back blankly.

When Augustus sat down, his suit jacket parted. His torso was covered in guns. *He's just pretending to be a professor. Remember, he's in the Assembly of Death. He's the oldest Chthonic heir. Don't forget who he really is.*

The reminder was chilling.

Poco climbed under the table and disappeared. Fangs flashed in the shadows at the three men's feet.

Laughter boomed as they picked at a spread of cheeses, fish, and fruits.

Just Chthonics enjoying the disturbing ambiance of one another's company.

Drex said something and followed the rest of the initiates to a table near Augustus. I went in the opposite direction.

Stumbling, I pushed past men speaking Latin with birds perched on their shoulders. Their eyes widened as they realized I was a girl, but none of them tried to stop me as I cut across the room.

An empty booth was hidden in the corner, covered in food.

Perfect.

Sinking as low as possible into the leather, I scooted until I was completely swathed in shadows and stared, unseeing, at the monotony that had spelled my demise. Nyx moved in her sleep, and I clung to her.

Augustus's booth erupted yet again with rowdy laughter. I shifted so they were in my blind spot.

My cheeks flushed from the heated temperatures. My fingers and soul tingled as they slowly thawed.

You're still alive. It's okay. You're going to survive this hellscape, get back to Charlie, and never see Augustus ever again.

Dark woods, rich leathers, and warm colors filled the room.

Whiskey and cigars filled my senses.

This is what Augustus called dangerous? He wouldn't last a second in the trailer park.

In one corner, an average bartender served drinks to extraordinary men.

Across the room, a freshly polished grand piano gleamed in the firelight. A figure, hidden behind a column, set up sheets of music, then started to play a mellow melody.

Men held their drinks up and bowed their heads to the pianist. Then they clinked their glasses together and threw the contents back.

Dice were thrown.

Cards were played.

An heir tossed his head back as he laughed, laurel crown gleaming.

Turning away from the joyous scene, I picked at the platter of food, eyes closing with each savory bite as I tried to commit the flavors to memory.

Time passed. I lost myself in the luxury of food and music as I tried to forget about Augustus's glowing crimson eyes.

My mind is my own. I shoved him out. He didn't win. He won't. I will survive.

I hummed softly in the back of my throat, and my eyes fluttered as I fought off sleep.

"Here she is, sir," someone sneered.

Theros—Drex's mentor and heir to the House of Zeus, also part-time egomaniac who could create a shield—gestured, with a golden vulture on his shoulder, from me to a Goliath of a man.

Then Theros bowed his head deeply, shot me a withering glare, and moved a discreet distance away.

"I've been looking for you," the Goliath said, voice dripping with accusation. An oversize laurel crown glittered with jewels atop his head.

He was the only House leader at the symposium. From what I could tell, everyone else was heirs and mutts.

Sighing, I sat up and pulled my elbows off the table. So focused on eating, I'd forgotten about Augustus's original message.

Electricity sparked as storm-gray eyes sized me up.

Zeus towered above me, firelight illuminating his famous features. A golden lion stood beside him with matching eyes.

I sank back into the shadows.

Without invitation, Zeus sat down in the booth, and I scrambled away so we were across from each other.

The lion bared its teeth threateningly and took a step back.

I made a face at it. *Get in line—the cheetah hated me first.* Its eyes narrowed as it slowly settled down onto its belly.

"So," Zeus said without preamble, "you grew up in the human world?"

"Yep, I d-did."

His eyes narrowed, brow furrowing. "Have you always had that stutter?"

There'd been a time—a hazy memory of peace—when words fell easily from my mouth, smooth and unbothered, but that was before the beatings had started. Long before I'd become who I was.

That time didn't count.

"Yes."

"Can you control it at all? Or do you always have it?" he asked judgmentally.

"I always have it."

"Have you taken speech therapy, or worked on yourself?"

I ground my teeth together. "Nope."

Funnily enough, speech therapy wasn't an option for a poor orphan in the protected zones. Neither was food. Or shelter.

Zeus frowned. "Interesting."

Is it really?

Awkward silence spread between us.

He grimaced and looked at something over my shoulder, unable to hold my gaze.

It was so darn predictable—my own blood found me lacking.

Father John said the only father that mattered was God. Charlie said we were better off without our birth parents, and he would have already signed at Zeus to get lost (with a lot more creative language).

I snickered at the thought.

Zeus's frown deepened. Lines creased golden skin, which shone a lighter shade of mine.

I ate the last piece of meat off the plate before he could take it.

Gray eyes sharpened. "Are you eating enough? Why are you so skinny? My stock are usually built strong and wide, not so—"

"Tall?" I offered as he said, "Wimpy."

I choked on the food.

The man before me had never hidden food vouchers in a cardboard box while counting down the days until he could eat, and it showed.

He raised a golden brow. "Why are you like this?" His nose wrinkled with disgust.

He waited for an answer.

Oh, it's not a rhetorical question? Rude.

"No clue," I lied, dragging the cheese knife across the plate so I could get the leftover bits.

Phantom pain shot in my wrists. Old cigarette burns ached on my torso.

Zeus's lips pursed as he watched the knife scrape loudly.

I sucked on it and glared.

He took one long-suffering breath, then pulled at his diamond cuff links and sat up straighter.

"You'll need etiquette lessons after the crucible," he said.

He spoke like it was a foregone conclusion, my survival and my need to learn the rules of high society.

I grunted eloquently.

"However, I'm *not* surprised about your test scores," Zeus said, either unaware of my body language or uncaring. "The House of Zeus is known as one of the brightest Houses for a reason. That a…mutt like you could score so high is a further testament to our genius. You should be proud."

Our genius? When did this become a group project?

Zeus smiled widely, eyes glinting with excitement. "All of Sparta is talking about the first female mutt in centuries, who beats the other initiates—with her fists and her scores."

My knife clattered.

I do what?

Golden curls shook as Zeus puffed up his chest. "Keep this up and there will most certainly be a place for you in our House. Who knows—" he grinned "—I might just train you alongside my heir."

He must be really desperate for children.

In my peripheral vision, Theros whipped his head around, posture straightening, mouth opening with indignation. His golden vulture glared.

"Maybe," I said, neutrally. "Or maybe n-not," I muttered under my breath.

The man across from me was a stranger.

He couldn't even look at me, let alone *see* me.

"Good." Zeus clapped his hands and stood up.

His lion followed suit, growling.

"Bad kitty," I whispered.

It snapped at the air.

I rolled my eyes. I'd always been more of a dog person anyway.

"It's interesting. You have my eye for sure," Zeus said as he tapped his knuckles on the tabletop to get my attention. "But I don't remember a woman with heterochromia…or eyes so—black." He tapped below his right eye.

Flickering green lights—broken glass—repeated blows to the face.

I rubbed at my wrists. "How strange."

"It is," Zeus agreed without inflection. "Keep up the good work. I recommend the soup—you can never go wrong with a good soup, if ya know what I mean." He winked and chortled.

I squinted with confusion. *How is soup funny?*

He walked away, his lion trailing, head turned back with its hackles raised. Theros ran up to his side and spoke frantically, waving his hands. They were built wide, with heavy muscle mass, but I was taller than both of them.

Men bowed low as Zeus passed. The room focused on him.

A god among gods.

I wrapped a hand around my bicep, grimaced as my fingers touched. Hair ties covered bony wrists. "C+A" stood out stark and squiggly against my dirt-streaked forearm.

It was strange; I'd never worried about what I looked like before. I'd been too concerned with making sure Charlie and I didn't starve to death.

For the first time, I felt…ugly.

Inadequate.

"Fuck that douche," Nyx said, her tongue flickering across my cheek. "He has his own head so far up his ass he can't see greatness when it's staring at him."

I laughed wetly, wiping my eyes, knowing she had to say that as my best friend.

My fingers came back pink.

"I hate this place," I whispered. "I wish I was just a stupid human living in a cardboard box. It was easier back then."

Nyx nuzzled her head against the side of my face. "If it makes you feel any better, kid, I also wish we were back in the forest."

Sighing, I rubbed my finger through the berry juice left on the plate and sucked on it.

"Screw these men," I whispered.

"Yeah," Nyx said enthusiastically. "Fuck them. Give me the signal and I'll bite all of them into comas. It will be my pleasure."

I laughed, and for the first time all night, I felt like I could breathe.

"You're not allowed to fall asleep ever again," I whispered to Nyx. "Things got rough out here."

"No." She gasped. "What happened? Give me all the tea."

Grinning despite it all, I retold the tale of Augustus butchering my mind like it was exciting and not deeply traumatic.

Nyx oohed and aahed appropriately.

Then she told me the mysterious Montana plague (which became a national news story on the radio and hit the trailer park when I was eleven) was really her biting all the neighbors who were mean to me. I prayed she was joking, but I feared she wasn't.

Still, I laughed (panic-cackled) along with her, because that was what friends did.

The room buzzed with conversation.

Drinks flowed.

The piano music was bright and airy.

And then, just when the despair had leached away, the fireplaces went out in a dramatic whoosh.

The room was dead silent.

Darkness reigned.

Low lights flicked on. Embedded in the floorboards, they cast everything in shades of crimson. Men smiled and leaned back in their chairs with anticipation.

A hauntingly seductive melody began to play.

Then…

They came out.

The sirens.

Beautiful men and women sauntered into the room, clothed only in their shimmering naked skin. More breathtaking than the supermodels in vintage magazines.

Even in the muted light, their hair sparkled like diamonds.

Pastel eyes dazzled in shades of colors I'd never dreamed could exist.

Their faces had symmetry beyond compare, and their bodies were sculpted curves that only a master artist could imagine.

Each siren who sauntered out from the back room was somehow more perfectly unique than the last.

Dozens of the ethereal creatures spilled into the room.

Spartans leaned toward the sirens, eyes greedily tracking as they spun sensually around the space.

They were thoroughly enraptured.

Hypnotized with lust.

Nyx slid around my neck to get a better view, and I stroked her warm scales.

A laugh bubbled in my throat.

The irony was undeniable: I was literally falling apart while angels spun around me.

Oh, to be a siren, dancing in a symposium in front of adoring Spartan men.

Some moments punched the breath from your lungs and dragged you through the mud, reminding you why life sucked. Other moments stole your air in a glittering swirl and reminded you why life was magical.

This was the latter.

It was art.

And then—it wasn't.

A Spartan wrapped his arm around a female siren's waist and pulled her to his lap. His tongue dragged across her throat, and she tipped her head back with a grin, expression changing to ecstasy as he licked across her nipples.

I blinked in shock.

A different Spartan fell out of his chair, knees hitting the ground and expensive suit jacket pulling tight as he crawled across the floor to a male siren with his mouth wide open, and he… *Oh wow.*

The energy shifted.

As if a switch had been flipped, the sirens and Spartans collided in carnal abandon.

I sank lower into my booth, grateful for the darkness.

Face flushing.

Across the room, in dim red light, a siren male and female crawled over the laps of my fellow initiates. The boys hastily pulled off their togas as the two creatures licked and sucked at their exposed skin.

I quickly looked away.

Mental note—buy bleach and drink it. Also, never look Maximum in the eye ever again.

A Spartan pulled off his pants a few feet away from me (*help*), then pressed himself against a female siren, who shivered with delight and opened her legs.

A male siren joined, and the amorous trio fell onto the floor in a tangle of thrusts and limbs.

Averting my gaze from the aggressive copulation occurring at my feet (that could not be sanitary), I accidentally looked over at where my mentors sat—Patro and Achilles were in the booth, but Augustus had disappeared somewhere.

He's probably naked with a group of sirens right now. I fought the irrational urge to look around for him.

In contrast, my mentors were the only Spartans I'd seen who were completely ignoring the sirens.

Maybe romance isn't dead?

Achilles looked up—vermilion eyes locked with mine—and Patro turned his head to see what Achilles was staring at.

My heart skipped a beat.

Patro smirked. Then he turned back around and dragged his tongue possessively across Achilles's throat. He licked at the edge of where skin met muzzle.

I blushed and looked down.

When I glanced back, they were both laughing at me.

Patro blew me a mocking kiss, then winked and lowered his head to Achilles's lap. My blush became a full-body flush, and this time, I kept my eyes averted.

The problem was, there was nowhere safe to look.

A sea of naked bodies engaged in obscenities.

Everyone was *jiggling* in ways I never could have imagined.

"Look away, kid." Nyx coiled around my head, covering my eyes. "You're too innocent for this."

I tugged her back down to my neck.

"Oh, please," I whispered. "I'm gonna be twenty soon."

Nyx shuddered. "Kid—you keep flinching every time you see a penis."

"Well," I said. "Have you seen them? They're horrifying."

"I'm looking at one right now," Nyx hissed. "Unfortunately."

We both recoiled as a Spartan in a laurel-wreath crown walked butt naked by our table, family jewels swinging.

We need to bring back people having shame.

"Is it supposed to curve to the left like that?" I whispered.

Nyx made a choking noise. "I don't know. Do I look like a penis expert to you?"

We both grumbled, overwhelmed by the sheer imagery of the room. I racked my (traumatized) brain for a safe conversation topic.

"What are those people doing?" I asked as I pointed at where male and female sirens, as well as a few Spartans, were crawling naked across the top of the piano.

"I think they're—trying to seduce the musician," Nyx said. "And failing."

We both gaped.

The pianist was still mostly hidden behind the thick column next to his bench. He was nothing but a flash of wide shoulders and a dark suit.

Whatever he looked like, he had the room going *feral*.

A Spartan crawled beneath the piano and was kicked away. A female siren sidled up next to the bench and was shoved off. A male siren lay exposed on the piano top (points for creativity) and was ignored.

"The pianist is probably just one of those asexuals," Nyx said. "Like spiders."

I pursed my lips and narrowed my eyes. "Do you mean—*arachnids*?"

"Exactly," she hissed.

Overall, I would not classify us as doing well.

"I think this is rock-bottom," I whispered.

The trio on the floor stood up, naked bits on full display, and then began aggressively doing *it* against a wooden pillar less than a foot away.

"I agree," Nyx said. "This is a new low."

A manic chuckle burst from my lips.

The female siren pulled away from her two lovers and pointed at me.

"I think she's laughing at us," she said to the male siren, who nodded before falling back to the floor with the male.

"We were just talking about..." *Damn you, Nyx, for being invisible.* I looked even more crazy than I was.

"Uh, sorry." I held up both my hands like I was at gunpoint. "I wasn't laughing at you, just the s-situation in general."

I pointed at a Spartan's penis as he walked past, just so there were no doubts what the situation was.

"Oh," the female siren said. "No worries, honey."

"Oh, I'm not worried." I waved my hand dismissively as the two men moaned loudly at her feet.

I've never been more worried.

She smiled and opened her mouth. Then her eyes widened, and she froze. Long seconds passed, and she didn't move.

I looked around awkwardly.

Before I could find out why she was freaking out, she lunged forward and grabbed my face.

Stranger danger. Stranger danger. Someone who is not *naked, please help.*

Pastel eyes stared deeply into mine, and her fingers trembled where they cupped my cheeks.

Wait—are we falling in love?

"You can...understand what I'm saying?" she whispered in awe.

Never mind.

"Uh, yeah? Can you understand me?" I asked as I tried to tug out of her grasp.

She pulled me closer.

"You're a Spartan?" she asked.

"Y-yeah." I tugged harder, neck straining. She held me immobile. *How strong is this woman?*

She flung her head back, long, silky hair sparkling, and then—she burst into tears. "I've—" gasp "—always —" gasp "—wanted to be able to—" gasp "—talk to someone in Sparta." Falling onto my lap, she convulsed with sobs (still very naked).

I didn't do it.

I patted her back awkwardly. "Let it out, s-sister."

She cried harder.

In my defense, it was my first time dealing with a randomly sobbing woman. I'd never had a sister.

"Uh—Alexis," Nyx said. "When did you learn to speak siren?"

"I don't speak siren," I said in a *duh* tone, grimacing as three sirens and two Spartans started having (aggressive) sex in the booth across from us.

Nyx tightened around my neck like she was reeling back. "Then how the heck are you *speaking to a siren right now*?"

My hand stilled as I stared down at the crying woman languishing naked on my lap.

"I can speak siren?" I asked.

Oh my god. Augustus said they only speak one unique language. It was why they were subjugated by Spartans.

"And you can speak to me..." Nyx said slowly. "Do you know what this means, kid?"

I narrowed my eyes. "I'm trilingual?"

Nyx hissed, fangs snapping the air. "It means you've found your power—you can talk to sentient creatures."

"But my brain doesn't feel...euphoric?" I pursed my lips. "Like it's supposed to."

To be fair, there was still blood seeping out of it, so that might not be helping.

Also, if I had to classify my mental state, it would be—depressed, with a smidge (immense amount) of anxiety.

"You're probably just a little messed up in the head." Nyx sighed heavily. "Honestly—I always thought it was weird that you could talk to me."

I reeled back. "And you didn't say anything?"

Nyx tightened around my neck. "Well, I'm saying something now."

"Nine years later," I said indignantly.

The table shook from the force of the thrusts occurring in the adjacent booth, and the siren sobbed harder on my lap.

I grimaced as I patted her head.

This is getting weird.

"Uh—madam, do you need anything?" I asked the siren. "Water, a shirt? Pants?"

Watery pastel eyes peered up at me. "I'm good. Thank you for caring about me. You're so gracious and beautiful."

I made a face.

"What is she saying to you?" Nyx asked curiously.

"That I'm—gracious, and beautiful?"

"Hmm," Nyx said skeptically. "Are you sure you can understand her?"

I slapped at her, but she dodged. "I'm pretty sure," I said. "I know when someone is telling me I'm beautiful—it doesn't happen often."

"Is this a cry for help?" Nyx asked. "Are you not coping well?"

I didn't respond.

A smile split my cheeks wide.

This was really happening.

Laughter exploded from my lips.

I'm not powerless.

Tears of happiness streamed down my face.

I will never be powerless ever again. I know what I am.

Happiness shimmered inside my soul, and I hugged Nyx tight, kissing her invisible head as she struggled.

This was just the beginning.

"Want to play a game?" the siren asked as she abruptly lifted off my lap, still crying as she spoke, which was very relatable.

I opened my mouth to say no, then remembered I had nothing to lose. I was here, and I was powerful.

"Sure," I said, and we grinned at each other. "I'll play."

The pianist missed a key.

19
THE DEVIL YOU DON'T KNOW

ALEXIS

"I can't believe you grew up with humans," said Lena, the siren who'd cried naked in my lap but now sat on my right side at the end of the circular booth.

Her words sounded normal to me, but Nyx said they sounded like inarticulate rasps.

Apparently, when I spoke, I was also rasping, which was bizarre because it didn't feel any different from my usual speech.

It suddenly made sense why everyone always gave me weird looks when I talked to Nyx.

I couldn't even imagine how strange Nyx's language sounded to others.

No wonder everyone in high school thought I was a freak.

"Your childhood must have been wild," Lena said, leaning into me.

I coughed awkwardly.

Oh yeah, starvation, abusive parents, and homelessness. So wild.

The siren was still butt-crack naked (free the nips and lips) and was now stacking a pile of knives in the middle of the table, which were apparently part of a card game? I was too scared to ask.

Seductive piano music played.

On my left, seven other sirens were crammed into the booth with us. Yes, all of them were naked.

"The human world really must have been so cool." Lena wiggled her eyebrows suggestively, her beauty shining in the darkness.

"Yeah," I whispered. "It was—interesting." Phantom pain shot down my wrists. "You know, because of the Titans, and the f-fall of civilization."

She shrugged like that part didn't matter.

"Are all humans really sexually repressed prudes?" she asked.

Oron, who was the only male siren at the table, leaned over me—since he sat on my left—and high-fived Lena. "That's a good question." He winked at me.

I grimaced back.

His thigh pressed flush against mine (*do not look down, Alexis—don't do it*).

"Stop glancing at his engorged penis," Nyx hissed, and she tightened around my throat.

If she says "engorged" ever again, I will kill us both. No questions asked.

My cheeks flushed because apparently, I was a pervert.

It didn't help that around the room, sirens and Spartans were still coupled and moaning. Hips thrust. Skin slapped. If anything, the fervor had gotten more aggressive.

Naked sirens and Spartans were still clamoring around the piano, now performing lewd acts.

Lena saw where I was looking.

"Now, that is a *real* man," she whispered as she nodded to the pianist. "Every siren knows what happens if you have the honor of touching him. He's a legend in our community. His powers are…toe-curlingly delicious." She sighed dreamily. "If you know what I mean."

Nope.

I had no clue what she meant.

Maybe sirens are just really into music?

Lena snapped her fingers to get my attention. "Back to the main question, Alexis—are all humans prudes?"

"No," I said as I tried to ignore (watch) the unholy acts occurring near the piano bench. "Some humans are closed-minded, but a lot are very open—sexually."

Too sexual.

People had forgotten that Tim-Tom announced in homeroom he could pick up a ruler with his ass and then spent ten minutes trying to give a demonstration.

Sadly, I couldn't forget.

However, Lena didn't look convinced by my answer as she dealt cards to everyone at the table.

"Are you sure?" she asked. "I've heard humans are afraid to have sex with all different types of people. It scares them."

I shook my head. "That's not true."

A part of me was surprised that I was talking so freely to them. This was the most I'd conversed with anyone. *Weird.*

"So, how many men have you had sex with?" a siren asked from the end of the booth, large breasts jiggling as she jumped up and down with excitement.

"Oooooooh." The sirens clapped eagerly. "Another good question," someone said.

Laughing (whimpering), I waved my hand dismissively.

The siren winked, her hair glittering. "I see…you lost count. I respect that *so* much."

I pursed my lips. "Not—exactly."

Lena wiggled her brows again. "At least tell us how many women you've been with?"

I winced and shook my head.

"Creatures? Spartans? Centaurs?" Lena asked, eyes narrowing like she was studying a bizarre creature.

"Wait, centaurs are real?" I asked. "So, do they have horse heads or h-horse bodies?"

Many debates on the subject had been held in the high school halls. Tim-Tom was team horse head.

"Obviously a horse head." Lena rolled her eyes, like she hadn't just blown my mind. "Now answer the question, woman. How many people have you had sex with? Anyone counts. Please, mother of spirits, tell us."

"Wait." I blinked, unable to let it go. "So, centaurs have a *human* body...with a *horse* head?"

This was life-changing information.

Lena slammed both her hands on the table, scattering cards. "Alexis," she warned. "Answer the question."

"Why are all the sirens looking at you with horror?" Nyx hissed. "Did you tell them about your Emmy and Carl fanfic? I told you it makes you weird and unlikable."

She doesn't understand mathematicians like I do.

Lena slapped me on the arm. Hard. She gazed up at me expectantly and waited.

Might as well rip the bandage off.

Picking at the lacquer on the wood table, I sighed heavily and whispered, "I've n-never had sex."

The sirens all nodded in understanding, because abstinence was sexy and mysterious. At least in my mind, that was what I thought would happen.

In real life—

"NO!" Lena cried out like someone had been shot. Then all the sirens in the booth started wailing. Nyx joined, just for the drama.

I sank lower into the booth and wished I could disappear off the face of the earth.

Nearby Spartans paused fornicating to see what all the commotion was about.

I should have kept the bandage on.

Lena pointed at me accusingly. "So *you* are the repressed prude. Why have you chosen to live such a miserable life?"

Because I'm scared of people. Touch. Sexuality.

Shrugging, I mumbled under my breath, "There wasn't much choice involved." The phantom aches worsened.

It wasn't easy to lose your virginity when you lived in a cardboard box and absolutely loathed being touched.

Instead of letting it go, the sirens perked up at my answer.

"We can change that. Do you want to fuck? Now?" Oron placed his hand on my thigh.

Jumping away from his hand, I nearly crawled out of my skin. "No."

Oron shrugged, still smiling.

"Can we please play the card game?" Changing the subject, I looked at Lena pleadingly.

"Of course." She nodded, expression grave. "Oh, big, beautiful prude."

I pursed my lips and decided to be flattered.

At least I'm big and beautiful. It could be worse...maybe.

"So the eight knives go in the middle of the table," Lena explained. "But there are nine of us, so we pass around the cards until people get four siren spirits or four Spartan Houses of the same colors. If you do, you snatch up a knife, and anyone can grab one—the person who doesn't get a knife must do a dare set by the rest of the table."

"So we fight over knives?" I asked, sure I was misunderstanding.

All the sirens nodded with excitement.

"Exactly," Lena said. "The fun part is when it gets violent and people tussle."

"Oh," I said, unsure how to put my feelings into words.

This is either going to be great fun—or a bloody disaster.

Two hours later, I screamed with laughter as I wrenched the last knife out of Lena's hands before she could fully get it.

"Not fair!" she yelled. "How the heck do you keep grabbing them by the sharp side?"

I shrugged and wiped my hand off on my toga. A few cuts on the fingers were nothing in the grand scheme of things. Heck, I barely noticed them.

"Why do I feel so—bubbly?" I asked no one in particular.

"Oh, that's the ambrosia in the food and drinks," Lena said casually.

I turned to her. "The what?"

"Ambrosia—it's a tasteless spice in all the food that acts as an upper, but don't worry, your half-human heritage should neutralize the effects. It impacts full-blooded Spartans the worst."

"Oh, that's good." I grinned (I had no clue what I was saying).

One siren at the end of the table yelled to Lena, "I dare you to go make out with a Spartan—then tell him he's ugly to his face."

Everyone burst into laughter.

"You gotta do it," I said. "That's the rules."

Lena rolled her eyes, flouncing out of the booth into the darkness. She pushed a random Spartan against the wall and kissed him thoroughly. The man melted in her arms.

"You, sir—are hideous!" Lena yelled into his face.

Our table erupted into laughter.

Tears streamed out of my eyes as the Spartan looked at her with adoration. *What an idiot.*

"Do you want a drink?" Oron asked me as the bartender passed out shots at our table.

"No." I tried to smile, but it ended with a grimace.

"How about a smoke?" The siren at the end of the table offered a cigarette.

"Nah." I laughed. "I'm good—I feel great already."

"Want to do Spartan drugs?" Another siren held up a white pill. "They make you hear colors and see music."

Honestly tempting.

"Maybe later." I laughed louder. Even feeling as good as I was, I was still aware that I wasn't emotionally ready to dabble in hard drug use. It wasn't my time—yet.

"She's our big prude," Lena said proudly as she slung her arm around my shoulder.

"Okay, next round!" Oron gathered the bloodstained knives and put them back in the center of the table. Cards were passed around, and we started to play.

Mid-game, he put his free hand on my arm. His chunky gold rings—decorated in siren spirit symbols—dug into my skin.

"You must try my drink," he whispered. "It's so good, you'll love it." He winked. "Just a sip."

The bubbly feeling fizzled slightly. "No, th-that's okay," I stuttered.

"YOU LOST!" Lena shoved at my shoulders and hooted. "Finally." The sirens held up their knives.

Darn it.

"As a punishment—" Lena tapped her lip "—you have to get naked, like the rest of us." The table laughed and heckled.

I rolled my eyes. "Oh, please."

"Do it! Do it! Do it." They drum-rolled their hands on the knife-covered table. One siren winced, then laughed, showing off a cut from where she'd accidentally hit a knife.

"Fine." I held up both my hands, then slowly lowered them to my thighs.

They leaned forward with anticipation.

In one swift move, I stood up awkwardly in the booth and yanked up my skirt—everyone screamed.

Laughing, I shimmied my hips, showing off the unflattering shorts that were built in under the toga, preserving my modesty.

"I've lost all respect for you," Nyx said dryly.

With a grin, I kissed her invisible head before she could recoil, and I put my skirt back down. She slithered down into the top of my toga to hide from my attention.

"Noooooo," Lena screamed good-naturedly as I sat down,

laughing so hard I couldn't breathe. *Everything really is hilarious these days.*

Everyone resumed chanting. "Do it! Do it! Do it."

"Wahoo," I shouted while laughing. Grabbing the short sleeve of my toga, I pulled the ultra-stretchy material down so my arm was out.

The table oohed and aahed appropriately as I showed off my shoulder and my elbow.

Apparently, I had a knack for performance theater (stripping). *This feels like a very lucrative talent. I should pursue this.*

I pulled out the other side so both my arms were free.

Everyone clapped, and I laughed. As a naturally introverted person, there was something strangely intoxicating about all the attention. I was soaring through the sky, light as air.

Slowly I pulled at the stretchy material that covered my chest and made faces as the table laughed harder.

The piano music stopped.

There was a commotion in the far corner of the room.

The bench went flying, knocking over three naked sirens on their knees, as the pianist stood up.

Still dragging my toga lower, I recoiled in horror as glacial blue eyes flashed.

Tattooed letters stretched across a pale throat, and shadows were stark on a sharply defined face. A weapons holster stretched across a white silk shirt with blue diamond buttons—it was full of guns.

Kharon stalked across the room toward me.

Death in his eyes.

He shoved away a naked Spartan male who approached. Then he did the same to a siren.

Oh my god, he's *the pianist.*

Why was everyone trying to get to him and not away from him?

It hit me: after the massacre, while recovering at Corfu, I'd thought I'd hallucinated piano music, but it had been real.

Kharon had been playing in the house.

Distractedly, I stretched my toga fabric lower and—

"What the fuck are you doing?" Augustus's calloused hand wrapped around my neck. His fingers dug possessively into my sensitive skin. His other hand roughly yanked the straps of my toga back up.

Kharon stopped, still halfway across the room. He watched, unblinking, as Augustus touched me. His expression was unreadable.

I forgot how to inhale.

"It was a simple question." His breath tickled my ear as he squeezed my neck tighter. "Why are you taking your clothes off in public?"

"Professor," I whispered as he choked me. "*What* are you doing?"

He leaned close, dark eyes feral.

"I'm taking control—Alexis," he said silkily.

"Why?" I swallowed thickly.

He made a harsh noise in the back of his throat. "I'm done pretending."

His thumb stroked softly down the column of my throat, fingers burning against my much colder skin. His dark green dress-shirt sleeves were rolled up, showcasing a tan forearm covered in thick veins.

My stomach fluttered. *Am I into older men?*

Yep—ambrosia was 100 percent a drug. There was no way I'd think that in a sober state of mind.

I gasped for air as his grip tightened.

His lips hovered next to my ear. "This isn't a game, Alexis." My name rolled off his tongue like a confession of sin. "I know who you are."

Is this about my meeting with Zeus?

He didn't remove his fingers from my neck.

I was at his mercy.

Caught in his snare.

Heat pooled in my lower stomach, and everything got hazy in a dreamlike way. The scent of ozone filled my nose, and invisible electric sparks leaped between us.

Warm lips brushed against the shell of my ear. "You have no idea just what you've done with your little display. What you've started..."

Goose bumps exploded down my spine.

He inhaled deeply, then let out a guttural moan, like he couldn't help himself.

After a long moment of breathing harshly, like he was struggling to compose himself, he said, "You fucking infuriate me."

His words jolted me out of my trance.

I wrenched my neck out of his hold and fell back into the booth. "Leave me a-alone," I said, barely able to speak in his presence.

"Hey, get off her!" Lena shouted, and flung her elbows forward.

Since Augustus was leaning over her to get to me, he grunted in surprise and staggered back.

"Thanks," I whispered to her, hands shaking.

"What did he say to you?" Lena asked curiously, but I kept my gaze on the table, since *he* was still standing behind her. Watching. Waiting.

He was ready to break my mind and crush my will.

"Nothing good." *Nothing that makes any sense.*

Oron threw his arm around my shoulder and pulled me back against his naked self so he was flush against me. *He's touching me. He's touching me a lot.*

I froze.

It got even harder to breathe. My heart felt like it was going to explode out of my chest. My vision warped.

"I got you, Alexis, don't worry," Oron said. "We won't let him hurt you."

I grimaced and tried to sit up, but he held me down in the booth.

Sweat poured off my temples, and I breathed shallowly, vision blurring further. A weak feeling washed over me.

Sirens and Spartans stared at me.

The room spun.

"Are you okay, kid?" Nyx asked. "Do you want me to bite him?"

The panic worsened.

"I need to get out of the booth," I whispered.

Lena quickly made room, and her gentle hands guided me out.

I stood up shakily.

The problem was, Oron also escorted me out of the booth. He held on to me from behind as he whispered platitudes into my hair.

Before I could do anything, Augustus grabbed Oron by the back of the neck and ripped him away.

"How *dare* you touch her?" Augustus snarled. Then he chucked the siren across the room like he weighed nothing. "IF ANYONE IN SPARTA LAYS A SINGLE FINGER ON ALEXIS—THEY ANSWER TO ME!" he roared into the room.

I blinked up at my professor—the man who hated me—in horror.

What the heck is he doing?

He shrugged into his suit jacket, flashing the weapons holstered across his chest.

Panic filled my lungs.

I staggered back.

Gasping, hands on my knees, I greedily sucked in air and whispered, "Sorry, sorry, sorry," to Lena. Something was happening to me—I'd lost all control.

I was no longer flying.

I was plummeting.

What the freak does ambrosia do to a person? It felt like adrenaline but ten times worse.

Spartans and sirens turned toward the commotion.

Embarrassment burned my chest.

Before I could come up with some explanation (remember how to speak), Augustus stepped into my personal space.

Tension crackled in the air. "Alexis, you better leave the symposium, now," he commanded. "Or else…" He trailed off dangerously.

The shame intensified.

Head low, I tripped toward the exit as I tried to leave.

Lena stepped in front of my path. "I don't know what's happening," she said. "But if you need help, I'm here. You're not alone. Don't let anyone treat you less than you deserve, great one."

She looked at me like she thought I was powerful. Only Charlie had ever looked at me like that.

Breathing deeply, I nodded.

Tried to gather courage from her.

The room spun faster.

"I'm not leaving," I whispered to Augustus, eyes still focused on my new friend. *I won't let him boss me around. I need to speak up and stand up for myself.*

She smiled at me encouragingly.

Brutal hands grabbed my waist and threw me into the air.

I screamed and blinked in shock as Augustus's shoulder slammed into my stomach.

He'd thrown me over his shoulder.

He was carrying me toward the door.

"Stop him!" Lena screamed, but Spartans held her back as she tried to run after us.

The rest of the booth stood beside her with angry expressions, holding the bloodstained knives threateningly.

A few feet away, Patro arched his brow at Augustus like he was surprised by his actions, but he leaned against Achilles and didn't intervene.

The rest of the Spartans fell over themselves to get out of Augustus's way. Everyone respected him and thought he was fair.

No one was going to help me.

Lifting my head, I gave Lena a watery smile. "I'll be fine," I mouthed, not wanting to scare my new friends with the dark reality of my life.

But the sirens must not have believed me, because shouts echoed, and a shoving match broke out.

I panicked for my new friends. Pain spiked through my already pounding chest, bright and hot.

Am I dying?

Augustus slammed open the door to leave the symposium—the last thing I saw was a Spartan shoving a siren and her falling to the ground, screaming, foam bubbling at the corner of her mouth.

"We need to help her!" I said to Augustus as I waited for him to put me down, banging at his back. Panic intensified.

"Someone else will assist her," he growled. "The best Olympian doctors in the world are inside."

He's right.

The white-hot pain in my chest slowly dissipated, and I stopped struggling, but he still didn't release me.

Just stalked down the steps, then across the fields silently.

It took me a second to realize the blob on his leg was Poco. The raccoon was wrapped around his calf, staring up at me with a curious expression.

Augustus carried us both like it was nothing, his steps large and powerful.

His right arm pressed against my legs, and his hand gripped my right thigh.

My head spun faster.

Nothing felt real.

Calluses scraped against skin as his grip tightened—*he probably got them fighting Titans.*

I shivered.

My skin tingled.

His breathing was loud and ragged in the night, and his chest heaved with every step. But he didn't seem tired—he seemed wild, like he was trying to get control over himself.

Moonlight cast strange silver shadows, and I shivered in the cold.

"Put me d-down," I demanded when the shock wore off enough that I could speak.

His grip on my thigh tightened.

That was his only response.

A strange queasiness burned me alive, and dark butterflies fluttered inside my stomach.

"Uh—should I do something?" Nyx asked around my neck, and even she sounded unsure, like she didn't know what to do.

Her voice pulled me out of my shock. "No," I said. "I'll do it."

After a deep, calming breath, I beat my fists against his back and wiggled as much as possible.

"Release me!" I demanded, punching with all my might, fighting for freedom.

Muscles bunched beneath my fists, but Augustus's steps didn't falter.

He didn't even grunt.

I fought harder and screamed with everything I had, bucking and kicking. Desperate to get free.

Minutes later, I hung limp.

Panting with exhaustion, I was too tired to fight anymore. Poco tittered up at me—I made a face at the raccoon.

Your taste in Spartans sucks. How could you bond with him?

Poco hissed.

I hissed back.

Fingernails dug harder into the back of my thigh as he carried me, hard enough to bruise. I shifted slightly, and Augustus made a rough noise in the back of his throat.

"One hour," he said silkily. "Kick me one more time, and

I'll add another hour on top of the one hour of punishment you've already earned."

I froze, leg stilling.

"What punishment?" I asked. It was the first time he'd spoken since the symposium. "One hour of what?"

"I warned you," he said softly, his voice vibrating with rage. "You've pushed me too far this time."

"Wait—what did you warn me of?" I asked, genuinely confused.

He didn't answer.

Not cryptic and creepy at all.

Great, he's definitely going to torture me.

"Uh—kid," Nyx whispered as she clung to my upside-down neck. "I think Augustus really is into you, like *really* into you."

I shook my head and breathed deeply. "No way," I said softly. "He hates me."

"Yes, way." Nyx shivered. "He's wild for you—practically savage. You're in deep shit, sister. This is way worse than I thought. He hates you so much that he wants to fight—in the bedroom."

I choked. A manic bubble of laughter burst out my throat, and tears of despair streamed out of my eyes.

"Carl Gauss would never treat me like this," I whispered miserably. "What happened to nice men who love math and treating a woman right?"

Nyx scoffed. "They died out because they were pathetic and embarrassing losers. No woman wants a nerd."

"I do," I said.

"No—you just think you do," Nyx hissed. "What you want is a real man who wants to slaughter for you."

I shook my head. "You need help." Tears dripped down my face.

"Well—you need to get dicked down."

I cried harder because it was official: my best friend was a perverted lunatic. It was all too much. I couldn't keep living like this.

My bones were rubber, muscles ridiculously weak.

Lena thought I was powerful; she'd looked at me with hope, like she'd believed in me. But some opponents were too heartless, too ruthless, to keep fighting. Sometimes, there was only one way forward.

I closed my eyes and hung limp.

Sometimes all you could do was play dead and wait for the storm to pass.

It hurt less that way.

Two voices whispered at the edge of my subconscious.

They were watching me.

Staring.

Stalking.

With a gasp, I woke up. My heart pounded painfully inside my sternum.

Nyx mumbled but didn't awaken.

I was alone.

The soft *plop, plop, plop* of candle wax and the crackling of fire were the only sounds.

Rubbing my eyes, I tried to orient myself.

Distantly I recalled falling asleep while Augustus carried me back to the academy. I smiled as I remembered the events of the symposium before he'd ruined it.

You finally discovered your Spartan ability. You're not powerless. You can talk to sentient creatures.

Relief made me lightheaded.

That siren was screaming—she got hurt because of you.

I felt sick.

Sitting up, I took in the grandeur of the academy library.

I was sprawled out on a velvet chaise in front of a hearth, and someone had placed a knit blanket around me. The soft material was wrapped tightly around my feet, like the person had tucked me in.

A blanket was worth its weight in gold, since the fall temperatures had made the already chilled mountain miserable.

Had Augustus done it? *No, he wouldn't have. He hates me.*

I checked my thighs and sighed heavily. Sure enough, there were purple bruises where he'd gripped me.

At least my ears aren't bleeding anymore.

The bar was set alarmingly low.

Carefully I pulled my new treasure around my shoulders and hobbled to my feet.

With a yawn, I checked the clock on the wall; it was only three in the morning. The sun hadn't risen yet, which was why the other initiates weren't back from the symposium.

I had a few hours to myself.

Sighing again, I slumped into the seat I always studied in, and fingered the corner of my Thagorean textbook, where I'd written my name on the cover.

I might as well use this time to do a little studying.

I'd never admit it to the other initiates, because they complained about the class constantly, but I really enjoyed how complicated the Thagorean equations were.

I loved the rush of untangling the steps and finding the solution.

That was the nice thing about math: there was always a right answer. The process might have been messy, but the solution was black-and-white.

Nothing else in life was as simple.

Ever since the stupid Spartan merit test, everything was confusing.

The back of my neck prickled, and I groaned but refused to look around.

No one is watching you. It's all in your head.

Ignoring my deteriorating mental state, I cracked open the textbook, desperate for a distraction.

An index card fluttered out.

I turned it over with a yawn. Words were scratched messily across it in ink:

Leave Sparta now or there will be dire consequences for you. You have until the January Initiation Ball to disappear. Fail to heed this warning, and you will regret it.

Rolling my eyes, I tucked it into the flap at the back of the book.

What a corny threat.

It felt like something a child would do if they were trying to scare someone.

I was trapped at an academy, starving to death and studying until I couldn't trust my thoughts. The fact that someone wanted me gone was the least of my problems. Jessica had been meaner with her insults.

Titus or Alessander had probably done it.

They both had access to my books and had been way too quiet after the library incident, but I'd been expecting a much harsher form of retaliation.

Chuckling to myself, like I'd lost my mind (I had), I tucked the blanket tighter around my shoulders and repositioned my chair. It knocked against something heavy.

I bent over and picked up the offending object.

It was a medium-sized box.

It was wrapped in red velvet, a black silk bow with gold trim tied at the top. My name was written in neat cursive on a tag.

Oooh, a present.

I'd never actually gotten one before. It was a luxury Charlie and I never bothered to talk about. When you were starving, you knew the score; there were priorities, and frivolous gifts weren't one of them.

Maybe it's from the same person who gave me the blanket?

Slowly unwrapping the perfect edges, I couldn't keep the smile off my face. *Maybe my luck is finally turning around.*

After the dramatic (horrifying) events of yesterday, I needed a win.

Slowly I pulled the heavy lid off.

The smile slid off my face.

Seconds turned into minutes as I stared blankly down at the contents.

I was frozen.

Unable to move.

Water dripped onto the table, and I realized I was crying.

Scales slid against my throat, and I jumped up, nearly falling out of my seat, heart pounding. A scream burned the back of my throat. *It's just Nyx shifting in her sleep.*

Blinking, I slowly leaned closer to the box and gasped, because it was exactly what I'd thought it was.

There were four objects on top of wadded-up black tissue paper: two eyeballs covered in red veins, a smashed nose, and a severed male finger with chunky gold rings. Blood was splattered across all of them.

The eyes were pastel.

The rings had the symbol of the spirit of sirens on them.

It was Oron—*parts* of him.

Suddenly, the note in my textbook no longer felt like a children's game. Someone had murdered him. Torn him to pieces. Just to warn me away from the academy.

My hand spasmed with horror, and the box knocked over.

Something glinted underneath the body parts.

I was too sick to look.

Numb all over, with shaking fingers, I placed the lid back on the box and rewrapped it with the bow.

Like a zombie, I walked out of the library and up the stairs, out into the night. Around the side of the mountain, I found a large rock in the grass. Heaving, I rolled the rock over and revealed fresh soil.

Then I dug.

When there was a small hole, I put the box in and covered it with soil.

For a second, I thought about saying words. *He's dead because of you. What are you doing? You're losing it.*

Eyes widening, I turned and sprinted as fast as I could back to the academy.

Straight to the bathroom.

Collapsing onto the rusted toilet seat, I pulled my knees to my chest and rocked.

Teeth chattering from shock.

Paralyzed.

Hours later, boys laughed raucously as they came back from the symposium.

In a stupor I got to my feet, wiped my eyes, and stumbled to the library.

"Dude, that was crazy. I can't believe Professor Augustus carried you out like that." Drex ran over to the entrance as I walked in. "Everyone is talking about it—did you see the way he was staring at you all night? He literally stood in the corner just watching, not touching anyone. It was creepy."

I looked at him blankly, unable to speak.

He must have seen something in my expression, because he waved his hand dismissively. "But it's not a big deal. Honestly, everyone was freaking out about the siren who died."

My head snapped up. "What happened to him? Who d-did it?"

They already knew Oron was dead.

I received his parts in a box. Help.

The urge to confide burned the tip of my tongue, but I didn't know enough about Sparta. The underworld seemed like a heinous place; they could blame me and send me away.

Drex furrowed his brow with confusion. "Him? No—everyone's talking about that female siren who dropped dead after you were carried out."

The numb feeling became a crushing avalanche.

"Everyone thinks she must have been poisoned." Drex grimaced. "It was probably another siren. They have rivalries. Or maybe a dark creature, or a Chthonic—they've been known to attack other Spartans. Maybe they were trying to poison an Olympian but got her."

I staggered backward into a bookcase and collapsed to the floor.

Drex's eyes widened, and he offered me a hand up.

I didn't take it.

"Sorry," he said in a rush. "I shouldn't have said anything. But it's not your fault—even if Augustus hadn't taken you away, they probably would have snapped and killed her later. Chthonics don't need reasons."

I gasped for air as I got to my feet.

The only Chthonics in there were my mentors, Augustus, and Kharon. I couldn't see them killing her.

When I finally regained the ability to speak, I whispered, "Why do you speak like that when you're C-Chthonic?"

Drex recoiled. "No, I'm not."

"I saw you…during the massacre," I whispered.

He blanched. "What are you talking about? I didn't do anything."

Why is he lying?

Drex leaned closer and whispered conspiratorially, "Don't tell anybody, but my ability is endurance. My mind gets all euphoric, and I go into a trancelike state. I can run for *miles*…it's crazy." He grinned, clearly proud of what he could do.

Then who killed those three boys in the massacre?

I could have sworn his hand had been extended, eyes glowing red in the strange fog.

The hairs on my neck stood up as strange voices whispered.

"Do you hear that?" I pointed toward the sound.

"Hear what?" Drex asked.

The voices got louder. "There—that voice." I pointed again.

Drex peered in the direction. "I don't hear anything at all," he said. "Nothing."

My hand dropped.

How long have I been losing my mind?

Everything was falling apart around me, and nothing made any sense.

Do I have a brain tumor? Aren't women at risk of schizophrenia until they're twenty-six? Were my eye and ear not the only thing affected by the beating—did it permanently damage my brain?

"Never mind," I whispered to Drex.

"Are you feeling okay?" he asked as he reached for me. "You look really pale."

I recoiled against the bookshelf to avoid his touch.

Drex put his hands up in a surrender gesture.

"Try to take some deep breaths. It's going to be okay," he said kindly. "I know it's been hard for you lately—with Augustus causing a scene like he did. But he'll probably forget about it in a day or two."

Drex peered down at me, and I realized he was waiting for me to do something.

I nodded at him. "Yeah," I lied. "I'm s-sure he will."

Pushing myself back up to my feet, I tried to look normal, like I wasn't crumbling inside.

"Can you tutor me a little before class?" Drex asked hopefully.

I swallowed a whimper. "Sure."

Numbly I sat back down at the seat where I'd found the box of Oron's body, and opened the textbook, which still had the awful note tucked into it.

With cold lips, I talked Drex through concepts and drew them out.

At one point, Maximum Hera, the friendly initiate with blue highlights in his blond hair, sat down next to me and asked to study with us. Drex agreed before I could say no.

Maximum made small talk the entire time.

I wanted to die.

Hours later, I stared numbly at the rock floor of the classroom as Augustus told an ancient Latin tale about bull jumping.

He stopped mid-story and said, "Alexis—where did I say this took place?" His voice whipped cruelly.

"Mycenae," I answered without inflection. It sounded foreign. Barren and cold.

A long beat passed as Augustus furrowed his brow and stared

at me. Soulless black eyes narrowed like he was trying to solve a puzzle.

I stared back.

Numb.

Frozen.

Barely alive.

Break my mind. Take over my will. I dare you.

For the first time, he looked away first.

I didn't feel any satisfaction.

In fact, I felt nothing at all.

20
THE PIANIST

KHARON: A FEW HOURS EARLIER, AT THE SYMPOSIUM

I leaned forward at the piano and watched my prey.

Alexis was sitting at a table, surrounded by sirens. She smiled and laughed freely as she talked with the naked creatures. *What other secrets do you have, carissima?*

The male siren sitting next to her shifted closer, staring at her with pure lust.

I ground my teeth together.

Missed a note.

My thigh muscles bunched. It took every ounce of control I possessed not to stand up and throw my dagger into his throat.

Play the long game, Kharon.

Don't ruin all your carefully laid plans.

I slammed my fingers down across the ivory keys, pressing the pedal with so much force the piano creaked.

Another Olympian Spartan crawled toward the piano bench,

and I kicked him away with disgust. I wasn't interested in playing with weak bitches; I had singular tastes.

Once I made up my mind, nothing could change it.

I was looking at what I wanted.

Hell and Hound lay at my feet, hackles rising with annoyance as a constant stream of sirens and Spartans crawled forward, trying to seduce me.

I regretted ever wasting my powers on them.

None of them deserved it.

Breathing deeply, I focused on the music and nothing else.

Fingers moving quickly across the keys, I lost myself in the flow of a faster melody. Plans and moves played out before me, and I studied each one carefully.

There was no room for error.

Not with what was on the line.

There was an explosion of laughter across the room, and I leaned forward to look around the column. Unable to avoid the magnetic pull Alexis had on a room.

My fingers stilled.

She was standing up at the booth, skin gleaming like polished gold, her mismatched eyes crinkled with laughter.

Dried blood was crusted across her perfectly curved lips, her arms were streaked with dirt, and curls were wild around her face—she looked like a disheveled angel.

I'd never met anyone who was such an intoxicating combination of shy and bloodthirsty.

I loosened my diamond-encrusted belt to release the pressure in my pants.

Alexis smiled seductively, slowly tugging down one of her toga sleeves.

I palmed myself through my pants.

I stared, entranced.

Hell growled, deep in his throat, and startled me out of my trance. *What the fuck is she doing?*

I stood up and threw the piano bench back. People grunted in pain, and I ignored them.

I need to stop her. If the sirens see her naked flesh, so help me Kronos, I'll kill them all.

Stalking across the room, I shoved a Spartan out of the way.

Halfway toward my prey, I stopped.

Augustus grabbed her neck and stopped her.

He was choking her.

Gently.

His dark eyes were wide with rage. He leaned close and whispered something into her ear, his long black-and-white hair hanging between them like a silk curtain. The scar across his cheekbone and nose was an angry slash.

The lust intensified tenfold.

They were devastatingly handsome together.

Both were vicious.

Both uniquely attractive.

Augustus and I had shared hundreds of people over the years. We preferred fucking together. It kept people from getting too attached, and it was fun to make people sob with unimaginable ecstasy.

But I'd never felt like this before.

Pride filled me as I watched Alexis melt beneath his touch.

Heat flashed in both their gazes.

I smiled.

Things were progressing faster than I expected; the timeline would need to be accelerated.

Slowly I grabbed my throbbing shaft and stroked.

The pleasure was otherworldly.

I squeezed.

A male siren whimpered as he pressed himself flush against me.

Growling, I pulled my hand away and shoved the man off me. He fell to the ground, and I kicked him, then grabbed a drink off a tray and threw it back. The ambrosia burned deliciously.

It was time to get to work.

I had prey to ensnare.

21

TITAN ATTACKS

Alexis: Late November

Golden light glittered across the Ionian Sea as the sun set in Corfu.

The late November breeze blew through the open French doors with a slight chill, and male voices laughed raucously somewhere in the house. I was lying on my bed.

I hadn't felt like laughing since I'd received the terrifying gift two months ago.

I can't believe I go back to that hell tomorrow.

I groaned in frustration because time was passing with disturbing quickness.

Life was a blur of torturous monotony.

Mostly because I was a coward and had opted out of attending the symposia for the last two months.

Every week I starved, suffered from dehydration, cried while running the now freezing circuit, wished I could shower because I felt grimy, and studied until I wanted to die.

This might be worse than high school. Maybe.

Jessica and Tim-Tom had been their own special breed of torment.

Now—stretched out across my bed, graphing the Riemann Hypothesis—I aggressively popped a grape into my mouth.

Classical music played on the radio tilted against my pillow.

I'd been trying to relax all weekend, but my thoughts kept getting away from me.

One hour of running? One hour of doing push-ups? A one-hour test?

Augustus's disconcerting threat still haunted me weeks later.

Over the last two months, the professor had given no indication of what he'd meant while he'd carried me over his shoulder like a barbarian.

I rubbed my neck and thigh where his grip had bruised.

Strange nausea rolled low in my stomach, and I breathed deeply through my nose as I waited for it to pass.

Dark butterflies fluttered.

Everything about the man confused me.

He'd made a point of snarling with disgust every time my name was read off first after tests and shooting me a poisonous glare. If looks could kill, I'd be six feet under.

Shouldn't a professor favor the top student?

The truth of my existence was becoming depressingly obvious: people didn't like me.

There was something off about me.

I was defective.

Drapes fluttered as wind gusted, and shadows elongated with the setting sun, so I pulled up the hood of my oversize emotional support sweatshirt.

Nyx snored and shifted underneath it.

Someone had left the black garment on the chair in my room weeks ago, right after the box incident, and since the material was ridiculously soft (the nicest thing I'd ever felt or worn), it was now mine.

The skull on the front—which was sticking up its middle finger—had grown on me.

Fluck the flucking world. Life's a biatch like that.

Yes, I was in my emo era.

No, I didn't want to talk about it—that was the point—however, as a commitment to the lifestyle, I was experimenting with swearing in my mind.

I was making some (no) progress.

Years of associating vulgar language with the foster parents was a hard habit to break. Still, I was trying to push past the mental block.

I don't want to go back to that freakin' sucky academy tomorrow, I practiced in my mind.

Outside my room, the male voices got louder, and someone bellowed with laughter.

Putting my pen down, I turned down the radio dial so I could eavesdrop.

On my days off, I usually avoided my mentors, especially since *he* was always hanging around.

"Achilles, did you see *The Falcon Chronicles* for last month? Helen gave it to me," Patro said loudly in the kitchen. "Kharon, you made the front page. So, you finally chose a betrothal? Was it one or two Olympians? Who are they?"

A feminine voice oohed loudly, and I perked up with interest. They hadn't had a woman over the entire time I'd been staying with them.

A raspy voice chuckled darkly. "Something like that," Kharon said.

Speak of the devil.

My jaw dropped.

Satan has a lover? Maybe two? Those poor freakin' Olympians. Praying for them.

More words were said that I couldn't hear. Then it got quiet as the men went back to the other side of the house.

Stomach growling, I shoved the last bite (half the block) of cheese into my mouth and tiptoed to the door with my empty plate.

After checking to make sure the coast was clear, I hurried into the kitchen.

Piling my plate high with the food that was always spread across the counters, I turned to leave, but a yellow scroll on the table caught my attention. It was partially unrolled and covered with colors.

I sat down and hesitantly opened it.

The Falcon Chronicles was written in bold text at the top. "Sparta's top news source."

A colorful picture of Kharon, wearing a suit in a grand ballroom, took up most of the scroll.

His glacial blue eyes glowed menacingly on the page, lips pulled down in a frown. A silver crown gleamed with rubies atop his styled dark hair.

The devil really is gorgeous.

In thick black ink, it read, "Chthonic bad boy: Sparta's most eligible bachelor was seen sending betrothal jewelry last month. Who is the lucky Olympian heir or heiress?"

Below it, a story detailed,

> Kharon's blue eyes flashed with longing at the annual House of Dionysus ball. He refused to dance with any eligible Spartans and instead brooded about, head clearly full of thoughts of his love(s). Our sources can confirm he sent the customary three betrothal gifts, and one of them was the priceless blue diamonds from the House of Artemis. Ladies and gents, the courtship of the century has begun.
>
> Who is the lucky citizen of Sparta? We have no doubt they opened the jewels, therefore accepting the betrothal. What lucky Olympian(s) is Sparta's most eligible bachelor going to devote his life to? The marriage law has been

a smashing success, motivating young Spartans to find true love.

I snorted and popped a grape into my mouth.

His lovers are going to need a lot *more than jewels. Most likely a lobotomy, and a gun for safety. Who would voluntarily sleep next to that psycho at night?*

The rest of the story was equally ridiculous, filled with flowery language about pining and a secret great romance.

Who believes this crap?

Although when Patro had asked about it, Kharon hadn't denied it.

Maybe he really is in love?

I shivered with horror. Some people should spend their lives alone; he was some people.

Unrolling the scroll further, I choked at the next story. Grape bits lodged in my esophagus.

Coughing, I stared at the picture in disbelief.

It was me, sitting by myself in a dark booth at the symposium. I was slumped over, looking miserable, and the whitish-gray of my one eye contrasted harshly with my dark eye and gave me a menacing look.

Darn, my hair really is frizzy.

The bloodstains underneath my nose and eyes were also not attractive.

I sighed. They couldn't have found an uglier picture if they'd tried.

Rude.

Beneath the image, bold text said, "Meet Alexis Hert, the newest Olympian prodigy. Zeus confirms the abandoned mutt is his, and her classmates tell all."

Feeling violated, I skimmed the story.

"No, she's not as attractive as people are saying," says her classmate Titus. "Her eyes are freaky, and she's overhyped. She got lucky in the fight, and her test scores are barely beating out the rest of the class."

Of course they'd interviewed Titus, of all people.

Mental note—stare at him as much as possible this week. I hoped my eyes disturbed the crap out of him.

Fluck him.

"Holy Kronos, it's you!" a girl yelled from the doorway, and I shrieked with surprise.

Clutching my chest, I slumped at the table as I tried to ride out the heart attack.

"My brothers didn't tell me you were over. I totally would have introduced myself," the girl said enthusiastically, like my presence was exhilarating. "I'm Helen." A ruby crown glittered on her head.

"Your brothers?" I asked, jaw dropping as my brain caught up with what she was saying.

She's the heiress to the House of Aphrodite.

Everyone knew who she was.

"Patro is my half brother on my mom's side. Augustus is my full brother, and *very* overprotective." Helen sighed dramatically, then moved to my left and mumbled something inaudible about boys.

I couldn't picture Augustus having a younger sister.

He probably just growls at her like a beast.

The daughter of the most beautiful woman in the world stood before me (a girl impersonating a mountain troll).

"Oh, c-cool," I said, eloquent as ever. At that exact moment, my stomach let out a loud gurgle.

"I won't bother you," Helen said. "I know you're training right now and doing the crucible, which is literally insane. You probably have to meditate and study. You must be sooooo mentally strong."

I choked on the pastry I was shoving down my throat.

I wouldn't say "strong" was an apt descriptor.

Helen respectfully averted her gaze as I hacked, and waved her hands in the air.

"Keep up the great work," she said. "Maybe we'll see each other around. That will be so fun. I swear there're like no women in all of Sparta—especially not younger like us. Ya know?" Nodding, I grunted in agreement, even though I didn't know.

Anything.

At this point, I was 50 percent convinced I was hungry in a cardboard box, lucid dreaming about Sparta. Everything seemed surreal, and it was getting more extreme by the minute.

Helen stepped closer. "It's crazy! There's especially no young Chthonic women. I'm the only one. It sucks. The Great War killing all the Chthonics really was terrible for dating and friendships—especially since the Chthonic men can be *so* stifling. You've met Augustus. You know what I mean."

You mean the fact that he's the rudest, most belligerent man on earth?

I nodded at her, dumbstruck.

She was the most normal Spartan I'd met yet.

"Well." Helen shrugged dismissively. "At least Chthonics are strong, and we've really banded together. Everyone's super protective of each other. It's kind of nice, if you get past all the blustering and broodiness."

I think she's confusing psychosis for protectiveness. Poor thing.

Helen must have misread the horror in my expression, because she patted my arm. "Don't worry—you're not a weak Olympian like the rest of them… I can tell from the way you carry yourself—you remind me of my brother. You're strong like a Chthonic."

"Thanks?" I said.

Your brother terrifies me, so that's alarming.

Unaware of my panic, Helen shuffled out of the kitchen with a glass of water in her hand. "Just keep up the mental strength," she yelled from the hall. "Stay mentally calm. That's def the key."

My eye twitched.

The key was *def* killing myself before I had to go back.

But I loved her fighting spirit.

In my peripheral vision, the unrolled scroll proclaimed Kharon's betrothal and showcased my bad hair day. I frowned as Titus's words came back to me.

Spitefully I grabbed more food off the counter and shoved it all in my mouth at once.

Back in my room, I angrily picked up a pillow and drop-kicked it across the room. Screaming through gritted teeth, I fell face-first onto the bed, then pummeled the mattress with my fists.

It helped marginally (not at all).

Helen would not have been impressed.

As I lay on the bed, impersonating a cadaver, two voices whispered in the corner of my room.

No.

Absolutely not.

NO!

I was not doing this.

Throwing myself off the bed, I stalked over to the corner and pointed at the chair. "I don't know who you are," I said to the voices. "Or why you're constantly whispering and following me around, but I've had it. Knock it off!" I made an X with my hands.

The chair didn't move.

Drapes fluttered as a breeze gusted.

The room was silent.

You're losing your mind again, Alexis. Get it freakin' together, woman. No voices are whispering. You're imagining things.

Sanity was easier said than done these days.

Pulling at my curly (frizzy) hair, breathing erratically, I slowly backed away from the inanimate object I'd just scolded.

There were cries for help. Then there were *cries* for help. This was the latter.

I fell to my knees.

Buried my head in my hands.

"Freak, fluck, biatch, crud, darn, flippin', shrit," I wailed despondently, but my eyes were bone-dry because emo girls didn't cry (I'd cried yesterday).

The despair continued.

I missed Charlie and Fluffy.

With every cell in my body, I wished I was back starving in the woods.

That night, I dreamed of piano music, a box full of body parts, glowing red eyes, skeletal monsters, a strange obsession tinged with possessiveness, a skeleton holding up its middle finger, scratchy writing on a note, and calloused fingers digging into my skin.

The devil called me carissima and whispered that he was going to take care of me from now on.

I woke up screaming.

The next morning, I reluctantly took off my emotional support sweatshirt, then met up with Patro and Achilles in the kitchen to have food (eat as much as possible in five seconds) before going back to the academy.

Patro made small talk about a new Spartan gun they were releasing, but Achilles said nothing, because he literally couldn't, and Nyx snored around my neck.

Helen walked into the kitchen, then pulled the seat out right next to mine.

"Hi again!" she said.

I waved awkwardly, then wanted to end myself for being so socially weird. *She's a foot away. Why would you wave?*

This was definitely why people hated me.

"How did you sleep?" Helen asked, completely unaware that I was mentally spiraling. "I slept great—the mattresses in this little cottage are amazing."

Little cottage? This is a mansion.

She blinked expectantly, and I realized she was waiting for a response.

"Horribly," I said truthfully.

She grimaced. "Sorry about that. A good night's sleep is crucial to cognitive functioning."

I nodded. "That w-would explain a lot of things."

She pursed her lips like she couldn't decide if I was joking or not.

I shoved half a loaf of bread in my mouth, then washed it down with butter and a handful of grapes.

Helen used a fork and knife to delicately cut a date into tiny pieces.

She was so ladylike; it was cute.

"All right, let's go. We can't be late," Patro ordered. Internally whimpering, I grabbed another handful of food and ate it as quickly as possible.

"Good luck! Knock all those boys dead!" Helen cheered as we disappeared in a crack of smoke.

Unfortunately, that will probably happen.

Her enthusiasm for life was extremely unrelatable, and slightly off-putting, but also sweet.

She inspired me to want to kill myself less. Maybe.

The Crimson Duo left me on the front lawn.

When I entered the icy darkness of the mostly empty classroom, General Cleandro sat at the desk with his feet up, and Augustus was smiling while chatting to Cassius.

His face dropped when he saw me, and he scowled.

I flipped him off and said, "Get freakin' lost."

In my head.

In real life, I averted my gaze and collapsed onto the floor where I always sat, groaning as a rock bit into my left butt cheek.

"I can't do this again," Nyx moaned around my neck. "It's sooooo cold in this awful mountain."

"You're telling me," I whispered as softly as possible, hyper-aware that I was probably speaking some freaky snake language.

In the front of the room, Augustus whipped his head around. Soulless black eyes narrowed on me as Poco climbed onto his shoulder.

Cassius followed his gaze, then looked back at the professor with confusion.

"Yep," Nyx said. "Those are bedroom eyes. This is not a drill. It's happening. Augustus is giving you bedroom eyes. Wow—this is escalating."

I choked on air. "If by bedroom, you mean the eyes you give someone who's manacled in your dungeon—then yes, that's exactly what's happening."

"Oh yeah," Nyx hissed. "That could also work. If the dungeon has red lights, whips, and chains everywhere. Also, seductive music and chocolate."

I closed my eyes and pinched the bridge of my nose. *Please, God, bring me a new best friend. Make her less of a horny pervert. Thank you.*

When I opened my eyes, Augustus had turned back to Cassius, and his smile had returned.

Bas-turd.

I slumped onto my side and fantasized about all the creative ways I could off myself. Frankly, at this point, I didn't care if Carl Gauss thought I wasn't accomplished in the afterlife (I cared).

Carl can suck on my…stuff.

"Why am I actually so lame?" I whispered to Nyx, wishing I could swear like a sailor.

A thin tongue flicked against my cheek. "I fear it's my fault for sheltering you," Nyx said seriously. "I should have bullied you more. Instead, I let you grow up into a weirdo. I'm sorry."

I choked.

Why does everyone always answer my facetious questions?

"Alexis, you're here early too!" Blond hair gleamed with blue highlights.

NO. God no. I can't do this. Please Lord. NOOOOOOO. This is NOT the friend I wanted. I take it all back.

Maximum smiled down at me like we were best friends (we weren't).

"Not him again." Nyx groaned around my neck.

He was the type of person who woke up with a smile and journaled every day what he was grateful for. Someone needed to tell him an *apocalypse* had happened.

People needed to learn how to act appropriately.

"This is actually perfect," Maximum said as he sat down on my left, forcing me to shift over my textbooks so there was room. "I wanted to move back a row and sit next to you—now that we've been studying together for months."

He wiggled his brows and winked.

What he forgot to mention was that we studied together for months *against* my will.

I tutored Drex because of our alliance, and Maximum sat there being annoying the entire time because he was uncomfortable sitting with his own thoughts and wanted to tell everyone how happy he was 24/7.

He needed a shovel to the head.

My neck ached as I turned my head so I could keep Maximum in my field of vision.

"Uh, are you sure?" I asked skeptically.

They never said we had assigned seating, but it was kind of inferred.

"Of course it's fine," Maximum said as he made a show of stacking his books next to mine. "So, how was your time off?

I saw there was a whole exposé on you in *The Falcon Chronicles*—did you see it?"

Sighing heavily, I nodded.

Yes, I saw the picture where I looked like a swamp monster. Yay.

"It's so cool. You have no idea how much everyone in Sparta is talking about you. People in my House keep asking me about you. They freak out when I tell them we're close friends. Isn't that so awesome?"

I grunted noncommittally.

Drex entered the classroom. "Did you move seats?" he asked Maximum with a furrowed brow.

I slumped back with relief as their attention turned away from me.

A few minutes later, all seven of us were seated, and Augustus started lecturing about Cyclopes.

Focusing on my posture, I wrote neat notes in Latin. They'd be illegible by the end of the two weeks, but for now it gave me something to do.

An elbow nudged my ribs.

"I met a Cyclops once," Maximum whispered, his voice barely audible in my left ear.

Don't talk to me. I nodded but said nothing.

He nudged me again. "Have you met one?" he asked.

Don't touch me.

Eye twitching, I shook my head and kept taking notes.

A few minutes later, he nudged me again. This time, his breath was hot on the side of my face as he leaned close. "Did you know that the—"

"Maximum and Alexis." Augustus slammed shut the textbook he was reading from. "Get the *fuck* away from each other. This is a classroom, not a symposium."

Maximum squealed and sidled away from me, clearly shocked by the professor's harsh countenance.

Titus and his cronies chuckled in the back row.

Finally, some personal space.

"Wait," Augustus said menacingly. Soulless black eyes glittered with danger, and his jaw clenched. "Why the fuck did you switch seats? This is *my* classroom, not yours."

Initiates shifted with confusion as the normally calm professor lost it; however, as someone who'd been personally victimized by his freaky mind powers, I was not surprised.

"Everyone, up!" Augustus roared. "You're running the crucible."

What?

Never mind. This was a lot, even for him. Usually he gave people warnings and tried to minimize how many times we ran, especially since it had gotten so cold outside.

General Cleandro sat up with a maniacal grin and hit his pager. His hawk screeched.

None of us dared make a noise of complaint.

BOOM.

A fierce-looking man with long blond hair appeared. An albino crow sat on his shoulder.

"Ryax, heir to the House of Dionysus," said General Cleandro. "Your mentee took it upon himself to switch seats and bother his classmates. Lead them through the circuit."

"Yes, General." Ryax bowed his head, then straightened with a snap. He did not look happy.

"Go!" Augustus roared. "What are you waiting for?"

Initiates physically recoiled at his foul mood, then ran out of the room as fast as possible.

I went with them.

Hours later, my breath came out in ragged, frosty puffs. Teeth chattering, I rubbed at my arms for warmth as I ran up the mountainside. Ice and snow were frigid against my numb toes.

The sky was a miserable shade of gray.

Late November up in the mountains felt like the ninth layer of hell.

Snow flurried, and I shivered harder.

The flimsy material of my toga was not warm. My arms and legs had turned a concerning shade of gray.

Everything ached.

I missed the stifling heat of summer.

Drex jogged beside me with a placid expression, his eyes slightly unfocused as he used his powers. "You're doing great," he said. "A little bit more, then it's all downhill."

A little bit more, then I kill us both.

"It's so cold," Nyx moaned.

Drex kept jogging serenely, lost in his head, unaware of my struggles.

Coughing miserably, I pumped my frozen legs and tried to stay beside him.

Ryax had disappeared up the mountain, but the rest of the initiates were only a few yards ahead. Bloody footprints stained the snow behind them.

"AHHHHHH." A loud, high-pitched scream echoed from somewhere to the right.

I tripped.

Drex barely caught me as he also stumbled.

Everyone stopped running.

We whipped our heads around.

The noise sounded again, much closer, like it was fast approaching.

"Titans!" Cassius yelled, and there was a long pause of horror. Then everyone panicked.

Arms pumping, legs flying, the seven of us sprinted up the narrow mountain path as fast as we possibly could. Icy drops slammed against us, somewhere between ice and snow, as we neared the peak.

"I'm watching your back!" Nyx shouted. "Just concentrate on running. I'll let you know if anything approaches."

I grunted in acknowledgment and kept sprinting.

"Titans on the path!" Cassius yelled loudly when we finally saw Ryax waiting for us at the top, his albino crow circling in the air above his head.

Ryax's eyes widened, and his crow cawed as it dove onto his shoulder. "I'll alert the Assembly of Death."

BOOM.

He leaped away.

Cassius stumbled, and for a second, the seven of us stopped and stared, disbelieving that he'd left us all *alone* on the mountain without protection.

A Titan's scream echoed loudly.

"I'll try to get to the lake and alert Kharon!" Cassius yelled. Wings fluttered on his feet. Then he resumed sprinting, this time at an impossibly fast speed as he hovered over the ground.

He disappeared.

There were six of us left.

"FUCK," Titus screamed, which was the most relatable thing he'd done to date, as the six of us ran down the path where Cassius had disappeared.

Arms pumping.

Legs pounding.

We sprinted down icy rocks at full speed.

Mid-stride, Leo tripped over a boulder in front of me.

His leg cracked horribly as it bent at an awful angle, foot stuck beneath it.

He screamed as he fell.

I stumbled to a stop and reached for him.

Everyone else kept running.

"Shit, kid," Nyx shouted. "It's approaching behind you!"

I looked back and gasped.

A Titan was about a hundred yards up the path.

Tall and skinny, its pale skin was covered in mottled black veins, and its humanlike features were hollowed and misshapen. Ragged scraps of clothes hung off it.

It resembled a rotting corpse.

I gaped.

In a blur, it sprinted forward.

Veined eyes were wide. Sharp teeth were bared. Black talons flashed.

It was fast approaching.

Dangerously close.

Standing beside Leo, I grabbed his hand and tugged on his arm to try to help him up. The Titan leaped forward from an impossible distance, its talons flashing.

Please budge. Freakin' come on!

I yanked on Leo's arm with all my might as he groaned, trying desperately to free him from where he was trapped.

Air whooshed.

Red splattered across me.

Close enough to touch, the Titan crouched over Leo and ripped out his throat with its teeth.

Leo didn't make a single noise.

The hand clutching mine spasmed. Leo's head flopped back, eyes unseeing, fingers slipping through mine.

I just held his hand as he died.

I backed away in horror, unable to comprehend the sheer brutality of what had occurred.

I kept backing away from the monster, down the mountain.

The Titan smacked its lips, spittle made of gore splashing out.

Abruptly—like it was hit by an invisible force—the Titan staggered back, swinging its arms wildly as its black blood sprayed.

Deep, hair-raising growls echoed.

Where are those noises coming from?

The Titan kicked its foot forward with unnatural speed, and there was a thud and a whimper, like something invisible had attacked it and been hit aside. I patted my throat. Nyx was still there. *What the heck?*

The Titan lifted its head and stared.

Directly at me.

I sprinted down the mountain and looked back over my shoulder.

The Titan was still looking directly at me.

Freak, this REALLY isn't good.

Scales slid against my neck. "I'll slow it down. Get to safety!" Nyx shouted. Then she disappeared off my neck.

"No." I stretched for her—fingers missing her invisible body as she flung herself off me and back up the mountain toward the monster.

I slowed, waiting for Nyx.

A few seconds later, marks appeared on the Titan's neck, and it grunted and slapped at its body with its claws.

Nyx shouted as the Titan stumbled around in confusion.

"Nyx," I called as I stopped moving. "Get back here!"

"RUN!" she yelled.

"Not without you!"

I glanced back. The rest of the class had disappeared. In the other direction, Leo was sprawled dead.

Shaking from cold, adrenaline, and abject fear, I vibrated in place.

All I wanted to do was turn and run.

But I couldn't.

"I'm not leaving without you," I called out, praying she was close. The Titan kept stumbling around, like her venom had weakened it.

Cold scales wrapped around my ankle, and I sighed with relief. "What are you doing?" Nyx screamed as she climbed up to my neck.

The Titan stopped stumbling.

My breath caught.

It turned toward me and stared—teeth parted like a wild

animal, eyes impossibly wide. Leo's blood coated the bottom half of its face.

The Titan was twenty feet away.

In a blur, it lunged forward.

There was no time to turn and run.

It would catch me.

Shrieking between gritted teeth, I bent down and picked up a heavy ice-covered rock.

With trembling arms, I held it above my head and waited. Every cell in my body screamed at me to run for my life, but I ignored the instinct.

Ten feet away.

I widened my stance.

Frick, this is going to hurt. Frick. Frick. Frick. Frick.

Five feet away.

You can do this.

Chucking the rock into the Titan's face, I leaned back and turned as its claws swiped. The razor-sharp points grazed lightly across my shoulder.

Hot pain exploded.

I ignored it.

The Titan fell back, clutching at its broken face, black blood gushing all around it.

Scrambling for my rock, I picked it up and lunged forward. Slammed it down against its head.

The Titan moved with impossible speed, but the rock grazed the side of its face. Growling, it rolled to its feet in a crouched position.

On my knees, I didn't have time to reach for the rock again.

Gritting my teeth, I got ready to throw myself at it. I had nothing but fingernails and rage. Nyx reared back on my neck, like she was preparing to bite.

It was hell.

But we were in it together.

The Titan let out a heinous wail as it lunged toward me. I squeezed my eyes shut and did the same.

BOOM.

Pop. Pop. Pop. Pop. Pop. Pop. Pop.

The collision never came.

I stumbled to my feet and righted myself.

A dark cloak billowed in the icy wind.

A Spartan straddled the Titan, chest heaving, two shiny guns extended.

Bullet after bullet unloaded.

"Glad you're okay. Don't touch him—he's mine." The Spartan turned to his right as he spoke, which was confusing because I was on his left.

Who is he talking to?

"I said, stay back," the Spartan ordered.

No worries, I was actually not *going to intervene. He's all yours.* I struggled to process what I was seeing and hearing.

Black blood splattered.

The Titan gurgled and twitched.

Click. Click.

The Spartan jammed in two fresh clips and resumed shooting.

Long minutes passed; he didn't stop.

"Holy crap," Nyx whispered with alarm as she reared back on my neck. "Are you seeing this?"

I nodded, unable to speak.

"Hot with a capital *H*, if you catch my gist," Nyx hissed.

I grimaced because I assuredly did not catch her gist. Also, I was starting to seriously worry about my taste in friends.

The Titan had stopped twitching or making noise. It was a limp carcass of mutated flesh, but gunshots still echoed loudly.

Finally, the Spartan threw both smoking guns to the side.

Nyx and I sighed (me with relief, her with an uncomfortable sexual undertone).

He pulled out a wicked dagger, knelt over the carcass, and started stabbing violently. Gore flew.

Eyes wide, I backed away down the mountain.

Maybe I can get away before he notices—

"Where do you think you're going?" the Spartan rasped darkly. This time, he turned his head and stared directly at me.

Glacial blue eyes were on fire.

I froze.

"Shit—it's *him*," Nyx said.

I was jealous of her ability to swear. This was the perfect moment for it.

The Spartan got to his feet, cloaked head rising as he turned to me, sharp knife still clutched in his hand.

Kharon's muscles bunched, chest heaving, as he pointed the knife at me.

Black blood was splattered across the shadowy planes of his sharp features.

He looks possessed.

No. He *is the thing that possesses people.*

I took another step back.

"Um," I whispered articulately.

"Shit, shit, shit," Nyx said. Now she was just showing off. Her scales slid against my neck as she slithered down into my toga to hide. "You need to run, kid. As fast as you can."

I shook my head slowly and held up both my hands in a surrender gesture.

Rule number one of surviving in rural Montana: you never run away from the predatory wildlife. If you do, you die. They like the chase.

"Thanks for taking c-care of the Titan," I whispered as I shuffled slowly backward. My chest burned with pain, and I winced as the motion opened my wound.

Kharon stalked toward me, long legs eating up the ground, holsters stretching across his chest and bulging thighs.

His tattered black creature cloak fluttered behind him, and his gait had a hitch to it, like he was limping slightly.

It didn't slow him down.

A wicked blood-covered knife was pointed forward—directly at my heart.

Shuffling back faster, I whimpered when he got close, and my eyes squeezed shut on instinct as I waited for the blow.

Warm fingers brushed beneath my chin.

I squinted my eyes open.

Kharon tipped my head up slowly, thumb trailing gently against the edge of my jaw. His right hand cupped my face, and his left hand still gripped his knife.

He leaned close—his mouth hovered inches from mine.

I parted my lips.

The strange queasiness churned deep in my stomach, and a flush burned across my skin.

His breath hitched.

A calloused thumb dragged slowly across my jawline.

"Alexis," he rasped softly, fingers still stroking with unbelievable gentleness, his face close to mine.

"Kharon?"

"This is your last warning. If you *ever* put yourself in harm's way like that again—" his voice shook "—there will be…consequences."

"Why do you care?" I whispered. "You hate me—we're enemies."

He inhaled sharply. "Carissima, don't test me." His voice strummed with viciousness, lips centimeters away. "Please," he begged.

"What?" I asked with confusion.

The fingers tightened into a vise, and I yelped as he squeezed painfully. His pupils dilated. "Why the FUCK DID YOU NOT RUN AWAY WITH THE REST OF THE INITI-

ATES? YOUR LIFE WAS IN DANGER—CHTHONIC FUCKING LIFE!"

I blinked up at him as he bellowed into my face, numbness washing over me in an icy wave. *He's mad that I put my mentors' statuses as generals at stake.*

Breath caught in my throat.

"EXPLAIN YOURSELF," he roared.

Phantom pains shot up both my wrists.

Flickering green lights—fists—ropes—pain—Mother screaming in my face.

Muscle memory took over.

I froze.

How to Take a Beating 101: stay still and minimize damage. Don't complain. Don't flinch. Don't react. Suffer in silence.

Everything warped and twisted.

My vision blurred.

I was insensate.

"Breathe through your nose," Nyx said soothingly. "He's locked away, and she's dead. You're safe, kid. I promise."

Glacier-blue eyes widened as they stared into mine.

Paralysis locked my limbs into place. I couldn't move, couldn't breathe—couldn't feel. Anything.

Kharon stumbled away.

He dropped his knife and swore under his breath, dragging his hands roughly through his short hair.

"FUCK," he bellowed as he pulled harder at his hair and looked at me. "I didn't mean to do that—I'm sorry, are…are you okay? Alexis?"

I tried to speak, but my lips didn't work.

Kharon swore vehemently, looking more distressed by the minute.

He stared at the mutilated Titan. "I need to take it to the underworld—NO," he shouted and turned back to me. "I need to get you away from here—I need to get you somewhere safe. You're hurt. SHIT."

Limbs locked; paralysis intensified.

"I need to take you back to the academy. He'll know what to do." Kharon's words were raspier than usual, and his eyes crinkled with distress. "Can I—" He reached for me slowly. "Can I touch you? Just so we can leap."

I gave a jerky nod.

Gently, like I was made of glass, he grabbed my biceps.

"Come here, guys," he said. *To who?*

The world exploded.

I barely noticed.

A muse yelped as we knocked into her, fireplaces crackled, and candles glowed in the hazy darkness.

Smoke billowed around us.

We'd leaped into the library.

Initiates and a few familiar Spartans with weapons drawn stood in a huddle. They must have come back before us.

Thank goodness everyone else is safe.

My stomach rolled.

But you couldn't save Leo.

Kharon bellowed something as he laid me gently down on a chaise lounge, but all I could hear was a sharp ringing in my ears.

There was a commotion.

Patro and Achilles were leaning over me with panicked expressions. Patro yelled something in my face. Someone ripped him away and leaned toward me, but everything blurred.

"How the fuck did a Titan get all the way out here? It doesn't make sense," a masculine voice growled.

I drifted in and out of consciousness.

My eyes opened a tiny crack—a doctor knelt over me, wearing medical gloves.

Aren't doctors not allowed in the crucible?

I tried to speak, but I was locked in some sort of sleep paralysis.

"What the fuck do you think you're doing?" a voice whipped cruelly from somewhere beside me.

The doctor froze. "I'm p-putting our newest healing cream on her wounds? You asked me to treat her. This should close the skin in hours."

"Lay a finger on her," the voice said calmly, "and I'll cut off both your hands. Then I'll shove them down your throat. Then, while you're busy choking, I'll skin you alive."

The doctor recoiled and dropped the tub of cream.

"Calm down. There's no need to worry," said a second, more reasonable voice. "If he touches her, I'll stab him. You put the cream on her."

Never mind, not reasonable.

The doctor left.

Who named two psychopaths as my medical proxies?

My lids shut, and I couldn't open them.

Hands delicately brushed hair off my forehead. "Be gentle with her," the second voice said.

"Obviously," the first voice responded. Fingers gently glided across the wounds on my chest, like I was a doll that would break under any pressure.

The hands on my forehead kept smoothing my hair back tenderly.

Maybe they aren't so bad.

"That doctor pulled her toga down when everyone was present," the second voice said softly. "If you hadn't moved in front of her, they all would have seen her exposed chest. He would have dishonored all three of us."

How does flashing my nipples affect them? Classic men, making everything about themselves.

"I know. I'll handle him tonight," the other man said as fingers carefully tucked a curl behind my ear.

"Use your sharpest knife."

"Of course."

Wait. What?

Hours later, I gasped awake.

I was sprawled on a chaise lounge in front of a fireplace, with bandages around my chest. A luxuriously soft black blanket was tucked around my shoulders.

The rest of the initiates were seated at the tables, studying.

Everything seemed normal.

Calm.

I must have imagined the voices threatening to stab people. *Thank God.*

With a yawn, I hobbled over to my usual seat.

"She's alive!" Maximum smiled widely as I sat down, then grimaced when everyone glared at him.

Leo's dead.

I rubbed my temples, wondering if it had all been a bad dream.

"It was crazy," Maximum whispered in a loud voice (he literally couldn't speak quietly if held at gunpoint). "Patro, Achilles, and Augustus leaped onto the mountain and took us all back to the library. But Augustus absolutely lost it when he realized you weren't with us and were in danger. I thought he was going to murder everyone."

"He's just worried about my mentors becoming generals," I whispered, and Drex gave me a weird look.

I shivered and pulled the soft blanket tighter around my shoulders.

Maximum narrowed his eyes like he wanted to say something.

"Can you help me with this problem?" Drex asked, and I was grateful he changed the subject.

When we resumed class a few hours later, Augustus was a

dark cloud of fury. He screamed at initiates and glowered the entire time.

At least he's angry at everyone, not just me.

"Alexis!" His voice cracked like a whip.

Never mind.

"Are you paying attention, or are you too busy daydreaming about your idiotic stunt on the mountain? Here's some advice—next time, when you see a Titan approaching…try to run *away* from it, not to it."

Titus chuckled and whispered something derogatory under his breath.

I stared at the floor and fisted my hands.

And the torment continued.

22

TWISTED JUSTICE

AUGUSTUS: A FEW HOURS EARLIER

Alexis was fast asleep.

I left her side.

Moving silently behind the library stacks, I grabbed the unsuspecting doctor by the back of the neck.

"Domus," I whispered as he struggled.

BOOM.

We leaped away from the academy in a cloud of smoke.

Throwing the pathetic man down onto the rough concrete floor, I locked manacles around his wrists before he could react.

He squinted up at me and visibly relaxed. "Oh thank Kronos, I thought you were Kharon."

I stared down at him in silence.

Slowly, he tensed as he took in my unmasked expression.

"Fronti nulla fides," I whispered viciously.

Do not trust the appearance.

His eyes filled with terror.

I was done pretending.

He shouted and yanked, steel chains rattling as he fought to get away from me.

"Do you treat all your female patients so roughly?" I asked, my voice echoing around the cavernous room of my dungeon. "You didn't need to expose her *FUCKING BREASTS*," I bellowed in his face, "to treat her shoulder wound."

He whimpered and pissed himself.

"P-p-p-please, on Kronos's honor, I won't do it again," he said.

The House of Hermes's fish flashed on his white coat pocket as he trembled with fear.

"Don't hurt me," he begged. "She's just an Olympian mutt. She doesn't matter—she didn't even know. It wasn't a big deal. I just wanted to see her chest. Just a glimpse. There are so few Spartan women," he babbled.

I tasted bile.

To think what he would have done if we hadn't been there to stop him. What he could also do to Helen.

He was a highly respected doctor who often worked closely with all the Houses.

"Kronos, please," he begged, tears pouring down his face. "It wasn't a big deal. She doesn't matter."

"Kronos won't save you," I said darkly. "He doesn't care about dirty, dishonorable perverts like you."

Pain scoured my chest as I activated my powers.

He struggled harder and screamed. *"Someone h-help me! Please!"*

I grabbed his chin roughly and yanked his head back, staring into his eyes.

"I'll let you in on a secret," I said, my voice flat and cold. "Alexis Hert matters more than you could ever imagine—and she's mine to protect. Do you know what that means? You violated one of my own."

His eyes went impossibly wide. He whimpered louder as he realized the gravity of his mistake, and the true nature of the man in front of him.

Pain burned in my chest.

I slammed past his barely existent mental defenses and speared into his mind. His eyes exploded from the force of my intrusion.

"TEAR YOURSELF TO SHREDS," I bellowed inside his head.

Chains rattled.

He ripped at his own flesh.

I stood still and watched as justice was served.

And smiled.

23

Twisted Rage

Kharon

"The doctor better be near death," I called out to Augustus as I leaped into the dungeon. Smoke billowed at my feet.

Rage seethed dark and hot in my chest, and my vision warped in and out of focus as I kept activating my powers.

The urge to kill—everyone—burned me alive.

I'd left Hell and Hound back in the library; their broken bones would heal in about a day.

My poor darling was in a lot of pain.

So were the hellhounds.

My knuckles cracked as I fisted my hands. *Alexis almost died on that mountain. A Titan almost tore her to shreds. We almost lost her. Forever.*

I stalked forward, deeper into the dungeon.

Augustus was standing in the shadows, eyes gleaming with danger as he stared at the unmoving, mutilated carcass of the doctor.

His expression was vicious.

He'd dropped the mask of fake pleasantness that he always wore around Olympians.

On the other side of the spacious room, chains rattled, and a second man moaned in pain.

We both ignored the noise.

"Good work." I stood beside Augustus and admired his kill. "I'll scatter the doctor's pieces so he can't regenerate."

"No!" Augustus shouted.

I turned to him in confusion.

"I want to—keep him for some time," he said, voice sharp. "He doesn't deserve a quick death. I want to make it hurt." He vibrated with intensity.

I narrowed my eyes. "What did the doctor…tell you?"

"He did it on purpose. He wanted to see her chest." Augustus spat onto the ground with disgust. "He said there are so few Spartan women to look at, so he wanted to *fucking* see. Imagine what he would have done if we weren't there."

My thoughts blanked.

Chains rattled.

Unthinking, I palmed my gun with my left hand. Pointed it at the far corner. Shot the other prisoner until he went still.

I didn't feel any better.

The gun smoked in my hand, and the fury ate me alive.

"On the mountain," I said quickly, needing to get the horrible realization off my chest. "There was a moment where I yelled at Alexis, and she…disappeared—just like I used to."

Augustus went unnaturally still.

As I gasped for air, the twisted memories suffocated me, and my ruined leg throbbed.

"Someone hurt her," I whispered as I clawed at the neck of my shirt with my right hand, popping buttons so I could breathe. "Badly. Very—fucking—badly."

Diamonds scattered around the dungeon.

"I don't know...about our plan," I said as I waved the gun and tried to breathe. "If she's been hurt before, maybe we should—"

"The plan goes forward." Augustus cut me off harshly. "It's more reason for us to act quickly. She needs our protection, and we'll fucking give it to her."

I stood up straight, inhaling deeply.

Chains scraped against the floor in the corner, and there was a long, pained moan.

"We will protect her," I repeated, tightness loosening in my chest.

Just the idea of abandoning our scheme had caused me physical pain.

Staring at each other, we nodded.

Unspoken promises drifted between us.

Power was a dangerous game—but we were dangerous men. We knew exactly how to get what we wanted.

We knew what it took—audentes fortuna iuvat.

Fortune favors the bold.

Chains rattled. Without looking away from Augustus, I pointed my gun to the corner and unloaded until the prisoner finally shut the fuck up.

"The plan *must* go forward," Augustus said, voice smooth as silk. "Sparta is on the line."

"For—Sparta," I said slowly, and Augustus's eyes flashed with sinful satisfaction.

What we really meant was left unsaid.

It lingered between us, slow and poisonous, like nightshade.

24
SUFFERING

Alexis: The beginning of December

I blinked and tried to focus my vision as we waited for the next class to start.

It didn't work.

The early December temperatures were beyond punishing. Another week of the crucible (hell on earth) had passed, and I was starving and sleep-deprived.

At this point, it was just a normal day in my life.

The six of us sat silently in semicatatonic states as our breaths puffed frosty. Everything was a hazy blur of chattering teeth and hellacious suffering. Cold gnawed at my frozen bones.

Leo had been dead for a few weeks.

I held his hand while he died and his fingers spasmed in my grip.

My lashes fluttered, and white obstructed my vision where frost stuck to them.

Nyx was a heavy frozen block wrapped around my waist. She'd moved from my neck to my torso. She said it was slightly warmer beneath the loose fabric of my toga—now deep in brumation, she didn't so much as twitch.

I rocked back and forth, missing the summer heat, and fantasized about food.

This is officially worse than high school.

At this point, I'd sell both of my kidneys on the black market for a chance to hug Charlie and have Jessica tell me I smelled.

In the front of the room, General Cleandro wore a heavy black coat, and his hawk sat in the furry hood on the back of his neck. There were dark circles under his eyes, and he wore a permanent frown.

Everyone had been on edge since the Titan incident.

Voices whispered, and I snapped my head to the right (barely moved an inch). In my peripheral vision, a blurred skeletal monster flashed dagger-sharp teeth.

Eyes widening in horror, I gaped at the—empty space.

There was nothing there.

Just ice-covered rocks and Titus, who was trying to eviscerate me with his eyes. He'd resumed heckling me after Leo had been brutally murdered; apparently the death of his friend had inspired him to bully others.

The male mind was fascinating (horrifying).

"What the fuck are you looking at?" Titus sneered with pale blue lips.

I blinked slowly. "A w-waste of oxygen."

Wow—did I actually say that out loud? Holy crap. I'm amazing. I wish Carl Gauss was here to see me shine.

Titus was a blurry smudge of manic energy as he leaned toward me. "Say that again, bitch. I fucking dare you. See what happens."

"You're a waste," I said slowly. "Of oxy—"

The door slammed open, and Augustus barked, "Alexis, turn the fuck around and stop flirting with Titus or you'll all run the crucible—again."

Titus snapped his jaw shut, and the rest of the class whimpered.

A scream of despair filled my chest as I forced my frozen neck to turn back forward.

The only thing I'm flirting with is cardiac arrest.

In the front of the dimly lit room, Augustus wore nothing but a toga—his tan arms were on display, muscles bulging obscenely (not that I noticed)—and yet again, he was glaring at me.

Apparently he had a personal vendetta against me living a good life.

People really need to focus on themselves. Ever heard of self-improvement?

I rubbed at the hair ties on my wrists and averted my gaze. The back of my neck prickled like he was still staring.

"Leaping, like oaths and bonding, is all about having a strong concept of home," Augustus said in Latin as he lectured. "It's all about *focusing* on the feeling of safety and protection—most Spartans imagine a person. Now close your eyes and focus."

Luckily my eyes were already closed (I was going into a coma).

Immediately Charlie popped into my head.

My chest twisted with heartsickness. Sternum burning with misery, I forced my thoughts blank because it hurt too much to think about him.

I didn't have a home, not anymore.

"Open your eyes. What do you envision?" Augustus asked.

No one spoke.

"Alexis," he said. "Who did you picture?"

Nails gouged my forearm, and I jolted. I hadn't realized I was clutching at my tattoo. "I s-saw Charlie. He's my—" I cut myself off, horrified by how much I was speaking. *Don't tell the Spartans about him. Pull it together, woman.*

Augustus's expression twisted with madness.

Poco hissed.

"Who the fuck—" he walked forward and stopped an inch away from where I sat "—is Charlie?"

His stance was wide, and he loomed above me with his hands fisted.

Why does he freak out about everything I say?

Swallowing thickly, I tipped my neck back. "No one."

Long, painful seconds passed as he towered in front of me like he was trying to intimidate me with his size.

I rocked back and forth faster.

Augustus unfurled one fist, then leaned forward with his hand extended. He was reaching toward me. My eyes widened, breath hanging in the air between us as he neared in seemingly slow motion.

Everyone in the class stared with anticipation.

I waited (eagerly) for him to strangle me to death.

General Cleandro cleared his throat.

Augustus's arm snapped back to his side, fingers flexing, and he shook his head like he was coming out of a daze. Poco screamed and stuck out his tongue at me.

I would have screamed back, but I was too exhausted.

Augustus turned around and stomped back to the front of the classroom, without a word of explanation for his bizarre behavior.

"What was that?" Drex whispered under his breath, eyes wide as he looked back and forth between me and Augustus.

That was a rabid raccoon and a foiled assassination attempt.

I opened my mouth to respond, but I forgot how to speak, and no sound came out.

Foreign voices whispered in my periphery.

My vision unfocused.

I couldn't see a darn thing.

Manic laughter trickled from my lips, but it wasn't funny. Nothing was.

Reality was unraveling at the seams.

At the front of the classroom, Augustus cleared his throat and resumed lecturing. At least, that was what I assumed was happening, because his mouth was opening and closing, and he was writing on the chalkboard.

I blinked.

Time twisted and warped.

"Alexis, can you help me with this for a second?" Drex called.

I startled awake and realized we were on a break, studying in the library (the other boys were sitting at the table; I was lying in front of the fire, studying the backs of my eyelids).

Groaning, I got to my feet.

"Noooo," Nyx moaned beneath my toga as I moved away from the warm hearth.

Shuffling behind a bookcase, I pulled her out of my toga (while trying to make it look like I was just stretching). I laid her in front of the fireplace. "I'll return for you."

"Please don't," she hiss-mumbled.

I chose not to be offended as I staggered over to Drex.

A few hours later, everything got hazy again.

I was walking (stumbling as Drex pulled me forward by the front of my toga) down the narrow dark corridor toward the menagerie.

How did I get here? Are we going to see the animals again?

Augustus led at the front, and the six of us followed. He stalked through the icy darkness, unbothered like the cold didn't dare touch him.

My teeth chattered so hard my jaw ached.

Every step sent sharp pain jolting down my spine, which was abused from sitting hunched over for hours.

Augustus stopped abruptly, and the six of us bumped into one another. Moans echoed in the dark.

No one was well.

Augustus threw open the menagerie door. "Everyone inside," he ordered.

We shuffled forward.

"Except Alexis," he said.

Despair punched me in the gut as my feet stilled.

The rest of the class entered through the brightly lit door, but Drex shifted in front of me protectively.

It was just the three of us.

Augustus cracked his neck loudly and took a single step toward us. "Drex—get inside, now."

Sunlight illuminated the scar across his sharp cheekbone, and his black eyes smoldered with mania.

How does anyone actually believe that he's a nice guy?

There was a long tense moment as Drex stared up at him. Then my friend nodded and gave me an apologetic look as he walked away into the menagerie.

Augustus pulled the door shut behind him with a crack.

Just the two of us were left.

In the dark.

Before I could move (sprint as fast as possible straight into the wall and knock myself out), a force slammed into me. *Oh nice, the wall ran into me. How convenient.*

The wall was warm, and it moved.

It smelled dangerous and intoxicating.

I gasped in confusion.

Tingles sparked along my nerves, and I struggled to orient myself as my vision cleared.

Augustus's neck blinked into shadowy focus.

I yelped.

His fingers were wrapped tightly around my upper arms, and his hard chest was heaving. He was pressed flush against me, and his hot breath was the warmth tickling my ear. He was pinning me against the wall with his body.

Prickles exploded across my frozen skin.

Help?

His heartbeat pounded through the thin material of both our togas and mingled with my own.

He inhaled loudly, and his steel stomach muscles rippled against my torso. The strange sensation caused a burning to start in my lower stomach.

Butterflies fluttered.

"Professor?" I asked slowly, unable to put anything else into words.

"Alexis," Augustus growled my name darkly, shifting his head so his stubble scraped against the side of my face.

Every muscle in my body tensed.

Heat pooled low as the butterflies turned vicious and ravaged me from the inside out.

"I'll give you *one* more chance to answer." Augustus's knee wedged between my legs and forced them apart as his heavy weight leaned into me and pinned me harder against the rocky wall. "Who the fuck is Charlie?"

I couldn't tell where he began and I ended.

A lot is happening right now.

The killer butterflies multiplied inside my stomach, and my knees trembled.

Clearing my dry throat, I struggled to speak. "Why d-do you care?" I whispered into the dark.

A sinful, humorless laugh echoed, and his chest vibrated against mine. Sharp sensations traveled from my chest to my core.

Everything was on fire.

His lips lingered dangerously close to my ear. "Because—no other man is allowed to have you," he said silkily.

The words were a punch to the gut, and my eyes slammed open.

I reared back and hit my head against the rocks by accident. A loud crack echoed, and Augustus swore.

Just what I needed on top of everything else, a concussion.

He pressed me harder against the wall so I couldn't move. His grip was hard enough to bruise.

"What are you talking about, Professor?" I asked with genuine confusion.

What game is he playing?

The scent of electricity burned caustic in the air, like lightning had struck between us.

His fingers flexed and held me still.

"When Chthonic lives are at risk, it's my job as eldest heir to know everything," Augustus said darkly. "Answer the question. Now."

This is about my mentors. Why is everything always about Patro and Achilles becoming generals?

Blood-covered eyes glowed faintly in the dark, the only source of light.

Pressure burned behind my eyes. There was a stabbing sensation. *"Tell me!"* a foreign voice demanded inside my skull.

I ripped my gaze away and stared at the floor as throbbing pain pierced my head.

He's trying to break my mind again.

Trembles shook my limbs, and my teeth chattered.

Long, tense moments passed.

"Look at me!" Augustus ordered silkily out loud.

I didn't obey.

Staring at the floor, I focused on not becoming a mindless zombie, which was surprisingly hard these days.

The tension between us was a live wire of electricity, and our breaths were loud and labored.

I waited for him to attack.

He waited to make his attack.

His fingers dug harder into the bare skin of my biceps.

Everything was so confusing—my head spun.

I'm too tired for this.

I slumped back against the icy wall.

Augustus whispered something about Chthonics into my left ear, but I couldn't hear it. Also, I'd forgotten what we were talking about.

Exhaustion hammered mercilessly.

Where am I?

Gently he pulled me away from the wall and down the dark hall.

A door opened, and there was a bright, blinding light. He whispered something about taking care of myself and gathered the extra material of his toga. He softly dragged it over my face.

Either he's cleaning off dirt or getting ready to suffocate me?

Either way, I stood still and let it happen.

"Do you need me to get you anything?" His voice sounded far away. "I can't do much to help—but I can try."

"A lobotomy," I mumbled.

He muttered something about a "difficult, exhausted pain in his ass." *They sound cool.*

Suddenly he scooped me up into his arms and carried me through the door. Then he placed me down gingerly. "Sit here—do *not* move a muscle. You'll only hurt yourself," he ordered, which was ironic because he'd just tried to *break* my mind.

"You better not move," I countered smartly, then fell over. Defying gravity was hard work.

"Seriously, Alexis, just stay here and wait for me to come back," Augustus said. "Please don't move."

He backed away, and the door closed.

I was alone.

It was just me, myself, and my insightful thoughts.

I have a feeling the earth is actually flat.

It was hard being so wise all the time.

Time fractured around me.

Everything blurred.

I blinked—I was lying spread-eagle on a snow-covered bank of a familiar lake. The water was frozen, and so was I.

Birds flew overhead, and my classmates' voices sounded from a tree line nearby.

I sat up with a moan.

Oh, look, I was back in the menagerie.

There was dirt and blood all over my bare knees, and a trail of red covered the snow behind me, like I'd been crawling.

Faintly I remembered Augustus ordering me to not move.

Oopsie.

Stretching, I winced as my spinal cord popped like machine-gun fire.

Rolling my aching neck from side to side, I marveled at the unnatural patch of white on the top of my hand.

Oh yay, frostbite.

It was official: I was not living a good life.

God, is this because of that one M-rated Carl Gauss fanfic I wrote? Please forgive me. I knew it was wrong when I was writing it, but I couldn't stop myself.

There was a loud hacking noise.

Understood, God, I will be better.

The noise repeated, and I turned. The cheetah creature from before crept over to where my blood covered the snow and sniffed it.

It lifted its head up with its pupils blown out. All the hair on its body stood on edge. Then it yowled as it sprinted away.

"Rude—I bet I taste delicious," I called after it. "You're missing out."

A hiss echoed from the trees.

"That's just unnecessary," I grumbled under my breath.

Apparently I wasn't good enough to befriend or to eat. It shouldn't have hurt so badly, but it did.

It was the principle of things.

I poked miserably at the patch of frozen skin on my hand.

Fluffy Jr. suddenly sprinted out from behind dead grasses toward me, wagging his tail (if that was what you could call the white thing that trailed behind him).

He turned his head. A stick was halfway down his throat, jutting out of his muzzle like a point.

He was so beautiful.

"Hey, little guy." Tears poured down my cheeks. "I really—missed you. Are you okay? How have you been? You're so gorgeous."

It was great to see a friendly face.

I needed this.

"Things have been really—hard for me lately, especially since Nyx is always asleep," I confessed with a sniffle as I wiped my blurry eyes. "You being here right now means a lot. I can't even tell you."

Fluffy Jr. wiggled his body, then tipped his head down and stabbed the end of the stick deeper.

He choked and fell over.

Stressful minutes of CPR later, I was on my hands and knees, gasping from exertion, clutching a saliva-covered stick.

Fluffy Jr. celebrated surviving his near-death experience by running in a circle and chasing his misshapen butt.

I debated crossing the menagerie and begging the monstrous creature to end me. *Lord knows the cheetah's too cowardly to do it.*

But it was a long walk.

Would it kill the beast to be a little more conveniently located?

"Time's up!" Augustus roared from the doorway. "Everyone out in five minutes or you're running the crucible. Alexis—where the fuck did you go? I told you not to move!" His rage echoed through the cavernous menagerie.

Oh, that can't be good.

Fluffy Jr. used my momentary distraction to run up and grab the half-digested stick back out of my hand.

I stared at him.

He stuck it back down his throat.

Apparently, everyone is struggling with their mental health these days. Who am I to judge?

Groaning, I staggered to my aching feet, then shuffled toward the door, leaving Fluffy Jr. to his own morbid devices.

I smiled and limped casually by Augustus, who was waiting for all of us at the door. He had a fluffy hunchback—Poco's tiny hands were clutched together at the front of his neck.

Augustus stared down at my bloody knees.

Tan features turned purple, his hands fisted, and a vein pulsed on his forehead. His jaw was clenched so tightly I could practically hear his teeth grinding together.

Luckily he said nothing. Just whirled around and marched back along the path as we all hurried to keep up with him.

Poco turned his head and hissed at me.

"You have rabies," I mouthed silently.

Poco showed how *not rabid* he was by shoving half of Augustus's ponytail into his mouth and screeching at the top of his lungs.

"Real mature," I said.

Drex looked over at me with concern.

Time shifted.

Hours later, I rocked back and forth as Pine lectured about the number zero.

"Alexis," he said. "What did I say a month ago is a tenet of Thagorean ethics that allows you to divide fractions of zero?"

The rest of the class looked at me with panicked expressions.

"Unreal n-numbers," I said numbly as my teeth chattered. The answer was so obvious I didn't even have to think about it, which was good because at the moment, a lot of thought processing was not happening.

Pine beamed. "Correct—right again. Your mind is truly impressive."

Carl Gauss would push me to be better, not praise me for answering stupid questions.

The class relaxed.

I remained tensed (half-catatonic).

Voices whispered behind me, and my neck prickled. *The voices aren't real. Pull it together, Alexis.*

I blinked.

Drex was pulling me into the library. "Come on, we have four hours to study," he said as he pushed me gently into my usual chair.

Time is strange.

I fell out of it and sprawled onto the floor.

Alessander crawled past on his hands and knees, with blue lips and eyes bloodshot from sleep deprivation.

We nodded at each other.

Real recognized real.

Drex hauled me up by the front of my toga, sat me down in the chair, then pushed it in tightly before I could fall out of it.

"T-t-tanks," I garbled.

He grunted and nodded, then collapsed into his own seat across from me.

Shaking, I could barely grab my textbook and open it.

An index card fluttered out.

Messy words were scratched hastily in ink:

This is your last warning.

Leave Sparta now or there WILL be consequences. The Titan was just a taste of what I'll do. You better disappear by the January Initiation Ball.

I stared at it.

Oh.

My.

God.

Leo was dead because of me.

A person purposefully set the Titan free.

I'm being hunted.

After the momentary shock passed, I felt—absolutely nothing. Yep, it was official. I was too exhausted to care.

Nihilism (the crucible) had robbed me of all emotions.

Life was meaningless.

Death wasn't scary because… I wasn't alive.

Slowly I tucked the paper away in the back of the book. Then I gingerly kicked my feet back and forth to check, but there was nothing under my chair.

Nice. It was just a note this time.

"Are you okay?" Drex asked, and I realized I'd been staring down at the tabletop with wide eyes.

I looked up at him. "No."

He blanched. "Uh—do you not want to study today? I understand it's been a lot. Maybe we should sleep in front of the fire and—"

"Give me your textbook," I ordered and cut him off as Maximum sat down next to me.

Drex pushed it forward.

"Ugh, this is miserable," Maximum said as he slumped next to us.

I ignored him.

With unfeeling lips, I walked Drex through equations. Every few seconds, he glanced at me with a worried expression, like he was concerned for my well-being.

Who's going to tell him that ship sailed nineteen years ago?

Hours later, General Cleandro screamed something, and Drex dragged me back into the classroom.

Unfortunately, no one remembered to get Alessander.

The general grinned and announced we were running the circuit.

Augustus looked at me with an intense, worried expression, so I gave him a thumbs-up to show that everything would be all right. His frown deepened, and I realized I was holding up my elbow, not my thumb. *Awkward.*

I blinked.

Wind howled, and snow whipped in a frenzy.

Visibility was zero.

I was 99 percent sure my eyeballs were also freezing, because it was hard to move them.

Bloody feet slipped on ice as I struggled to keep up with the group. If Drex hadn't run slightly in front of me, pulling me forward, I would have 100 percent fallen off the mountain into the ravine below (on purpose).

Sadly, he wouldn't leave me alone.

The misery continued.

When we finally got to the bottom of the mountain a million years later, my jaw dropped—in my head, because I couldn't move my face muscles. They'd broken a path through the frozen lake so we could swim through it.

It had Kharon written all over it.

Why are Spartan men like this? God forbid anyone try to live a somewhat good life these days.

Kharon stood on the river in a boat. A thick fur coat hung around his wide shoulders. His jaw was clenched, and he stared at me with a strange expression.

He almost looked—worried?

Just like Augustus, deep lines marred his forehead.

They had good reason to worry.

Hours later, I crawled onto the frozen bank, head hanging low, eyes twitching, limbs tingling, gasping for air. I was numb all over.

The icy swim had easily been the worst experience of my life.

Hands-down.

Being Spartan meant we'd survive when humans would go into shock, but it didn't make it hurt any less. It just meant we could suffer more.

Lucky me.

I crawled toward the mountain entrance as initiates stumbled to their feet around me. We staggered down to the library, and I collapsed in front of the hearth I always lay in front of.

I landed on a warm block, which moaned.

"Nyx?" I asked, remembering I had a snake bestie. *Ever almost abandon a friend? Same.*

She hissed and slithered around my neck. Her warm scales felt divine, like a toasty scarf.

I opened my mouth to thank her, but passed out from exhaustion.

"Alexis," someone shouted. "Shit!"

Time got fuzzy again.

Everything was spinning in muted shades of red.

Maybe this is the afterlife? And we've forgotten what came before? Maybe it's all a simulation, and that's why math makes so much sense?

My head lolled back, and I stared up into the glacial blue eyes of a murderer. Fur was draped over my shoulders. Kharon was carrying me across his chest, and Augustus had his hand on my forehead.

They were both glaring down at me.

What did I do now?

I glimpsed a muzzle, and Patro said something. *When did my mentors get here?*

There was a loud gurgling sound.

Water.

They're going to make me swim it again. No. No. No.

I struggled to get away from the icy River Styx, but Satan

flexed and held me tight. I couldn't even move an inch. He was merciless.

He lowered me down into a tub.

Hot water surrounded me.

I sighed at the heat, and Nyx let out a low hiss of contentment as she slithered away.

Abruptly, prickling exploded across every one of my nerves.

I was boiling alive.

Screaming, I tried to get away from the pain, but Kharon and Augustus held me down. Their expressions were strange.

Patro kept saying something behind them, but I couldn't hear him over my agonized shrieks. A muzzle moved in my peripheral vision as Achilles dragged his hands roughly through his hair.

Tears streaked warmly down my frozen cheeks, and I pleaded at them nonsensically.

They didn't release me.

Monsters without empathy.

Darkness pulled me under, and blessedly I finally died.

I awoke with a start. I'd just passed out. *Another disappointment.*

Warm bubbly water sloshed around me as I moved. I was lying fully clothed in a grand marble tub.

The dark bathroom was unfamiliar. Moonlight streaked through a closed window, and a light prickling sensation tingled along my limbs, but for the most part, I felt nothing.

I was fully numb.

The physical pain had passed.

Whispers echoed, and I gripped my hair-tie-covered wrists as old aches burned my forearms.

The door creaked open slowly, and I slid lower into the water.

Black eyes met mine. Augustus was holding a steaming mug and a bottle of medicine.

He startled when he realized I was awake, watching him.

"You need to drink this," he said softly, his eyes narrowed with concern. "And take this nutrient pill so you can regain strength. It's imperative that you—"

"Leave," I interrupted him with a raspy croak, the harsh sound unnaturally loud in the quiet.

I didn't want his help, or his stupid mug of whatever.

The memory of frigid, icy, dark water haunted my thoughts. The mental pain from the endeavor persisted.

Augustus straightened up taller under my scrutiny, silver crown gleaming. "I will leave—after you've drunk this and taken your medicine." Black eyes narrowed.

I stared down at the water and avoided his monstrous gaze.

His footsteps echoed softly.

They stopped inches away; he was close enough that I could smell electricity and musk.

He fell to his knees beside the tub.

"Tip your head back—Alexis," he said. "Don't make me ask again."

I wanted to grab the cup from his hand and throw it in his face. But I'd never been great at conflict.

Tilting my head, I stared down at the soapy water as he gently pressed the steaming mug to my lips. It tasted earthy and a little sweet.

"Good job, my carus," he said as I took a big gulp.

I choked at the Latin endearment.

A strange heat warmed my stomach. "Don't c-call me that," I whispered, voice tremulous. "I'm not *your* anything—you don't even know me."

"Are you sure about that?" he asked slowly, voice smooth and dangerous. "Nota res mala, optima."

An evil thing known is best.

His hand spanned the back of my skull as he cradled my head and tipped the mug back. Heart pounding painfully in my chest, I drank quickly, disturbingly aware of the fingers pressing against my scalp.

When I'd taken the medicine and drained the mug, I bolstered my courage and asked, "Which one of us is the evil thing?"

He laughed, a dark, silky sound.

"Go to sleep. I'll watch over and protect you," he said. "I'm not going anywhere."

It sounded like a threat.

My lids felt impossibly heavy, and I closed my eyes.

He never answered the question.

That was the last thought I had.

25
Bonding with Protectors

Alexis: Late December

We waited in frigid silence for the next class to begin.

Time passed strangely in the mountain. The days went by with painful slowness, but the months blinked by.

It was already late December.

I shivered harder.

There was one more month until the Initiation Ball and graduation ceremony. One month until I turned twenty and was apparently immortal.

It didn't feel real.

I'd almost survived, but the problem was, I hadn't even been alive to begin with.

No part of me felt like celebrating.

The days were getting harder to endure.

My spirit was deteriorating.

Ever since Augustus had knelt beside me while I slept in a bathtub, things had been strange between us. He still was a grumpy bastard, but every time I looked up during his lectures, he was staring at me.

It was weird.

Now, teeth chattering uncontrollably, I held my knees to my chest and rocked back and forth. My breath lingered in a frosty cloud.

Nyx's scales were still icy beneath my toga.

The classroom was darker than usual; the only source of light was a single torch burning on the wall above the chalkboard.

All the candles had extinguished a week earlier.

Icicles hung off them.

Drex moaned beside me as he curled tighter in on himself. Maximum looked back at us and smiled—his lips were white, and there was a square patch of frostbite on his cheek.

I tried to grimace, but my face was frozen.

Someone groaned behind me.

The six of us who remained huddled low as we tried to conserve as much body heat as possible. Our breaths were loud and labored, skin unnatural shades of ice.

December was trying to kill us.

"Your teeth chattering is obnoxious," Titus whispered behind me. "Do you now see why women should never do the crucible? You're too weak."

Since I'm still alive (against my will) and a bunch of dudes are dead, that makes zero sense.

Alessander laughed beside him, but it was a strangled, pained sound.

Drex and I both rolled our eyes (our eyelids barely twitched, but we understood what we meant).

Maximum turned around at the noise and shuffled closer to me and Drex. "Guess what I heard?" he whispered conspiratorially.

Neither of us responded.

Unfortunately, he took that as an invitation to continue.

"The Houses aren't happy so many initiates have died this year." Maximum shook his head and made a dramatic face. "About three die on average, and they're especially pissed about the Titan attack. Apparently one hasn't happened in centuries."

Yeah, because someone did it on purpose. Also, they keep leaving me notes, which is not weird, unsettling, or concerning at all.

Neither Drex nor I reacted.

Maximum deflated.

Here's a crazy idea—if they wanted people to live, they shouldn't have held a massacre to begin with. Just saying.

Instead of turning around and letting us suffer in peace, Maximum turned his full attention to me and shuffled closer. "Are you doing okay, Alexis? I know you have less muscle than the rest of us."

Wow.

That was a bold statement, especially since he was shorter than me.

I narrowed my eyes and grunted eloquently.

"Do you want me to rub your arms, to warm you up?" Maximum smiled as he held out his hands.

"No." I reeled back. *I'd rather die.*

"Okay." He winked and kept his hands extended toward me. "Offer's still on the table."

That's too bad.

The door was thrown open.

Augustus stalked into the room with Poco sitting on his shoulder.

He looked down at where Maximum was leaning toward me, and his expression contorted with fury.

Black eyes flashing, he clenched his jaw.

Poco clapped and poked his cheek.

Pine hurried in after him.

Everyone sat up straighter because unless they were reading test scores, both professors were never in the classroom at the same time.

We held our breath.

If they made us run the crucible right now, I would perish from hypothermia (throwing myself off the top of the mountain).

The only good part about this week was that we'd meditated a lot because we were learning about leaping, so I hadn't had to take many notes.

But overall, the last week at the academy had been the worst one yet.

So far.

It will probably get worse.

Everything in life does.

A chair scraped at the front of the class as General Cleandro stood up beside Pine. Both men wore long, heavy coats.

Augustus was still the only one dressed in a toga. His bare, vein-covered arms were crossed nonchalantly—biceps bulging obscenely—like he wasn't even cold.

I rocked faster to warm myself.

"Today is an important day for all of you," Augustus said with a serious expression, and Poco nodded his head in agreement. "Today is the day you bond with your chosen protector."

I stopped rocking.

This isn't good.

We'd been to the menagerie a few times over the last few months, and each time, the animals had reacted the same way.

They hated me.

Freezing, and sick to my stomach with nerves, I followed the rest of the initiates down the narrow ice-covered hall.

General Cleandro held open the door to the menagerie. "Remember, animals can sense your powers and your soul. Tread carefully. You have one hour to bond with an animal," he said harshly. The *or else* hung unsaid in the frosty air.

Inside, the trees were barren of leaves.

A light covering of snow dusted everything. Birds cawed loudly and flew around, bright swaths of color on a barren landscape.

The larger animals moved silently, concealed behind the trees.

Everyone spread out as they looked up at the birds.

I rubbed at my temples. I had no idea what I was going to do.

Since it was probably best to try out a new area, I walked to the far right and sat down on a stump in the middle of a clearing.

Birds cawed aggressively from the air, warning me off.

Protracted minutes passed as I waited for a mythical animal to come out and love me.

None did.

One by one, the other initiates cheered and whooped with excitement as they bonded.

A falcon with an impressively long silver tail puffed up proudly on Cassius's arm, and he beamed with pride.

Then, a few minutes later, a squat purple bird with two heads squawked on Alessander's shoulder, and he pumped the air.

There was a smattering of applause.

I didn't clap.

Drex held up the golden toucan he always sat with. "Look, Alexis!" he called.

I gave him a thumbs-up, and a fake smile hurt my cheeks.

Time kept passing.

Panic set in.

Standing up, I wandered toward the forest. Birds took flight, a deer with strange horns sprinted away, and a red possum scurried up a tree as it hissed in my direction.

Maybe I can lie and say Nyx is my protector? She was sleeping around my waist, but if I could just get her to show herself, it could work.

It was the only plan I had.

Fluck my life.

"Wow—I'm not surprised none of the animals wanted to bond with you." Titus slunk around a tree. His chest was puffed up with pride. An eagle with neon-green markings and long gold talons was perched on his shoulder. "Now they're gonna kill you for not bonding with a protector."

He laughed and approached.

His eagle screeched but stayed put. For some reason, bonded animals didn't freak out around me as much as unbonded ones did, although they still weren't happy with my presence.

Of course, Titus thought that was hilarious, and he laughed even harder.

I wish I was back in the stupid frozen lake.

Fisting my chilled hands, I breathed roughly through my nose to calm myself down.

Titus got closer, and his eagle turned its head away like it couldn't stomach looking at me. *Right back at you, robot.*

There was a sudden blur near my legs, and Titus fell back screaming.

The eagle flapped its wings aggressively.

Menacing growls echoed.

Fluffy Jr. stood in front of me protectively. His head was at my thighs, and his strange white tufts of fur stood on end as he vibrated with rage.

Has he grown since I last saw him? Was he always this big?

Titus pointed at my hero. "Get that thing!"

Before the bird could react, I swooped down and picked up Fluffy Jr. protectively with a loud grunt. He was not light, and I had to use both hands.

Are the twigs making him fat?

"That thing bit me," Titus growled, pointing at his bloody leg.

Kissing Fluffy Jr. on his forehead, I whispered, "Good boy."

His misshapen body trembled with excitement, and he turned his head up, then licked my cheek.

I gagged—his breath was rancid.

"Give me that thing," Titus ordered. "You know the rules. If a Spartan is attacked by an animal, he has the right to exact revenge. Give it over. Now."

I held Fluffy Jr. tighter and took a step back. "Oh, please," I said. "You barely have a s-scratch."

Titus stuck out his leg and showcased what was left of his shin. "You can see my bone!"

Holy crud. Did he literally bite a chunk out of him, then swallow it?

I gave Fluffy Jr. another kiss on the head. This time for bravery and daring to do what needed to be done during a stressful time.

"If you don't give it over—right now," Titus said threateningly, "I'll take it from you forcibly." His eagle flapped its wings and leaned forward like it was getting ready to attack.

It was a *big* bird.

My stomach dropped, heart pounding, because I knew what I needed to do. *Nyx is going to be so mad when she wakes up.*

"You can't," I said. "Because he's my—protector."

Titus's jaw dropped.

"Bullshit," he said. "You're just saying that. No fucking way will you bond with that thing."

"Back up." I pointed at him and moved away. "Let us bond."

Fluffy Jr. squirmed and yipped in my arms, licking my chin with excitement like he knew what was going to happen.

"If you reject me and boil my brains," I whispered to him, "I will *not* forgive you."

He licked me again.

"You better think my soul is beautiful."

After a deep, steadying breath, I awkwardly held up Fluffy Jr.'s heavy body out in front of me and stared into his eyes like we'd been taught.

I cleared my thoughts.

Focused on the feeling of home. Laughter, solving equations, cuddling under a tarp, music, Charlie.

"Domus," I whispered.

Nothing happened. *Well, that was anticlimactic.*

Sighing, I began to lower my arms—

Pure energy exploded in my chest. I was falling and flying at the same time.

Something new, a strand of light, unfurled inside my sternum, and it strummed with loyalty, aggression, and the urge to protect. It felt violent.

The cord burned impossibly hot, and my heart pounded like I was having a heart attack as I struggled to breathe.

It was a panic attack.

The connection was overwhelming.

All-consuming.

Intense. Dangerous. Volatile.

I collapsed onto my knees and clawed at my sternum.

Shaking.

Gasping.

Everything got blurry.

A horrible stench brought me back to consciousness. Wetness licked my nose. Then Fluffy Jr. stepped back and stared down at me.

He had two-colored eyes.

One a pale white, the other midnight-black.

"Are you blind?" I whispered as I fingered his mashed-up little ear. He spun in a circle and barked, the sound loud and dangerous. *We'll deal with that later.*

Groaning as the icy snow burned my exposed skin, I hobbled to my feet.

There was a new throbbing ache in my chest, and while it was no longer debilitating, it was *heavy.*

Titus stood a few feet away with his jaw hanging open. He stared at me like I was an idiot.

It was the perfect moment for me to practice vocalizing.

"Frick you," I said to him, then stomped (shuffled) away, with Fluffy Jr. at my heels.

"YOUR TIME IS UP!" General Cleandro shouted from the doorway a minute later. "Everyone out."

I ran (hobbled forward with more intensity), and Fluffy Jr. sprinted past me.

He wiggled his lumpy butt with excitement and looked back to make sure I was following. I smiled at him.

"You have five hours to study in the library," General Cleandro announced as we trudged through the dark hallway. "Use the time wisely."

When we finally got back to the library, my smile fell.

Augustus blocked the door. Poco was still seated on his shoulder.

The other initiates had already entered the room.

"What…is that?" Augustus pointed to Fluffy Jr., and Poco also pointed.

"This is Fluffy Jr.," I said confidently. "My protector."

Poco hissed.

Augustus took a step forward, and blood pooled in the whites of his eyes.

Pressure spiked painfully in my skull.

I ripped my gaze away.

Staring at the floor, I gasped for air. *He tried to violate my mind again. What the actual hell? I thought he wanted to* protect *me, not boil my freakin' brains.*

Augustus's breathing was loud and harsh. In my peripheral vision, he clenched and unclenched his fingers like he wanted to hit something (I was definitely the something).

"Is there a p-problem, Professor?" I whispered calmly, like I didn't want to throw up from fear.

The initiates are a few feet away. I can scream for help, and they'll know what he's doing.

We both knew no one would do anything to stop him.

He was a famous full-blooded Chthonic heir, and I was an abandoned Olympian mutt. He was ancient royalty. I was nothing.

Fluffy Jr. growled. The sound was low and menacing, the noise of a much larger predator.

The cord in my chest burned with heat, and the urge to *protect and kill* thrummed through me.

Poco flashed razor-sharp fangs.

Augustus muttered something under his breath about Chthonics, dishonor, and women who couldn't take care of themselves.

Finally he gritted his teeth and said, "No. That is…all, Alexis." Once again, Augustus said my name with a strange inflection, like it meant something to him.

He gestured as he stepped aside so I could enter the library. There wasn't enough room to pass.

Girding my lady loins, I pushed past him.

Goose bumps exploded across the right side of my body—his muscles flexed beneath my touch, and Augustus made a low, throaty noise in the back of his throat.

The strange queasiness in my stomach spiked hot.

An inferno raged.

Poco leaned out and grabbed for my curls with both of his little hands.

I stumbled into the room.

It was a second of contact between us, if that, yet my heart raced like I'd run the circuit.

Augustus stalked away without another word, and I slumped with relief.

Something about him drives me crazy.

Whatever it was, I had a bad feeling it was going to spell my demise.

26

GIFTS

Alexis

Augustus left me reeling.

When I regained my wits enough to walk (stumble in a forward direction), I hurried over to the study tables where the rest of the boys were spread out in their usual spots.

Initiates recoiled as I passed with Fluffy Jr., and Titus shot us both death glares, his leg still bleeding.

If there was any justice left in the world, he'd get gangrene.

When I finally got to my seat, I fell into it. The luxurious throw blanket that someone had gifted me was draped across the back, and I wrapped it around my arms gratefully.

"Wow. You bonded with that thing?" Drex whispered as his golden toucan glared at me.

I repositioned Fluffy Jr.'s head on my lap. He was not a thing; misshapen creatures deserved love too.

"Yep," I said as I busied myself pulling out textbooks. I didn't want to talk about it.

"Look." Maximum held up his arm and showcased a yellow squirrel creature with five legs. It screeched when it saw me and climbed under his shirt.

Never mind, that thing is weird and does not deserve love.

"Very...nice?"

Maximum beamed and pulled his seat closer to mine.

I tried to scoot away, but there wasn't any room with the chair on my other side.

"Wasn't it crazy?" he said. "I can still feel his presence right now, a hot pressure at all times in here." He tapped at his forehead.

"Yeah," Drex responded. "My head is low-key killing me ever since we bonded. The heat is constant. It's almost like when I use my powers but a little more intense."

I looked back and forth between the two boys, stomach dropping.

"Did you feel anything in your chests?" I asked, trying to look casual.

"No," Maximum said.

"No. Why?" Drex asked.

I opened my textbook. "No r-reason," I muttered. The throbbing cord in my chest was unmistakable.

There was nothing in my head.

Nada.

Zilch.

Why can nothing in my life be normal? Can something go right for once? Is that really too much to ask for?

Apparently it was.

Six hours later, we ran the circuit in a blizzard.

Snow whipped in a frenzy, burning my eyes, and the visibility was zero. I could barely see my arms as I pumped them. Nyx was an icy block around my stomach.

Patro and Achilles jogged on either side of me. Nero and

Poppae ran at our feet, easily navigating the mountain, like they were born to run.

The rest of the initiates were in front of us, except Titus, who limped behind us with a wounded leg.

My neck prickled under the weight of his glare.

He was furious.

Get in line, buddy.

I was 99 percent sure we were only running right now because Augustus was trying to kill off Fluffy Jr.

An hour ago, while we were meditating and envisioning leaping, Fluffy Jr. had barked, and Augustus had announced that I was "purposefully trying to disrupt the class with my idiotic, useless protector."

Then he'd ordered us to run the circuit, and General Cleandro summoned my mentors.

The kicker: Augustus had let everyone else's animals stay behind but made Fluffy Jr. run it with me as "his punishment."

The joke was on Augustus—Fluffy Jr. seemed to be having the time of his life.

He ran ahead of us, body quivering with his head flung back as he tried to catch every single snowflake. He'd been doing it for hours and showed no signs of slowing down. His oversize paws and surprisingly powerful legs ate up the climb like it was nothing.

At least someone was having fun.

Breathing shallowly, gums aching from inhaling freezing air, eyelashes frozen over, I pushed my burning muscles forward.

"So," Patro asked casually, like he wasn't even exerting himself, "have you noticed anything off about Augustus lately? I've known him my entire life, and he's usually a very calm guy, but he seems a little—different."

I choked on saliva and spat it out.

The wind whipped it right back into my face, and it froze across my cheek.

The universe hates me.

"Have you?" Patro asked again, clearly not letting it go.

"He's a dick," I said, then tripped with excitement because I'd finally done it; I'd sworn aloud.

Fluffy Jr. barked loudly and jumped around as the cord in my chest strummed. He was happy for me. *Adorable.*

"It's weird." Patro shook his head slowly like he was leisurely thinking and not climbing up the side of a mountain in a blizzard, trying to survive. "Has he said anything to you?"

I shook my head.

Yeah, he threatened me, then smashed my brain to bits. He's also held a mug to my lips, potentially called me evil in Latin, and promised to protect me. Pinned me against a wall. Stalked me with his eyes.

"Are you sure he hasn't done anything…dramatic? Like given you anything?" Patro was staring at me like he wanted to ask something specific, but then Achilles shook his head, and he closed his mouth.

"No," I said. *The only thing he's given me is PTSD.*

A beat passed.

"He's the s-son of Ares," I continued, like it explained everything. He'd chosen to be heir of the lineage nicknamed the *House of War*; that was all I needed to know about his mental health.

My mentors looked unconvinced.

"On another topic," Patro said, "you never told us—did you ever figure out what your power is?"

I stumbled again.

Achilles caught me. His calloused fingers lingered on my arm as he slowly released me, like he didn't want to let go.

I tilted my head toward him questioningly, but he fisted his hands and glanced away.

"Did you figure it out?" Patro repeated as he looked down at me expectantly.

"Yeah, I did," I said with a gasp. "I can talk to sentient creatures in their language. I can talk to sirens, and some…other creatures I've met."

Patro's face transformed with excitement. He'd never done this around me.

I choked again. He was breathtaking when he smiled.

The longer I survived the crucible, the nicer he seemed to get.

"Wait—that's actually amazing!" Patro said. "That's the least lame Olympian power I've ever heard of, congrats."

I nodded exhaustedly.

Patro slapped my back. "We're gonna make a Spartan out of you yet. I always knew we got lucky when we got you as our mentee."

Achilles made a sound of disbelief in his muzzle, and judging from his narrowed red eyes, unlike Patro he was not feeling grateful to have me around.

Sure.

We'll pretend that's what happened.

A thought hit me. I took the opening. "Patro," I asked between pants, "what's your power?"

Green eyes glowed bright as snow whipped between us.

For a second, I thought he wouldn't answer. But then he said softly, "If I'm touching someone, I can tell if they're lying or telling the truth."

My stomach twisted into knots. That was why "Liar" was tattooed across his knuckles. He was the *L* in *WSDL*.

He could easily uncover all my secrets.

I feigned casualness. "That's cool."

He winked down at me, and my breath caught. "So," I said awkwardly, "do you and Achilles know who you're going to marry when you turn twenty-six?"

The two of them straightened and looked at each other. "We have an idea," he said cryptically.

I nodded and resumed focusing on running.

He cleared his throat.

"I just want to thank you," Patro said, his expression uncharacteristically solemn. "For not—coming on to Achilles."

I coughed. *What?*

"A lot of women and men," he said bitterly, "harass him because of his muzzle and inability to talk. We assumed because of how you'd grown up that you would be like the other human girls we've met."

I grunted and nodded, unsure of what to say.

"We're together," Patro blurted. "But since we're bisexual—no one seems to fucking respect that we're a couple. So, thanks again." He nodded down at me, then looked away, like he was embarrassed.

I shrugged (tried to move my shoulders but failed).

"We're usually not interested in other people," Patro continued with a blush. He glanced at me like he was trying to convey something important. "But we've recently..."

Achilles shook his head.

I waited, but Patro never finished his sentence.

They're acting weird.

To change the subject, I asked something that had been bothering me for weeks. "What does Hades's power do? The fog during the massacre was...strange."

Patro arched his brow and looked down at me. "It torments you with the worst thing you've ever done."

The boy with horns screaming for mercy as he beat himself with his own fists.

There had been so many voices.

None of them made sense.

"Is the fog—confusing?" I asked, unsure how to verbalize the jumble of noises I'd experienced.

Patro shook his head. "No, it's painfully clear."

My sternum went cold, and it had nothing to do with the icy conditions.

We ran the rest of the way in silence.

When we finally got to the bottom of the mountain, the river was iced over so thickly that they couldn't clear a path.

Tears streamed down my face with relief. They froze and made my face hurt.

Drex grinned at me.

The other initiates slumped over with gratitude.

Patro announced we would be running the mountain pass for a second time because we couldn't swim. Any congenial feelings I had for him extinguished.

I cried again, this time from misery.

When the suffering was over, we staggered back down the stairs into the mountain. All of us were near comatose.

Fluffy Jr. led the way, his fur covered in snow and ice.

Augustus's face fell when he saw him outside the classroom, and he glared down at my protector with a murderous expression.

Fluffy Jr. growled back.

General Cleandro stepped out of the room and announced we had a break in the library.

The six of us turned and stumbled in that direction. Titus moaned, dragging his wounded leg behind him.

No one went to the tables.

We all collapsed in front of the different fireplaces spread around the room.

I stuck both of my feet, which were a sickly pale blue color, near the flames.

If I was fully human, they'd need to be amputated. Since I was part Spartan, I'd recover.

Lucky me.

Voices whispered nearby, and the hairs on my neck stood up like I was being watched.

I gritted my chattering teeth and ignored it.

Fluffy Jr. licked my face (it smelled like something had *died* in his mouth) as I lay on the floor in front of the fireplace. Then numbness turned into an awful prickling sensation, and I convulsed on the rug.

In a daring show of solidarity, Fluffy Jr. fell asleep. He snored. Loudly.

When the shakes finally passed, I pulled my feet away from the fireplace and staggered upright.

I collapsed back into a chaise, eyes closing.

Classical music filtered in softly from outside.

"Alexis?" Maximum said, and the cushion moved beneath me.

Hey, God, it's me again.

Please help.

I cracked open my right eye. He was sitting next to me on the chaise, leaning forward.

Maximum's face hovered inches in front of mine. "I know it's not a great time, but… I've been wanting to get you alone—so I could tell you this."

"Hmm?" I grunted noncommittally.

"I really like you," Maximum whispered, leaning even closer. "Like, a lot. You're the coolest girl I've ever met."

He must not know a lot of women.

"Uh, okay?" I said awkwardly, still leaning back, unsure what he wanted me to do. *Why is he leaning closer?*

The back of my neck prickled.

Icy lips pressed softly against mine.

Shocked, eyes wide open, it took me a second to realize that he was kissing me. A boy was kissing me.

The kiss was sort of…nice? It really didn't feel like much of anything.

My face was still numb.

A ferocious animal growl echoed. Fluffy Jr. must have woken up.

I sat still and waited for the kiss to pass.

Finally Maximum pulled back and opened his eyes.

Up close, he had a dark freckle on the top of his lip, and his eyes were a soft brown with small gold flecks.

His smile was blinding. "That was really nice," he whispered as he pinched a curl that had sprung free against my neck with his thumb and pointer finger.

I grunted.

"Let's do it again sometime." He winked and kissed my forehead before I could pull away. Then he sauntered off to a fireplace on the other side of the library.

I blinked in shock.

Fluffy Jr. snored loudly.

Dazed and more than a little confused, I slid down onto the carpet and stuck my feet over the open flame.

This time, I felt the fire. It was a pleasant distraction from my racing thoughts.

After the kiss incident, the rest of the days passed in a blur.

Once again, Augustus announced I'd scored first in the class, but this time, a muscle in his forehead jumped, and his eyes narrowed as he glared at me. There was more malice in his black eyes than usual—which was saying something.

When Patro and Achilles returned, I was desperate to leave the icy mountain.

I sighed with relief as we leaped away.

The temperature was mild on Corfu, but an icy chill pervaded my bones. My bedroom was heated, so I stood over the vent, thawing from the week in my skull sweatshirt.

Helen stopped by once and gave me a rose-scented body wash and a cream that she said was a gold-infused moisturizer for my face.

I used it on my chapped feet.

Nyx finally woke up. She took one look at Fluffy Jr.—and immediately went back into brumation to stop herself from killing him.

At least, that was what I thought she said.

It was hard to tell.

Poppae ran away when she saw Fluffy Jr., and Nero snapped his teeth at him.

Meanwhile, I spent the time shoving as many pastries into my mouth as possible and chugging water, all while standing over the heated grate.

Classical music played.

Male voices shouted, but I didn't bother to listen. At this point, I didn't want to know.

It was now January, which meant only fourteen days until the Initiation Ball and the Assembly Ceremony.

Then I'd be free.

I was *so* close to surviving the crucible.

All too soon, it was time to go back to the academy.

Patro and Achilles gently grabbed me and Fluffy Jr. as we leaped away from Corfu.

I crept with trepidation back into the freezing classroom.

Sat down with a bone-weary sigh.

"Where is Maximum?" Augustus's voice cracked like a whip. There were purple smudges beneath his eyes and shadows beneath his sharp cheeks, like he hadn't slept since we'd last seen him and was losing weight from stress.

Drex looked over at me in the freezing cold, and I shrugged back as we waited for our last two weeks of hell to start.

General Cleandro pushed a button on his pager, and Ryax Dionysus appeared.

"Where is your mentee?" the general demanded.

Ryax bowed his head low, and the albino crow on his shoulder did the same. "He went home this weekend, and he never returned. I reached out to the House of Hera, and they said he defected. I've not seen or heard anything of him since."

The general scoffed. "What a coward. You're dismissed."

"Yes—General." Ryax leaped away in a cloud of smoke.

Drex and I looked at each other with wide eyes.

There's no way he defected this close to the end. My stomach sank to the floor, and I held Fluffy Jr. close to my chest.

Classes passed in a blur. I barely heard anything.

When the general gave us time off in the library, I stumbled blindly inside. Collapsed into my seat.

My foot hit an object.

No.

Please no.

I stilled.

Everything spun, and I fell out of my chair.

"Are you okay?" Drex asked.

Fluffy Jr. whimpered and sniffed my face.

I was on the floor.

There was a medium-sized box under my chair.

It was wrapped in red velvet, and a black silk bow with gold trim tied it off at the top.

Crawling forward like a zombie under the table, I shredded the wrapping, yanked roughly at the bow, and pushed off the top.

I needed to know.

I had to.

Slowly I inched forward.

Two veiny eyeballs—soft brown with gold flecks—sat above lips with a dark freckle on the top corner. A bloody severed thumb and finger were touching on the side, like they were pinching something.

Pieces of Maximum were sitting on top of wadded-up black tissue paper. Something glinted beneath the gory parts.

He's dead.

And for some reason, it's because of me.

Bile burned my throat, and I choked it down.

With shaking hands, I put the lid back on the box and shoved it into a storage cubby under the table.

Then I pulled myself back into my seat.

"Are you okay?" Drex asked with a worried expression.

I shook my head at him and slowly opened my textbook. This time, there was no note.

My neck prickled like I was being watched. Voices whispered.

Drex said something else, and I nodded, but I couldn't hear him.

Internally, I was screaming.

27

THE SPARTAN BALL

Alexis: Two weeks later

I'd made it to mid-January.

Somehow.

Surprisingly, the crucible had ended with a whimper, not a bang. Just another week of studying, lectures, starvation, and a test. Just like that, we were done.

I'd survived.

Then why do I feel dead? Can I really endure an immortality with these emotions?

I rubbed at my tired eyes as I stared at the rack bursting with ball gowns.

They can always cut you into tiny pieces or starve you into a coma.

The thought calmed me.

Outside the open French doors, the Ionian Sea glittered. Streaks of sunlight reflected across the luxurious fabrics.

Green foliage fluttered outside as Corfu's mild breeze filled my bedroom.

All I wanted to do was crawl into bed and sleep for days, but the Initiation Ball was tonight.

The ball was supposed to introduce us to all of Sparta. It was a celebration for completing the crucible. Then, tomorrow at dawn, we'd have our graduation ceremony in the Dolomites Coliseum.

I groaned with exhaustion.

Shivering, I blew into my hands to warm them up.

Even though the temperature was pleasant on the island, my fingers and toes still felt frozen. They'd yet to fully thaw.

"What do we think?" Helen asked as she gestured to the rack of dresses with a Chthonic crown sparkling atop her head.

She'd burst into my room this morning. I'd groggily sat up in bed, and then she'd screamed in horror.

I'd thought we were under attack.

When she'd started wailing about frizzy hair, I'd slumped back into the soft pillows with relief.

She'd finally calmed down enough to speak and had explained that Patro put her in charge of making me presentable for the Initiation Ball.

Now I stood in my oversize emotional support skull sweatshirt and waited for instructions.

Nyx was wrapped around my neck, snoring.

"Here are all your options for the ball," she said. "Do you have any questions? Concerns? Ugh—I know, it's not enough choices...you're probably freaking out right now. But don't worry, everyone will be disguised. So you can mingle with everyone in Sparta without worrying about House biases. Since the Great War, they love to do masquerade balls to promote unity."

Dozens of diamond bracelets clacked together on her wrists as she gestured.

"Oh, Kronos," Helen said before I could respond. "Now I'm

freaking out too. We are both really panicking." She fanned her face. "This can't be good for our pores."

Personally, I felt very calm.

This is the least stressful thing that has literally ever happened in my life.

"Do you have any wrinkle cream?" Helen grimaced. "I keep tensing accidentally. All the stress is getting to me."

Do they really make a cream for wrinkles? Why?

I stared at her perfectly smooth skin. "How old are you again?"

"Sixteen—duh." She shrugged a dainty shoulder. "But don't worry, I help my brother dress for events all the time. I might be young, but I'm a professional."

Actually, now I'm worried.

At that exact moment, Fluffy Jr., who was lying on my bed, gnawing on his oversize front paw, let out a burp.

If that doesn't sum up my life.

Helen burst into laughter and plugged her nose. "Your protector is so cute." She made a kissy face at Fluffy Jr. (he didn't notice; he wasn't the brightest). "He's so…*real.* Ya know? His energy is like—fierce. In a relatable way. He's not stuffy or pompous. He's down-to-earth. Troubled but strong."

No, I didn't know.

I was not getting any of that from him.

My bewilderment must have shown on my face, because she turned back to the rack of dresses. "Okay, time to focus." She waved her hand at me. "Have you gotten your color analysis done this season by a professional? I don't want to guess."

I choked.

"No," I said, ignoring my deteriorating mind. "I haven't."

She reeled back and gasped, sheer terror in her eyes. *Did a Titan break in?* I whirled.

We were alone.

My heart pounded erratically, and I breathed deeply, trying to calm down. Lately it felt like I was living on a razor's edge.

The only thing I'd done "this season" was freeze to death, starve, receive gifts of body parts, run the circuit, and study until I wanted to die.

I'd also daydreamed about Carl Gauss shirtless, secretly started writing another fan fiction about him, and gone nonverbal for two weeks after Maximum's death because I didn't want to talk to anyone.

We all coped with horrors in different ways.

As if on cue, voices whispered at the edge of my subconscious.

"You've never been color analyzed?" Her jaw dropped. "What do you wear each day? How do you know what to put on?" She looked down at my skull sweatshirt. "Actually—that makes sense."

I looked down too. "What's wrong with it? It's c-cozy."

Helen burst into surprisingly deep throaty laughter. "You're a funny one. Everyone in Sparta takes themselves way too seriously, especially the women, ya know—cause we're so rare. It gets *very* catty out there. But you seem chill… I think we're gonna be good friends."

I rubbed at my aching temples.

She seems to be confusing exhaustively traumatized for chill.

"Actually, now that I'm looking at it…" She tapped her glossy pink lips. "I think I've seen that sweatshirt before?"

"Probably Patro's." I'd found it in his house after all.

"No, it's definitely not his—even though it has a horrifying graphic, which he would like. That's an expensive cashmere blend from the Himalayas… I'm pretty sure it's custom-made. He never splurges on clothes like that."

"Oh." I shrugged.

"You say you found it. Are you sure someone didn't leave it for you? It can actually be a big deal in Sparta, gifting—"

"No, I found it." I cut her off because once she started on a topic, she tended to get stuck.

Also, it was just a sweatshirt. It wasn't that deep. It was soft and almost hung to my knees; that was the important part.

"Okay." She clapped her hands. "I always get distracted—I've diagnosed myself with like a million things—but let's stay focused. You are the talk of Sparta—the abandoned female mutt from the House of Zeus who has crushed all the boys in the crucible. You're an icon of womanhood, and you need to dress like it."

Stifling another yawn, I chuckled.

She stared at me with an intense expression.

Wait, is she not joking?

"You know—you've inspired me," she said quietly, her voice serious. "I want to participate in the massacre and crucible, just like you. All the bullshit in the Houses about preserving heiress honor is so stupid. The men get so mad whenever I bring it up, especially Augustus. But you understand."

I choked on spit.

I'm not the hero you think I am.

She looked at me with wide emerald eyes, like I was her savior and not a deeply troubled, slightly older teen with psychological, physical, and abandonment issues.

"I think," I said slowly, "you should s-stay honorable."

Her face fell, shoulders slumping with dejection.

"Or…not?" I grimaced. "I guess if you wanted to—you could? It's not that serious," I lied.

Death and torture should never be taken lightly.

She looked up hopefully, flashing brilliantly white teeth. "You really think I could survive the crucible?"

I pursed my lips. "It's not just if you could s-survive. It just sucks. Why would you want to?"

"Because I want to prove I don't need Augustus to look after me." She gritted her teeth. "He's so annoying—they *all* are. Chthonic men are so overbearing. Like ten times worse than Olympians, especially when it comes to their loved ones. They're psychotic. And since I'm their only heiress, they act like I'm made of *glass*."

I nodded like I understood, but I didn't.

Helen leaned closer. "But my power is—dark," she whispered conspiratorially. "I can do things…bad things, if you get my gist." She winked.

"Oh," I said eloquently.

Mental note—stay on her good side.

"Helen, focus!" She hit herself in the face, then dug through a big box beside the rack of clothes. "So obviously, you're wearing this as your mask." She held up what looked like the headpiece of a costume. It was a giant lion's head.

I was?

Four hours later, I stood in front of the bedroom's full-length mirror as the setting sun cast golden streaks across the room.

Fluffy Jr. snored loudly on the bed.

"Are you sure you don't want to wear any of the colorful dresses?" Helen asked for the millionth time. She pulled out a sparkly pink strapless dress and held it up. "How about this?"

"No."

"Ugh." She pouted. "You're no fun."

I shrugged and admired my reflection. A long-sleeved black dress hung to my feet, covering every inch of skin.

It was a little clingy around the torso for my taste, but compared to the other—plunging—dresses, it was perfect.

Studying myself in the mirror, I frowned as I realized what it was missing. "Helen, I need a bra."

"No, you don't." Her smile was diabolical.

"Yes." I pointed at my chest. "I do."

"No." She smirked evilly. "You have a small chest, which is absolutely perfect for this style of dress. The material is so thin and tight that bra lines would ruin the effect. Plus—a little nipple is hot."

"I agree with her," Nyx said.

Now she wakes up.

"Uh, no," I sputtered, crossing my arms over my chest protectively. "It's not the look for me."

The free the nips (and lips) campaign was a mindset, not necessarily a reality.

Helen crossed her arms and stuck her nose in the air. "You refused to take the hair ties off your wrists or wear any of the heels. This is the least you can do—for women everywhere."

That seemed slightly dramatic.

I pointed down at the gold ballet flats on my feet. "Because my feet are bruised and my toes are covered in blisters. The heels hurt way too much."

"Well," Helen huffed. "Do your *nipples* hurt?"

"She has a point," Nyx said as she slithered around my neck.

Dear God, it's me again.

Before I could argue with a literal youth about the sensitivity of my nipples (this was my personal hell), Helen picked up the lion disguise and put it over my head.

Nyx hissed as the bottom of the mask hit her. *Karma.*

She slithered down my body, then coiled tightly around my ankle and calf. Thankfully the dress flared enough around my lower body that it concealed her.

"Perfect," Helen squealed. "I'm a genius. Everyone's gonna lose it when they see you." She clapped. "Cunt—absolute cunt, served."

Excuse me? What did she just call me?

Youth culture was upsetting.

"Go, go, go." She pulled an elephant mask over her head, adjusted the thin straps of her white gossamer gown, then pushed me out the door with surprising strength. "We're gonna be late."

We ran into my mentors in the hall. Apparently we had a safari theme going on.

Patro was in a dark blue suit with a boar headpiece. Achilles stood next to him in black, wearing a hyena mask.

They both went unnaturally still.

They stared at me for a long, drawn-out moment.

Helen clapped her hands, and the strange tension broke.

The men reached for us. "Domus," Patro muttered.

BOOM.

The world contorted in darkness.

We leaped away.

I staggered and tried to catch my breath, smoke billowing.

We were in a grand ballroom, straight off the pages of a fairy tale. The walls were gilded, and the floor was polished black marble. Ionic colonnades, covered in ivy, wrapped around the perimeter of the room.

Holy crud.

Shimmering crystal chandeliers hung from a frescoed ceiling depicting clouds and cherubs.

A full orchestra played in the corner.

Hundreds of people milled about in formal wear, all sporting various headpieces representing every sort of animal imaginable, many of them much more intricate than mine.

Creatures walked past with tails and strange appendages peeking out beneath their black cloaks.

Based on the large numbers, all of Sparta was present. But one thing was the same among the different immortal groups—everyone was dripping in jewels.

Since protectors weren't allowed at the ball and no one's crowns were visible, it was virtually impossible to differentiate people.

The entire affair seemed like a lot just for five initiates.

Helen had said something about Spartans loving any chance to celebrate, so that must be it.

The air whooshed, and I stumbled out of the way as Spartans spun around the dance floor near where we stood.

"Some people have voice modifiers in their masks," Helen said, her elephant tusk bobbing. "So don't expend energy trying to identify people. It's a masquerade for a reason, and Spartans take being incognito *very* seriously."

"Helen, why are you advising *our* mentee?" Patro asked, boar head tilting to the side. His hand rested possessively on my shoulder, and my stomach pinched with queasiness.

A long beat passed, and I realized what was so strange about the gesture.

Patro's touch wasn't unpleasant.

"She's fine," I said defensively as I pulled away from him, disturbed that I *wasn't* disturbed by his casual display of affection. She was the first person in Sparta who actually bothered to explain anything.

"Come on, we need to mingle." Helen grabbed my hand and tugged me toward the tables.

Hours later, my head spun with exhaustion. Spartans sure loved to brag about themselves.

"You're funny," Zeus said through his snake head. He'd found me hours ago and was holding me hostage. Electricity sparked on his suit, making him unmistakable, and his booming laughter echoed.

I just asked if there was any food here?

Zeus had been laughing ever since he realized it was me in the lion's head.

A man nearby in a jaguar mask snapped his head around. Black diamond eyes stared at us.

"I see you've already got the House pride." Zeus clapped me on the shoulder, and I flinched. "I told you to keep up the great work, and you did. After tomorrow's graduation, you'll be an official member of my House. I have *big* things planned for you."

I coughed, back aching from where he'd hit me.

"Who knows!" Zeus shouted. "You might even earn a crown."

Spartans clapped around us, and he turned to greet them. I awkwardly extracted myself, stumbling away.

I turned around to ask Helen if there were seats open anywhere, but she was gone. My mentors had also disappeared.

They'd probably wandered off when Zeus had grabbed me.

Sighing, sweat dripping down my sides from the stress of having to talk to people, I wandered aimlessly toward chairs in the back corner. Drex was probably around somewhere, but finding him in the crowd would be difficult.

My legs ached from standing.

The grand clock on the high wall showed it was already the early hours of the morning.

The graduation ceremony would be held at the Dolomites Coliseum in less than three hours.

As far as I could tell, all of Sparta attended that too. Which meant everyone at this ball would be there, yet no one seemed in a hurry to leave.

Are Spartans against sleep because they're immortal?

Personally, exhaustion was hitting hard.

Two weeks straight of sleep deprivation made it hard to keep my eyes open.

It didn't help that there seemed to be no food or refreshments at the ball, probably because of the intricate masks.

What's a little more starvation after a lifetime?

I sighed again, then stumbled as I almost careened into a dancing triad—two men spun around a curvaceous woman in a sheer red dress.

Moving hastily, I flinched as I almost ran into four men dancing together in a circle.

The orchestra music was loud, and the lion's head had limited visibility. A dull ringing echoed in my ear, and I struggled to orient myself.

Jewels sparkled on large swathes of exposed skin.

I rubbed at my aching wrists.

You don't belong here.

The crucible had been horrible for a million reasons, but it had been isolated in the mountains.

Now an ancient culture glittered around me.

One I knew next to nothing about.

The hair on my neck stood up like I was being watched, and a scream bubbled in my throat.

You are in control of your thoughts. Keep it together, woman.

"Would you like to dance?" a modified voice asked.

A tall, powerfully built man in a perfectly tailored black suit—wearing a wolf's head with crystals for eyes—stood before me.

Immediately my mouth went dry, and I shivered with unease.

The stranger was waiting for me to speak.

After coughing to clear my throat (and making it very weird), I finally found my voice. "Nope," I said as I went to move around him, off the dance floor.

He shifted and blocked my path. "I insist." He extended a black-gloved hand and bowed deeply like I was royalty.

My palms instantly started to sweat. *Does he think I'm someone I'm not?*

"Still a n-no," I said as I tried to shove past him. It was like pushing against a brick wall. He didn't budge.

"We're going to dance now." There was an edge of violence in his modified voice, something I didn't like.

My instincts were telling me to run. "I don't think you want to dance with me," I whispered, not taking his hand and hoping to defuse whatever tension was building between us.

He stood where he was, perfectly still, crystal eyes focused on me. "I know," he said slowly, "exactly what I want."

The tension tripled.

I took a step back, jumping as I stepped straight into someone else.

Strong hands grabbed my shoulders and steadied me.

"Sorry," I sputtered, dipping my head as I moved to the side.

Both men moved swiftly.

They blocked my path.

Each wore gloves and a wolf head—one had emerald eyes and the other crystals—and they both towered above me in bespoke suits.

I swallowed thickly.

Suddenly I wanted to sprint in the other direction. As fast as I could.

"I'm gonna go sit down." I pushed my shoulders back and tried to convey authority.

Neither moved out of my way.

"No, you're not," said the man with the emerald-eyed mask. His voice was also modified.

I glanced around, desperately searching for Helen or my mentors. The room had gotten fuller, and it was impossible to see anything over the crush of bodies.

When I turned back, the men were inches away.

My stomach fluttered as they crowded my personal space. I had a bad feeling I knew who they were.

"We're going to dance with you now," one of them said.

It wasn't a question.

It was a command.

Before I could take a breath, the man with the emerald eyes placed his hand in mine and fanned his other hand across my waist.

Butterflies fluttered.

The other man stepped behind me and grabbed the indent above my hips with both his hands.

The butterflies exploded, and I inhaled shakily.

This isn't good.

They twirled me around before I could say or do anything.

With me pressed between them, they spun me around the ballroom like it was second nature. All I could do was hang on and let them lead.

We danced.

It was terrifying; it was exhilarating.

The orchestra switched to a softer song, and I exhaled with relief as the ringing in my ear dissipated.

Fingers pressed harder into the tops of my hips, and the hand holding mine clenched.

Both men took a step forward. They had already been extremely close to begin with.

Now we were pressed flush together.

It was obscene.

My uncovered nipples rubbed against the hard planes of a muscular chest.

Heat blazed across my cheeks and traveled down my neck. The strange queasiness twisted painfully inside my lower stomach.

I shivered.

The hands gripping my hips from behind moved slowly forward across my torso.

Inch by inch they trailed higher.

I'd never been touched so intimately before.

Their bodies shifted as we spun faster, blocking me from everyone's view.

Gloved fingers traveled up.

Higher.

Higher.

Higher.

They brushed across my nipples possessively.

I gasped.

White-hot pleasure burned from my chest to my core.

"Why the fuck," said the man pressed against my front, "are these out? You really can't take care of yourself, can you?"

At that moment, the man behind me tweaked his fingers

wickedly across my chest, and it was unmistakable what he was referring to.

Stars sparkled in my vision.

I moaned and tipped my head back, rested it against a muscled chest.

Both men groaned roughly.

The man in front leaned closer. "I'm going to have to torture every man and woman who's looked at you tonight," he whispered. "Carissima."

The man in back once again dragged his fingers across my chest.

Everything was on fire.

The Latin endearment wasn't funny.

"I'm not your dearest," I muttered, head still tilted back, boneless, as they held me up between them.

Pleasure sparkled through my veins.

"Yes, you are," they said in unison.

They spoke like they knew something I didn't.

Hands trailed away from my chest down my stomach, and I whimpered. Foreign sensations tingled across my nerves.

They both took a step back as we spun.

They resumed holding me at a respectful distance, like we were just strangers dancing and they hadn't just set my body on fire.

"Why," said the emerald-eyed man casually, "did you not take out the jewels?"

It took me a second to remember how to speak. "What are you talking about? What jewels? Out of where?"

What a strange question.

Exhaustion, dizziness from spinning, and the warm sensations twisting in my lower stomach made it hard to think.

Something strange was happening.

They must think I'm someone else.

My first event in the Spartan world, and I'd stolen another woman's lovers.

“Uh—I’m poor,” I blurted out, needing to ruin whatever disillusion they were under about my identity. “I don’t have jewels.” The truth seemed the easiest way.

The men stilled again. Fingers gripped my skin harder, and for a second, they trembled—with something volatile. Vibrations shook through me.

“No, you aren’t,” the man behind me said forcefully, like he was gritting his teeth. “Not anymore.”

Excuse me? Are they mocking me?

I scoffed and tried to pull my hand out of the front man’s grip. “Yes, I—I am.”

I wasn’t ashamed of who I was or how I’d grown up.

As far as I could tell, Spartans had no ability to comprehend what it was like to be at the bottom of the food chain. Dirty, in the woods, under a tarp. *Charlie is still there waiting for me.*

I wouldn’t let this place make me forget.

I struggled harder, but the men just stepped closer and resumed dancing. Their hips pinned me in place.

“Let me go.” I yanked at my arm as I tried to gain control of the situation.

They chuckled darkly and held me tighter as the three of us twirled.

“I don’t think we will,” said the front man harshly. “Non ducor, duco.”

I am not led, I lead.

The man at my back leaned close. “My carus.”

Goose bumps exploded down my arms because he called me his dear in Latin, like it meant something.

My feet stopped, but their tight grips kept me moving between them. They spun, dragging me across the packed dance floor.

They’re playing with you. This is all a game.

I felt sick.

“I have a question.” I asked softly.

Both men bent down to listen, wolves leaning closer to devour.

I slammed my knee up (the leg Nyx wasn't on) into the front man's crotch, then rammed my elbow back.

Powerful legs clamped around my raised thigh so my knee was pressed against hardness, and I couldn't move—the man in front let out a throaty groan.

That wasn't supposed to happen.

Fingers spasmed where they held me, but they didn't release.

The man behind me pushed his hips forward—a bulge dug into my lower back. His chest vibrated against me.

I was wedged in place.

Unable to move.

All pretenses of dancing were gone.

They hadn't even flinched at my violence. If anything, it had turned them on.

These weren't normal men.

Monsters.

"What—was your…question?" the man behind me asked wickedly, his hips flexed.

My heart pounded painfully inside my chest.

They had me trapped.

I tilted my head back, gritted my teeth, and forced out what I wanted to say.

"Who *the fuck*," I whispered, "do you two think you are?"

They laughed louder, crueler.

"Oh—don't you know? We belong to *you*, carus."

My breath left in a whoosh because the game wasn't funny anymore. It was horrifying.

"Let me go," I demanded, and I tried to pull away, but once again they didn't budge an inch. They groaned wantonly.

The butterflies in my stomach fluttered.

"We're never letting you go," one said harshly. "You already belong to us. And we've decided that we're going to take care of you—someone has to do it, because clearly you can't do it yourself."

Why does that sound so familiar?

"No one owns me but myself." I shook my head. "And I've been doing just fine for years."

"What an adorable perspective," the other man said with a raspy chuckle. "But your actions speak differently."

Shifting, I tried to kick at them. "Release me now, or I'll cause a scene. This isn't f-funny anymore."

The man in the back slowly rolled his hips. "We've never been more serious about anything in our fucking lives."

"Carissima," said the man in front throatily. "We'd *love* to cause a scene with you." Hardness pulsed against my thigh.

Hands trailed wickedly back up toward my chest.

They tweaked my nipples.

Drifted back down and grabbed the indent where my waist met my hips. Fingers spread possessively across my lower stomach and pulled me back flush against a hard male body.

Chills erupted across my skin.

Everything blurred.

A modified voice whispered seductively, "Carissima, why don't we—"

"Am I interrupting something?" Patro asked loudly, and I gasped for air as the two men in wolf masks took a step away from me.

Head dizzy, I nearly passed out with relief at the familiar voice as two jungle-themed masks came into focus.

"Yes—you fucking are," the man behind me said harshly.

Patro took a step forward.

The man in front turned his head toward my saviors. "We were just…talking." Since he flexed his hands, then graphically readjusted the bulge in his pants and tightened his belt, his words were not convincing.

Liar.

Patro took another step toward me.

"I've been looking for you!" Helen said as she ran forward out of seemingly nowhere, elephant trunk bobbing. "I have someone who really wants to dance with you—let's go."

She dragged me away across the dance floor and left the four men standing together.

I tried to look back, but she tugged me forward.

"That was insane—the chemistry," she said. "Holy Kronos...*everyone* in Sparta is talking about your dance." She gasped and fanned at her mask dramatically. "I had to get you out of there before they started talking about dishonor and betrothal contracts—although...since you're a mutt, you probably don't need to worry about that until you're twenty-six. Still. Wow."

I felt like I'd been struck by lightning. "I don't even know who they are," I whispered. The lie tasted poisonous, but I didn't let myself think about who they were.

If I did, I'd fall apart.

A part of me was wildly alive, and the other part of me was screaming in terror.

Butterflies danced like knives in my stomach.

Helen scoffed. "Well, one thing's for sure—those men knew *exactly* who you were." She stopped abruptly on the edge of the marble floor and gestured to a man in an elk head. "Here's the person who wanted to see you. He says he's one of your professors."

I froze.

Held my breath.

"Alexis!" Pine's voice was unmistakable as he offered his hand. "How are you? I wanted to talk with you."

It's just him.

I exhaled with relief.

"Of course, Professor." I took his hand.

He held me at a respectful distance and led me across the dance floor, talking about Thagorean and advanced math concepts. Other dancers swirled around us.

I couldn't concentrate on a single word.

My head swiveled.

Searching for... I didn't even know.

Just calm down. It's over now. Don't think about the men. Worry about it tomorrow after the graduation.

The problem was, it didn't feel over.

The song ended, and both of us stopped dancing.

"Alexis," Pine said slowly, and I instinctually took a step away from him. Stomach twisting with unease at his tone. "Now that we are no longer professor and student, I want to say that I—"

A wicked dagger pressed against the front of his throat exposed beneath his mask, hard enough to draw blood.

Pine gurgled.

Crystals flashed, and a wolf mask shook as the dagger pressed harder into skin. "Finish that sentence, and I'll put you into a coma—and I'll keep you there for the rest of immortality. I warned you not to fucking speak to her. Don't test me." A second wolf head loomed behind him.

A woman screamed.

"We're under attack!" a male bellowed. "Titans!"

People shrieked.

All hell broke loose.

Explosions echoed as Spartans leaped away.

I turned and ran, shoving through the crowd of bodies and smoke.

"Alexis!" Helen shouted, and I whirled to see an elephant mask pushing forward.

I reached for her.

A strange man in a jaguar mask grabbed me roughly—Helen threw herself toward us—the world disappeared in a flash of black agony.

I staggered and fell to my knees.

Something yanked at my arms—harsh material scraped against my wrists.

The man grunted and moved away, and a feminine yell echoed. There were loud smacking sounds.

Disoriented from leaping without warning, I blinked through

the heavy lion's mask. I waited for my vision to clear and the ringing in my ear to stop.

When it finally did, I tried to move.

I couldn't.

Freezing temperatures bit through the flimsy material of my gown, and I looked down in horror. The pressure wasn't phantom—coarse rope was twined tightly around my wrists.

The line was also attached to a thick metal hook, which was welded into the wall of a shed.

Kneeling on the dirt floor, I yanked with all my might, shoulders burning. The hook didn't budge an inch. If anything, the knot around my wrists tightened.

The rope was extremely strong.

I was stuck.

Gasping for air, I swiveled my head.

Across the room, Helen's arms were also tied off in front of her by a rope attached to a metal wall. She was slumped on the ground, unconscious, elephant head still on.

What the hell is happening?

Debris was piled around the small shed. Moonlight cast silver shadows through broken glass windows, and icy tree branches clattered outside.

The dark sky had a grayish tint as night began to make way for dawn.

The Assembly Ceremony would start soon.

How long was I dancing?

"I warned you what would happen, but you didn't listen," said a modified voice. "Now—you're going to pay. And so is your idiotic friend."

My captor took off his jaguar mask.

I stared up in shock.

"You?"

28

THE SLAYER

ALEXIS

Sitting in dirt, wrists bound before me, I peered up at my kidnapper through the heavy lion's head.

"I warned you, multiple times—I told you to leave Sparta if you wanted to live," my captor said bitterly. "But you didn't listen...you had to try and usurp me."

I blinked again.

Unable to process what was happening.

"Now you'll die, just like the rest of them." He gestured at the piles of debris along the walls of the small space. "And so will she. Your idiot mutt friend tried to save you by grabbing me as I leaped. Well, now you're both dead."

My eyes widened at a skull leaning against the wall.

It wasn't junk piled around us; it was bones. Frayed, rotting ropes were tethered to the walls next to them.

He murdered them.

He's going to kill us.

"But wh-why?" I croaked on dry lips, brain frozen in shock. None of it made any sense.

Storm-gray eyes narrowed, deep golden skin was drenched in shadows, and a laurel crown gleamed atop blond hair.

Theros smiled cruelly.

"Because I am the heir to the House of Zeus." His expression was sick. "Only I will wear a crown. I'm the one who inherits our House's legacy and brings our family honor...no abandoned, *mangy* mutt is going to take my birthright."

Months ago, when the doctor had said the House of Zeus's mutts "struggled," I'd thought it was a strange choice of words.

These bones are the mutts.

The House of Zeus didn't have a fertility issue—it had a murder issue.

I struggled to put all the pieces together.

It still wasn't adding up.

"But why the siren? Why did you kill Maximum?"

The boxes of body parts didn't make any sense.

"What are you talking about?" Theros asked. "I didn't kill them. I know you read my note—a muse told me—so don't pretend you weren't warned."

Wait, he didn't leave the boxes?

The handwriting on the note had been different from the box, but I'd assumed that was some type of mind trick to throw me off.

I had two separate stalkers.

Yanking at my restraints, I screamed through gritted teeth at the injustice of it all. Helen was still not moving on the ground.

Theros clicked his tongue. "There's no use struggling. I've done this...many times. As you can see, I have a system in place."

He knelt and picked up a rusty crowbar.

Eyes widening, I struggled harder.

Theros turned and slammed the iron against the metal wall.

He banged loudly, a harsh sound echoing through the silent forest.

Far away, something screamed.

Theros smiled at me as he dropped the iron.

"This time," he said, "it was almost too easy…all I had to do was shout that Titans were attacking, and here we are—where the actual Titans will attack. This unprotected area is crawling with them. It was almost as easy as leaping, getting that Titan to attack the circuit—evil Chthonic bastards had to interfere."

He killed Leo. He was the one who set the Titan after us.

The scream echoed louder.

I struggled harder.

Closer.

He ties them up, then lets the Titans kill them.

He was a monster.

I was going to die.

Yanking at the rope, I screamed, "NYX, WAKE UP!"

She moaned sleepily, then hissed as she realized something was wrong.

"Attack him!"

Theros's eyes widened—he took a step back.

Icy scales slid across my calf as she launched herself forward.

The air distorted.

A dull sound echoed. Nyx moaned and fell to the dirt with a thud. Behind his shield, Theros looked around nervously. *BOOM.* He disappeared in a cloud of smoke.

"COWARD," I shrieked at the empty space where he'd leaped away.

Outside, bone-chilling screams echoed louder, and Nyx groaned and whispered something inaudible.

Stuck in a lion's head, I whimpered with dread.

This was really happening.

I was surrounded by the corpses of people who'd been in the same position before me. Helen had tried to help me, and now she was going to die.

I was trapped.

Nyx was incapacitated.

No one knew where we were.

No one was coming to save us.

Bird sounds echoed as dark gray lightened with sunrise.

Dawn had arrived.

Another horrible noise echoed through the woods, much closer than the last. A Titan was fast approaching.

With us tied up like this, it would rip us both apart with its talons.

We'd be easy to kill.

You can do this, Alexis. Think. Think.

I looked around, but there was nothing I could reach to help me. No sharp edge to saw the rope against. There was no slack around my wrists—they were bound painfully tight. Theros knew what he was doing.

Breathing roughly through my nose, I bowed my head and muttered a prayer.

You know exactly what you need to do. It's your only chance of saving Helen. Charlie is waiting for you to come home.

I did.

But I didn't want to do it.

It's not fair.

The Titan screamed. It was approaching. Fast.

DO IT.

Clenching my jaw as tightly as possible, refusing to think about it, I lifted my tied hands above my head and slammed them down as hard as I could against the floor.

Shrieking, I did it again.

And again.

Time distorted in a blur of déjà vu.

I was ten years old, banging my wrists against rocks to get out of ropes; I was almost twenty years old, slamming my hands down against the ground to dislocate my thumbs; *I sobbed, snot running down my face*; I bellowed through the pain.

Again and again.

Pulling, I yanked while I fractured bones.

I shrieked at the blinding agony, then tugged harder.

Shattered bones poked through rope-burned skin.

Millimeter by millimeter, mangled hands slipped through a much too small opening.

Helen woke up and started shouting something, but I couldn't comprehend anything she was saying over the screaming pain.

My vision blurred like I was going to pass out, and I blinked rapidly.

No. Stay awake. Keep it together. She needs you.

I pulled with all my might. Shaking, panting, covered in sweat, I kept bludgeoning myself for what felt like an eternity.

Helen screamed.

Yelling, I yanked with everything I had—bloody hands *finally* slipped out—I threw myself across the shed.

On my knees, I swiped at the patch of disturbed dirt until I felt Nyx. Jerkily I grabbed her and pushed her into the front of my dress so I couldn't lose her. As I stumbled to my feet, she moaned in pain but slithered down and wrapped tightly around my leg.

I was free.

But Helen was still tied up, and I had no way of getting her out. The crowbar was the only instrument, and it wasn't sharp enough to cut through the rope.

She shouted something, but my ear rang louder.

I couldn't understand.

Moaning in pain, I ripped off her elephant head. Her wide, tear-filled eyes stared at my ruined hands with horror.

A long moment passed. Then she shook her head like she was coming out of a daze.

"Knife!" she said, and I read her lips. "I have a knife on my inner thigh. Patro makes me carry it for protection."

God help me.

I jerkily pushed up her dress and stared down at my mangled

hands, then at the thin weapon. There was no way I could hold it. Not like this. It wasn't humanly possible.

You're not fully human.

You're Spartan.

I didn't move.

Pain throbbed in both my hands. My vision blurred. The world spun.

Just fucking do it, Alexis. Don't you dare think about it.

I was paralyzed.

Helen stared at the weapon, then at my bloody hands. Her lips quivered with sorrow.

A Titan screamed outside, the sound close. Very close.

Tears filled her eyes, and she slumped with despair, like she knew she was doomed.

Don't think. Just fucking act. Right now. Or she's going to die.

I forced my fingers to pick up the knife.

Shrieking through gritted teeth, I clenched my ruined hand tighter around the thin hilt and started sawing at the piece of rope between Helen's hands.

The knife was sharp, but the rope was thick, and the cutting motion sent unimaginable waves of agony streaking up my forearm. My fingers slipped up the hilt. Sharp pain stung as I accidentally grabbed the blade.

Blood from the fresh cuts made the handle slippery, so I had to flex my hand to grip it.

Sawing at the rope, I screamed and pushed harder.

This was hell.

The world spun, tears streamed down my cheeks, and darkness made the edges of my vision fuzzy.

CLANG.

The metal shed rocked—something slammed against it from the outside.

I sawed with everything I had, digging the knife into the fraying rope. Ignored the pure agony eating away at my nerves as the world spun faster. Sweat dripped down my face. Black clawed at the edges of my consciousness.

Don't you fucking dare pass out.

There was a horrible noise, and I whipped my head around.

A creature was framed in the door.

Morning light illuminated its gruesome visage. It was tall and skinny, its pale skin covered in dark veins. A mouth wide with serrated teeth, bulging eyes, and razor-sharp talons completed the horrifying picture.

No. No. No. No.

I cut harder, and Helen yanked with all her might, shouting as she slipped free.

There was no time to celebrate.

The Titan lunged.

Turning, knife extended, I slammed it into the monster's eye. Nails raked across my arm like hot coals, and I screamed.

The Titan stumbled and shrieked, tripping back and falling onto the dirt floor as it clawed at the hilt protruding from its face.

I used the opening.

Grabbing the door of the shed, bloody fingers slipping as I tried to get purchase, I threw my body against the door—slammed it closed on the Titan's head. Black blood splattered. Again and again I threw myself forward and jammed it.

Helen shouted, and the sound pierced through the haze.

Turning, I staggered over to her.

Grabbed her.

Behind me, there was a loud shriek as the Titan started to rise. Without Spartan weapons, there was no way to stop it.

My vision tunneled.

Everything spun.

It felt like I was drowning underwater.

You're trapped. You're doomed. You have no options left.

But there was one possibility.

A long shot.

More theory than reality.

It shouldn't have been an actual option.

My thoughts blanked.

I focused only on a singular destination—the feeling of home.

The Titan lunged at us.

"Domus," I whispered—claws missed us by a fraction of an inch as the world disappeared in an explosion of blinding darkness, and agony tore me to shreds.

I blinked, and I was kneeling on the sands of the Dolomites Coliseum in a cloud of dissipating smoke.

Helen was sobbing beside me.

Nyx grumbled something about being smushed, and she slithered off my leg onto the sand.

I'd somehow leaped with all three of us. I'd done the impossible.

Two men in full-length black togas with long fur capes stared down at us.

Snow flurried.

"Alexis? Helen?" Glacial blue and soulless black eyes widened as they took us in.

I staggered to my feet. Helen remained kneeling, whimpering.

Kharon took a step forward, face contorted as he stared down at my ruined hands and clawed-up arm. Augustus went unnaturally still beside him, and his face paled until his scar was a stark slash of red.

"Who. The. Fuck. Did. THIS. TO. YOU?" Kharon's raspy voice increased in decibels until he was shouting at me at the top of his lungs. "GIVE ME THEIR NAME."

Augustus pulled out a gun and unclicked the safety, his eyes wild.

Helen sobbed harder into the sand.

I turned away from the men, searching through the faces standing on the sands.

Fury was a living, pulsing thing.

My blood boiled as my frosty breath lingered in the chilled air.

How dare he. He thinks he can just get away with this?

Members of the twelve Houses were spread out along the oval perimeter of the coliseum sands. House flags waved behind each group.

It was dead silent.

Snowflakes drifted softly.

In the middle of the arena, Drex, Cassius, Alessander, and Titus stood in a line. General Cleandro, Professor Augustus, and Professor Pine, who had a white bandage wrapped around his throat, stood beside them.

Everyone was dressed in long togas with animal furs, and just like at the Initiation Ball, no protectors were present.

The graduation ceremony hadn't started yet.

But I didn't care.

That wasn't why I was here.

Drex gestured at me to come join them, and I looked away.

Still searching.

There.

Kharon lunged for me. "ALEXIS—TELL US WHO DID THIS TO YOU!"

I dodged his grip because this was my anger. Not his.

I pointed with a bloody, mangled finger and stalked across the sand toward the fluttering flag that displayed the golden lion of the House of Zeus.

Adrenaline, pain and rage made me shake.

My target's jaw dropped as he saw me stalking across the sands toward him, covered in blood.

You should be very afraid.

Zeus frowned. "What is the meaning of this? What are you—"

I ripped the lion off my head and lunged.

29

THE CONSEQUENCES

ALEXIS

Before Theros or anyone realized what was happening—no one would dare attack a precious Olympian heir in front of everyone—my bloody hands were wrapped around Theros's throat.

He staggered back.

There was a loud pounding noise as Zeus tried to get to us. Men joined him, pummeling frantically. Then bodies were everywhere. Eyes glowed bloody as two men attacked the others.

I ignored them all.

Let them worry about their precious heir. Let them panic.

None of them could get through Theros's shield.

The outside world was nothing but muffled sounds and a blur of colors.

We were trapped.

Together.

Perfect.

Theros fell backwards.

"You tried to murder us," I spat as I threw myself on top of him. "You left us tied up to die."

We grappled, my hands and shoulders throbbing unmercifully, but I didn't care.

"You don't…want to do this," he said, grunting as we rolled in the sand. "Think about the House honor."

Wrestling, I laughed harshly.

"I don't care about your stupid House honor—I grew up *homeless*, you prick."

I reared back and slammed my head into his nose.

He whimpered as blood exploded.

I bared my teeth. "What I've endured for years—would kill you in a day."

I did it a second time, and he screamed with pain; I screamed with satisfaction.

An uppercut caught me in the gut, and I gagged. Ears ringing, eyes rolling, I struggled to stay conscious.

Theros twisted and slammed me back against the sand, gray eyes wide and manic as he straddled me.

His hands slipped against my neck as he choked me.

I slammed fists up into his face, and broken pieces of bone scourged his skin. *"Coward!"* I shrieked.

Blood rained down.

He squeezed my neck harder.

Choking, I forced my lips into a smile. "Now—all… know—" I gasped "—what a monster—you…are." I laughed with a mocking rasp.

His nose flared, and he bellowed, rearing his fist back.

Pain exploded in my chest—but Theros was frozen. His fist was reared back like he was getting ready to punch, but he wasn't moving.

The sharp pain stabbing my chest was from an unknown source.

White-hot agony.

With labored breaths, I clutched at my chest.

Am I having a heart attack?

Above me, Theros started screaming.

His eyes rolled back. Foam dripped from his lips as he convulsed.

Agony in my sternum intensified.

Theros shrieked louder, and the sound was horrific.

In slow motion, he fell back off me. His shield crumbled, and the outside world came back into sharp focus.

Everyone on the sands had moved to surround us. Dozens of Spartans stared down at me.

Olympians stepped forward, but two figures yanked them back.

"Stay away from her!" someone shouted. Then there was a blur of grunts as the Spartans turned to defend themselves against attackers.

Theros bellowed louder on the ground.

"Alexis!" Patro knelt before me, blocking my view of the commotion. "Stop it—let him go!" he yelled at me.

Achilles was beside him with a furious expression.

What is he talking about?

Theros let out a skull-breaking scream.

"Focus on breathing slowly," Patro said, reading the confusion on my face. "Imagine the pain in your chest dissipating—just focus on each breath." He inhaled deeply to demonstrate.

I followed his motions.

Slowly the stabbing pain in my sternum lessened.

The awful pressure released.

Theros stopped howling. He moaned weakly as he slowly sat up, still twitching in the sand.

"Great job, you're doing it," Patro said as he rubbed my back. "Just like that, good girl. I'm so proud of you."

I leaned into his touch.

"She—she—she was..." Theros stammered as he crawled away from me. Foam still dripped out the side of his mouth.

I glared at him and bared my teeth.

He yelped.

"Don't worry about him. He doesn't matter," Patro said soothingly. "Focus on me—focus on taking deep breaths until the pain in your chest is fully gone. Just like that. You're doing so well. Unlike Olympians, our power is in our heart."

What power?

I nodded shakily and kept breathing slowly as I leaned against him, even though I didn't understand.

"She...she...she," Theros shouted between coughs as he pointed at me. "Her eyes were bloody—she's one of them—she was killing me—arrest her—she's a monster—she was—"

"SILENCE," a hair-raising voice bellowed.

The coliseum went dead silent, and the men stopped fighting around us.

You could have heard a pin drop.

"What—is the meaning of this?" Hades enunciated each word with painstaking slowness as he walked across the sand toward us. Inky fog trailed around his feet like smoke.

No one moved.

No one breathed.

Midnight-black eyes flashed with warning. "Someone better explain *right now*—what I just saw."

Patro swallowed thickly, then stood up in front of me. His body blocked mine from Hades's line of sight.

"Our mentee, Alexis Hert," Patro stated loudly, voice ringing with confidence, "disappeared last night with my sister, Helen Aphrodite, in the chaos of the Initiation Ball...they both arrived here this morning."

Theros gasped with surprise at Helen's surname, then whimpered in pain. Everyone whispered.

Good, I hope he realizes how dead he is. They won't let him get away with hurting her.

Patro continued, "My sister is in shock and struggling to recover, but from what she's told me, this man attacked them." He pointed at Theros, eyes full of blood. "And Alexis sacrificed herself to save my sister, then leaped both of them to safety."

The whispers increased.

Patro cleared his throat and took a deep breath. "What we saw here was Alexis confronting my sister's attacker, and during the altercation, her eyes filled with blood. She activated Chthonic powers she didn't know she had, and from what I saw… I believe her blood *is* her power—she can cause others pain with it."

What?

Patro looked back at me with a pleading expression, like he was begging me to understand something unsaid.

The whispers turned into outright shouts.

Zeus recoiled like he'd been struck, electricity sparking frantically around him.

"She's a powerful Chthonic heiress—and she saved Helen!" Patro shouted proudly, then raised his fist into the air. "She's a hero!" Achilles stood up and did the same.

The shouts turned into a roar as all of Sparta lost their minds.

Theros wailed.

Sharp feedback rang through my left ear.

I stared down at my ravaged hands—shattered bones visible through ruined skin—as everything spun around me.

I inhaled sharply.

Oh my god.

No.

Please no.

It hit me like a punch straight to the face—exactly what

Patro meant about the power in my chest. It was the reason I'd felt pressure in my chest when I'd bonded with Fluffy Jr., when the other initiates had only felt it in their heads.

Patro had said Olympians felt their power differently from him and Achilles.

I was like them.

I was Chthonic.

No. No. No. No. No. No.

God help me.

There were four times in my life I'd felt the blinding chest pain I'd felt today.

One.

Foster Mother had died after I'd scratched at her face with bloody nails. She'd screamed something about a red-eyed devil while staring straight at me.

Two.

Boys pleading and convulsing during the massacre, foam dripping from their lips, after I'd clawed at their wounds with my bloody fingers. Them staring up at me with horror. A red glow reflected in the fog.

Three.

Christos splashing in the water, foaming at the mouth as he screamed and tried to get away from me—after we'd shaken bloody hands.

Four.

The siren, wincing as she'd cut herself on a knife that was covered in my blood. Her dying shortly after.

Each time, I'd felt excruciating pain in my chest like I was having a heart attack.

It hadn't been panic.

I'd been killing them, murdering them.

Unlike this time, there'd been no one there to talk me down, to teach me how to control my powers.

"YOU SLAUGHTERED THEM. SINNER!" Father John screamed in my mind as he pointed at me.

Patro said Hades's fog shows you the worst thing you've ever done.

You heard Mother screaming.

The fog attacked you at the end because you *were killing those boys.*

I clutched my head with ruined hands and opened my mouth to beg for mercy, but no sound came out.

The animals in the menagerie hated me because they saw what I truly was.

My head was underwater.

My soul was in hell.

I'd been delusional this entire time, hoping my ability was mundane.

The reason I felt no euphoria when I spoke to Nyx and the sirens was because it wasn't my Spartan powers that let me converse with them. It must have been something else.

Drex had never been the Chthonic monster.

It had always been me.

Too much was happening—I was free-falling, unable to slow down as I plummeted to ruin.

Oh my god.

Patro's pleading expression made sense. Because of him, everyone thought my power just caused pain—it didn't.

It killed.

And I would have murdered Theros if Patro hadn't helped me calm down. I would have killed an *immortal.*

It shouldn't have been possible.

It was.

If evil is unnoticed, does it still exist?

I was boiling apart at the seams, falling back into the sand, sprawled brokenly. The drowning sensation intensified.

What am I?

Inky fog rolled in as dark robes approached.

How do I live with myself?

How do I live with what I've become?

"But that's not possible," Hades said loudly, and all of Sparta fell silent. "She can't be a Chthonic heiress. We would know if a child was birthed to—"

He stopped talking and reared back.

The face of a haunted man.

"ZEUS," he bellowed abruptly. "You *said* she was dead… you said you knew for a fact that the Titans killed her. We held a funeral together!"

Zeus stepped forward, electricity sparking all around. "She was! Vyco of the House of Hermes—where are you? Explain yourself!"

An older man jogged forward.

"Patro," Hades ordered. "Touch him right now—we need to know if he's lying or not."

My mentor nodded and hurried over to the man who'd stepped forward. Achilles stood protectively at his heels, like a muzzled sentinel.

"KNEEL," Zeus commanded, and Vyco fell to his knees. "Explain again—*exactly* what happened the day Hercules was killed." Storm-gray eyes rolled with fury.

I sat up straighter.

Hercules was the eight-letter word embroidered on the fabric I'd been found in as a baby. It was a name, not a label.

The hairs on my arms stood up.

A bad feeling rolled through me.

Everything was happening in slow motion, like I was in the middle of a car crash.

Vyco raised his head.

"There was a Titan attack at the House of Zeus during a federation meeting," he said. "The Spartans were all meeting in the other room, and I'd just arrived and was in the hall. Hercules's nurses died in front of me. In the chaos, I grabbed the baby and leaped. I ended up in a rural wasteland—then there was blood everywhere, and I was convulsing—I passed out… when I woke up, I was alone, and the baby was gone. I assumed it had been killed by Titans or a wild creature."

Patro looked up, eyes blazing red. "He's telling the truth."

"You said you saw the baby die!" Zeus bellowed as he rounded on Vyco.

Vyco shook his head. "I thought I did. It was an *unprotected* baby—there was blood, and monsters were attacking. It's what I thought happened."

"That's the truth," Patro announced, eyes still bloodred.

Zeus turned to Hades, who had fog pouring off him.

They shared a long look.

At that moment, the scar on my sternum prickled, and I rubbed at it. My hand stilled. I'd had the mark since I was a baby.

It's a perfectly straight line.

Someone tried to stab me.

Shivers traveled down my spine, and my gut told me that Vyco's story wasn't the entire truth.

Something else was going on here.

Something bigger than what was being said.

Zeus's voice rang out, his gaze still locked on Hades. "Vyco—you withheld information about the kidnapping of my goddaughter. You will be dealt with later."

Wait, if he's my godfather, then who's my…

Hades walked toward me. His midnight-black eyes and tall, lean build were uncannily familiar. Snow swirled around him.

He stopped in front of where I was sitting, then fell to his knees.

"Daughter—it's really you?" Tears shone in his eyes, and long, pale fingers shook as they reached slowly for a curl that had escaped. "You look so much like your mother."

"Hercules!" Persephone flung herself to her knees before me. Her dark gold skin was a familiar shade.

Her mane of blond curls matched mine; it was just lighter. Wide blue eyes stared at me as she clutched my face. Then she burst into sobs.

"They made my baby do the crucible," she wailed as she clutched at me. "You poor darling angel." She brushed curls back off my forehead. "You must have been so scared."

I stared back at her.

Frozen.

Unable to find any words.

She held me like she loved me. No one had ever done that before.

Mom?

Dad?

Tears streamed down my cheeks.

They were both holding me with such tender emotions, and I was kneeling in their arms, a monster.

Long moments passed as the three of us embraced on the sands.

Zeus stepped forward, casting a shadow across us.

His voice shattered the moment.

"Since she's an honorable heiress who was forced to endure the savage crucible—per our customs, something must be done to right the grave dishonor that she's suffered… I propose an alliance with my house. A marriage."

Wait, what?

Hades and Persephone stilled in my arms. Together they launched to their feet.

I staggered up behind them, nearly passing out from the pain of movement. Everything spun. The urge to collapse was immense.

Adrenaline was wearing off.

I blinked rapidly, forcing myself to stay conscious.

"You dare propose a betrothal with the boy who hurt her and Helen?" Hades asked, voice crackling with violence.

Persephone shouted and stepped forward. "Look at my daughter's ruined hands and arm—look at what he did to her! Helen is inconsolable over the attack…how *dare* you—" Hades held her back.

Zeus held up his hands in a surrender gesture. "I didn't mean to insinuate my goddaughter would marry Theros. I misspoke. My gravest apologies—Theros will be dealt with."

He held a hand over his heart.

"A grave dishonor has been done to both women," Zeus continued. "Helen's honor is also at stake, through her association. You know this—it is our laws. Any Olympian House will do. Are there any heirs that will step forward for her hand?"

Why would Helen be punished for being kidnapped? Why would I be dishonorable when they *forced me to participate in the crucible?*

I wanted to scream and pull at my hair. The Spartan laws were archaic and psychotic.

Dozens of men stepped forward, and I took a step back.

No. Please no.

I'd rather fight a Titan.

I shook my head as Persephone turned back to me. Hades released her, and she went to my side.

"*My* daughter will not be selecting any marriage contracts at this moment," Persephone scoffed, voice full of vitriol. "Step back, you fools. She's bleeding and injured—where is your honor? You embarrass us all."

Men bowed their heads in shame.

I sidled closer to her. The throbbing pain in my hands was making everything hazy, and it was getting harder to see.

"There's one problem here," a raspy voice called out.

Kharon stepped forward.

He sauntered across the arena, fur cape dragging through the sand, silver crown askew atop his head.

Blood was splattered across his face, and his knuckles were bruised like he'd been fighting.

Ice-blue eyes locked on mine.

"She's already betrothed," he announced.

Murmurs erupted.

Persephone looked up at me with confusion—I stared at Kharon.

What is he doing?

His smirk was wicked. "She's already betrothed to me and my partner. In accordance with the new marriage law, she is the one we've decided to wed."

The murmurs became shouts.

"Excuse me?" Hades snarled. "What did you just say about my daughter?" Inky fog rolled.

No, I'm not.

Why is he lying?

I narrowed my eyes at him and shook my head, trying to get him to stop whatever ploy he was pulling.

"I can prove it!" he shouted, and the sands fell silent.

He arched a dark brow, like he was daring someone to call him out on his bluff.

Hades gestured to Patro. "Check if he's lying."

Green eyes widened. Then Patro slowly moved over to his friend like he wanted to be anywhere else.

I scoffed. *They're probably in on it together. It's all an act.*

Kharon smiled, still staring directly at me. "My partner and I sent Alexis Hert two betrothal gifts—two boxes," he said proudly.

The world shook.

My knees gave out.

Everything spun.

Kharon smirked like he had me pinned, right where he wanted me.

"Each box was wrapped in red velvet, and a black silk bow with gold trim was tied at the top—each contained two of the three customary gifts. Symbols of our protection were laid atop priceless heirlooms."

I tasted bile.

Symbols of protection. He means body parts.

I'd never looked beneath the tissue paper, but something had glinted.

Kharon continued, "We also gifted her a priceless blanket and clothes straight off our backs—she opened both boxes, used the blanket, and wore the clothes. *Unequivocal* acceptance of the betrothal."

Sparta erupted with a roar.

People shouted and talked, and everyone clamored like I'd done something shocking.

Betrayer eyes sparked with satisfaction—I glared back.

Screw you.

He knew I'd had no idea that I was accepting anything by opening a box. He'd backed me into a corner and played me. Just where he wanted me.

His smile was sinful.

Pure male satisfaction oozed off him, like he'd played the long game and won.

Another horrible realization punched me.

No.

Holy shit.

It can't be.

He'd stared at me with interest while Christos drowned. My eyes must have been bloodred.

He'd known I was Chthonic.

All along.

He fucking knew from the beginning.

His puzzling comments about secrets and backing me into a corner the first time we'd met didn't seem so cryptic anymore.

When he'd talked about me staying safe, I'd assumed he was just worried about my mentors.

He wanted me unharmed.

Because he knew *I* was Chthonic.

He'd wanted to marry me as soon as he found out.

I'm the fucking loophole. I'm how he gets around the law and doesn't have to marry an Olympian.

Bile filled my throat.

I'd felt so bad for the poor person he was going to marry.

The Falcon Chronicles had said they'd seen him sending betrothal jewelry at the same time I'd received my box.

I was the betrothed they'd written about.

He's been playing me all along.

"SILENCE," Hades bellowed, and once again the coliseum went silent. "Patro—is it true?"

Green eyes glanced at mine, full of apologies. "Yes, he spoke the truth." Patro grimaced like it pained him to say the words.

Hades turned to me. "Daughter, do you deny what he says? You can speak freely. Please, be honest. If he's lying, I can—"

"He's telling the truth," I said numbly, cutting him off.

Bone-deep agony mixed with exhaustion.

It was all too much.

I was sick with nausea.

There was no fight left in me.

"A betrothal is sacred," Kharon announced gravely. "The federation cannot interfere once it has been accepted. Not only am I in compliance with the marriage law, but it will also save her honor *and* Helen's honor." His face was full of sympathy, like he was just trying to help.

"I have—come to care for Alexis...greatly," he said, voice shaking with emotion.

Liar.

LIAR!

He's putting on a show.

It's all a game.

I'm just a loophole.

Persephone must have sensed my agitation, because she wrapped her arms around my shoulders and cradled me against her. "It's going to be okay, honey. I'll make sure of it."

Tears filled my eyes because no one had ever said that to me before, and it had never been less true.

Zeus stepped forward, his face full of outrage. "Who is this partner you speak of also marrying?"

Kharon stepped to the side.

Augustus stepped forward, crown glinting atop two-toned hair. Just like Kharon, he was splattered in blood.

No.

Not him.

Anyone but him.

Voices muttered.

Someone said, "The heir to the House of Artemis *and* the heir to the House of Ares—holy Kronos."

"Both Chthonic heirs?" someone gasped. "That's insane."

Augustus stared across the sand at me with the eyes of a killer. He held my gaze, unblinking.

Kharon told him what I was after that first week. That's why he glared at me accusingly in class. That's why he made perplexing comments about my power and dishonor. That's why he said Chthonic lives mattered—I was the Chthonic life, not my mentors.

They were using me.

That was it.

Helen looked up from where she was kneeling in the sand with Patro now by her side, and her eyes were wide with sympathy. They shone with misery.

The chatter intensified all around.

"We have betrothed her together," Augustus announced, voice silky smooth and full of confidence. "That is why two boxes were sent, and both were opened. She accepted both of us."

Never.

Unlike Kharon, he didn't smirk. His expression was stoic.

Zeus frowned. "But the federation stated in the marriage law you cannot marry a Chthonic. It is unacceptable that you three would—"

"It stated," Augustus interrupted him smoothly, "that we could not marry *only* one of the ten Chthonic names that were listed in the law. Alexis Hert was not on that list."

"But," Zeus sputtered. "The purpose of the law—"

Kharon interrupted him. "The purpose of the law does not matter. What matters is that we have obeyed the letter of the law in exactitude. As Alexis is *not* listed, there should be no problem."

Zeus clenched his hands into fists, face reddening, but he said nothing.

Air left my lungs—the two men in wolf's heads had asked me where my jewels were.

It had been them.

They'd wanted to know why I wasn't wearing their horrid gifts.

And they'd touched me so...intimately.

The worst part? I'd enjoyed it. A part of me had known. But like a fool, I'd ignored the warning signs.

They probably laughed about it afterward.

They'd been playing a twisted game for months.

Setting me up for marriage.

Using me.

To avoid a marriage law.

There's something wrong with them. They're...sick in the head.

I could feel their feral energy from yards away in the way they watched me. Their eyes were a little too wide, postures a little too stiff.

They used charisma to hide what they really were.

Father John was mistaken. The devil wasn't a lone figure—

he was two men, and both were standing across from me, splattered in gore.

Savage promises glinted in their expressions.

The emotions were suddenly too much.

I'd never had a romantic relationship, and now *this* was happening to me. I was in way over my head.

My lower lip trembled as I glared at them, and Augustus's face fell.

He looked shattered.

I looked away.

Everything blurred, and time was fuzzy on the edges as my head spun with blood loss.

Zeus cleared his throat, an edge of spite in his gaze as he looked at me. "Under the article three amendments," he said harshly, "the law states clearly that all Chthonics are required to join the Assembly of Death if they survive the crucible. It is our law—she must join. As a Chthonic, she also…must compete in the upcoming Gladiator Competition."

Persephone cried out as Zeus and Hades started arguing.

Helen sobbed harder in the sand.

Bone-weary, just wanting the day (life) to be over with, I staggered to the group.

"I'll do it," I said.

Nothing matters anyway. I'm already dead.

"Daughter," Hades said, "you don't have to."

"No way in fucking Kronos will you make our betrothed have to fight Titans and compete in that savage tournament," Augustus spat with disgust. "She'd be the first young heiress in decades—it's preposterous and dishonorable. I will *never* allow this."

Kharon nodded beside him. They looked apoplectic.

If one more man spoke for me, I was going to lose it.

"Technically…" Zeus frowned. "Under Article Three of the Great War Reparations Act, she does have—"

"I'll do it!" I screamed at the top of my lungs, chest heaving as my vision blurred. "I said I'll fucking do it." I waved mangled hands.

Sparta fell silent.

No one spoke.

I staggered over to where the initiates were standing waiting for the graduation ceremony to begin.

I wanted to fight.

To kill.

To die on a battlefield.

Chop me into little pieces. Put me into a coma. I dare you. PLEASE DO IT, YOU FILTHY LIARS.

Zeus and Hades shouted at everyone to get back into positions.

Time warped.

I was standing beside Drex and the other initiates in the middle of the arena. Snow fell quietly all around.

Titus looked down the line at me. His expression was horrified, like he felt bad for me.

I stared back blankly.

Dead.

Numb.

A murderer.

Poisonous blood dripped from my ruined hands, the hands of a killer.

When the other initiates' names were read, General Cleandro announced they had graduated and were citizens of Sparta.

But when he read mine, he paused.

"Alexis… I mean—Hercules," he said reluctantly. "Do you accept a life of servitude in the Assembly of Death, fighting Titans and…defending Sparta?"

He waited, his expression grim.

I smiled coldly. "I do. Gladly."

He grimaced and looked away—like he couldn't stomach the darkness in my eyes. I scoffed and staggered back into line.

I was what they'd made me into.

And they hated it.

I chuckled brokenly to myself as we graduated from the crucible with all of Sparta staring at us.

No one cheered.

Hades and Persephone ran over to me, while Achilles and Patro knelt with Helen and whispered to her. My mentors looked up and made eye contact, their expressions intense. I looked away.

I wanted to go over and make sure she was okay—but I could barely stand.

Kharon and Augustus stalked behind my parents. Nyx reappeared with an exhausted hiss, and she slithered around my throat.

Villains.

Enemies.

My betrotheds.

The world spun faster.

"What happened to your eye?" Persephone asked as she hurried up to me and tipped my chin back. "It wasn't like that when you were a baby."

Kharon and Augustus snapped their heads in my direction.

"I don't know," I mumbled numbly, the lie unconvincing.

Then Patro, Kharon, Achilles, and Augustus turned toward Theros with murder on their faces.

I pulled away from my parents. "I have to go."

They reached for me.

But they were too late.

"Domus," I whispered brokenly, with one face in my mind.

The world exploded as I leaped away.

30

CHARLIE

ALEXIS

Everything was dark as I leaped.

"Are you there?" I shouted, my breath a frosty puff as I staggered to my feet and narrowly avoided slamming into a tree trunk.

The Montana forest was dark.

It was the middle of the night, and thick snowflakes fell.

Turning in circles, vision blurring, I desperately tried to orient myself among the frost-covered tree branches.

Half-unconscious, delirious with pain, I stumbled forward with snow crunching beneath my ruined flats.

"Charlie?" I shouted as I ripped through the forest.

Twigs cracked loudly, but I didn't care that I was waking the nightlife. For the first time in my life, Titans didn't feel like an overwhelming threat.

There were bigger monsters in the world.

I was one of them.

Nyx mumbled in her sleep as she shifted on my throat, and my heart pounded erratically inside my chest, pumping poisonous blood through my veins.

You murdered them all.

"Charlie!" I screamed, desperation making me sick.

He was there when you killed your first victim. He was crying in the corner as you tore your mother to shreds. How dare you soil him with your corrupt presence?

Tears froze as they streaked across my face.

Everything ached.

My black soul was on fire.

I pushed through icy branches, uncaring as they scratched against my skin and opened new wounds.

"Charlie," I whispered dejectedly, giving up hope. *He doesn't want to see you. You abandoned him. He hates you now.*

Sobbing, I bounced against a tree and fell to the forest floor.

You're actually evil. God can't save you now. Carl and Emmy would be disappointed.

On my hands and knees in the shallow snow, I opened my mouth to cry, and a scream came out.

"Alexis?" an unfamiliar male voice called, and heavy footsteps crunched.

I cried harder because Charlie didn't speak. *The Spartans found me before I could ever get to him.*

The Spartan approached quickly as he ran deftly through the forest—nothing but a shadow.

"Alexis!" the strange man cried out as he fell to his knees next to me.

Moonlight kissed pale skin, sharply angled features, messy blond hair, and piercing yellow eyes.

"Charlie," I whispered hoarsely.

Long fingers moved rapidly. "Sister," Charlie signed. Then he gently wrapped his arms around my shoulders and hugged me tight.

Nyx hissed as he bumped her, but Charlie didn't seem to notice. He was too busy holding me like he was afraid I'd disappear.

Surrounded by ice and snow, warmth exploded in my sternum—I was finally home.

We trembled as we held each other.

Ignoring my protests that I could walk, Charlie picked me up into his arms and carried me through the trees.

Time passed in a blur.

The world warped.

I was sitting on layers of old rugs. A patched blanket was wrapped around my shoulders and Charlie's. He'd grown taller and wider since I'd seen him, and we barely fit within the dilapidated box.

Cardboard and tarp were draped over our heads. Icy branches clattered against the sides of the structure as the wind howled.

The flickering green light of the broken lantern illuminated the harsh planes of Charlie's face.

His bone structure had grown, but he didn't have muscle and fat to go with it.

His features were hollowed and emaciated.

Despair burned in my sternum.

"I'm so sorry," I whispered. "For leaving you. I took the test, and it all happened so fast. They took me—it was a massacre—then the crucible—then I found out…my blood—they used me." I gasped for air, unable to get my thoughts in order.

Charlie shifted closer so we were leaning fully against each other.

His body was trembling.

"I was so scared," he signed. "Everyone at school was talking about how you were a lost female Spartan, and that they'd taken you to Italy. I tried to find a way to get to you—but there's no human travel across the Atlantic. There was no way to reach out. I've been sick with worry every day—I *should* have been there to protect you. You were never the fighter. It shouldn't have had to be you… I'm so sorry."

Tears streamed down his face.

I threw myself forward and wrapped my arms around him.

His skin was ice-cold, like he hadn't been warm in weeks, and I wanted to scream at the unfairness of it all.

We held each other with desperation.

"If there was a choice between me and you having to do the crucible," I whispered shakily, "I'd do it every time—you're not a fighter either. Not really. Neither of us should have to live this way. We both deserve better."

Long moments passed as we embraced.

I pulled back slightly.

"Where's Fluffy?" I whispered in confusion, looking around the small, empty structure.

Charlie bowed his head low.

"I tried," he signed slowly. "I gave her all the jerky—but it wasn't enough."

My vision blurred over.

Nyx wasn't here, so there was no one to feed her.

"She didn't survive the early winter." He buried his head in his hands and cried out, a heart-wrenching wail.

"It wasn't your fault," I gasped on a watery sob. "Please, it wasn't your fault. Please. Please listen to me. Please." Once again, I wrapped my arms around my younger brother and held him tight.

The wind howled sharply.

Branches clattered.

We were nothing but two broken souls trying our best to survive in a cruel, unforgiving world.

In that dark of night, we mourned together.

For Fluffy, who'd been nothing but a bright, shining light of love in a heartless place.

For each other.

For the horrible days we'd spent apart.

I whispered into the flickering green light, "I promise—I'll never leave you again. You'll always be by my side."

"Always," he signed.

Curled up under a stolen blanket, we fell asleep shivering in each other's arms. Pain throbbed through my limbs, but I easily ignored it.

There was nowhere else I'd rather be.

I woke to the angry sound of dogs barking off in the distance.

Charlie moaned in his sleep and twitched.

"Wake up," I whispered as I elbowed his shoulder.

He sat up with a gasp. "What is it?" he signed, blond hair disheveled, yellow eyes sleepy.

"Listen." I pointed outside the box.

The barks increased.

"Who are they?" he signed. "What do they—"

Our covering was ripped away.

Bright morning rays reflected off the snow with blinding intensity.

Four towering men stood in the forest. They wore togas and long furs.

A gun was drawn.

Poppae knelt at their feet, and Nero was standing still, sniffing the air like something was there.

Before I could react, Charlie threw himself in front of me, shielding me with his much larger form.

"Why the *fuck* are you in a cardboard box—and who the fuck is this?" Kharon rasped. "Actually, don't tell me. I'd rather shoot first and then find out."

A safety was clicked off.

"Don't you d-dare," I shouted and tried to push Charlie away from me, but he flexed and didn't budge. "It's my little brother—Charlie!"

There was a long moment of silence.

"That is your little brother?" Patro asked, voice full of disbelief. "Is *this* where you live?"

Someone swore violently.

"Charlie, get off me," I said as I pushed at his back. "I need to talk to them."

He shook his head and didn't budge.

I stretched up and peeked over his shoulder—Kharon had a gun extended, inches away from Charlie's forehead.

Glacial eyes burned with fury.

Beside him, Augustus wore a similar expression of rage. His long, two-toned hair was messy, like he'd been continually running his fingers through it. Poco sat on his shoulder, pointy teeth bared with aggression.

A few feet away, a smoking cigarette hung between the grates of Achilles's muzzle, and his red eyes were molten. His fists were clenched tightly, chest heaving.

Patro stood next to him, glaring. Any trace of the congenial man I'd gotten to know over the last few weeks was gone.

He was furious.

"Move aside," Augustus said with deceptive softness. It was the tone he always used before he absolutely lost it. "We need to get Alexis medical help—she spent the night bleeding in this absolute *disgrace* of a fucking shelter."

He pointed down at the red-stained blanket.

Charlie blanched.

Oh my god, I could have hurt him. I'd been so upset, so concerned with getting back to him, that I'd forgotten I was putting him at risk. *Thank God he's okay. Thank God I didn't accidentally use my powers.*

Charlie turned to me with concern and shuffled back.

Augustus seized the opening. He moved with impossible swiftness and threw me over his shoulder. Nyx moaned in her sleep as I was flung through the air.

Charlie lunged for me, but Patro and Achilles stopped him.

For a second, I was stunned.

I exploded into action.

"NO!" I shrieked at the top of my lungs, fighting with everything I had. "CHARLIE HAS TO COME WITH ME. IF YOU LEAVE HIM HERE, I'LL KILL US ALL!"

Augustus wrapped his arm around the back of my legs in a steel vise. His hand gripped my thigh through the thin material of my dress.

He squeezed, hard enough to bruise.

"I promise," I gasped for air as I struggled. "I *promise*, if you leave him right now—I'll never forgive any of you. I'll chop myself into little pieces. I'll poison your food with my blood. I'll bring us all d-down and then—"

"For Kronos's sake," Patro shouted, interrupting my tirade. "While Kharon was tracking you here, Augustus told us you had a brother. We were always planning on bringing him back—we're not monsters."

I stopped struggling.

Tilted my head to look at Kharon's face. "You promise," I said, needing to know it wasn't a sick joke and they wouldn't separate us. "Please."

I didn't trust any of them, especially not him.

Glacial eyes narrowed. "So you're not blood-related?" Kharon asked skeptically.

I snarled, "He's my fucking brother. How *dare* you?"

Kharon clicked on the safety of his gun and put it in his thigh holster. "Calm down—carissima. We'll bring him with us."

"No," I spat. "I don't think I will calm down. Why are you even here?"

Augustus's fingernails dug into my thigh.

Kharon's smile was all teeth. "The real question is, why is our betrothed living in a fucking box? We will be addressing this later. For now—run away from us again, and we'll chain you to our bed. Forever."

I held up two broken fingers and flipped him off.

"We'll get to that part later as well," Kharon said with a depraved smirk.

I scoffed at his hubris.

Patro's lips thinned, and Achilles's eyes flashed with vitriol. My mentors were suddenly glaring at Kharon like they wanted to murder him.

Why are they so angry?

"Domus," Augustus whispered, nails stabbing deeper like he was trying to burrow himself under my skin.

The world twisted with darkness.

All six of us leaped away.

31

WICKED BONDS

ALEXIS: END OF JANUARY

Some revelations you could never recover from.

You're a murderer. A butcher. You've slain multiple people. How can you live with yourself?

The thoughts—the truth—wouldn't stop stabbing through my skull.

Guilt was a boulder on my shoulders.

Crushing me.

Face numb, body frozen, I plodded down the aisle with a bouquet of black calla lilies clenched between my fingers as harp music played.

All of Sparta turned to stare at me, their crowns and jewels gleaming. Hundreds—Spartans, protectors, and creatures—were crammed into the grand palace. Most were standing, but the Chthonics, crowned guests, and Charlie were seated.

At least he's here. You'll never be apart again.

It wasn't enough.

I wanted to murder everyone, and the kicker was—I actually could.

They won't even be your first, second, or third victims.

I'd done the impossible—I'd accidentally become a serial killer.

Help?

A spiky, ruby-covered silver crown was heavy on my head.

Ribbons were tied around my throat in a delicate noose, a white diamond-encrusted toga draped off my shoulders, and matching silk flared into a cape, dragging across the floor.

My will to live dragged with it.

War paint completed the pretty (morose) picture: blush colored a corpse's cheeks, mascara brightened dead eyes, and lipstick kept the screams inside.

Chandeliers sparkled over black marble floors in the high-ceilinged atrium, and grand windows framed the snow-dusted banks of Lake Como.

Where are the pitchforks? The fire? The ghouls? The blood? The demonic energy?

Hell looked different from what I'd imagined.

Up ahead, my birth people—my parents?—sat with a three-headed dog and dragon at their feet. Persephone leaned into the petal-covered aisle and mouthed, "I love you." She wiped at her eyes, lips quivering.

Hades wrapped his arms around her and mouthed, "I'm so proud of you, daughter." Male twins with unique crowns sat on his other side.

Hades smiled at me.

I wouldn't be.

I wasn't smart enough to see the trap they'd laid.

I'm just a loophole.

Forcing my lips up, I gave them a reassuring smile.

Internally, I was raging.

Screaming.

My birth people looked so hopeful.

Over the last two weeks, they'd let Charlie stay with us and had nursed my hands to health. They'd even remembered it was my twentieth birthday.

They'd done everything they could to help me "move forward" past the kidnapping, and Hades took great pleasure in telling me that Theros had mysteriously "disappeared."

No one was searching for him.

While the likely torture of my kidnapper was a positive, it wasn't enough to fix the overarching problem—me.

My smile dropped as I walked past them.

I could only pretend for so long.

In the next row, eleven Spartans wore large jeweled crowns and exquisite finery. All the House leaders were in attendance. Zeus glowered, and his lion showed its teeth. I resisted the urge to bare mine back.

The House leaders frowned at me, and I let them see the misery in my eyes.

I'd never been a big fan of tyranny.

This wedding is a sham.

Because of your stupid law—my life is ruined.

On the other side of the aisle, Patro's expression was furious, and Achilles's posture was rigid. His arm was stretched across Patro's chest like he was physically restraining him from causing a scene.

Charlie sat stiffly beside the two of them. His yellow irises were wide with concern.

Helen was next to him with a shell-shocked expression, like she couldn't believe this was happening.

That makes two of us.

At the front of the aisle, Fluffy Jr. slept on the floor with an invisible Nyx wrapped around his neck.

In the last week, he'd grown three sizes larger and one hundred pounds heavier.

I couldn't be sure, because his features were still lumpy and covered in tufts of fur, but I'd potentially bonded with a hideous horse.

Dark times indeed.

During Fluffy Jr.'s sudden growth spurt (early-onset obesity?), he'd formed a friendship with Nyx—she tried to strangle his thick lumpy neck, and he wagged his gnarled tail, thinking they were playing. Thus her current position wrapped around him.

Poco sat next to my murderous animals, chewing on both his hands at the same time.

Every few seconds, for seemingly no reason, the raccoon would let out a loud, ear-piercing screech.

We were all trying our best.

After all, I was walking toward *them.*

My steps faltered.

Silk cloaks and long black togas did nothing to civilize the unhealthy glint in their unblinking eyes. They were beasts masquerading as men.

Kharon's short, usually messy, hair was perfectly slicked back under his crown. He swallowed thickly, and the black ink of his neck tattoo—"Furia"—was stark against his pale skin.

Beside him, Augustus wore glasses, and his two-toned hair hung under his crown, down to his waist in a silky sheet.

The new looks did nothing to soften either of them.

They were wolves in sheep's clothes—in the sense that they'd gutted the sheep, put its severed parts in a box, and then gifted them to me so they could maintain their sick lineages.

Augustus's jaw ticked as he glared, perpetually furious with me, and Kharon cracked his neck like he was getting ready for battle.

That can't be good.

I stopped at the end of the aisle, and the music cut off.

The silence was charged.

Cruel satisfaction flashed in their eyes as they flanked me.

I was trapped.

The familiar elderly officiant stepped forward, her eyes a startling shade of violet and hair pure white.

Up close, her features were eerily familiar.

My stomach dropped to my knees.

That's why I recognized her after the massacre. She delivered Charlie to the trailer, ten years ago.

I was free-falling, arms wide, unable to slow my sharp descent into madness.

She gestured to the men. "I'm glad that you took a chance on the killers—great choice," she whispered to me.

I stared back, unamused.

Is this lady for real right now?

She ignored my general aura of disdain, unrolled a scroll, then squinted with surprise like she was seeing it for the first time.

Long, awkward moments passed, and as we waited, I stewed.

There was no choice involved in this sham of a marriage.

While the Houses were against the union of three Chthonics, they'd pushed it forward as quickly as possible to mitigate the scandal of a precious heiress taking part in the crucible. Everyone wanted to save my feminine "honor" so I could remain "pure."

Too bad I was filthy.

I'd been rolling in the mud for years: starving, using illegal food stamps, *killing*, lying, pretending, doing anything I could to survive.

There was nothing honorable left to save.

The urge to leap away was overwhelming, but I bit down on my tongue to stop the word from tumbling out.

My parents were watching with hopeful expressions, and Sparta would never let me leave, not now that they had their precious Chthonic heiress back. Not now that they thought my "sacred" betrothal was voluntary. Helen's honor was also somehow "smeared" by her association with me.

She's only sixteen. She doesn't deserve to suffer because of me.

Also, Kharon and Augustus would hunt me down—they'd stalk me to the ends of the earth—if I tried to run away.

So there was that.

The noose tightened around my throat.

My betrotheds shifted closer, like they could read my mind.

I should have worn a bomb.

Their hands rested possessively on my lower back—one on top of the other. Body heat burned through thin layers of silk.

I tried to inch away from their touch.

They leaned into me.

Salt and musk mixed with the scent of electricity, and I shivered.

I was standing in the middle of a hurricane, waiting for the eye wall to hit.

Kharon dipped his head to my ear. "Are you okay?" His voice was a throaty rasp.

No. I'm cheating on Carl Gauss. I'm an unloyal whore.

Memories of fingers dragging across my chest scoured my brain, and butterflies fluttered.

He tangled a finger around the one curl that hung freely down my back and tugged sharply, smirking. "Are you, carissima?" he repeated.

He's mocking me.

I glared up at him. "No," I whispered. "No, *dearest.* I'm not."

Kharon's smirk fell. "You will be," he said through gritted teeth.

The pretense of civility was gone.

"No," I said. "I won't."

Augustus shifted closer. "Pay attention—don't do this now," he whispered, glaring at both of us, black eyes flashing.

"You would say that." I scoffed.

Fingers flexed across my spine, pressing harder into skin.

Augustus ducked his head low, breath hot against my ear. "What's that supposed to mean, *Alexis*?"

The ends of his silky hair brushed across my collarbone, and the butterflies exploded. Queasiness twisted deep in my stomach.

I hated the way he said my name.

Like it was a sin.

Like it meant something to him.

"Or," Augustus whispered huskily against the shell of my ear, "should I call you—Hercules?"

A lily stem snapped in my hand.

I turned toward him. Our faces were inches apart, disconcertingly close.

"How about you call me nothing—*Professor.* I'm only here because you tricked me."

Black eyes pooled into a bottomless abyss.

"You're here because you accepted our gifts," he said harshly. "I warned you that someone would step in with how reckless you were acting, and *you* agreed that we would be the ones to take care of you—Kronos fucking knows you need the help."

I choked. "You're delusional—I'd never choose you two… not in a m-million years. You trapped me."

Kharon stiffened, jaw clenching beside us.

"That's not true, Alexis," Augustus said darkly, his nails digging harder into my lower back. The man had a thing for scratching me.

"It is. I'm positive," I snarled. "Don't touch me."

I stepped away—Augustus grabbed my bicep and yanked me back between them.

"But you belong to us," he said silkily. "You've shown it. Acta, non verba."

Deeds, not words.

Trying to yank away, I snarled up at him, "In your dreams. I haven't shown you anything."

"Oh, Alexis, you don't want to know the wicked things I dream about—don't test me," Augustus whispered ominously. "Not here, not now—you won't like the result."

I scoffed in his face. If he attacked, I'd kill him with my blood powers.

Great, I'm embracing murder.

The officiant cleared her throat, and the three of us looked up with annoyance.

Augustus dropped my arm.

She gaped, scroll trembling in her hands.

"Oh my," she said, blinking rapidly. "This union is definitely going to be—intense. Better get on with it before..." She trailed off.

Before what?

Her violet eyes started to glow an electric shade of blue.

"We're here today," she bellowed, her voice three octaves too deep to be natural, "to witness the most sacred Spartan oath, which will unequivocally chain these three souls together... for all of immortality!"

A trickle of fear skittered down my spine.

Not unite.

Not tie.

Chain.

I'm only standing here because they didn't want to do this with an Olympian.

Her head snapped forward. "Look into one another's eyes," she commanded.

Augustus and Kharon shifted in front—I reluctantly looked up.

Glacial blue.

Soulless black.

"Now repeat after me!" The officiant's voice was muffled, like we were all deep underwater, drowning.

"Omnia causa fiunt. Vi et animo. Sic itur ad astra."

My lips were numb.

"Everything happens for a reason. With heart and soul. Such is the way to the stars," we said in Latin, voices mixing.

The officiant threw her arms above her head.

"Stet fortuna domus!" she shouted.

We repeated in unison, "Let the fortune of the House stand."

The last syllable rang through the silent atrium.

The storm slammed into me.

White-hot pain seared my heart. I was skewered on a phantom sword. Gasping for air, bent over, I clutched at my sternum as agony burned relentlessly.

The pressure was astronomical. Unfathomable.

Harsh grunts echoed as Augustus and Kharon leaned back, jaws clenched as they gripped their chests.

The three of us burned together.

Abruptly, as quickly as it had begun, the pain stopped.

All was still.

What did I just do? I should have run.

But a dull ache still simmered deep within my heart, like the calm was just an interlude, not the end.

The worst is still to come.

Hands on my knees, I coughed as I struggled to catch my breath. Someone rubbed my back soothingly.

When I finally found the strength to stand straight, Kharon and Augustus had recovered. They stared at me with laser focus.

I grimaced.

Why aren't they blinking?

The officiant exhaled loudly, scroll clattering.

"I knew you three would be electric, but that was…unexpected." Her voice was grave. "What a—powerful union…

There will be consequences for sure—dark consequences." She shivered. "There always are."

Numbness spread.

If I hadn't been experiencing the worst panic attack of my life, I might have worried about her unsettling abstruse comments.

As it was, I felt nothing.

I'd reached my limit.

She clapped her hands together and smiled widely, like she was overcompensating. "Now you may exchange rings."

Augustus pulled a long, thin velvet box out of his toga.

Inside were two matching black bands of snakes eating their own tails, with rubies for eyes. Attached to the bands were chains of blue diamonds that formed bracelets at the end.

Augustus and Kharon put the serpent bands on each other's ring fingers and clasped the attached bracelets around their wrists.

The jewelry pieces were much flashier than a human wedding band.

"Now—I will attach them, permanently," the officiant said as she stepped forward with a metal tool.

The men held up their wrists, and she clamped the glowing end of the tool around the bracelet clasps. There was a hissing sound as the metal heated and the clasp disappeared.

Wonderful, permanent jewelry you can't remove. What's next? A collar and leash?

I felt sick.

The men clapped each other on the back and embraced.

Kharon pulled out a larger velvet box.

An oval blue diamond, blindingly large, sat on a thin gold band, and a long, dainty chain of matching blue diamonds hung off it.

I blanched at how ostentatious it was.

Augustus grabbed my left wrist firmly like he could sense

my hesitation, and his calluses scraped across my skin as he held my hand up for Kharon.

The hairs on the back of my neck stood up, and I tried to wrench my hand out of his grip.

His fingers flexed, and I couldn't move an inch.

As we grappled, Kharon slipped on the extravagant diamond, which covered the entire lower part of my finger.

Everyone who saw my hand would know what it represented.

Their eyes flashed with primal satisfaction as Augustus positioned the long, thin chain across the top of my hand, pushing my sleeve back so he could clasp the attached bracelet.

He stilled.

Augustus's fingers spasmed, and Kharon inhaled sharply through clenched teeth.

Since the healed skin was still sensitive, I hadn't been able to cover my wrists with hair ties like usual.

Old white scars crisscrossed with new red marks. The skin was ravaged.

No one moved.

"These are old—what the actual fuck?" Augustus growled, clenching his jaw tightly. "How did you get these?"

"It's nothing," I whispered as I tried to tug my arm away, but this time, Kharon held my hand still. His scowl was dangerous.

Augustus took a deep, steadying breath as he clasped the bracelet. "We'll talk about this later." His eyes burned with violence.

"No," I said through gritted teeth, "we won't be talking about anything."

The whites of Augustus's eyes filled with blood.

I bared my teeth.

Before things could escalate (things being homicide), the officiant stepped forward and melted the clasp.

When she was done, I yanked my hand back to my side protectively.

Augustus stared at my arm, like he could see through my sleeve and was trying to memorize my scars.

The blue diamond was heavy on my finger, and the chain prickled against my oversensitive flesh.

It's permanent. I really can't take it off.

The world wobbled.

"Now," the officiant said, "you may kiss the bride."

My heart raced, skin tingling with strange anticipation. *Sorry, Carl.*

"But wait." The officiant held up both her hands and chuckled awkwardly. "Let me get out of here with everyone else before you…kiss."

Why would she need to leave?

I turned around, and my stomach twisted with confusion. Most of the guests were already walking down the aisle, out the front door. Only a few men remained seated.

Persephone waved from the front lawn, Lake Como sparkling behind her. Then she and Hades disappeared in a cloud of smoke.

Muffled booms echoed as guests disappeared.

Only a few lingered in their seats.

"Everyone, out!" Kharon shouted at them, his raspy voice snapping like a whip. "Now."

Why?

Some of the remaining men jumped to their feet and left.

Achilles had to drag a fighting Patro away, and Charlie reluctantly followed them.

Only one man stayed. A gold laurel crown sat atop his blond hair, and he kicked his feet up, lounging back.

"Leave," Kharon demanded as he took a step toward him threateningly, and Augustus held him back.

The blond man grinned cockily. "It's the laws of Sparta," he said. "A marriage kiss may be witnessed by a member of the public if they desire to stay." He put his hands behind his head. "And I desire to stay."

Kharon clenched his hands into fists. "Is that so?"

Augustus stepped off the dais and slowly sauntered toward the man.

Then, moving quicker than my eyes could follow, he lunged and grabbed him by the throat.

Augustus's eyes glowed crimson red, and he stared at him for long, tense moments.

A silent battle waged.

The blond man whimpered, and phantom pressure pulsed behind my eyes as I remembered the feeling.

Augustus released him. Standing up straight, he adjusted his toga. A slight flush across his cheeks was the only sign he'd done anything.

In contrast, the blond man staggered to his feet, eyes unfocused, blood gushing profusely from his eyes, nose, and ears. Then, like a zombie, he turned and stumbled down the aisle, out the front door.

There was a commotion outside as he collapsed, and a boom echoed as someone took him away.

Augustus smirked up at us, eyes still bloodred. Kharon chuckled darkly.

Two monsters sauntered toward me.

I took a step back, bumping into the stone altar.

32

But You Belong to Us

Patro

My knees cracked against the floor of our home.

Smoke billowed.

Launching myself upright, I grabbed Achilles by the front of his shirt and shoved him into our bedroom so we could have privacy from Alexis's brother. I kicked the door behind me, and it shut with a loud bang.

"You should have let me stay," I said through gritted teeth, jaw aching from the force of my rage. "We should have intervened."

Maroon eyes flashed with warning; Achilles pushed back at me, and we grappled. Our breath was harsh and ragged in the quiet room.

"She didn't want to marry them—it's not fucking right," I said as Achilles thrust my back flush against the wall.

Stars exploded in my vision.

The pain grounded me.

"Fuck," I whispered brokenly. "She's *our* mentee—not theirs…she…she…"

I struggled to put into words the confusing jumble of emotions I felt for Alexis Hert. She was supposed to be just a nuisance, the annoying girl we had to mentor.

I should have hated her.

The problem was… I didn't hate her, not at all.

"What do we do?" I asked, desperation making my voice crack.

The question hung between us like a grenade.

Achilles slowly signed, "We find a way—to take her away from them."

I inhaled sharply, rubbing at my chest. The branded scar tissue was lumpy beneath my touch.

"She'll be ours?"

Achilles's eyes blazed with fire as his fingers moved quickly. "She already is. She just doesn't know it yet."

33

CARNAL DELIGHTS

ALEXIS

We were alone.

Long, tension-filled moments passed as the three of us stared at one another, not moving, not speaking, just breathing heavily.

The anticipation was a live wire.

My skin prickled from the weight of their stares.

"May I—" Kharon rasped, breaking the spell. He reached forward and cupped my face. "Kiss the bride?" His thumb stroked slowly against my jawline.

My head was under icy water, heart in my throat. Two new cords pulsed faintly inside my sternum.

All the lines had blurred.

I swallowed thickly.

The damage is already done. There's nothing left to lose. It's just a stupid kiss.

I nodded jerkily.

Kharon's smirk was sinful as he stepped closer.

Crack. The heir of Artemis, the son of Erebus, the Hunter, fell to his knees in front of the altar.

I stared down at his bowed form.

Augustus stepped closer; in one swift movement, he grabbed my hips, and lifted me so I was seated on top of the altar—Kharon's face was level with the juncture of my thighs.

A sacrificial bride.

Augustus's fingers lingered where he grabbed me.

"May I kiss the bride?" Kharon said again, slowly lifting the hem of my toga and exposing my legs. Fingers dragged across sensitive skin.

"What?" I whispered as my vision warped.

Everything was out of focus.

Kharon arched a dark brow, his sharp cheekbones glinting as he challenged me with his eyes.

Kharon wet his lips.

Leaning forward, breath hot against my exposed thigh, he pushed up the last inch of my silk toga over my hips.

The material bunched at my waist.

His intention was obvious.

Queasiness burned deep in my stomach, and the room spun.

Butterflies fluttered.

Kharon lingered over the thin fabric that covered my core. "May I kiss the bride?" he repeated with a rasp.

Oh my god.

The butterflies spasmed.

He looked up at me, brow arched mockingly. There was laughter in his eyes, like he didn't think I'd agree.

This was all a game to them—they were playing with me.

You're already dead.

I sank deeper into the murky water, into the consequences.

Look what you did to all those people.

I needed a distraction; I needed to forget that I was a serial killer.

"Yes," I breathed out on dry lips, before I lost my nerve.

His pupils expanded, eyes widening with surprise.

Black nails grabbed my thighs and wrenched them open, hard enough to bruise.

Kharon's expression was feral.

He leaned forward, pulled silk to the side with his teeth, and dragged his tongue wantonly through my core.

My eyes rolled back.

I gasped with pleasure.

Augustus stepped into my personal space, his hand wrapped around the back of my neck, fingernails digging into the front of my throat.

He squeezed, holding me still.

"Shhh," he whispered in my ear as his calloused thumb pressed into my lips and forced my jaw open.

Then Augustus's open mouth hovered over mine. "This is your punishment, my carus," he said. "I told you… You have one hour—only then will you be allowed to come."

Wait, didn't he say something similar months ago?

Warning bells went off in my head, but I couldn't concentrate on them.

Kharon sucked on my clit—stars exploded as he slowly pressed his finger inside me.

The infamous hunter, the son of Artemis, pulled his head back from between my thighs, finger still buried deep, and slowly licked his lips.

"Dulce periculum," Kharon said with a wicked smirk, mouth glistening. "Carissima." His breath was hot as he lapped at me softly.

"Danger *is* sweet," Augustus said. Then he slammed his tongue deep into my throat, like he was trying to devour me with his kiss.

Kharon pushed his finger even deeper and blew on my clit—I screamed into Augustus's mouth.

Both men groaned.

The butterflies were on fire.

Kharon tortured me with his tongue and fingers, bringing me to the brink of ecstasy but pulling away at the last moment.

It was hell.

Augustus pulled down my toga. He lapped and sucked at my nipples as Kharon flicked his tongue against my clit.

Everything tingled, and I forgot how to breathe. How to think. How to care.

This is heaven.

They traded places. Augustus fell to his knees in front of the altar and lifted my butt with both his hands. Then he licked me, ass to core, like he owned my flesh.

Kharon bit down around my nipple.

I screamed.

The men devoured me.

Time got hazy.

Panting, struggling to see or hear, covered in sweat, I grabbed at their hair and begged. Pleaded for mercy as I writhed beneath them. Words and noises tumbled from my lips.

I was nothing but theirs.

"Fuck." Kharon's raspy voice broke through the pleasurable fog. "We lost track—it's been an hour. What do you want to do?"

The men pulled away, and I whimpered with desperation.

Cool air burned overstimulated flesh.

"You get between her legs," Augustus ordered, and once again Kharon fell to his knees before me, his breath tingling across my heat.

But this time, glacial blue eyes filled with blood.

"I'll hold her," Augustus said from where he stood next to

Kharon's kneeling form. He gripped the back of my neck, turning my face toward his. I whimpered louder.

Black eyes stared into mine.

"Alexis—I need you to look at me, my carus. You did such a good job," Augustus praised me. "Your punishment is over."

I blinked in confusion.

Kharon licked my clit—foreign sensations coursed through my body, lighting every nerve on fire.

It was my pleasure, but more.

Smug male satisfaction mixed with ecstasy.

Holy crap. I'm feeling mine and *his pleasure at the same time.*

Waves of rapture built higher, and I tipped my head forward, screaming.

I doubled over from the ripples—Augustus yanked my neck back so I wouldn't fall. Bloodred eyes held my shuttering gaze.

Pressure tingled behind my eyes.

Instinctively, I tried to yank away, but he held me still.

His voice pounded inside my skull. *"Feel ecstasy,"* he commanded. Just like that, pure rapture exploded inside my mind.

I screamed with pleasure.

Time didn't exist.

As I panted and shook, my vision slowly refocused.

The men were still fully clothed.

My toga was bunched up at my waist, and I was leaning forward, slumped against Augustus. My chin was on his shoulder.

"Such a good carus," Augustus praised as he rubbed circles on my back.

Kharon was resting his head against my thigh, tracing his fingers over my calf.

Either I was hallucinating, or two ferocious-looking skeleton dogs were sleeping in the middle of the aisle.

I tried to speak, but my throat was hoarse.

After a couple of attempts, I whispered, "What are those skeleton dogs?"

Kharon's teeth grazed across my inner thigh as he nipped at me. Augustus kissed the side of my neck and kept drawing circles.

"Those," Kharon said as he kissed my leg, "are my two protectors. They're hellhounds."

His neck tattoo. That was what I couldn't remember. "Furia" was slang for hellhound.

"But why have I never seen them before?" My voice was raspy from screaming.

The world had a dreamlike quality.

Nothing felt real.

"They're invisible to Spartans," Kharon said. "It's a gift from my creature heritage—I can see them." He kissed my thigh.

Persephone is part creature. Is that why I can understand animals when others can't?

I drowned in my thoughts.

Kharon continued, "And since I'm using my Spartan power right now—which lets whoever I'm touching see and feel what I do—you can now also see my hellhounds."

"Oh," I mumbled articulately.

Head swimming, I tried to process everything.

Kharon's pleasure had combined with mine into unimaginable ecstasy.

Is that why I felt strange pleasure whenever he touched me in Corfu? Was I feeling what he *felt all this time?*

Oh god.

"No wonder you're such a hit at the symposium," I whispered as I lay my head against Augustus, who played with the ends of my hair.

Both men stilled.

"I wouldn't bring up your—performance at the symposium," Augustus growled. "After you've just been punished for it."

I grunted in annoyance, too boneless to do anything else.

Kharon bit my thigh, hard enough to leave marks, then lapped at it.

"That's why my nickname is Sex," he rasped.

I startled.

It really is Sex.

I whispered shakily. "So does the *W* stand—"

"War," Augustus cut me off, kissing my temple softly. "I'm War—because of what I can do to people's minds."

Shivers exploded down my spine.

One hellhound woke up, dagger-sharp canines flashing as it yawned, a shadowy tongue stretching. Ice-blue flames burned where its eyes should have been.

It turned and whispered something to the other dog. It was too far away for me to hear what it said.

It sounds exactly like the whispers I've been constantly hearing.

The urge to scream hit me.

"They can speak," I said on numb lips.

"No," Kharon said. "They just make strange grunting sounds."

No.

They're speaking a language.

An icy sensation washed down my spine like someone had dumped a bucket of cold water over my head.

"Did you have th-them—" I struggled to calm my racing heart "—following me?"

His nails bit into my ankles. "Maybe," Kharon said with feigned casualness.

He was a terrible liar.

My neck was prickling constantly. I heard them everywhere for months.

The voices weren't in my head—they were real. Kharon had been stalking me.

Nightmares of glowing red eyes, pressure on my foot, a

strange obsession, skeletal creatures, and whispers had plagued me every time I slept.

In the dreams, the devil had warned me he was going to take care of me.

Oh my god, was Kharon touching me while I slept, and I could feel his obsession with me and see his hellhounds? Sometimes there were two men—was that them?

Was it all real?

As I hyperventilated, my eyes widened. "Did you w-watch me sleep at Corfu?"

Kharon's fingers stilled where they were trailing over my skin.

"Maybe," he said.

I wanted to die.

He's been stalking me.

Every. Single. Night.

I gasped for air. "Did you both—ever…watch me?"

Kharon gently kissed the sensitive flesh of my inner thigh. "Maybe," he rasped again.

It was more horrible than I could have ever imagined.

They were actually villains.

"I need to leave," I said shakily as I struggled to calm down. A panic attack burned inside my sternum.

Augustus picked me up into his arms. "Shhh. Relax, my carus. This villa is our home." He cradled me against his chest. "It's now your home as well—you will *never* spend the night in a cardboard box ever again. We're going to take care of you."

I fought to get out of Augustus's hold, but steel muscles flexed. His grip was painful as he pinned me to his chest.

The panic attack got ten times worse.

Why won't he let me go?

The edges of my vision got fuzzy, heart hammering, fear choking me.

"Breathe slowly, please," Augustus begged. "You're hurting yourself."

"Let me go," I gasped, voice far away as the world collapsed around me.

Augustus's arms flexed, holding me in place.

"Never," they replied in unison.

It was too much.

All of it.

The room spun unmercifully, and my vision faded. This time, I didn't fight to stay awake—I let the darkness pull me under.

I passed out.

34
THE STALKER

KHARON: FIVE MONTHS EARLIER

THE INITIATES' FIRST LAP OF THE CRUCIBLE (KHARON'S OMITTED REALIZATION)

An *insane realization* hit me, and my breath left my lungs like I'd been punched as Alexis and the drowning boy splashed in the water.

No.

It can't be.

It's not possible.

Alexis's eyes were bloody and glowing.

They were *Chthonic* red.

I quickly did the math in my head—there was only one Chthonic child who'd died as a child.

Hercules.

My jaw dropped.

She was the famous daughter of Persephone and Hades.

Everyone in Sparta knew how they'd tragically lost her after Titans attacked.

Plot twist—she was very much alive.

The boy screamed louder in the water like he was being torn to pieces as they tussled.

Oh my Kronos—she's killing him.

The boy splashed harder, and Alexis yelled something, but I couldn't hear it over the rushing in my ears.

The federation doesn't know.

They don't know she's Chthonic.

No one can know.

I smiled so widely that it hurt my face—she was the solution to the marriage law; she was the loophole we'd been searching for.

I call dibs.

Pure euphoria filled me.

She's going to be ours. Augustus is going to be thrilled.

I had to make it look like I killed the boy before someone realized what she was. I had to keep her identity hidden.

She would be our dirty little secret.

Kneeling, I touched the boy's forehead. Pain stabbed through my chest as I unleashed my Chthonic powers. His screams intensified as I let him see my protectors, and he flailed while Hell and Hound jumped in to feast, but all my attention was still on her.

A plan unfolded before me.

A scheme.

Alexis had been raised in the human world.

She didn't know our customs.

She wouldn't know that merely opening a betrothal box was an acceptance of a union.

In contrast, everyone in Sparta knew the first step was to discover the sender.

Her ignorance was perfect.

We could exploit it.

Ruthlessly.

Then, at her graduation ceremony, we'd reveal to all of Sparta that she'd accepted our gifts.

She'd be ours.

Eternally.

The federation couldn't do anything to stop the ceremony if all of Sparta knew she was already ours. It would be the highest dishonor to intervene.

We could trap her in marriage.

It would work.

It had to.

Who ruled Sparta was on the line.

I was the hunter of my generation because I knew how to play the long game—I always caught my prey.

Alexis Hert is going to be ours. She's going to be between us. Underneath us. On her knees. On a marriage altar with her thighs spread wide while we feast on her. We're going to devour her.

Our power is going to be unprecedented.

The three of us will be the villains of this new age.

The federation will fall.

I stood up, the boy forgotten, as I slowly turned my boat toward her.

Alexis's stunning blood-filled eyes flashed. Then she swam away frantically.

Tipping my head back, I roared with laughter.

I followed her closely.

When she finished the swim and crawled onto the bank, I sat down in the boat, and I used the other dark gift from my creature heritage.

I pushed my consciousness into my protectors.

"Follow Alexis. Watch her. Don't leave her side," I commanded them.

Hell and Hound stalked forward into the mountain entrance, invisible to everyone but me.

I sat down in the boat and focused on the connection with my protectors that pounded through my sternum.

Whatever they saw, I saw.

We were one.

Being in two places at once could be disconcerting, but it was easiest when I had nothing to do. Lucky for me—my schedule was free for *months.*

Hell and Hound slunk into the back of the dark classroom—making creature noises that only I could hear—as they zeroed in on Alexis, who was hunched over, shivering.

She whipped her head around and squinted directly at where they were.

My breath caught.

Can she see them?

She slumped lower and looked away, shaking her head like she was imagining something.

She doesn't know I'm watching her.

Chuckling, I lounged back in the boat and spread my arms wide as I enjoyed the view.

Alexis Hert didn't know it yet, but she'd enthralled a monster.

Things were about to get *very* messy.

I laughed harder.

The stalking had begun.

35
THE PLAN

AUGUSTUS: PRESENT DAY

Click. Click. Click.

My dress shoes echoed against Italian marble. I carried my new bride against my chest, up the grand stairway of our villa.

Kharon walked beside me, and his expression was smug.

My face mirrored his.

We'd won.

Our plan had come to fruition.

We were married to Alexis—bonded for life with a Chthonic Spartan who was our equal. We were more powerful than ever. It was the most glorious feeling in the world. She was perfect for us.

Perfectly *ours.*

My smile fell.

Pride morphed into rage.

Alexis had panicked when she'd realized the depths we'd sunk to in order to wed her. Her pupils had blown wide, and she'd tried to get away from us. Her fear had been unmistakable, and I was glad she'd passed out before she'd hurt herself.

That wasn't all.

Her wrists were covered in old, jagged scars, and Persephone had said she hadn't been born with two differently colored eyes. We'd also found her sleeping in a Kronos damned *cardboard box* with her brother.

Alexis was keeping things from us—unseemly things—things we needed to slaughter people over.

Her silence was unacceptable. She would reveal every one of her secrets, and then we would torture whoever hurt her. Brutally.

That was how this was going to work.

My hands cramped, and I forced myself to soften my punishing hold. I didn't want to hurt her. I didn't want to scare her. The problem was, I didn't want to do a lot of things in life, but I still did them.

I hadn't asked to be born with such…*violent* inclinations.

But I had been.

Kharon leaned down and petted the invisible heads of his vicious hellhounds.

We had both been raised in the crucible of power. Kronos had forged us with wrath and savagery.

I had a feeling that when Alexis woke up—it would be war.

Guns were strapped to our thighs beneath our ceremonial togas for a reason. We were always ready for conflict. She would learn there was no escaping us.

Ever.

"Amore et melle et felle es fecundissimus," I whispered down to the sleeping angel in my arms.

Kharon nodded in agreement as he adjusted the weapon holster under his toga.

Love is rich with honey and venom.

It had never been more true.

36
THE MONSTER

ALEXIS

My eyes shot open.

I woke up with a broken gasp.

Sleep paralysis locked my limbs, and every cell in my body screamed with pain. I was still in my wedding toga, tucked beneath silk sheets.

Deep male snores echoed around the cavernous room. The three of us were lying in a decadent four-poster bed.

Memories of my husbands' smug expressions stabbed at me. Hellfire ignited in my chest, and it burned hot.

Hatred filled me.

They won't get away with this. They'll pay for tricking me.

Two new cords—chains—scorched my chest, singeing as they wrapped tighter around my heart like the marriage bond could feel my displeasure.

Augustus and Kharon moaned with pain in their sleep.

There were consequences to marrying a monster.
They'd begun.
For them.

★ ★ ★ ★ ★

Exclusive Bonus Scene

Hades

A week before the wedding...

"Should we be concerned?" Persephone asked as she looked across the room at their daughter.

Hercules, or "Alexis," as she liked to be called (an undignified commoner name that Persephone was still grappling with) was lying starfished on the floor in front of the extravagant black marble fireplace.

The turquoise water of the Adriatic Sea sparkled outside their palatial villa on Crete.

Persephone's concern was not prompted by her daughter's spread-out position on the floor. Nor was it the misshapen white fluff laying across her legs that she called a protector. It wasn't even the fact that she hadn't spoken a word to anyone in an entire week.

Hades also went nonverbal when stressed, which he was often.

No. Persephone's concern was borne from the pieces of black tape her daughter had pasted across her face in a massive X.

Hades looked up from the book on theoretical physics that he was reading. He pulled down his glasses and squinted over at the hearth.

"Why would we be concerned?" he asked with confusion. "She's perfect."

Persephone sighed, because while she agreed with the perfection of her daughter, there were definitely red flags to the situation that her husband was missing. Like usual.

"The tape over her eyes and mouth?" Persephone asked with a dramatic hand flourish around her face.

Hades scoffed. "We've all been there—she's probably just suffering from a slight case of prewedding jitters. Remember that time I was stressed about the Cyclops invasion and I wore a helmet without eye or mouth holes for a week? She's just coping."

Persephone rubbed at her temples.

"I also remember," she said dryly, "that you went on a murderous rampage the next day and slaughtered a dozen Cyclops by yourself when you were supposed to be waiting for backup."

Hades smiled. "Good times."

Hydra, her dragon protector, let out a sigh (of fire) as she groaned with exasperation. Marriage to the leader of the illustrious House of Hades was not for the faint of heart.

Persephone considered herself a stalwart, no-nonsense, strong-willed lady who could handle difficult personalities.

Still, her husband and newly reacquainted daughter were testing her nerves.

"Should we do something?" she asked with growing exasperation. "We finally have our child back—we need to help her."

Hades grunted and put his book down. Black fog swirled

around him in a silky fog. He looked less like a man and more like a monster from another world.

"Fine," he said. "I will help our daughter." He rose to his full height and Cerberus wagged its three tails as it also stood up. "Alexis," he called over to the other room.

Alexis lifted her head. Two-colored eyes (that she refused to talk about despite Persephone's insistence) were partially obscured behind the taped X, but the parts that were visible were filled with heavy emotions.

Persephone's chest ached as she recognized the helplessness in her daughter's gaze. Once upon a time, she'd felt trapped by her mother, Demeter, and had been drowning in angst. Now her child's suffering was killing her.

Hades's expensive Italian loafers clicked against the marble floor as he walked toward his daughter.

"Your mother is worried about you—she wants us to help you," Hades said, stating the obvious with zero tact.

Persephone sighed again. Her husband and "discreet" were not two words she'd ever used in the same sentence.

"So." Hades smiled down at his—still lying on the floor looking extremely unwell—daughter. "Do you want to wear a helmet of mine? It has no eye and mouth holes, and I've found it helps in times of extreme duress."

"Uh, wait." Persephone stood up. "Darling, that wasn't what I meant when I said you should—"

Alexis nodded her head.

Hades beamed and clapped. "Perfect."

Cerberus sniffed the white lumpy mass her daughter referred to as Fluffy Jr., then it let out three loud yips of excitement, hunched low, and jumped back and forth like it wanted to play.

Fluffy Jr. laid its head down on Alexis's torso like it, too, was suffering from depression.

A few minutes later, Persephone was nursing a violent migraine with ambrosia.

Alexis, her precious miracle, was lying next to the fireplace with a golden helmet completely obscuring her face.

Meanwhile, her lovely (clueless) husband was kneeling beside Alexis, laughing and demonstrating the helmet's durability and protectiveness by hitting it with various objects.

"Hades, can you not terrorize her, please?" Persephone called out with exasperation.

Both her family members turned toward her: the man and the faceless helmet.

"I'm helping her," Hades said, his lips pursed with genuine confusion. He whacked the helmet with a spoon. "See."

Persephone did not see.

"Raise your thumb if this is helping," Hades said to his daughter.

Rubbing her aching head, Persephone opened her mouth to inform him he was—

Alexis held up her thumb.

Hades beamed.

Persephone picked up a shot of pure ambrosia and threw it back. Somehow, she'd birthed a girl version of Hades.

Kronos help her.